THE WORLD'S CLASSICS

SELECTED STORIES AND SKETCHES

BRET HARTE was born Francis Brett Hart in Albany, New York, in 1836. In 1854 he joined his mother and her second husband in San Francisco. Employed as an apothecary clerk, miner, teacher, expressman, and printer's devil, Harte found his true calling in journalism and became the founding editor of the *Overland Monthly* in 1868. In that year he also published 'The Luck of Roaring Camp', the story of hearts and miners of gold that catapulted him into fame. The centre of a community of writers that included Mark Twain, Ambrose Bierce, Joaquin Miller, and Henry George, Harte had to look East rather than West for literary acclaim. He never returned to California after his departure for Boston and a $10,000 contract in 1871. His inability to produce under the pressure of this unprecedented sum forced him to turn to lecturing and, in 1877, to leave the United States. After serving as a US commercial agent in Prussia and Consul in Glasgow, Harte settled in London in 1885. In his increasingly comfortable exile Harte continued to write and gather his short stories into a book a year. He died in Camberley, Surrey, in 1902.

DAVID WYATT is a professor of English at the University of Maryland, College Park. He is the author of *The Fall into Eden: Landscape and Imagination in California* and *Out of the Sixties: Storytelling and the Vietnam Generation*.

THE WORLD'S CLASSICS

BRET HARTE

Selected Stories and Sketches

Edited with an Introduction by
DAVID WYATT

Oxford   New York
OXFORD UNIVERSITY PRESS
1995

Oxford University Press, Walton Street, Oxford OX2 6DP

Oxford New York
Athens Auckland Bangkok Bombay
Calcutta Cape Town Dar es Salaam Delhi
Florence Hong Kong Istanbul Karachi
Kuala Lumpur Madras Madrid Melbourne
Mexico City Nairobi Paris Singapore
Taipei Tokyo Toronto

and associated companies in
Berlin Ibadan

Oxford is a trade mark of Oxford University Press

British Library Cataloguing in Publication Data

Data available

Library of Congress Cataloging in Publication Data
Harte, Bret, 1836-1902.
[Short stories. Selections]
Selected Stories and sketches/Bret Harte; edited with an
introduction by David Wyatt.
p. cm.—(World's classics)
Includes bibliographical references.
1. Western stories. I. Wyatt, David, 1948- . II. Title.
III. Series.
PS1822.W93 1995 813'.4—dc20 94-14749
ISBN 0-19-282354-X

1 3 5 7 9 10 8 6 4 2

Typeset by Pure Tech Corporation, Pondicherry, India
Printed in Great Britain by
BPC Paperbacks Ltd
Aylesbury, Bucks

CONTENTS

INTRODUCTION

IN 1860 the 23-year-old Francis Brett Hart found himself the temporary editor of the *Northern Californian*, a newspaper published near the modern town of Eureka. He had been hired by the paper as a printer's devil, but, as luck would have it, the owner took a trip to San Francisco and left Hart in charge. In February of that year a band of white men, armed with knives, axes, and the strong support of the local community, attacked a nearby tribe of Indians during a religious ceremony and killed some sixty people. Most of the dead were women and children. Three days later Hart's paper carried this headline, in the largest possible type:

INDISCRIMINATE MASSACRE OF INDIANS WOMEN AND CHILDREN BUTCHERED

Hart left Uniontown a month later.

Harte's would prove a career of sudden rises and falls. The Uniontown incident revealed not only his responsiveness to the racial politics of the frontier and his belief in language as a weapon of social change but a gambler's ability to profit from shifts of fortune. The loss of his newspaper job sent him back to San Francisco and straight into a staff position on the *Golden Era*, the leading literary weekly of the day. In the following months he published his first short story and adopted the pen name Bret Harte. Within eight years he would found and edit the *Overland Monthly*, a magazine as influential on the west coast as the *Atlantic* was on the east. As the decade ended he began publishing the stories that brought him a national reputation and even the offer of a professorship of Recent Literature at the newly founded University of California across the bay.

Yet for all its early fame the name of Bret Harte survives in association with diminutives: sentimentality, local colour, the short story. The twenty volumes of the Standard Library Edition (1896–1904) have come down to us as a vast, unread falling off. Harte's stories, it is claimed, offer not feeling but its pretence. The California materials do not rise to the level of a universal or at least a national vision. And the one attempt at a novel, *Gabriel Conroy* (1876), only demonstrates by its failure Harte's inability to extend his fictions into the most capacious and demanding forms.

Harte is unlikely to regain a place in the canon remotely close to the position he held, in the early 1870s, as the most well-paid and widely read author in the United States. In 1871 he was offered $10,000, an unprecedented sum, for the exclusive publishing rights to a year's worth of his work. In that year he delivered the Phi Beta Kappa poem at the Harvard commencement, a triumph that may have offset his misgivings about the wild success of the 'worst poem I ever wrote'.[1] Popularly known as 'The Heathen Chinee', the sixty-line satire had swept the English-speaking world after Harte had rescued it from a drawer in the previous September. The *New York Globe* ventured to say that 'there is not a secular paper in the United States which has not copied it'.[2] Yet by 1877 Harte had confessed, in a letter to his wife, to being 'penniless'.[3] In that year he secured an appointment as the Commercial Agent of the United States at Krefeld, Germany; in the next he left the country that had made him famous, never to return. England eventually took Harte in, and he kept writing. Except for a few tales, he could not regain his early form. 'I grind out the old tunes on the old organ and gather up the coppers,'[4] he wrote as he prepared to leave the country. By the 1950s, Harte had been reduced to one story routinely included in high school anthologies as an example of regional realism. By 1990 the *Heath Anthology of American Literature* had dropped him altogether.

George Stewart writes in his sympathetic biography of 'two outstanding "problems" in Harte's artistic development—his rapid rise in the late sixties, and his almost equally rapid decline

[1] George Stewart, *Bret Harte: Argonaut and Exile* (Houghton Mifflin: Boston, 1931), 181.
[2] Ibid. 180.
[3] Ibid. 243.
[4] Gary Scharnhorst, *Bret Harte* (Twayne: New York, 1992), p. ix.

in the middle seventies'.[5] Stewart sensibly reduces the matter of Bret Harte to one of development. And Harte did prove awkward in managing his success. He diminished the rate of his steady, scrupulous output; he turned from his proven medium, the short story, to the writing of ungainly plays; he failed to develop new fictional material; he overspent on clothes, his family, lavish hotels. Some have argued that his departure from California in 1871 deprived him of the intelligence of sustaining soil. The reasons for Harte's decline are many, and he no doubt bears responsibility for the career he made and unmade with such astonishing speed. Harte deserves a place in literary history as more, however, than a magnificent failure. His story can be read as less a tragedy of development than one of reputation, a reputation that in his life and in the century to follow remained stubbornly bound up with that unique and collective American literary construct, Mark Twain.

Twain was born in 1835; Harte, a year later. The two met in San Francisco in 1864, where Harte acted as contributor to and occasional editor of the weekly *Californian*. The two men were already linked by their ambition to transform Far Western materials into adequate forms, and they remained linked as well, until their final break in 1877, through the editing, publishing, and co-authoring of various projects.

Twain first fulfilled the ambition by publishing 'The Celebrated Jumping Frog of Calaveras County' in 1865 in *Saturday Press*. Harte claimed to have solicited the story for his magazine, where it was later republished; Twain disputed the claim. 'The Jumping Frog' was a critical success, but one Twain denigrated; he called the story 'a villainous backwoods sketch'.[6] When Harte attempted to publish his big story of the West three years later, the female proof-reader objected to its immorality and tried to stop the printer from proceeding. But his readers loved it, including the editors of the *Atlantic Monthly*, who wrote immediately asking for a story 'similar to the "Luck" '.[7] The

---

[5] Stewart, *Bret Harte*, p. viii.

[6] Bernard De Voto, *Mark Twain's America* (Houghton Mifflin: Cambridge, Mass., 1932), 175.

[7] Stewart, *Bret Harte*, 167.

relative acclaim accorded both stories more than justified Twain's assertion in 1866 that 'though I am generally placed at the head of my breed of scribblers in this part of the country, the place properly belongs to Bret Harte'.[8]

Margaret Duckett gives a compelling account of this 'strange and finally painful relationship'[9] in her authoritative *Mark Twain and Bret Harte*. Collaboration did not bring the two men close. As Twain wrote in 1870:

Indeed Harte *does* soar, & I am glad of it, notwithstanding he and I are 'off,' these many months. It happened thus. Harte read all of the MS of the 'Innocents' & told me what passages, paragraphs & chapters to leave out—& I followed orders strictly. It was a kind thing for Harte to do, & I think I appreciated it. He praised the book so highly that I wanted him to review it *early* for the *Overland*, & help out the sale there. I told my publisher. He ordered Bancroft to send Harte a couple of books before anybody else. Bancroft declined! . . . Well, Sir, Harte *wrote me the most daintily insulting letter you ever read*—& what I want to know, is, where *I* was to blame?[10]

Harte's *Overland Monthly* did eventually give Twain's book a favourable review, and Twain's gratitude and admiration continued to shade into anger. In the same year he was to deny hotly that he had produced a parody of 'Plain Language from Truthful James', the formal title of Harte's 'The Heathen Chinee'. Some have read 'Tennessee's Partner', published in October 1869, as an allegory about the decline of the Twain–Harte friendship. The story did get a rise out of Twain. In the margin of his copy, he jotted notes that questioned Harte's 'clear knowledge of human nature' when he has the partner *'welcome back* a man who has committed against him that sin which neither the great nor the little ever forgive'.[11]

Twain's publication of *Roughing It* in 1871 was overshadowed by Harte's record-breaking contract with Fields, Osgood and Company. That year at a luncheon in Boston attended by the

[8] Margaret Duckett, *Mark Twain and Bret Harte* (Oklahoma University Press: Norman, 1964), 8.

[9] Ibid., p. vii.

[10] Ibid. 34.

[11] Ibid. 50.

city's literary élite Harte condescendingly put his hand on Twain's shoulder and said, 'This is the dream of his life.'[12] Five years later, down on his luck and in need of funds, Harte invited Twain to collaborate on a play dramatizing aspects of 'The Heathen Chinee'. *Ah Sin* toured Washington and New York but did badly with both the critics and the public. 'The piece perished,' Twain wrote.[13] Harte had borrowed from Twain and not repaid the debt; in the wake of the play's failure Twain took umbrage at a purported remark by Harte about Mrs Clemens. The affair of the play was placed in the hands of attorneys; after 1877, Harte and Twain never again met.

Harte never wrote of Twain with bitterness; it is Twain's anger that has come down to us. In his *Autobiography*, Twain reserves a place of special scorn for his one-time partner. 'Bret Harte was one of the pleasantest men I have ever known. He was also one of the unpleasantest men I have ever known.'[14] Twain presents Harte as a creature of surfaces, a man who had the bad taste to have 'good taste in clothes'.[15] There is no depth: 'I think he was incapable of emotion, for I think he had nothing to feel with. I think his heart was merely a pump and had no other function.'[16] Twain proceeds to imply that Harte is a plagiarist, spendthrift, and general '*Son* of a ——!' More damaging to Harte's future reputation were the repeated claims about the attenuation of emotion that we label 'sentimental'.

As American literature became codified and canonized in the 1920s and 1930s, the only American humorist to achieve the rank of a 'major' writer was Mark Twain. In the process, his work became the centre of a debate between Van Wyck Brooks and Bernard De Voto about the status of money and culture in American life. The attack on Twain's 'craving for success'[17] was

---

[12] Ibid. 69.
[13] *The Autobiography of Mark Twain*, ed. Charles Neider (Harper & Brothers: New York, 1959), 250.
[14] Ibid. 125.
[15] Ibid.
[16] Ibid.
[17] Von Wyck Brooks, *The Ordeal of Mark Twain* (Dutton: New York, 1920), 198.

so vigorous that fifty years of scholarship went into proving him not only a spokesman for American democracy but a skilled ironist and a stylist that any New Critic could rewardingly unpack. Having made the case so well for Twain, the critics might have paused to realize that they had also made the case against Harte. Not only because Harte was the competitor with whom Twain was most closely associated and for whom he felt the most unaffected scorn but because the very literary strategies and values that make Twain—his 'aggressive' rather than a coolly distanced humour, his command of extended as well as brief fictions, his insistence on vernacular rather than conventionalized speech, his attention to the specificity rather than the iconography of setting and place—are largely absent in Harte. The critics did their job so well that in 1935 Ernest Hemingway was able to claim that 'all modern American literature comes from one book by Mark Twain called *Huckleberry Finn*',[18] and this despite the fact that the first story in the 1925 edition of *In Our Time* unfolds as a canny revision of 'The Luck of Roaring Camp'.

In *Understanding Fiction*, Cleanth Brooks and Robert Penn Warren engage in an extended critique of 'Tennessee's Partner' and 'The Outcasts of Poker Flat'. They judge both stories to be sentimental, and they define sentimentality as 'emotional response in excess of the occasion'.[19] 'Excess' is the key word here; it speaks of something faked or unearned, of the desire to enjoy a feeling, as James Joyce has it, without incurring the immense debtorship for a thing done. Nineteenth-century sentimentality exaggerated the capacities of its characters. The sentimental in our time often takes the opposite form, one caught by Wallace Stevens's maxim that 'sentimentality is a failure of feeling'.[20] The exhibition of too little feeling is surely as sentimental as the display of too much, yet the twentieth-

[18] Ernest Hemingway, *Green Hills of Africa* (Scribner's: New York, 1935), 22.

[19] Cleanth Brooks and Robert Penn Warren, *Understanding Fiction* (Appleton-Century-Crofts: New York, 1943), 608.

[20] Wallace Stevens, *Opus Posthumous* (1957; rev. edn. Alfred Knopf: New York, 1989), 189.

century repression of feeling has been glamorized as irony or minimalism or existential angst, while the 'excess' remains, simply, sentimental. It was precisely through an inversion of Harte that Hemingway, who owned a volume of *The Luck of Roaring Camp and Other Tales*, invented his early literary style. 'Indian Camp' owes more than a thematic debt to its literary namesake. Not only do both stories depart from an Indian woman's birth cry, 'a cry unlike anything heard before in the camp' (p. 8–9). Not only in both do a group of bewildered men attend upon and attempt to comprehend the 'hard time' women go through 'having babies'.[21] Not only is each story more comfortable lingering over 'Deaths' than 'birth' (p. 7). In Dr Adams's wilful concentration on improvisational technique (see Harte's 'extempore surgeon' Stumpy, p. 8), in Nick's inability to 'watch',[22] in the displacement of the concrete obstetrical details into abstract nouns like 'it' and 'something',[23] in the whole uncanny sense of an emotion present but undescribed, Hemingway carefully inverts Harte's 'straining for an emotional effect',[24] as Brooks and Warren have it, into a studied numbness. What the stories share, in Harte's phrase, is a fascination with the male stance of 'demonstrative unconcern' (p. 10). So Nick Adams begins his sentimental education, one that will detour through irony and pity before the deliverance of the Hemingway hero into a life of feeling in *For Whom the Bell Tolls*.

A negative model, then, may serve as a valuable literary provocation. Yet the charges against Harte cannot be dropped simply because productive anxiety attends upon his influence. If we focus attention on his plots and their outcomes, the emotions his characters display can seem gratuitous or unearned. Harte's stories turn upon a moment of sacrifice in which an unpromising character experiences a sudden access of nobility: Mother Shipton saves her rations and then gives them, starving, 'to the child' (p. 26). Out of the violently competitive frontier life, Harte unfailingly extracts these melodramas of

[21] Ernest Hemingway, *In Our Time* (Scribner's: New York, 1925 and 1930), 19.
[22] Ibid. 17.
[23] Ibid.
[24] Brooks and Warren, *Understanding Fiction*, 219.

care. Three features of this pattern make, I think, for its sentimentality. First, the pattern is repeated in virtually all of Harte's work. The unlooked-for hero does not fail to present himself. The work thus takes on the quality of an apologue for an unvarying and innate human goodness across the many possible cases. The behaviour looks imposed on life rather than discovered in it. If Harte lacks a vision of evil, so, many have argued, does Emerson, a man who never stopped believing that we bring ideals to life by believing them true.

Speed is the second feature of Harte's plots that make them sentimental. Harte elected to work in *short* short stories. 'Tennessee's Partner' fills fewer than ten modern pages. A prose narrative of this length has room for the 'denouement' on which Poe insisted but for little else. Yet all the while that Harte prepares us for his climaxes he also indulges in claims about character change. In his best story, the word 'regeneration' gets repeated like a mantra. 'And so the work of regeneration began in Roaring Camp. Almost imperceptibly a change came over the settlement' (p. 13). By the end of the paragraph which these sentences begin a 'pastoral happiness' has descended upon the camp. Given the rate at which this evolution occurs, it must necessarily be described rather than dramatized. Like Mliss's 'great change' (p. 87), it is merely said to happen.

The key element in Harte's sentimental complex is his conviction in the signifying power of visible and dramatic incident. He lampoons the whole apparatus of plot-making in 'A Lonely Ride' ('As I stepped into the Slumgullion stage I saw that it was a dark night, a lonely road, and that I was the only passenger', p. 68), a story that delivers on the opening paragraph's promise that despite the portents nothing will happen. Yet Harte's best stories for the most part read like treatments for screenplays; he fills them with outward, describable event. No wonder that by the early 1930s Hollywood had produced three versions of 'Mliss'. What apparently counts as worth narrating for Harte is what is *apparent*. Hemingway called this 'the sequence of motion and fact which made the emotion'.[25] In the 1920s, this was called style. When Harte

<hr />

[25] Ernest Hemingway, *Death in the Afternoon* (Scribner's: New York, 1932), 2.

focuses on the outer rather than the inner life of his characters, the tactic is judged an evasion.

'But one must really make an end of incident.' The words are Mary Austin's, from her 1906 book *The Flock*. Austin was the most inspired inheritor of Harte's California materials, just as Louise Clappe, another woman who wrote cleanly about the West, was his most inspired source. In her 1903 volume *The Land of Little Rain*, Austin published a story called 'Jimville—A Bret Harte Town'. The story provides a brilliant critique of Harte's materials and methods, especially his tropism towards melodramatic event. Her anti-romance counters Harte's disposition to impose a narrative logic on the indeterminacy and accident of life in frontier towns. The residents of Austin's exemplary ghost town are 'untroubled by invention and the dramatic sense'.[26] The desire to narrate is like the desire to name; both can over-organize the world.

'Hear now,' Austin writes, 'how Jimville came by its name.'[27] Austin gives the subject two sentences. The town is named after three Jims—the two men who found the local mines and the one who opens the first hotel. *That* is Bret Harte material. Austin refuses to develop it and proceeds instead with a long paragraph about the 'origin of Squaw Gulch'. New Englander Dimmick's squaw—she has no name—is abandoned by him. She is pregnant. The prospecting Jim Calkins finds her dying in a ravine with 'a three days babe nozzling at her breast'. He buries the squaw, farms out the child, and then returns 'to Squaw Gulch, so named from that day', and discovers his mine. Jim regards 'this piece of luck as interposed for his reward'. Here is the sequence; a woman gets pregnant; a baby is born; the baby is discovered and given away; a mine is discovered. What is the story here? Austin continues, 'Bret Harte would have given you a tale. You see in me a mere recorder, for I know what is best for you; you shall blow out this bubble from your own breath.'

Names here judge the story. Jim's name goes to the town—and to Austin's 'tale'. Despite the fact noted early on that 'the

---

[26] Mary Austin, *Stories from the Country of Lost Borders*, ed. Marjorie Pryse (1903 and 1909; Rutgers University Press: New Brunswick, NJ, 1987), 69–70.
[27] Ibid. 68.

town looks to have spilled out of Squaw Gulch',[28] the name of the town still follows the male. Place for active men and for men, like Harte, who write about them, deserves a name or a narration if it can be commodified as gold or worked up into a marketable fictional subject. Austin attempts to shift attention towards the lives that go unnoticed or are lived largely from within. What would 'The Luck of Roaring Camp' have been if written from the squaw's point of view?

'Perhaps the less said of her the better' (p. 7). Harte's story can be read as about the elision of the female. He has also constructed it to be read far more easily as a sentimental tale about an all-male family romance. Harte's best stories offer their readers the option of identifying with their characters or listening to their narrators. As Harold Kolb argues, 'His crude and sentimental characters are surrounded by a narrative commentary that is refined, cynical, and aloof.'[29] That many readers will resist this tone and submit instead to having tears jerked is a human tendency Harte meant to expose as well as exploit. He is a virtual scientist of that reading practice we call identification, and he knew that the most powerful identifications are achieved not in the ironic transaction of asking a reader to think less of himself but in the sentimental encouragement to feel that one can be more. Harte thus chose to promote identification with characters who rise above themselves; the transfer of emotion is towards a character who achieves a moment of transcendence over limits. The transaction is sentimental because it assumes and plays upon a permanent human sense of defeat and self-pity, a burden that is relieved in seeing Harte's little characters lifted up. Along the way, however, Harte shadows this 'exaltation of feeling',[30] as he calls it in 'An Apostle of the Tules' with a voice that gently mocks it. A master of affective stylistics, Harte writes for a reader in whom he can provoke, more or less simultaneously, a sentimental response and its critique.

[28] Ibid. 67.

[29] Harold H. Kolb, Jr., 'The Outcasts of Literary Flat: Bret Harte as Humorist', *American Literary Realism*, 23 (Winter 1991), 56.

[30] *The Writings of Bret Harte*, Standard Library Edition (Houghton Mifflin: Boston and New York, 1896–1904), iv. 308.

The sentimental assumption in 'The Luck of Roaring Camp' is that men can domesticate a world without the significant assistance of women. The feminization of post-Civil War America is the specific cultural anxiety this fantasy is meant to combat. Readers may associate mining with the Gold Rush itself, but Harte saw the mines, if at all, in 1855, and remains, as George Stewart argues, 'the writer, not of California in '49 and '50, but of California in the middle fifties and even later'.[31] The informing vision was supplied by a man writing in the late 1860s and one well aware that his readership was largely female and that the culture of the manly Argonauts had been supplanted by one in which women were fighting for and gaining increasing power. Jane Tompkins has argued that the Western begins with Owen Wister as a male 'reaction against a female tradition of popular culture',[32] but the Western, both in its conventions and in the tensions that generate them, really begins with Harte.

'There was commotion in Roaring Camp' (p. 7). So the story begins. The word 'commotion' means violent agitation or noisy disturbance and is conventionally used, as Harte does here, as a high falutin and therefore diminishing term—as a word too big for the job. The word belittles. In using it, Harte forecasts the position from which he and those who choose to stand with him might view the story's action. At the same time, the word, in its root meaning, accomplishes a complex pun: Com / motion = to move together. The story will prove to be about a group of men who learn to do just that. Harte's 'sketch' also originates in an act of 'com / motion', the sexual union of Cherokee Sal with—and here, in the uncertainty of the child's paternity, the issue of moving together becomes at once absurd and deadly serious. As 'the only woman in Roaring Camp' (p. 7), and as its prostitute, Sal has in all likelihood endured a commotion with every man—'the father was unknown' (p. 12)—in the 'triangular valley' (p. 8).

Harte's story unfolds through a mixture of tones and implications that can be seen at work in the first sentence in a single

[31] Stewart, *Bret Harte*, 51.
[32] Jane Tompkins, *West of Everything: The Inner Life of Westerns* (Oxford University Press: New York, 1992), 132.

word. The opening pages extend this strategy to the matter of Cherokee Sal. Stewart observes that Harte's stories betray an absence of the 'mother *motif*'.[33] 'The Luck' can be read as a story about the fate of the mother in a world that lacks a language or a set of social practices that can give her a place. The men of the camp have virtually nothing to say about Sal except phrases like 'Sal would get through with it' (p. 8). Against this violent inarticulateness, Harte opposes a narrative voice of turgid solemnity. 'Dissolute, abandoned, and irreclaimable, she was yet suffering a martyrdom hard enough to bear even when veiled by sympathizing womanhood, but now terrible in her loneliness. The primal curse had come to her in that original isolation which must have made the punishment of the first transgression so dreadful' (p. 7). This language judges as it sympathizes, but the net effect is of a sermonizing rhetoric that gets no closer to Sal's inner life than miner Tipton's 'rough on Sal' (p. 7). Harte thus displays, with withering irony, the truth of the axiom with which he begins. Given the available verbal and emotional resources, 'perhaps the less said of her the better'.

Where, in such a discourse, is a reader to take up a secure position? Reading Harte at his best is like taking a projective test. The more comfortably we rest in an offered perspective, the more likely we are to have refused Harte's invitation to remain in a state of sceptical alarm over our values, capacities, and rhetorics. In the pages describing Sal, the words 'sin' and 'sinful' are prominently featured. The last sentence to do so is this one: 'Within an hour she had climbed, as it were, that rugged road that led to the stars, and so passed out of Roaring Camp, its sin and shame, forever' (p. 9). Few readers may avidly pounce here upon the three words 'as it were'. But they do undercut, for those who wish to notice, the expressed fantasy of deliverance. The words are also balanced by another three: 'sin and shame'. Harte here repeats the syllable 'sin' for the third time in the story. The repetition converts the term into a cliché. It becomes a label that goes with Sal, a character introduced to us as 'a very sinful woman'. Harte repeats the

[33] Stewart, *Bret Harte*, 240.

word in order to enact and expose the knee-jerk piety that presumes to so locate and label, a piety he has already traced back to the primal punisher himself. He also drops the phrase 'sin and shame' into the sentence about Sal's passing in a manner so offhand that one is free to nod at it in quiet agreement. Readers who take such judgements straight get the Sal and the heaven they deserve.

Once Sal dies, the camp becomes magically domesticated. The miners start cleaning and stop swearing. The lost mother is replaced by an ass—'the only other being of Cherokee Sal's sex and maternal condition in the settlement' (p. 9). An active womanly presence is further displaced and reintroduced under the cover of a persistent animism. 'Nature took the foundling to her broader breast' (p. 12). An early suggestion that 'female attention' (p. 11) for the baby should be procured meets 'with fierce and unanimous opposition', but, once the men have proven that they can father and mother alone ('They've got vines and flowers round their houses, and they wash themselves twice a day,' p. 16), the decision to invite some 'decent families' into the camp finally occurs.

The sacrifice that this concession to the sex cost these men, who were fiercely sceptical in regard to its general virtue and usefulness, can only be accounted for by their affection for Tommy. A few still held out. But the resolve could not be carried into effect for three months, and the minority meekly yielded in the hope that something might turn up to prevent it. (p. 16)

The story's action will resolve the threat: the flood comes and the Luck is swept away before 'the sex' can be granted entry. 'Something might turn up to prevent it,' the most resistant men hope. 'And it did' (p. 16). This sentence follows directly upon the expressed hope. *And it did*. In the sentence, Harte shifts from describing the wishes of his characters to forecasting the operation of his plot. It is at once a shift in tone and in perspective, one that suspends suspense and places us, with the maker of the plot, in a zone of some remove. Harte comes close to equating plot with wish-fulfilment: he produces, as if on cue, an ending that does 'prevent' the unwelcome female incursion. After this, the ending is largely epilogue. The more compelling event has been Harte's admission that 'something' (the author) willingly generates endings to satisfy a kind of desperate wishing. In 'The Luck of Roaring Camp', plot manages and allays male anxiety.

This is why Harte assigns Kentuck the role of camp spokesman. He voices the bulk of the reported dialogue because he epitomizes the superstition, verging on paranoia, with which the members of the camp interpret the world. Their gambler's mentality that everything signifies and can be read as predictive is projected both on to 'Nature' and the 'd——d little cuss' (p. 10). Thus the baby does not simply respond reflexively to Kentuck's poking hand; 'He rastled with my finger.' Thus Tommy does not merely respond to colour and motion; he is found 'a talking to a jay bird' (p. 15). Harte follows Kentuck's description of the incident with a characteristic 'Howbeit', a word providing a space in which less credulous readers can step back from the sentimental claim. He then slips back into Kentuck's sensibility and winds up the paragraph with an orgy of personification. 'To him the tall redwoods nodded familiarly and sleepily, the bumblebees buzzed, and the rooks cawed a slumbrous accompaniment.' Harte shifts so smoothly between pathetic fallacy and the discreet acknowledgement of it that a reader remains free to determine when and whether to suspend disbelief.

In *The Ordeal of Mark Twain*, Van Wyck Brooks writes about the evasions and poverty experienced by men living on the mining frontier. 'There were so few women among them, for instance, that their sexual lives were either stunted or debased; and children were as rare as the "Luck" of Roaring Camp, a story that shows how hysterical, in consequence of these and similar conditions, the mining population was.'[34] Brooks's sociology may be open to debate, but he does make the important point that Harte's story is hysterical in more than a funny way. Like Hemingway, a latter-day student of male hysteria, Harte is often mistaken for celebrating rather than analysing a deeply troubling and easily mystified complex of male attitudes. The love of understatement, the obsession with order and cleanliness, the humour bordering on cruelty, the homo-erotic bond-

[34] Brooks, *Ordeal of Mark Twain*, 201.

ing that cloaks itself in violence and expertise—all this is summoned in both writers as originating in a fear of female sexuality and power. Such repressions are abetted by the equation of feelings with women and actions with men, a split that not only opposes the genders but forces individuals to deny a part of their human selves. Since both writers were wise enough to acknowledge the return of the repressed, their stories are also haunted by the whole realm of emotion that has been banished and with which women are culturally associated. 'It seemed to relieve him of any unjust implication of sentiment, and Kentuck had the weaknesses of the nobler sex' (p. 10). Sentiment is a weakness, and a property of nobility; the deceptions and confusions in this sentence expose the deep ambivalence Harte's characters so often display in its presence. Harte understood sentimentality as inhering in the extremity as well as in the quantity of a response and so wrote that the extremes—especially in his male characters—often meet. The 'evasion of emotion peculiar to all brothers' (p. 251) (as Harte calls it in 'A Protegee of Jack Hamlin's') typically redounds upon itself. Exiled feeling comes surging back in distorted and melodramatic forms; Harte's men prove sensitive after all. His stories turn upon the big moment when a man acts like a 'woman'—when he feels.

In 1899 Harte published in the *Cornhill Magazine* an essay entitled 'The Rise of the "Short Story"'. He begins by admitting the 'custom of good-natured reviewers to associate the present writer with the origin of the American "short story"'. Harte modestly declines to claim such a position, but he does argue that until he began writing the American short story was 'not characteristic of American life'. (He lists Poe, Longfellow, and Hawthorne as precursors.) The expansion of the frontier and the Civil War offered writers new subjects, he continues, and the development of a unique American 'humour'[35] provided a successful angle of approach. Harte sees himself as a pioneer in this effort through his choice of 'distinctly Californian'[36]

[35] Bret Harte, 'The Rise of the "Short Story"', *Cornhill Magazine*, NS 7 (July 1899), 3.
[36] Ibid. 7.

subjects and characters. 'The secret of the American short story', he concludes, 'was the treatment of characteristic American life, with absolute knowledge of its peculiarities and sympathies with its methods.'[37]

'Unquestionably the influence of Harte upon the American short story has been greater', Fred Lewis Pattee argues, 'than that exerted by any other American author, always excepting Irving.'[38] Harte is the pivotal figure in the history of the short story, but not for the reasons he himself cited. His contribution had less to do with the discovery of an authentic content than with the refinement of a certain kind of effect. The most intelligent and persuasive writing about the American short story by its major practitioners has theorized it in formal rather than thematic terms. These writers view the form as uniquely suited to a highly controlled rhetorical transaction between author and audience. 'Effect', for instance, is the key word in Poe's speculations on the form. 'I prefer commencing with the consideration of an effect,' he writes in 'The Philosophy of Composition'.[39] 'In fiction the dénouement—in all other compositions the intended effect—should be definitely considered and arranged, before writing the first word; and *no* word should be then written which does not tend, or form a part of a sentence which tends to the development of the dénouement or to the strengthening of the effect.'[40] This effect is an emotional epiphany produced through strict authorial control of a reader's emotions. 'Without a certain continuity of effort—without a certain duration or repetition of purpose—the soul is never deeply moved.'[41] Poe's aim was to so move the soul, and he believed that he could do so best through a form that was plotted in a single motion and readable in a single sitting. While James sought, at times, a 'masterly brevity',[42] he came to prefer the 'liberty'[43] of the novel

[37] Ibid. 8.

[38] Fred Lewis Pattee, *The Development of the American Short Story* (Harper & Brothers: New York, 1923), 239–40.

[39] Edgar Allan Poe, *Essays and Reviews*, in the Library of America (1984), 13.

[40] Pattee, *Development of the Short Story*, 133.

[41] Poe, *Essays and Reviews*, 571.

[42] Henry James, *Letters*, vol. iii, ed. Léon Edel (Belknap Press: Cambridge, Mass., 1980), 360.

[43] Ibid. 58.

to the kinds of pleasure afforded by his 'short lengths'.[44] Within the long length, he believed, the attending mind had the freedom to revise its reactions and judgements. Harte, on the other hand, worked best within a form that confined and simplified. When he came to speculate about his chosen form, he lacked a language adequate to his own performance, one that had opened the short story to a wider audience while still deploying it as an inquest into the limits and powers of human attention. His is a work, as my reading of 'The Luck' has shown, about all that stands in the way of our being able to be moved and to respond.

This is not to say that Harte lacked a theme. Harte's work has been delimited as merely local, as in this squib from the high school textbook *United States in Literature* (1982): 'Harte was a journalist and prolific short story writer who became famous for his "reportorial" fiction of the West in the Gold Rush days. These stories are filled with *local color*, dramatic though artificial plotting, and endearing characters who have become Western stereotypes.'[45] Yet Harte's stories actually betray, in his own words, 'very little flavor of the soil'.[46] They display a minimal interest in weather and terrain. 'Though based upon local scenery and local subjects,' Harte wrote in the Preface to his *Condensed Novels*, 'no one is better aware than their author of their deficiency in local coloring.'[47] What they do capture is something else altogether more important and enduring—the recurring American situation of the frontier as a shifting and unlocalized scene of encounter. Harte's project was to open up the question of the Far West for the reading public and to do so by diverting its attention, through the rhetoric and structures of sentiment, from the by no means local or temporary conflicts along that frontier over gender and sex, money and race.

Cultural struggle over gender issues was the focus of Harte's most persistent enquiry. The word 'sex' appears often in Harte,

[44] Ibid. 240.
[45] *United States in Literature* (Glenview, Ill., 1982), 173.
[46] Standard Library Edition, vol. i, p. xii.
[47] *Condensed Novels* (G. W. Carleton & Company: New York, 1867), p. vii.

as in the phrase 'the fair sex'. The conflation of the meanings of 'sex' and 'gender' in such usages is consistent with Harte's interest in the ways in which our repressions of sexuality construct gender and the narratives that regulate it. But Harte also wrote directly about bodily passion and was rare in doing so. In looking back on the writers of his day, Henry Adams ventured the claim in *The Education* that 'all the rest had used sex for sentiment, never for force'.[48] Except, among American writers, he adds, Walt Whitman and 'Bret Harte, as far as the magazines would let him venture'. Harte was a student of the work of loving and how it makes us; hence his fascination with betrayal. 'A Passage in the Life of Mr John Oakhurst' represents love as a man's best work, and 'work' is a syllable the story compulsively repeats. 'How do you like your work?' (p. 219), the recovered 'sick woman' (p. 215) asks the smitten Oakhurst. The transformation of the gambler and the woman he has so discreetly loved is achieved without touching, but elsewhere Harte is less coy about the life of the body. In a story like 'A Protegee of Jack Hamlin's', Harte projects his hero into a world virtually saturated by sex in which women 'make the first advances' (p. 254) and where the most innocent social alliance reinserts Jack into a circuit of desire. The story's opening image of the paddle-wheel forecasts this:

It certainly was a fascinating sight—this sloping rapid, hurrying on to bury itself under the crushing wheels. For a brief moment Jack saw how they would seize anything floating on that ghastly incline, whirl it round in one awful revolution of the beating paddles, and then bury it, broken and shattered out of all recognition, deep in the muddy current of the stream behind them. (p. 233).

Jack gazes at the wheel through the eyes of a 'reckless' woman abandoned by a fellow-gambler. She sees in the promise of destruction a release from shame, but he, having lived and loved longer, sees something more like eternal return, not the manageable end of passion but its obsessive, inexorable churning.

Harte conflated money with gambling, and gambling became for him the figure for hope in a capitalist order. A man must

[48] Henry Adams, *Novels, Mont Saint Michel, The Education*, in the Library of America (1983), 1071.

'make' a living. In 'Bohemian Days in San Francisco', Harte recounts a story about the 'fearful joy in the gambling saloons'.[49] Lured into betting on a roulette wheel, greenhorn Harte, ignorant of the rules of the game, places a 'large coin—the bulk of my possessions'[50] on the table. 'It was not only my coin but my manhood at stake.' The first spin wins him three hundred dollars. Paralysed, he lets the money lie and loses it all. 'But what of that! I was a man!'[51] Harte here provides an ironic origin-tale for his many gambling stories. Gambling is a test of nothing—certainly not manhood—and in its chance operations it sadly approximates the connection between effort, merit, and success in the larger culture. 'Life was at best an uncertain game' (p. 19), he writes in 'The Outcasts of Poker Flat'. Its outcomes are mechanistic, largely a matter of luck. In 'How I Went to the Mines', Harte invokes the miner's belief that ' "luck" would inevitably follow the *first* essay of the neophyte or "greenhorn" ' (p. 290). Harte goes prospecting, immediately finds a nugget—and then nothing more. At the mines Harte witnessed the most brute and arbitrary form of capital formation, an extraction of wealth that had more to do with risk-taking and pure chance than labour or intelligence expended. Harte's first written 'essays' were also similarly lucky, and he knew, from hard and bitter experience, how quickly such luck could turn.

As a writer, Harte was to prove sympathetic to characters who lived on the margins. His lovable Jack Hamlin is a 'half-breed', of mixed white and Indian ancestry. Harte himself 'was by blood a quarter Hebrew',[52] as George Stewart puts it. After his paternal grandfather had married a Gentile, the family suppressed its Jewish heritage. As a newspaperman in the 1850s and early 1860s, Harte proved a staunch abolitionist. As a maker of fictions, he wrote about California as a collision of cultures. He was the first to consolidate the myth of Spanish California, but he was equally engaged by the violent injustices

---

[49] Standard Library Edition, xviii. 139.
[50] Ibid. 140.
[51] Ibid. 141.
[52] Stewart, *Bret Harte*, 16.

of the present, especially those visited upon the Chinese. America was not, in Harte's projection of the frontier, a pot that had melted, but rather the scene of disturbing and sometimes violent negotiations.

'I have read everything relating to the earlier colonial history of the western coast'[53] Harte once maintained. His work contains more than 100 Spanish, Spanish-American, and Mexican characters. Harte romanticized the pre-conquest California he also carefully studied, converting it into one long siesta of 'peaceful, pastoral days' (p. 262). Father Junipero Serra—the founder—haunted his thought. Modern-day American Automobile Association images of whitewashed missions surrounded by vaqueros and industrious Indians owe everything to Harte. Despite his consistently elegiac tone, Harte also proved 'tirelessly concerned', as Stanley T. Williams has written, 'with that moment . . . when one expanding culture overtakes another and leaves behind its engulfing waves islets of the old'.[54] Implicit within Harte's elegy for 'that glorious Indian summer of California history' (p. 107) then, is an awareness of the cost and workings of imperialism along that 'locus of first cultural contact'[55] that Annette Kolodny defines as a frontier.

Harte's 1870 volume was titled *The Luck of Roaring Camp and Other Sketches*, and I have included the complete text of that volume (pp. 1–150) in the present edition. The volume contains Harte's most famous 'sketches', but in the appended 'Stories' and 'Bohemian Papers' another tone intrudes. It is a kind of swelling racial sorrow. Here he renounces 'the attitude of deception kept up at the front windows' (p. 146) of our lives. 'Notes by Flood and Field' re-enacts the appropriation of Mexican ranchos by the invading Americans, and predicts, through the figure of the flood, the eventual engulfment of the invaders. 'The Mission Dolores' imagines the 'last Greaser' giving way to the bustling Yankee, a shift that involves a diminishment of speech. 'Gutterals have taken the place of

[53] Stanley T. Williams, *The Spanish Background of American Literature* (Yale University Press: New Haven, Conn., 1955), 215.

[54] Ibid. 233.

[55] Annette Kolodny, 'Letting Go Our Grand Obsessions: Notes Toward a New History of the American Frontiers', *American Literature*, 64 (Mar. 1992), 3.

linguals and sibilants' (p. 140). In the piece called 'John Chinaman', Harte concedes the 'delicate pliability of the Chinese expression and taste' (p. 143) while admitting 'the impossibility of determining' much of anything about their inner life. Harte condemns the 'vulgar clamor about servile and degraded races' (p. 144) just as the narrator of 'Wan Lee, the Pagan' draws us into a bemused tour of the exotic and then suddenly exposes us to the jingoism that 'set upon and killed unarmed, defenseless foreigners' (p. 208). Harte saw that the frontier would unfold as a struggle over race disguised as a romance about freedom and the purity of the national character; even in 'The Luck', he allows, 'No encouragement was given to immigration' (p. 15). Beyond this, in his lecture 'The Argonauts of '49', he locates and celebrates the acts of resistance displayed by the 'Spaniard' and the 'Heathen Chinee'. Both types represent what Harte calls 'available memory' (p. 278). Deprived of a public sphere in which they can distend their manhood, these figures become heroes of 'inner consciousness' (p. 278). Because he does not and cannot appropriate that inner life, Harte grants these figures a subjectivity that is not sentimentalized. He also shows how they 'get even' (p. 280) as in the Chinese citizen who opens a 'doctor's office' in San Francisco. *That*, Harte knew, was the future of California. In these deceptively modest pieces, Harte chooses to look through 'back windows' at the shadows of our lives, and if his critics have failed to see as far or feel as deeply, he did not fail to provide his readers with the means for doing so.

NOTE ON THE TEXT

THE present volume contains the entire text of the first edition of *The Luck of Roaring Camp and Other Sketches*, published in 1870 in Boston by Fields, Osgood, and Company. One misprint has been silently corrected, five commas have been added, and one deleted. No other alterations have been made to the text apart from the imposition of single quotation marks, and the removal of points after 'Mr', 'Mrs', 'Dr', and 'St'. In addition, I have reprinted five short stories, Harte's most popular lecture (first given in 1872 and printed here in the expanded, published version), and a personal narrative of his early days in California. The text of these seven works follows that of *The Writings of Bret Harte*, Standard Library Edition (Houghton, Mifflin and Company: Boston, 1896–1904).

SELECT BIBLIOGRAPHY

Place of publication is New York unless stated otherwise.

EDITIONS

'The Rise of the "Short Story" ', *Cornhill Magazine*, NS 7 (July 1899), 1–8.

Stegner, Wallace, *The Outcasts of Poker Flat and Other Tales* (NAL, 1961).

The Writings of Bret Harte, Standard Library Edition (Houghton Mifflin: Boston and New York, 1896–1904).

BIOGRAPHY, BACKGROUND, AND CRITICISM

Barnett, Linda Diz, *Bret Harte: A Reference Guide* (G. K. Hall: Boston, 1980).

Canby, Henry Seidel, 'The Luck of Bret Harte', *Saturday Review of Literature* (17 Apr. 1926), 717–18.

Clappe, Louise A. K. S., *The Shirley Letters* (1854–55; Peregrine: Santa Barbara and Salt Lake City, 1970).

Duckett, Margaret, 'Bret Harte and the Indians of Northern California', *Huntington Library Quarterly*, 18 (Nov. 1954), 59–83.

—— *Mark Twain and Bret Harte* (Oklahoma University Press: Norman, 1964).

Gaer, Joseph, *Bret Harte: Bibliography and Biographical Data* (California Research Project, 1935; rpt. Burt Franklin, 1978).

Kolb, Harold H., Jr., 'The Outcasts of Literary Flat: Bret Harte as Humorist', *American Literary Realism*, 23 (Winter 1991), 52–63.

The Letters of Bret Harte, ed. Geoffrey Bret Harte (Houghton Mifflin: Boston, 1926).

Morrow, Patrick, *Bret Harte: Literary Critic* (Popular Press: Bowling Green, Ohio, 1979).

Pattee, Fred Lewis, *The Development of the American Short Story* (Harper & Brothers, 1923).

Scharnhorst, Gary, *Bret Harte* (Twayne, 1992).

Stewart, George, *Bret Harte: Argonaut and Exile* (Houghton Mifflin: Boston, 1931).

Thomas, Jeffrey F., 'Bret Harte and the Power of Sex', *Western American Literature*, 8 (Fall 1973), 91–109.

Walker, Franklin, *San Francisco's Literary Frontier* (Knopf, 1939).

Williams, Stanley T., *The Spanish Background of American Literature* (Yale University Press: New Haven, Conn., 1955).

A CHRONOLOGY OF BRET HARTE

1836 Born Francis Brett Hart, 25 August, Albany NY, to Henry Philip Hart and Elizabeth Rebecca (Ostrander) Hart.

1854 Travels across Nicaragua and joins mother in San Francisco. Harte family settles in Oakland.

1855 According to 'How I Went to the Mines', visits the mining area near Robinson's Ferry (Melones) along the Stanislaus River.

1857 Works as Wells Fargo expressman 'for a brief delightful hour'. First of Harte's published writings to be preserved, the poem 'The Valentine', printed in the *Golden Era*.

1857 Moves to Uniontown; begins work as printer's devil and editorial assistant on the *Northern Californian* in 1858.

1860 Returns to San Francisco abruptly after printing protesting headline about massacre of a local Indian tribe. Typesetter and contributor on staff of the *Golden Era*. First uses signature 'Bret Harte'. Publishes 'The Work on Red Mountain', later called 'Mliss'.

1861 Clerk in US Surveyor General's office, San Francisco.

1862 Marries Anna Griswold, 11 August at San Rafael.

1863–9 Serves on Staff of US Branch Mint, San Francisco.

1864–7 Contributor to and occasional editor of the weekly *Californian*.

1864 Meets Mark Twain in San Francisco.

1866 Edits the controversial *Outcroppings, Being Selections of California Verse*.

1867 Publishes his first book, *Condensed Novels and Other Papers*.

1868–70 Founding editor of the *Overland Monthly*.

1868 Unsigned story 'The Luck of Roaring Camp' appears in the *Overland Monthly* in August.

1869 Publishes 'The Outcasts of Poker Flat' in January; 'Miggles' in June; 'Tennessee's Partner' in October; and 'The Idyl of Red Gulch' in December.

1870 Publishes 'Brown of Calaveras' in March and the poem 'Plain Language from Truthful James' ('The Heathen Chinee') in September. Publishes *The Luck of Roaring Camp and Other Sketches*. Declines offer of professorship of Recent Literature at the University of California, Berkeley.

1871 Leaves California with his family in February. Contracts with Fields, Osgood & Company to contribute exclusively to the *Atlantic Monthly* and *Every Saturday* for 12 months for $10,000. Delivers Phi Beta Kappa poem at Harvard commencement.

1872 Reluctantly begins lecturing throughout the eastern and southern United States. Richard Henry Dana introduces Harte and his 'The Argonauts of '49' in Boston.

1876 Publishes his only novel, *Gabriel Conroy*.

1877 Collaborates on the play *Ah Sin* with Mark Twain.

1878–80 Commercial Agent of the United States in Krefeld, Prussia.

1880–5 US Consul in Glasgow, Scotland.

1885 Harte removed as Consul. Moves into the home of Arthur and Madame M. S. Van de Velde in London. Contracts with A. P. Watt to handle his business affairs and resumes fulltime writing.

1898 Harte moves to rooms of his own; Harte's wife visits England; Harte continues to send her his monthly cheque.

1902 Dies of cancer of the throat on 5 May in Camberley, Surrey.

THE LUCK OF ROARING CAMP,

and Other Sketches

PREFACE

A SERIES of designs—suggested, I think, by Hogarth's familiar cartoons* of the Industrious and Idle Apprentices—I remember as among the earliest efforts at moral teaching in California. They represented the respective careers of The Honest and Dissolute Miners: the one, as I recall him, retrograding through successive planes of dirt, drunkenness, disease, and death; the other advancing by corresponding stages to affluence and a white shirt. Whatever may have been the artistic defects of these drawings, the moral at least was obvious and distinct. That it failed, however,—as it did,—to produce the desired reform in mining morality may have been owing to the fact that the average miner refused to recognize himself in either of these positive characters; and that even he who might have sat for the model of the Dissolute Miner was perhaps dimly conscious of some limitations and circumstances which partly relieved him from responsibility. 'Yer see,' remarked such a critic to the writer, in the untranslatable poetry of his class, 'it ain't no square game. They've just put up the keerds on that chap from the start.'

With this lamentable example before me, I trust that in the following sketches I have abstained from any positive moral. I might have painted my villains of the blackest dye,—so black, indeed, that the originals thereof would have contemplated them with the glow of comparative virtue. I might have made it impossible for them to have performed a virtuous or generous action, and have thus avoided that moral confusion which is apt to arise in the contemplation of mixed motives and qualities. But I should have burdened myself with the responsibility of their creation, which, as a humble writer of romance and entitled to no particular reverence, I did not care to do.

I fear I cannot claim, therefore, any higher motive than to illustrate an era of which Californian history has preserved the incidents more often than the character of the actors,—an era which the panegyrist was too often content to bridge over with a general compliment to its survivors,—an era still so recent that in attempting to revive its poetry, I am conscious also of awakening the more prosaic recollections of these same survivors,—and yet an era replete with a certain heroic Greek poetry, of which perhaps none were more unconscious than the heroes themselves. And I shall be quite content to have collected here merely the materials for the Iliad that is yet to be sung.

San Francisco, December 24, 1869.

SKETCHES

THE LUCK OF ROARING CAMP

THERE was commotion in Roaring Camp. It could not have been a fight, for in 1850 that was not novel enough to have called together the entire settlement. The ditches and claims were not only deserted, but 'Tuttle's grocery' had contributed its gamblers, who, it will be remembered, calmly continued their game the day that French Pete and Kanaka Joe shot each other to death over the bar in the front room. The whole camp was collected before a rude cabin on the outer edge of the clearing. Conversation was carried on in a low tone, but the name of a woman was frequently repeated. It was a name familiar enough in the camp,—'Cherokee Sal'.

Perhaps the less said of her the better. She was a coarse, and, it is to be feared, a very sinful woman. But at that time she was the only woman in Roaring Camp, and was just then lying in sore extremity, when she most needed the ministration of her own sex. Dissolute, abandoned, and irreclaimable, she was yet suffering a martyrdom hard enough to bear even when veiled by sympathizing womanhood, but now terrible in her loneliness. The primal curse had come to her in that original isolation which must have made the punishment of the first transgression so dreadful. It was, perhaps, part of the expiation of her sin, that, at a moment when she most lacked her sex's intuitive tenderness and care, she met only the half-contemptuous faces of her masculine associates. Yet a few of the spectators were, I think, touched by her sufferings. Sandy Tipton thought it was 'rough on Sal', and, in the contemplation of her condition, for a moment rose superior to the fact that he had an ace and two bowers* in his sleeve.

It will be seen, also, that the situation was novel. Deaths were by no means uncommon in Roaring Camp, but a birth was a new thing. People had been dismissed the camp effectively, finally, and with no possibility of return; but this was the first time that anybody had been introduced *ab initio*. Hence the excitement.

'You go in there, Stumpy,' said a prominent citizen known as 'Kentuck', addressing one of the loungers. 'Go in there, and see what you kin do. You've had experience in them things.'

Perhaps there was a fitness in the selection. Stumpy, in other climes, had been the putative head of two families; in fact, it was owing to some legal informality in these proceedings that Roaring Camp—a city of refuge—was indebted to his company. The crowd approved the choice, and Stumpy was wise enough to bow to the majority. The door closed on the extempore surgeon and midwife, and Roaring Camp sat down outside, smoked its pipe, and awaited the issue.

The assemblage numbered about a hundred men. One or two of these were actual fugitives from justice, some were criminal, and all were reckless. Physically, they exhibited no indication of their past lives and character. The greatest scamp had a Raphael* face, with a profusion of blond hair; Oakhurst, a gambler, had the melancholy air and intellectual abstraction of a Hamlet; the coolest and most courageous man was scarcely over five feet in height, with a soft voice and an embarrassed, timid manner. The term 'roughs' applied to them was a distinction rather than a definition. Perhaps in the minor details of fingers, toes, ears, etc., the camp may have been deficient, but these slight omissions did not detract from their aggregate force. The strongest man had but three fingers on his right hand; the best shot had but one eye.

Such was the physical aspect of the men that were dispersed around the cabin. The camp lay in a triangular valley, between two hills and a river. The only outlet was a steep trail over the summit of a hill that faced the cabin, now illuminated by the rising moon. The suffering woman might have seen it from the rude bunk whereon she lay,—seen it winding like a silver thread until it was lost in the stars above.

A fire of withered pine-boughs added sociability to the gathering. By degrees the natural levity of Roaring Camp returned. Bets were freely offered and taken regarding the result. Three to five that 'Sal would get through with it'; even, that the child would survive; side bets as to the sex and complexion of the coming stranger. In the midst of an excited discussion an exclamation came from those nearest the door, and the camp stopped to listen. Above the swaying and moaning of the pines, the swift rush of the river, and the crackling of the fire, rose a sharp, querulous cry,—a cry unlike anything heard before in the camp. The pines stopped moaning, the river ceased to rush, and the fire to crackle. It seemed as if Nature had stopped to listen too.

The camp rose to its feet as one man! It was proposed to explode a barrel of gunpowder, but, in consideration of the situation of the mother, better counsels prevailed, and only a few revolvers were discharged; for, whether owing to the rude surgery of the camp, or some other reason, Cherokee Sal was sinking fast. Within an hour she had climbed, as it were, that rugged road that led to the stars, and so passed out of Roaring Camp, its sin and shame, forever. I do not think that the announcement disturbed them much, except in speculation as to the fate of the child. 'Can he live now?' was asked of Stumpy. The answer was doubtful. The only other being of Cherokee Sal's sex and maternal condition in the settlement was an ass. There was some conjecture as to fitness, but the experiment was tried. It was less problematical than the ancient treatment of Romulus and Remus,* and apparently as successful.

When these details were completed, which exhausted another hour, the door was opened, and the anxious crowd of men who had already formed themselves into a queue, entered in single file. Beside the low bunk or shelf, on which the figure of the mother was starkly outlined below the blankets stood a pine table. On this a candle-box was placed, and within it, swathed in staring red flannel, lay the last arrival at Roaring Camp. Beside the candle-box was placed a hat. Its use was soon indicated. 'Gentlemen,' said Stumpy, with a singular mixture of authority and *ex officio** complacency,—'Gentlemen will please pass in at the front door, round the table, and out at the back door. Them as wishes to contribute anything toward the orphan will find a hat handy.' The first man entered with his hat on; he uncovered, however, as he looked about him, and so, unconsciously, set an example to the next. In such communities good and bad actions are catching. As the procession filed in, comments were audible,—criticisms addressed, perhaps, rather to Stumpy, in the character of showman,—'Is that him?' 'mighty small specimen'; 'hasn't mor'n got the color'; 'ain't bigger nor a derringer.' The contributions were as characteristic: A silver tobacco-box; a doubloon; a navy revolver, silver mounted; a gold specimen; a very beautifully embroidered lady's handkerchief (from Oakhurst the gambler); a diamond breastpin; a diamond ring (suggested by the pin, with the remark from the giver that he 'saw that pin and went two diamonds better'); a slung shot; a Bible (contributor not detected); a golden spur; a silver teaspoon (the initials, I regret to say, were not the giver's); a pair of surgeon's shears; a lancet; a Bank of England note for £5; and about $200 in loose gold and silver coin. During these proceedings Stumpy maintained a silence as impassive as the dead on his left, a gravity as inscrutable as that of the newly born on his right. Only one incident occurred to break the monotony of the curious procession. As Kentuck bent over the candle-box half curiously, the child turned, and, in a spasm of pain, caught at his groping finger, and held it fast for a moment. Kentuck looked foolish and embarrassed. Something like a blush tried to assert itself in his weather-beaten cheek. 'The d—d little cuss!' he said, as he extricated his finger, with, perhaps, more tenderness and care than he might have been deemed capable of showing. He held that finger a little apart from its fellows as he went out, and examined it curiously. The examination provoked the same original remark in regard to the child. In fact, he seemed to enjoy repeating it. 'He rastled with my finger,' he remarked to Tipton, holding up the member, 'the d—d little cuss!'

It was four o'clock before the camp sought repose. A light burnt in the cabin where the watchers sat, for Stumpy did not go to bed that night. Nor did Kentuck. He drank quite freely, and related with great gusto his experience, invariably ending with his characteristic condemnation of the new-comer. It seemed to relieve him of any unjust implication of sentiment, and Kentuck had the weaknesses of the nobler sex. When everybody else had gone to bed, he walked down to the river, and whistled reflectingly. Then he walked up the gulch, past the cabin, still whistling with demonstrative unconcern. At a large redwood tree he paused and retraced his steps, and again passed the cabin. Half-way down to the river's bank he again paused, and then returned and knocked at the door. It was opened by Stumpy. 'How goes it?' said Kentuck, looking past Stumpy toward the candle-box. 'All serene,' replied Stumpy.

'Anything up?' 'Nothing.' There was a pause—an embarrassing one—Stumpy still holding the door. Then Kentuck had recourse to his finger, which he held up to Stumpy. 'Rastled with it,—the d—d little cuss,' he said, and retired.

The next day Cherokee Sal had such rude sepulture as Roaring Camp afforded. After her body had been committed to the hillside, there was a formal meeting of the camp to discuss what should be done with her infant. A resolution to adopt it was unanimous and enthusiastic. But an animated discussion in regard to the manner and feasibility of providing for its wants at once sprung up. It was remarkable that the argument partook of none of those fierce personalities with which discussions were usually conducted at Roaring Camp. Tipton proposed that they should send the child to Red Dog,—a distance of forty miles,—where female attention could be procured. But the unlucky suggestion met with fierce and unanimous opposition. It was evident that no plan which entailed parting from their new acquisition would for a moment be entertained. 'Besides,' said Tom Ryder, 'them fellows at Red Dog would swap it, and ring in somebody else on us.' A disbelief in the honesty of other camps prevailed at Roaring Camp as in other places.

The introduction of a female nurse in the camp also met with objection. It was argued that no decent woman could be prevailed to accept Roaring Camp as her home, and the speaker urged that 'they didn't want any more of the other kind.' This unkind allusion to the defunct mother, harsh as it may seem, was the first spasm of propriety,—the first symptom of the camp's regeneration. Stumpy advanced nothing. Perhaps he felt a certain delicacy in interfering with the selection of a possible successor in office. But when questioned, he averred stoutly that he and 'Jinny'—the mammal before alluded to—could manage to rear the child. There was something original, independent, and heroic about the plan that pleased the camp. Stumpy was retained. Certain articles were sent for to Sacramento.* 'Mind,' said the treasurer, as he pressed a bag of gold-dust into the expressman's hand, 'the best that can be got,—lace, you know, and filigree-work and frills,—d—m the cost!'

Strange to say, the child thrived. Perhaps the invigorating climate of the mountain camp was compensation for material deficiencies. Nature took the foundling to her broader breast. In that rare atmosphere of the Sierra foot-hills,—that air pungent with balsamic odor, that ethereal cordial at once bracing and exhilarating,—he may have found food and nourishment, or a subtle chemistry that transmuted asses' milk to lime and phosphorus. Stumpy inclined to the belief that it was the latter and good nursing. 'Me and that ass,' he would say, 'has been father and mother to him! Don't you,' he would add, apostrophizing the helpless bundle before him, 'never go back on us.'

By the time he was a month old, the necessity of giving him a name became apparent. He had generally been known as 'the Kid,' 'Stumpy's boy,' 'the Cayote' (an allusion to his vocal powers), and even by Kentuck's endearing diminutive of 'the d—d little cuss.' But these were felt to be vague and unsatisfactory, and were at last dismissed under another influence. Gamblers and adventurers are generally superstitious, and Oakhurst one day declared that the baby had brought 'the luck' to Roaring Camp. It was certain that of late they had been successful. 'Luck' was the name agreed upon, with the prefix of Tommy for greater convenience. No allusion was made to the mother, and the father was unknown. 'It's better,' said the philosophical Oakhurst, 'to take a fresh deal all round. Call him Luck, and start him fair.' A day was accordingly set apart for the christening. What was meant by this ceremony the reader may imagine, who has already gathered some idea of the reckless irreverence of Roaring Camp. The master of ceremonies was one 'Boston,' a noted wag, and the occasion seemed to promise the greatest facetiousness. This ingenious satirist had spent two days in preparing a burlesque of the church service, with pointed local allusions. The choir was properly trained, and Sandy Tipton was to stand godfather. But after the procession had marched to the grove with music and banners, and the child had been deposited before a mock altar, Stumpy stepped before the expectant crowd. 'It ain't my style to spoil fun, boys,' said the little man, stoutly, eying the faces around him, 'but it strikes me that this thing ain't exactly on the squar. It's playing it pretty low down on this yer baby to ring in fun on him that he ain't going to understand. And ef there's going to be any godfathers round, I'd like to see who's got any better rights than me.' A silence followed Stumpy's speech. To the credit of all humorists be it said, that the first man to acknowledge its justice was the satirist, thus stopped of his fun. 'But,' said Stumpy, quickly, following up his advantage, 'we're here for a christening, and we'll have it. I proclaim you Thomas Luck, according to the laws of the United States and the State of California, so help me God.' It was the first time that the name of the Deity had been uttered otherwise than profanely in the camp. The form of christening was perhaps even more ludicrous than the satirist had conceived; but, strangely enough, nobody saw it and nobody laughed. 'Tommy' was christened as seriously as he would have been under a Christian roof, and cried and was comforted in as orthodox fashion.

And so the work of regeneration began in Roaring Camp. Almost imperceptibly a change came over the settlement. The cabin assigned to 'Tommy Luck'—or 'The Luck,' as he was more frequently called—first showed signs of improvement. It was kept scrupulously clean and whitewashed. Then it was boarded, clothed, and papered. The rosewood cradle—packed eighty miles by mule—had, in Stumpy's way of putting it, 'sorter killed the rest of the furniture.' So the rehabilitation of the cabin became a necessity. The men who were in the habit of lounging in at Stumpy's to see 'how The Luck got on' seemed to appreciate the change, and, in self-defence, the rival establishment of 'Tuttle's grocery' bestirred itself, and imported a carpet and mirrors. The reflections of the latter on the appearance of Roaring Camp tended to produce stricter habits of personal cleanliness. Again, Stumpy imposed a kind of quarantine upon those who aspired to the honor and privilege of holding 'The Luck.' It was a cruel mortification to Kentuck—who, in the carelessness of a large nature and the habits of frontier life, had begun to regard all garments as a second cuticle, which, like a snake's, only sloughed off through decay—to be debarred this privilege from certain prudential reasons. Yet such was the subtle influence of innovation that he thereafter appeared regularly every afternoon in a clean shirt, and face still shining from his ablutions. Nor were moral and social sanitary laws neglected. 'Tommy,' who was supposed to spend his whole existence in a persistent attempt to repose, must not be disturbed by noise. The shouting and yelling which had gained the camp its infelicitous title were not permitted within hearing distance of Stumpy's. The men conversed in whispers, or smoked with Indian gravity. Profanity was tacitly given up in these sacred precincts, and throughout the camp a popular form of expletive, known as 'D——n the luck!' and 'Curse the luck!' was abandoned, as having a new personal bearing. Vocal music was not interdicted, being supposed to have a soothing, tranquillizing quality, and one song, sung by 'Man-o'-War Jack,' an English sailor, from her Majesty's Australian colonies, was quite popular as a lullaby. It was a lugubrious recital of the exploits of 'the Arethusa, Seventy-four,' in a muffled minor, ending with a prolonged dying fall at the burden of each verse, 'On b-o-o-o-ard of the Arethusa.' It was a fine sight to see Jack holding The Luck, rocking from side to side as if with the motion of a ship, and crooning forth this naval ditty. Either through the peculiar rocking of Jack or the length of his song,—it contained ninety stanzas, and was continued with conscientious deliberation to the bitter end,— the lullaby generally had the desired effect. At such times the men would lie at full length under the trees, in the soft summer twilight, smoking their pipes and drinking in the melodious utterances. An indistinct idea that this was pastoral happiness pervaded the camp. 'This 'ere kind o' think,' said the Cockney Simmons, meditatively reclining on his elbow, 'is 'evingly.' It reminded him of Greenwich.

On the long summer days The Luck was usually carried to the gulch, from whence the golden store of Roaring Camp was taken. There, on a blanket spread over pine-boughs, he would lie while the men were working in the ditches below. Latterly, there was a rude attempt to decorate this bower with flowers and sweet-smelling shrubs, and generally some one would bring him a cluster of wild honeysuckles, azaleas, or the painted blossoms of Las Mariposas.* The men had suddenly awakened to the fact that there were beauty and significance in these trifles, which they had so long trodden carelessly beneath their feet. A flake of glittering mica, a fragment of variegated quartz, a bright pebble from the bed of the creek, became beautiful to eyes thus cleared and strengthened and were invariably put aside for 'The Luck.' It was wonderful how many treasures the woods and hillsides yielded that 'would do for Tommy.' Surrounded by playthings such as never child out of fairy-land had before, it is to be hoped that Tommy was content. He appeared to be securely happy albeit there was an infantine gravity about him, a contemplative light in his round gray eyes, that sometimes worried Stumpy. He was always tractable and quiet, and it is recorded that once, having crept beyond his 'corral,'—a hedge of tessellated pine-boughs, which surrounded his bed,—he dropped over the bank on his head in the soft earth, and remained with his mottled legs in the air in that position for at least five minutes with unflinching gravity. He was extricated without a murmur. I hesitate to record the many other instances of his sagacity, which rest, unfortunately, upon the statements of prejudiced friends. Some of them were not without a tinge of superstition. 'I crep' up the bank just now,' said Kentuck one day, in a breathless state of excitement, 'and dern my skin if he wasn't a talking to a jay-bird as was a sittin' on his lap. There they was, just as free and sociable as anything you please, a jawin' at each other just like two cherry-bums.' Howbeit, whether creeping over the pine-boughs or lying lazily on his back blinking at the leaves above him, to him the birds sang, the squirrels chattered, and the flowers bloomed. Nature was his nurse and playfellow. For him she would let slip between the leaves golden shafts of sunlight that fell just within his grasp; she would send wandering breezes to visit him with the balm of bay and resinous gums; to him the tall red-woods nodded familiarly and sleepily, the bumble-bees buzzed, and the rooks cawed a slumbrous accompaniment.

Such was the golden summer of Roaring Camp. They were 'flush times,'—and the Luck was with them. The claims had yielded enormously. The camp was jealous of its privileges and looked suspiciously on strangers. No encouragement was given to immigration, and, to make their seclusion more perfect, the land on either side of the mountain wall that surrounded the camp they duly preempted. This, and a reputation for singular proficiency with the revolver, kept the reserve of Roaring Camp inviolate. The expressman—their only connecting link with the surrounding world—sometimes told wonderful stories of the camp. He would say, 'They've a street up there in 'Roaring,' that would lay over any street in Red Dog. They've got vines and flowers round their houses, and they wash themselves twice a day. But they're mighty rough on strangers, and they worship an Ingin baby.'

With the prosperity of the camp came a desire for further improvement. It was proposed to build a hotel in the following spring, and to invite one or two decent families to reside there for the sake of 'The Luck,'—who might perhaps profit by female companionship. The sacrifice that this concession to the sex cost these men, who were fiercely sceptical in regard to its general virtue and usefulness, can only be accounted for by their affection for Tommy. A few still held out. But the resolve could not be carried into effect for three months, and the minority meekly yielded in the hope that something might turn up to prevent it. And it did.

The winter of 1851 will long be remembered in the foot-hills. The snow lay deep on the Sierras, and every mountain creek became a river, and every river a lake. Each gorge and gulch was transformed into a tumultuous watercourse that descended the hillsides, tearing down giant trees and scattering its drift and débris along the plain. Red Dog had been twice under water, and Roaring Camp had been forewarned. 'Water put the gold into them gulches,' said Stumpy. 'It's been here once and will be here again!' And that night the North Fork suddenly leaped over its banks, and swept up the triangular valley of Roaring Camp.

In the confusion of rushing water, crushing trees, and crackling timber, and the darkness which seemed to flow with the water and blot out the fair valley, but little could be done to collect the scattered camp. When the morning broke, the cabin of Stumpy nearest the river-bank was gone. Higher up the gulch they found the body of its unlucky owner; but the pride, the hope, the joy, the Luck, of Roaring Camp had disappeared. They were returning with sad hearts, when a shout from the bank recalled them.

It was a relief-boat from down the river. They had picked up, they said, a man and an infant, nearly exhausted, about two miles below. Did anybody know them, and did they belong here?

It needed but a glance to show them Kentuck lying there, cruelly crushed and bruised, but still holding the Luck of Roaring Camp in his arms. As they bent over the strangely assorted pair, they saw that the child was cold and pulseless. 'He is dead,' said one. Kentuck opened his eyes. 'Dead?' he repeated feebly. 'Yes, my man, and you are dying too.' A smile lit the eyes of the expiring Kentuck. 'Dying,' he repeated, 'he's a taking me with him,—tell the boys I've got the Luck with me now'; and the strong man, clinging to the frail babe as a drowning man is said to cling to a straw, drifted away into the shadowy river that flows forever to the unknown sea.

THE OUTCASTS OF POKER FLAT

As Mr John Oakhurst, gambler, stepped into the main street of Poker Flat on the morning of the twenty-third of November, 1850, he was conscious of a change in its moral atmosphere since the preceding night. Two or three men, conversing earnestly together, ceased as he approached, and exchanged significant glances. There was a Sabbath lull in the air, which, in a settlement unused to Sabbath influences, looked ominous.

Mr Oakhurst's calm, handsome face betrayed small concern in these indications. Whether he was conscious of any predisposing cause, was another question. 'I reckon they're after somebody,' he reflected; 'likely it's me.' He returned to his pocket the handkerchief with which he had been whipping away the red dust of Poker Flat from his neat boots, and quietly discharged his mind of any further conjecture.

In point of fact, Poker Flat was 'after somebody'. It had lately suffered the loss of several thousand dollars, two valuable horses, and a prominent citizen. It was experiencing a spasm of virtuous reaction, quite as lawless and ungovernable as any of the acts that had provoked it. A secret committee had determined to rid the town of all improper persons. This was done permanently in regard of two men who were then hanging from the boughs of a sycamore in the gulch, and temporarily in the banishment of certain other objectionable characters. I regret to say that some of these were ladies. It is but due to the sex, however, to state that their impropriety was professional, and it was only in such easily established standards of evil that Poker Flat ventured to sit in judgment.

Mr Oakhurst was right in supposing that he was included in this category. A few of the committee had urged hanging him as a possible example, and a sure method of reimbursing themselves from his pockets of the sums he had won from them. 'It's agin justice,' said Jim Wheeler, 'to let this yer young man from Roaring Camp—an entire stranger—carry away our money.' But a crude sentiment of equity residing in the breasts of those who had been fortunate enough to win from Mr Oakhurst overruled this narrower local prejudice.

Mr Oakhurst received his sentence with philosophic calmness, none the less coolly that he was aware of the hesitation of his judges. He was too much of a gambler not to accept Fate. With him life was at best an uncertain game, and he recognized the usual percentage in favor of the dealer.

A body of armed men accompanied the deported wickedness of Poker Flat to the outskirts of the settlement. Besides Mr Oakhurst, who was known to be a coolly desperate man, and for whose intimidation the armed escort was intended, the expatriated party consisted of a young woman familiarly known as 'The Duchess'; another, who had won the title of 'Mother Shipton'; and 'Uncle Billy,' a suspected sluice-robber and confirmed drunkard. The cavalcade provoked no comments from the spectators, nor was any word uttered by the escort. Only, when the gulch which marked the uttermost limit of Poker Flat was reached, the leader spoke briefly and to the point. The exiles were forbidden to return at the peril of their lives.

As the escort disappeared, their pent-up feelings found vent in a few hysterical tears from the Duchess, some bad language from Mother Shipton, and a Parthian volley* of expletives from Uncle Billy. The philosophic Oakhurst alone remained silent. He listened calmly to Mother Shipton's desire to cut somebody's heart out, to the repeated statements of the Duchess that she would die in the road, and to the alarming oaths that seemed to be bumped out of Uncle Billy as he rode forward. With the easy good-humor characteristic of his class, he insisted upon exchanging his own riding-horse, 'Five Spot,' for the sorry mule which the Duchess rode. But even this act did not draw the party into any closer sympathy. The young woman readjusted her somewhat draggled plumes with a feeble, faded coquetry; Mother Shipton eyed the possessor of 'Five Spot' with malevolence, and Uncle Billy included the whole party in one sweeping anathema.

The road to Sandy Bar—a camp that, not having as yet experienced the regenerating influences of Poker Flat, consequently seemed to offer some invitation to the emigrants—lay over a steep mountain range. It was distant a day's severe travel. In that advanced season, the party soon passed out of the moist, temperate regions of the foot-hills into the dry, cold, bracing air of the Sierras. The trail was narrow and difficult. At noon the Duchess, rolling out of her saddle upon the ground, declared her intention of going no farther, and the party halted.

The spot was singularly wild and impressive. A wooded amphitheatre, surrounded on three sides by precipitous cliffs of naked granite, sloped gently toward the crest of another pre- cipice that overlooked the valley. It was, undoubtedly, the most suitable spot for a camp, had camping been advisable. But Mr Oakhurst knew that scarcely half the journey to Sandy Bar was accomplished, and the party were not equipped or provisioned for delay. This fact he pointed out to his companions curtly, with a philosophic commentary on the folly of 'throwing up their hand before the game was played out.' But they were furnished with liquor, which in this emergency stood them in place of food, fuel, rest, and prescience. In spite of his remonstrances, it was not long before they were more or less under its influence. Uncle Billy passed rapidly from a bellicose state into one of stupor, the Duchess became maudlin, and Mother Shipton snored. Mr Oakhurst alone remained erect, leaning against a rock, calmly surveying them.

Mr Oakhurst did not drink. It interfered with a profession which required coolness, impassiveness, and presence of mind, and, in his own language, he 'couldn't afford it.' As he gazed at his recumbent fellow-exiles, the loneliness begotten of his pariah-trade, his habits of life, his very vices, for the first time seriously oppressed him. He bestirred himself in dusting his black clothes, washing his hands and face, and other acts characteristic of his studiously neat habits, and for a moment forgot his annoyance. The thought of deserting his weaker and more pitiable companions never perhaps occurred to him. Yet he could not help feeling the want of that excitement which, singularly enough, was most conducive to that calm equanimity for which he was notorious. He looked at the gloomy walls that rose a thousand feet sheer above the circling pines around him; at the sky, ominously clouded; at the valley below, already deepening into shadow. And, doing so, suddenly he heard his own name called.

A horseman slowly ascended the trail. In the fresh, open face of the new-comer Mr Oakhurst recognized Tom Simson, otherwise known as 'The Innocent' of Sandy Bar. He had met him some months before over a 'little game,' and had, with perfect equanimity, won the entire fortune—amounting to some forty dollars—of that guileless youth. After the game was finished, Mr Oakhurst drew the youthful speculator behind the door and thus addressed him: 'Tommy, you're a good little man, but you can't gamble worth a cent. Don't try it over again.' He then handed him his money back, pushed him gently from the room, and so made a devoted slave of Tom Simson.

There was a remembrance of this in his boyish and enthusiastic greeting of Mr Oakhurst. He had started, he said, to go to Poker Flat to seek his fortune. 'Alone?' No, not exactly alone; in fact (a giggle), he had run away with Piney Woods. Didn't Mr Oakhurst remember Piney? She that used to wait on the table at the Temperance House? They had been engaged a long time, but old Jake Woods had objected, and so they had run away, and were going to Poker Flat to be married, and here they were. And they were tired out, and how lucky it was they had found a place to camp and company. All this the Innocent delivered rapidly, while Piney, a stout, comely damsel of fifteen, emerged from behind the pine-tree, where she had been blushing unseen, and rode to the side of her lover.

Mr Oakhurst seldom troubled himself with sentiment, still less with propriety; but he had a vague idea that the situation was not fortunate. He retained, however, his presence of mind sufficiently to kick Uncle Billy, who was about to say something, and Uncle Billy was sober enough to recognize in Mr Oakhurst's kick a superior power that would not bear trifling. He then endeavored to dissuade Tom Simson from delaying further, but in vain. He even pointed out the fact that there was no provision, nor means of making a camp. But, unluckily, the Innocent met this objection by assuring the party that he was provided with an extra mule loaded with provisions, and by the discovery of a rude attempt at a log-house near the trail. 'Piney can stay with Mrs Oakhurst,' said the Innocent, pointing to the Duchess, 'and I can shift for myself.'

Nothing but Mr Oakhurst's admonishing foot saved Uncle Billy from bursting into a roar of laughter. As it was, he felt compelled to retire up the cañon until he could recover his gravity. There he confided the joke to the tall pine-trees, with many slaps of his leg, contortions of his face, and the usual profanity. But when he returned to the party, he found them seated by a fire—for the air had grown strangely chill and the sky overcast—in apparently amicable conversation. Piney was actually talking in an impulsive, girlish fashion to the Duchess, who was listening with an interest and animation she had not shown for many days. The Innocent was holding forth, apparently with equal effect, to Mr Oakhurst and Mother Shipton, who was actually relaxing into amiability. 'Is this yer a d—d picnic?' said Uncle Billy, with inward scorn, as he surveyed the sylvan group, the glancing firelight, and the tethered animals in the foreground. Suddenly an idea mingled with the alcoholic fumes that disturbed his brain. It was apparently of a jocular nature, for he felt impelled to slap his leg again and cram his fist into his mouth.

As the shadows crept slowly up the mountain, a slight breeze rocked the tops of the pine-trees, and moaned through their long and gloomy aisles. The ruined cabin, patched and covered with pine-boughs, was set apart for the ladies. As the lovers parted, they unaffectedly exchanged a kiss, so honest and sincere that it might have been heard above the swaying pines. The frail Duchess and the malevolent Mother Shipton were probably too stunned to remark upon this last evidence of simplicity, and so turned without a word to the hut. The fire was replenished, the men lay down before the door, and in a few minutes were asleep.

Mr Oakhurst was a light sleeper. Toward morning he awoke benumbed and cold. As he stirred the dying fire, the wind, which was now blowing strongly, brought to his cheek that which caused the blood to leave it,—snow!

He started to his feet with the intention of awakening the sleepers, for there was no time to lose. But turning to where Uncle Billy had been lying, he found him gone. A suspicion leaped to his brain and a curse to his lips. He ran to the spot where the mules had been tethered; they were no longer there. The tracks were already rapidly disappearing in the snow.

The momentary excitement brought Mr Oakhurst back to the fire with his usual calm. He did not waken the sleepers. The Innocent slumbered peacefully, with a smile on his good-humored, freckled face; the virgin Piney slept beside her frailer sisters as sweetly as though attended by celestial guardians, and Mr Oakhurst, drawing his blanket over his shoulders, stroked his mustaches and waited for the dawn. It came slowly in a whirling mist of snow-flakes, that dazzled and confused the eye. What could be seen of the landscape appeared magically changed. He looked over the valley, and summed up the present and future in two words,—'snowed in!'

A careful inventory of the provisions, which, fortunately for the party, had been stored within the hut, and so escaped the felonious fingers of Uncle Billy, disclosed the fact that with care and prudence they might last ten days longer. 'That is,' said Mr Oakhurst, *sotto voce** to the Innocent, 'if you're willing to board us. If you ain't—and perhaps you'd better not—you can wait till Uncle Billy gets back with provisions.' For some occult reason, Mr Oakhurst could not bring himself to disclose Uncle Billy's rascality, and so offered the hypothesis that he had wandered from the camp and had accidentally stampeded the animals. He dropped a warning to the Duchess and Mother Shipton, who of course knew the facts of their associate's defection. 'They'll find out the truth about us *all* when they find out anything,' he added, significantly, 'and there's no good frightening them now.'

Tom Simson not only put all his worldly store at the disposal of Mr Oakhurst, but seemed to enjoy the prospect of their enforced seclusion. 'We'll have a good camp for a week, and then the snow'll melt, and we'll all go back together.' The cheerful gayety of the young man and Mr Oakhurst's calm infected the others. The Innocent, with the aid of pine-boughs, extemporized a thatch for the roofless cabin, and the Duchess directed Piney in the rearrangement of the interior with a taste and tact that opened the blue eyes of that provincial maiden to their fullest extent. 'I reckon now you're used to fine things at

Poker Flat,' said Piney. The Duchess turned away sharply to conceal something that reddened her cheeks through its professional tint, and Mother Shipton requested Piney not to 'chatter.' But when Mr Oakhurst returned from a weary search for the trail, he heard the sound of happy laughter echoed from the rocks. He stopped in some alarm, and his thoughts first naturally reverted to the whiskey, which he had prudently *cachéd*.* 'And yet it don't somehow sound like whiskey,' said the gambler. It was not until he caught sight of the blazing fire through the still-blinding storm and the group around it that he settled to the conviction that it was 'square fun.'

Whether Mr Oakhurst had *cachéd* his cards with the whiskey as something debarred the free access of the community, I cannot say. It was certain that, in Mother Shipton's words, he 'didn't say cards once' during that evening. Haply the time was beguiled by an accordion, produced somewhat ostentatiously by Tom Simson from his pack. Notwithstanding some difficulties attending the manipulation of this instrument, Piney Woods managed to pluck several reluctant melodies from its keys, to an accompaniment by the Innocent on a pair of bone castinets. But the crowning festivity of the evening was reached in a rude camp-meeting hymn, which the lovers, joining hands, sang with great earnestness and vociferation. I fear that a certain defiant tone and Covenanter's* swing to its chorus, rather than any devotional quality, caused it speedily to infect the others, who at last joined in the refrain:—

> 'I'm proud to live in the service of the Lord,
> And I'm bound to die in His army.'

The pines rocked, the storm eddied and whirled above the miserable group, and the flames of their altar leaped heavenward, as if in token of the vow.

At midnight the storm abated, the rolling clouds parted, and the stars glittered keenly above the sleeping camp. Mr Oakhurst, whose professional habits had enabled him to live on the smallest possible amount of sleep, in dividing the watch with Tom Simson, somehow managed to take upon himself the greater part of that duty. He excused himself to the Innocent, by saying that he had 'often been a week without sleep.' 'Doing what?' asked Tom. 'Poker!' replied Oakhurst, sententiously; 'when a man gets a streak of luck,—nigger-luck,—he don't get tired. The luck gives in first. Luck,' continued the gambler, reflectively, 'is a mighty queer thing. All you know about it for certain is that it's bound to change. And it's finding out when it's going to change that makes you. We've had a streak of bad luck since we left Poker Flat,—you come along, and slap you get into it, too. If you can hold your cards right along you're all right. For,' added the gambler, with cheerful irrelevance,—

> ' "I'm proud to live in the service of the Lord,
>   And I'm bound to die in His army." '

The third day came, and the sun, looking through the white-curtained valley, saw the outcasts divide their slowly decreasing store of provisions for the morning meal. It was one of the peculiarities of that mountain climate that its rays diffused a kindly warmth over the wintry landscape, as if in regretful commiseration of the past. But it revealed drift on drift of snow piled high around the hut,—a hopeless, uncharted, trackless sea of white lying below the rocky shores to which the castaways still clung. Through the marvellously clear air the smoke of the pastoral village of Poker Flat rose miles away. Mother Shipton saw it, and from a remote pinnacle of her rocky fastness, hurled in that direction a final malediction. It was her last vituperative attempt, and perhaps for that reason was invested with a certain degree of sublimity. It did her good, she privately informed the Duchess. 'Just you go out there and cuss, and see.' She then set herself to the task of amusing 'the child,' as she and the Duchess were pleased to call Piney. Piney was no chicken, but it was a soothing and original theory of the pair thus to account for the fact that she didn't swear and wasn't improper.

When night crept up again through the gorges, the reedy notes of the accordion rose and fell in fitful spasms and long-drawn gasps by the flickering camp-fire. But music failed to fill entirely the aching void left by insufficient food, and a new diversion was proposed by Piney,—story-telling. Neither Mr Oakhurst nor his female companions caring to relate their personal experiences, this plan would have failed, too, but for the Innocent. Some months before he had chanced upon a stray copy of Mr Pope's ingenious translation of the Iliad. He now proposed to narrate the principal incidents of that poem—having thoroughly mastered the argument and fairly forgotten the words—in the current vernacular of Sandy Bar. And so for the rest of that night the Homeric demigods again walked the earth. Trojan bully and wily Greek wrestled in the winds, and the great pines in the cañon seemed to bow to the wrath of the son of Peleus.* Mr Oakhurst listened with quiet satisfaction. Most especially was he interested in the fate of 'Ash-heels,' as the Innocent persisted in denominating the 'swift-footed Achilles.'

So with small food and much of Homer and the accordion, a week passed over the heads of the outcasts. The sun again forsook them, and again from leaden skies the snow-flakes were sifted over the land. Day by day closer around them drew the snowy circle, until at last they looked from their prison over drifted walls of dazzling white, that towered twenty feet above their heads. It became more and more difficult to replenish their fires, even from the fallen trees beside them, now half hidden in the drifts. And yet no one complained. The lovers turned from the dreary prospect and looked into each other's eyes, and were happy. Mr Oakhurst settled himself coolly to the losing game before him. The Duchess, more cheerful than she had been, assumed the care of Piney. Only Mother Shipton— once the strongest of the party—seemed to sicken and fade. At midnight on the tenth day she called Oakhurst to her side. 'I'm going,' she said, in a voice of querulous weakness, 'but don't say anything about it. Don't waken the kids. Take the bundle from under my head and open it.' Mr Oakhurst did so. It contained Mother Shipton's rations for the last week, untouched. 'Give 'em to the child,' she said, pointing to the sleeping Piney. 'You've starved yourself,' said the gambler. 'That's what they call it,' said the woman, querulously, as she lay down again, and, turning her face to the wall, passed quietly away.

The accordion and the bones were put aside that day, and Homer was forgotten. When the body of Mother Shipton had been committed to the snow, Mr Oakhurst took the Innocent aside, and showed him a pair of snow-shoes, which he had fashioned from the old pack-saddle. 'There's one chance in a hundred to save her yet,' he said, pointing to Piney; 'but it's there,' he added, pointing toward Poker Flat. 'If you can reach there in two days she's safe.' 'And you?' asked Tom Simson. 'I'll stay here,' was the curt reply.

The lovers parted with a long embrace. 'You are not going, too?' said the Duchess, as she saw Mr Oakhurst apparently waiting to accompany him. 'As far as the cañon,' he replied. He turned suddenly, and kissed the Duchess, leaving her pallid face aflame, and her trembling limbs rigid with amazement.

Night came, but not Mr Oakhurst. It brought the storm again and the whirling snow. Then the Duchess, feeding the fire, found that some one had quietly piled beside the hut enough fuel to last a few days longer. The tears rose to her eyes, but she hid them from Piney.

The women slept but little. In the morning, looking into each other's faces, they read their fate. Neither spoke; but Piney, accepting the position of the stronger, drew near and placed her arm around the Duchess's waist. They kept this attitude for the rest of the day. That night the storm reached its greatest fury, and, rending asunder the protecting pines, invaded the very hut.

Toward morning they found themselves unable to feed the fire, which gradually died away. As the embers slowly blackened, the Duchess crept closer to Piney, and broke the silence of many hours: 'Piney, can you pray?' 'No, dear,' said Piney, simply. The Duchess, without knowing exactly why, felt relieved, and, putting her head upon Piney's shoulder, spoke no more. And so reclining, the younger and purer pillowing the head of her soiled sister upon her virgin breast, they fell asleep.

The wind lulled as if it feared to waken them. Feathery drifts of snow, shaken from the long pine-boughs, flew like white-winged birds, and settled about them as they slept. The moon through the rifted clouds looked down upon what had been the camp. But all human stain, all trace of earthly travail, was hidden beneath the spotless mantle mercifully flung from above.

They slept all that day and the next, nor did they waken when voices and footsteps broke the silence of the camp. And when pitying fingers brushed the snow from their wan faces, you could scarcely have told from the equal peace that dwelt upon them, which was she that had sinned. Even the law of Poker Flat recognized this, and turned away, leaving them still locked in each other's arms.

But at the head of the gulch, on one of the largest pine-trees, they found the deuce of clubs pinned to the bark with a bowie-knife. It bore the following, written in pencil, in a firm hand:—

BENEATH THIS TREE

LIES THE BODY

OF

JOHN OAKHURST,

WHO STRUCK A STREAK OF BAD LUCK

ON THE 23D OF NOVEMBER, 1850,

AND

HANDED IN HIS CHECKS

ON THE 7TH DECEMBER, 1850.

And pulseless and cold, with a Derringer by his side and a bullet in his heart, though still calm as in life, beneath the snow lay he who was at once the strongest and yet the weakest of the outcasts of Poker Flat.

MIGGLES

WE were eight, including the driver. We had not spoken during the passage of the last six miles, since the jolting of the heavy vehicle over the roughening road had spoiled the Judge's last poetical quotation. The tall man beside the Judge was asleep, his arm passed through the swaying strap and his head resting upon it,—altogether a limp, helpless-looking object, as if he had hanged himself and been cut down too late. The French lady on the back seat was asleep, too, yet in a half-conscious propriety of attitude, shown even in the disposition of the handkerchief which she held to her forehead and which partially veiled her face. The lady from Virginia City,* travelling with her husband, had long since lost all individuality in a wild confusion of ribbons, veils, furs, and shawls. There was no sound but the rattling of wheels and the dash of rain upon the roof. Suddenly the stage stopped and we became dimly aware of voices. The driver was evidently in the midst of an exciting colloquy with some one in the road,—a colloquy of which such fragments as 'bridge gone,' 'twenty feet of water', 'can't pass,' were occasionally distinguishable above the storm. Then came a lull, and a mysterious voice from the road shouted the parting adjuration,—

'Try Miggles's.'

We caught a glimpse of our leaders as the vehicle slowly turned, of a horseman vanishing through the rain, and we were evidently on our way to Miggles's.

Who and where was Miggles? The Judge, our authority, did not remember the name, and he knew the country thoroughly. The Washoe* traveller thought Miggles must keep a hotel. We only knew that we were stopped by high water in front and rear, and that Miggles was our rock of refuge. A ten minutes' splashing through a tangled by-road, scarcely wide enough for the stage, and we drew up before a barred and boarded gate in a wide stone wall or fence about eight feet high. Evidently Miggles's, and evidently Miggles did not keep a hotel.

The driver got down and tried the gate. It was securely locked.

'Miggles! O Miggles!'

No answer.

'Migg–ells! You Miggles!' continued the driver, with rising wrath.

'Migglesy!' joined in the expressman, persuasively. 'O Miggy! Mig!'

But no reply came from the apparently insensate Miggles. The Judge, who had finally got the window down, put his head out and propounded a series of questions, which if answered categorically would have undoubtedly elucidated the whole mystery, but which the driver evaded by replying that 'if we didn't want to sit in the coach all night, we had better rise up and sing out for Miggles.'

So we rose up and called on Miggles in chorus; then separately. And when we had finished, a Hibernian* fellow-passenger from the roof called for 'Maygells!' whereat we all laughed. While we were laughing, the driver cried 'Shoo!'

We listened. To our infinite amazement the chorus of 'Miggles' was repeated from the other side of the wall, even to the final and supplemental 'Maygells.'

'Extraordinary echo,' said the Judge.

'Extraordinary d—d skunk!' roared the driver, contemptuously. 'Come out of that, Miggles, and show yourself! Be a man, Miggles! Don't hide in the dark; I wouldn't if I were you, Miggles,' continued Yuba Bill, now dancing about in an excess of fury.

'Miggles!' continued the voice, 'O Miggles!'

'My good man! Mr Myghail!' said the Judge, softening the asperities of the name as much as possible. 'Consider the inhospitality of refusing shelter from the inclemency of the weather to helpless females. Really, my dear sir—' But a succession of 'Miggles,' ending in a burst of laughter, drowned his voice.

Yuba Bill hesitated no longer. Taking a heavy stone from the road, he battered down the gate, and with the expressman entered the enclosure. We followed. Nobody was to be seen. In the gathering darkness all that we could distinguish was that we were in a garden—from the rose-bushes that scattered over us a minute spray from their dripping leaves—and before a long, rambling wooden building.

'Do you know this Miggles?' asked the Judge of Yuba Bill.

'No, nor don't want to,' said Bill, shortly, who felt the Pioneer Stage Company insulted in his person by the contumacious Miggles.

'But, my dear sir,' expostulated the Judge, as he thought of the barred gate.

'Lookee here,' said Yuba Bill, with fine irony, 'hadn't you better go back and sit in the coach till yer introduced? I'm going in,' and he pushed open the door of the building.

A long room lighted only by the embers of a fire that was dying on the large hearth at its further extremity; the walls curiously papered, and the flickering firelight bringing out its grotesque pattern; somebody sitting in a large arm-chair by the fireplace. All this we saw as we crowded together into the room, after the driver and expressman.

'Hello, be you Miggles?' said Yuba Bill to the solitary occupant.

The figure neither spoke nor stirred. Yuba Bill walked wrathfully toward it, and turned the eye of his coach-lantern upon its face. It was a man's face, prematurely old and wrinkled, with very large eyes, in which there was that expression of perfectly gratuitous solemnity which I had sometimes seen in an owl's. The large eyes wandered from Bill's face to the lantern, and finally fixed their gaze on that luminous object, without further recognition.

Bill restrained himself with an effort.

'Miggles! Be you deaf? You ain't dumb anyhow, you know'; and Yuba Bill shook the insensate figure by the shoulder.

To our great dismay, as Bill removed his hand, the venerable stranger apparently collapsed,—sinking into half his size and an undistinguishable heap of clothing.

'Well, dern my skin,' said Bill, looking appealingly at us, and hopelessly retiring from the contest.

The Judge now stepped forward, and we lifted the mysterious invertebrate back into his original position. Bill was dismissed with the lantern to reconnoitre outside, for it was evident that from the helplessness of this solitary man there must be attendants near at hand, and we all drew around the fire. The Judge, who had regained his authority, and had never lost his conversational amiability,—standing before us with his back to the hearth,—charged us, as an imaginary jury, as follows:—

'It is evident that either our distinguished friend here has reached that condition described by Shakespeare as "the sere and yellow leaf",* or has suffered some premature abatement of his mental and physical faculties. Whether he is really the Miggles—'

Here he was interrupted by 'Miggles! O Miggles! Migglesy! Mig!' and, in fact, the whole chorus of Miggles in very much the same key as it had once before been delivered unto us.

We gazed at each other for a moment in some alarm. The Judge, in particular, vacated his position quickly, as the voice seemed to come directly over his shoulder. The cause, however, was soon discovered in a large magpie who was perched upon a shelf over the fireplace, and who immediately relapsed into a sepulchral silence, which contrasted singularly with his previous volubility. It was, undoubtedly, his voice which we had heard in the road, and our friend in the chair was not responsible for the discourtesy. Yuba Bill, who re-entered the room after an unsuccessful search, was loath to accept the explanation, and still eyed the helpless sitter with suspicion. He had found a shed in which he had put up his horses, but he came back dripping and sceptical. 'Thar ain't nobody but him within ten mile of the shanty, and that 'ar d—d old skeesicks knows it.'

But the faith of the majority proved to be securely based. Bill had scarcely ceased growling before we heard a quick step upon the porch, the trailing of a wet skirt, the door was flung open, and with a flash of white teeth, a sparkle of dark eyes, and an utter absence of ceremony or diffidence, a young woman entered, shut the door, and, panting, leaned back against it.

'O, if you please, I'm Miggles!'

And this was Miggles! this bright-eyed, full-throated young woman, whose wet gown of coarse blue stuff could not hide the beauty of the feminine curves to which it clung; from the chestnut crown of whose head, topped by a man's oil-skin sou'wester, to the little feet and ankles, hidden somewhere in the recesses of her boy's brogans, all was grace;—this was Miggles, laughing at us, too, in the most airy, frank, off-hand manner imaginable.

'You see, boys,' said she, quite out of breath, and holding one little hand against her side, quite unheeding the speechless discomfiture of our party, or the complete demoralization of Yuba Bill, whose features had relaxed into an expression of gratuitous and imbecile cheerfulness,—'you see, boys, I was mor'n two miles away when you passed down the road. I thought you might pull up here, and so I ran the whole way, knowing nobody was home but Jim,—and—and—I'm out of breath—and—that lets me out.'

And here Miggles caught her dripping oil-skin hat from her head, with a mischievous swirl that scattered a shower of rain-drops over us; attempted to put back her hair; dropped two hair-pins in the attempt; laughed and sat down beside Yuba Bill, with her hands crossed lightly on her lap.

The Judge recovered himself first, and essayed an extra-vagant compliment.

'I'll trouble you for that thar har-pin,' said Miggles, gravely. Half a dozen hands were eagerly stretched forward; the missing hair-pin was restored to its fair owner; and Miggles, crossing the room, looked keenly in the face of the invalid. The solemn eyes looked back at hers with an expression we had never seen before. Life and intelligence seemed to struggle back into the rugged face. Miggles laughed again,—it was a singularly eloquent laugh,—and turned her black eyes and white teeth once more toward us.

'This afflicted person is—' hesitated the Judge.

'Jim,' said Miggles.

'Your father?'

'No.'

'Brother?'

'No.'

'Husband?'

Miggles darted a quick, half-defiant glance at the two lady passengers who I had noticed did not participate in the general masculine admiration of Miggles, and said, gravely, 'No; it's Jim.'

There was an awkward pause. The lady passengers moved closer to each other; the Washoe husband looked abstractedly at the fire; and the tall man apparently turned his eyes inward for self-support at this emergency. But Miggles's laugh, which was very infectious, broke the silence. 'Come,' she said briskly, 'you must be hungry. Who'll bear a hand to help me get tea?'

She had no lack of volunteers. In a few moments Yuba Bill was engaged like Caliban in bearing logs for this Miranda;* the expressman was grinding coffee on the veranda; to myself the arduous duty of slicing bacon was assigned; and the Judge lent each man his good-humored and voluble counsel. And when Miggles, assisted by the Judge and our Hibernian 'deck passenger,' set the table with all the available crockery, we had become quite joyous, in spite of the rain that beat against windows, the wind that whirled down the chimney, the two ladies who whispered together in the corner, or the magpie who uttered a satirical and croaking commentary on their conversation from his perch above. In the now bright, blazing fire we could see that the walls were papered with illustrated journals, arranged with feminine taste and discrimination. The furniture was extemporized, and adapted from candle-boxes and packing-cases, and covered with gay calico, or the skin of some animal. The arm-chair of the helpless Jim was an ingenious variation of a flour-barrel. There was neatness, and even a taste for the picturesque, to be seen in the few details of the long low room.

The meal was a culinary success. But more, it was a social triumph,—chiefly, I think, owing to the rare tact of Miggles in guiding the conversation, asking all the questions herself, yet bearing throughout a frankness that rejected the idea of any concealment on her own part, so that we talked of ourselves, of our prospects, of the journey, of the weather, of each other,—of everything but our host and hostess. It must be confessed that Miggles's conversation was never elegant, rarely grammatical, and that at times she employed expletives, the use of which had generally been yielded to our sex. But they were delivered with such a lighting up of teeth and eyes, and were usually followed by a laugh—a laugh peculiar to Miggles—so frank and honest that it seemed to clear the moral atmosphere.

Once, during the meal, we heard a noise like the rubbing of a heavy body against the outer walls of the house. This was shortly followed by a scratching and sniffling at the door. 'That's Joaquin,' said Miggles, in reply to our questioning glances; 'would you like to see him?' Before we could answer she had opened the door, and disclosed a half-grown grizzly, who instantly raised himself on his haunches, with his forepaws hanging down in the popular attitude of mendicancy, and looked admiringly at Miggles, with a very singular resemblance in his manner to Yuba Bill. 'That's my watch-dog,' said Miggles, in explanation. 'O, he don't bite,' she added, as the two lady passengers fluttered into a corner. 'Does he, old Toppy?' (the latter remark being addressed directly to the sagacious Joaquin.) 'I tell you what, boys,' continued Miggles, after she had fed and closed the door on *Ursa Minor*, 'you were in big luck that Joaquin wasn't hanging round when you dropped in to-night.' 'Where was he?' asked the Judge. 'With me,' said Miggles. 'Lord love you; he trots round with me nights like as if he was a man.'

We were silent for a few moments, and listened to the wind. Perhaps we all had the same picture before us,—of Miggles walking through the rainy woods, with her savage guardian at her side. The Judge, I remember, said something about Una and her lion;* but Miggles received it as she did other compliments, with quiet gravity. Whether she was altogether unconscious of the admiration she excited,—she could hardly have been oblivious of Yuba Bill's adoration,—I know not; but her very frankness suggested a perfect sexual equality that was cruelly humiliating to the younger members of our party.

The incident of the bear did not add anything in Miggles's favor to the opinions of those of her own sex who were present. In fact, the repast over, a chillness radiated from the two lady passengers that no pine-boughs brought in by Yuba Bill and cast as a sacrifice upon the hearth could wholly overcome. Miggles felt it; and, suddenly declaring that it was time to 'turn in,' offered to show the ladies to their bed in an adjoining room. 'You, boys, will have to camp out here by the fire as well as you can,' she added, 'for thar ain't but the one room.'

Our sex—by which, my dear sir, I allude of course to the stronger portion of humanity—has been generally relieved from the imputation of curiosity, or a fondness for gossip. Yet I am constrained to say, that hardly had the door closed on Miggles than we crowded together, whispering, snickering, smiling, and exchanging suspicions, surmises, and a thousand speculations in regard to our pretty hostess and her singular companion. I fear that we even hustled that imbecile paralytic, who sat like a voiceless Memnon* in our midst, gazing with the serene indifference of the Past in his passionless eyes upon our wordy counsels. In the midst of an exciting discussion the door opened again, and Miggles re-entered.

But not, apparently, the same Miggles who a few hours before had flashed upon us. Her eyes were downcast, and as she hesitated for a moment on the threshold, with a blanket on her arm, she seemed to have left behind her the frank fearlessness which had charmed us a moment before. Coming into the room, she drew a low stool beside the paralytic's chair, sat down, drew the blanket over her shoulders, and saying, 'If it's all the same to you, boys, as we're rather crowded, I'll stop here to-night,' took the invalid's withered hand in her own, and turned her eyes upon the dying fire. An instinctive feeling that this was only premonitory to more confidential relations, and perhaps some shame at our previous curiosity, kept us silent. The rain still beat upon the roof, wandering gusts of wind stirred the embers into momentary brightness, until, in a lull of the elements, Miggles suddenly lifted up her head, and, throwing her hair over her shoulder, turned her face upon the group and asked,—

'Is there any of you that knows me?'

There was no reply.

'Think again! I lived at Marysville in '53. Everybody knew me there, and everybody had the right to know me. I kept the Polka Saloon until I came to live with Jim. That's six years ago. Perhaps I've changed some.'

The absence of recognition may have disconcerted her. She turned her head to the fire again, and it was some seconds before she again spoke, and then more rapidly:—

'Well, you see I thought some of you must have known me. There's no great harm done, anyway. What I was going to say was this: Jim here'—she took his hand in both of hers as she spoke—'used to know me, if you didn't, and spent a heap of money upon me. I reckon he spent all he had. And one day—it's six years ago this winter—Jim came into my back room, sat down on my sofy, like as you see him in that chair, and never moved again without help. He was struck all of a heap, and never seemed to know what ailed him. The doctors came and said as how it was caused all along of his way of life,—for Jim was mighty free and wild like,—and that he would never get better, and couldn't last long anyway. They advised me to send him to Frisco to the hospital, for he was no good to any one and would be a baby all his life. Perhaps it was something in Jim's eye, perhaps it was that I never had a baby, but I said "No." I was rich then, for I was popular with everybody,—gentlemen like yourself, sir, came to see me,—and I sold out my business and bought this yer place, because it was sort of out of the way of travel, you see, and I brought my baby here.'

With a woman's intuitive tact and poetry, she had, as she spoke, slowly shifted her position so as to bring the mute figure of the ruined man between her and her audience, hiding in the shadow behind it, as if she offered it as a tacit apology for her actions. Silent and expressionless, it yet spoke for her; helpless, crushed, and smitten with the Divine thunderbolt, it still stretched an invisible arm around her.

Hidden in the darkness, but still holding his hand, she went on:—

'It was a long time before I could get the hang of things about yer, for I was used to company and excitement. I couldn't get any woman to help me, and a man I dursent trust; but what with the Indians hereabout, who'd do odd jobs for me, and having everything sent from the North Fork, Jim and I managed to worry through. The Doctor would run up from Sacramento once in a while. He'd ask to see "Miggles's baby," as he called Jim, and when he'd go away, he'd say, "Miggles; you're a trump,—God bless you"; and it didn't seem so lonely after that. But the last time he was here he said, as he opened the door to go, "Do you know, Miggles, your baby will grow up to be a man yet and an honor to his mother; but not here,

Miggles, not here!" And I thought he went away sad,—and—and—' and here Miggles's voice and head were somehow both lost completely in the shadow.

'The folks about here are very kind,' said Miggles, after a pause, coming a little into the light again. 'The men from the fork used to hang around here, until they found they wasn't wanted, and the women are kind,—and don't call. I was pretty lonely until I picked up Joaquin in the woods yonder one day, when he wasn't so high, and taught him to beg for his dinner; and then thar's Polly—that's the magpie—she knows no end of tricks, and makes it quite sociable of evenings with her talk, and so I don't feel like as I was the only living being about the ranch. And Jim here,' said Miggles, with her old laugh again, and coming out quite into the firelight, 'Jim—why, boys, you would admire to see how much he knows for a man like him. Sometimes I bring him flowers, and he looks at 'em just as natural as if he knew 'em; and times, when we're sitting alone, I read him those things on the wall. Why, Lord!' said Miggles, with her frank laugh, 'I've read him that whole side of the house this winter. There never was such a man for reading as Jim.'

'Why,' asked the Judge, 'do you not marry this man to whom you have devoted your youthful life?'

'Well, you see,' said Miggles, 'it would be playing it rather low down on Jim, to take advantage of his being so helpless. And then, too, if we were man and wife, now, we'd both know that I was *bound* to do what I do now of my own accord.'

'But you are young yet and attractive—'

'It's getting late,' said Miggles, gravely, 'and you'd better all turn in. Good-night, boys'; and, throwing the blanket over her head, Miggles laid herself down beside Jim's chair, her head pillowed on the low stool that held his feet, and spoke no more. The fire slowly faded from the hearth; we each sought our blankets in silence; and presently there was no sound in the long room but the pattering of the rain upon the roof, and the heavy breathing of the sleepers.

It was nearly morning when I awoke from a troubled dream. The storm had passed, the stars were shining, and through the shutterless window the full moon, lifting itself over the solemn pines without, looked into the room. It touched the lonely figure in the chair with an infinite compassion, and seemed to baptize with a shining flood the lowly head of the woman whose hair, as in the sweet old story, bathed the feet of him she loved. It even lent a kindly poetry to the rugged outline of Yuba Bill, half reclining on his elbow between them and his passengers, with savagely patient eyes keeping watch and ward. And then I fell asleep and only woke at broad day, with Yuba Bill standing over me, and 'All aboard' ringing in my ears.

Coffee was waiting for us on the table, but Miggles was gone. We wandered about the house and lingered long after the horses were harnessed, but she did not return. It was evident that she wished to avoid a formal leave-taking, and had so left us to depart as we had come. After we had helped the ladies into the coach, we returned to the house and solemnly shook hands with the paralytic Jim, as solemnly settling him back into position after each hand-shake. Then we looked for the last time around the long low room, at the stool where Miggles had sat, and slowly took our seats in the waiting coach. The whip cracked, and we were off!

But as we reached the high-road, Bill's dexterous hand laid the six horses back on their haunches, and the stage stopped with a jerk. For there, on a little eminence beside the road, stood Miggles, her hair flying, her eyes sparkling, her white handkerchief waving, and her white teeth flashing a last 'good-by.' We waved our hats in return. And then Yuba Bill, as if fearful of further fascination, madly lashed his horses forward, and we sank back in our seats. We exchanged not a word until we reached the North Fork, and the stage drew up at the Independence House. Then, the Judge leading, we walked into the bar-room and took our places gravely at the bar.

'Are your glasses charged, gentlemen?' said the Judge, solemnly taking off his white hat.

They were.

'Well, then, here's to *Miggles*, GOD BLESS HER!'

Perhaps He had. Who knows?

TENNESSEE'S PARTNER

I DO not think that we ever knew his real name. Our ignorance of it certainly never gave us any social inconvenience, for at Sandy Bar in 1854 most men were christened anew. Sometimes these appellatives were derived from some distinctiveness of dress, as in the case of 'Dungaree Jack'; or from some peculiarity of habit, as shown in 'Saleratus Bill,' so called from an undue proportion of that chemical in his daily bread; or from some unlucky slip, as exhibited in 'The Iron Pirate,' a mild, inoffensive man, who earned that baleful title by his unfortunate mispronunciation of the term 'iron pyrites.' Perhaps this may have been the beginning of a rude heraldry; but I am constrained to think that it was because a man's real name in that day rested solely upon his own unsupported statement. 'Call yourself Clifford, do you?' said Boston, addressing a timid new-comer with infinite scorn; 'hell is full of such Cliffords!' He then introduced the unfortunate man, whose name happened to be really Clifford, as 'Jay-bird Charley,'—an unhallowed inspiration of the moment that clung to him ever after.

But to return to Tennessee's Partner, whom we never knew by any other than this relative title; that he had ever existed as a separate and distinct individuality we only learned later. It seems that in 1853 he left Poker Flat to go to San Francisco, ostensibly to procure a wife. He never got any farther than Stockton. At that place he was attracted by a young person who waited upon the table at the hotel where he took his meals. One morning he said something to her which caused her to smile not unkindly, to somewhat coquettishly break a plate of toast over his upturned, serious, simple face, and to retreat to the kitchen. He followed her, and emerged a few moments later, covered with more toast and victory. That day week they were married by a Justice of the Peace, and returned to Poker Flat. I am aware that something more might be made of this episode, but I prefer to tell it as it was current at Sandy Bar,—in the gulches and bar-rooms,—where all sentiment was modified by a strong sense of humor.

Of their married felicity but little is known, perhaps for the reason that Tennessee, then living with his partner, one day took occasion to say something to the bride on his own account, at which, it is said, she smiled not unkindly and chastely retreated,—this time as far as Marysville, where Tennessee followed her, and where they went to housekeeping without the aid of a Justice of the Peace. Tennessee's Partner took the loss of his wife simply and seriously, as was his fashion. But to everybody's surprise, when Tennessee one day returned from Marysville, without his partner's wife,—she having smiled and retreated with somebody else,—Tennessee's Partner was the first man to shake his hand and greet him with affection. The boys who had gathered in the cañon to see the shooting were naturally indignant. Their indignation might have found vent in sarcasm but for a certain look in Tennessee's Partner's eye that indicated a lack of humorous appreciation. In fact, he was a grave man, with a steady application to practical detail which was unpleasant in a difficulty.

Meanwhile a popular feeling against Tennessee had grown up on the Bar. He was known to be a gambler; he was suspected to be a thief. In these suspicions Tennessee's Partner was equally compromised; his continued intimacy with Tennessee after the affair above quoted could only be accounted for on the hypothesis of a copartnership of crime. At last Tennessee's guilt became flagrant. One day he overtook a stranger on his way to Red Dog. The stranger afterward related that Tennessee beguiled the time with interesting anecdote and reminiscence, but illogically concluded the interview in the following words: 'And now, young man, I'll trouble you for your knife, your pistols, and your money. You see your weppings might get you into trouble at Red Dog, and your money's a temptation to the evilly disposed. I think you said your address was San Francisco. I shall endeavor to call.' It may be stated here that Tennessee had a fine flow of humor, which no business preoccupation could wholly subdue.

This exploit was his last. Red Dog and Sandy Bar made common cause against the highwayman. Tennessee was hunted in very much the same fashion as his prototype, the grizzly. As the toils closed around him, he made a desperate dash through

the Bar, emptying his revolver at the crowd before the Arcade
Saloon, and so on up Grizzly Cañon; but at its farther extremity
he was stopped by a small man on a gray horse. The men
looked at each other a moment in silence. Both were fearless,
both self-possessed and independent; and both types of a
civilization that in the seventeenth century would have been
called heroic, but, in the nineteenth, simply 'reckless.' 'What
have you got there?—I call,' said Tennessee, quietly. 'Two
bowers and an ace,' said the stranger, as quietly, showing two
revolvers and a bowie-knife. 'That takes me,' returned Tennessee; and with this gamblers' epigram, he threw away his
useless pistol, and rode back with his captor.

It was a warm night. The cool breeze which usually sprang up
with the going down of the sun behind the *chaparral* *-crested
mountain was that evening withheld from Sandy Bar. The little
cañon was stifling with heated resinous odors, and the decaying
drift-wood on the Bar sent forth faint, sickening exhalations.
The feverishness of day, and its fierce passions, still filled the
camp. Lights moved restlessly along the bank of the river,
striking no answering reflection from its tawny current. Against
the blackness of the pines the windows of the old loft above the
express-office stood out staringly bright; and through their
curtainless panes the loungers below could see the forms of
those who were even then deciding the fate of Tennessee. And
above all this, etched on the dark firmament, rose the Sierra,
remote and passionless, crowned with remoter passionless stars.

  The trial of Tennessee was conducted as fairly as was
consistent with a judge and jury who felt themselves to some
extent obliged to justify, in their verdict, the previous irregularities of arrest and indictment. The law of Sandy Bar was
implacable, but not vengeful. The excitement and personal
feeling of the chase were over; with Tennessee safe in their
hands they were ready to listen patiently to any defence, which
they were already satisfied was insufficient. There being no
doubt in their own minds, they were willing to give the prisoner
the benefit of any that might exist. Secure in the hypothesis
that he ought to be hanged, on general principles, they indulged
him with more latitude of defence than his reckless hardihood

seemed to ask. The Judge appeared to be more anxious than the prisoner, who, otherwise unconcerned, evidently took a grim pleasure in the responsibility he had created. 'I don't take any hand in this yer game,' had been his invariable, but good-humored reply to all questions. The Judge—who was also his captor—for a moment vaguely regretted that he had not shot him 'on sight,' that morning, but presently dismissed this human weakness as unworthy of the judicial mind. Neverthe-less, when there was a tap at the door, and it was said that Tennessee's Partner was there on behalf of the prisoner, he was admitted at once without question. Perhaps the younger mem-bers of the jury, to whom the proceedings were becoming irksomely thoughtful, hailed him as a relief.

For he was not, certainly, an imposing figure. Short and stout, with a square face, sunburned into a preternatural redness, clad in a loose duck 'jumper,' and trousers streaked and splashed with red soil, his aspect under any circumstances would have been quaint, and was now even ridiculous. As he stooped to deposit at his feet a heavy carpet-bag he was carrying, it became obvious, from partially developed legends and inscriptions, that the material with which his trousers had been patched had been originally intended for a less ambitious covering. Yet he advanced with great gravity, and after having shaken the hand of each person in the room with labored cordiality, he wiped his serious, perplexed face on a red bandanna handkerchief, a shade lighter than his complexion, laid his powerful hand upon the table to steady himself, and thus addressed the Judge:—

'I was passin' by,' he began, by way of apology, 'and I thought I'd just step in and see how things was gittin' on with Tennessee thar,—my pardner. It's a hot night. I disremember any sich weather before on the Bar.'

He paused a moment, but nobody volunteering any other meteorological recollection, he again had recourse to his pocket-handkerchief, and for some moments mopped his face diligently.

'Have you anything to say in behalf of the prisoner?' said the Judge, finally.

'Thet's it,' said Tennessee's Partner, in a tone of relief. 'I come yar as Tennessee's pardner,—knowing him nigh on four year, off and on, wet and dry, in luck and out o' luck. His ways ain't allers my ways, but thar ain't any p'ints in that young man, thar ain't any liveliness as he's been up to, as I don't know. And you sez to me, sez you,—confidential-like, and between man and man,—sez you, "Do you know anything in his behalf?" and I sez to you, sez I,—confidential-like, as between man and man,—"What should a man know of his pardner?"'

'Is this all you have to say?' asked the Judge, impatiently, feeling, perhaps, that a dangerous sympathy of humor was beginning to humanize the Court.

'Thet's so,' continued Tennessee's Partner. 'It ain't for me to say anything agin' him. And now, what's the case? Here's Tennessee wants money, wants it bad, and doesn't like to ask it of his old pardner. Well, what does Tennessee do? He lays for a stranger, and he fetches that stranger. And you lays for *him*, and you fetches *him*; and the honors is easy. And I put it to you, bein' a far-minded man, and to you, gentlemen, all, as far-minded men, ef this isn't so.'

'Prisoner,' said the Judge, interrupting, 'have you any questions to ask this man?'

'No! no!' continued Tennessee's Partner, hastily. 'I play this yer hand alone. To come down to the bed-rock, it's just this: Tennessee, thar, has played it pretty rough and expensivelike on a stranger, and on this yer camp. And now, what's the fair thing? Some would say more; some would say less. Here's seventeen hundred dollars in coarse gold and a watch,—it's about all my pile,—and call it square!' And before a hand could be raised to prevent him, he had emptied the contents of the carpet-bag upon the table.

For a moment his life was in jeopardy. One or two men sprang to their feet, several hands groped for hidden weapons, and a suggestion to 'throw him from the window' was only overridden by a gesture from the Judge. Tennessee laughed. And apparently oblivious of the excitement, Tennessee's Partner improved the opportunity to mop his face again with his handkerchief.

When order was restored, and the man was made to understand, by the use of forcible figures and rhetoric, that Tennessee's offence could not be condoned by money, his face took a more serious and sanguinary hue, and those who were nearest to him noticed that his rough hand trembled slightly on the table. He hesitated a moment as he slowly returned the gold to the carpet-bag, as if he had not yet entirely caught the elevated sense of justice which swayed the tribunal, and was perplexed with the belief that he had not offered enough. Then he turned to the Judge, and saying, 'This yer is a lone hand, played alone, and without my pardner,' he bowed to the jury and was about to withdraw, when the Judge called him back. 'If you have anything to say to Tennessee, you had better say it now.' For the first time that evening the eyes of the prisoner and his strange advocate met. Tennessee smiled, showed his white teeth, and, saying, 'Euchred,* old man!' held out his hand. Tennessee's Partner took it in his own, and saying, 'I just dropped in as I was passin' to see how things was gettin' on,' let the hand passively fall, and adding that 'it was a warm night,' again mopped his face with his handkerchief, and without another word withdrew.

The two men never again met each other alive. For the unparalleled insult of a bribe offered to Judge Lynch—who, whether bigoted, weak, or narrow, was at least incorruptible— firmly fixed in the mind of that mythical personage any wavering determination of Tennessee's fate; and at the break of day he was marched, closely guarded, to meet it at the top of Marley's Hill.

How he met it, how cool he was, how he refused to say anything, how perfect were the arrangements of the committee, were all duly reported, with the addition of a warning moral and example to all future evil-doers, in the Red Dog Clarion, by its editor, who was present, and to whose vigorous English I cheerfully refer the reader. But the beauty of that midsummer morning, the blessed amity of earth and air and sky, the awakened life of the free woods and hills, the joyous renewal and promise of Nature, and above all, the infinite Serenity that thrilled through each, was not reported, as not being a part of the social lesson. And yet, when the weak and foolish deed was done, and a life, with its possibilities and responsibilities, had passed out of the misshapen thing that dangled between earth and sky, the birds sang, the flowers bloomed, the sun shone, as cheerily as before; and possibly the Red Dog Clarion was right.

Tennessee's Partner was not in the group that surrounded the ominous tree. But as they turned to disperse attention was drawn to the singular appearance of a motionless donkey-cart halted at the side of the road. As they approached, they at once recognized the venerable 'Jenny' and the two-wheeled cart as the property of Tennessee's Partner,—used by him in carrying dirt from his claim; and a few paces distant the owner of the equipage himself, sitting under a buckeye-tree, wiping the perspiration from his glowing face. In answer to an inquiry, he said he had come for the body of the 'diseased,' 'if it was all the same to the committee.' He didn't wish to 'hurry anything'; he could 'wait.' He was not working that day; and when the gentlemen were done with the 'diseased,' he would take him. 'Ef thar is any present,' he added, in his simple, serious way, 'as would care to jine in the fun'l, they kin come.' Perhaps it was from a sense of humor, which I have already intimated was a feature of Sandy Bar,—perhaps it was from something even better than that; but two thirds of the loungers accepted the invitation at once.

It was noon when the body of Tennessee was delivered into the hands of his partner. As the cart drew up to the fatal tree, we noticed that it contained a rough, oblong box,—apparently made from a section of sluicing,—and half filled with bark and the tassels of pine. The cart was further decorated with slips of willow, and made fragrant with buckeye-blossoms. When the body was deposited in the box, Tennessee's Partner drew over it a piece of tarred canvas, and gravely mounting the narrow seat in front, with his feet upon the shafts, urged the little donkey forward. The equipage moved slowly on, at that decorous pace which was habitual with 'Jenny' even under less solemn circumstances. The men—half curiously, half jestingly, but all good-humoredly—strolled along beside the cart; some in advance, some a little in the rear of the homely catafalque. But, whether from the narrowing of the road or some present sense of decorum, as the cart passed on, the company fell to the rear in couples, keeping step, and otherwise assuming the external show of a formal procession. Jack Folinsbee, who had at the outset played a funeral march in dumb show upon an imaginary trombone, desisted, from a lack of sympathy and appreciation,—not having, perhaps, your true humorist's capacity to be content with the enjoyment of his own fun.

The way led through Grizzly Cañon,—by this time clothed in funereal drapery and shadows. The redwoods, burying their moccasoned feet in the red soil, stood in Indian-file along the track, trailing an uncouth benediction from their bending boughs upon the passing bier. A hare, surprised into helpless inactivity, sat upright and pulsating in the ferns by the roadside, as the *cortège** went by. Squirrels hastened to gain a secure outlook from higher boughs; and the blue-jays, spreading their wings, fluttered before them like outriders, until the outskirts of Sandy Bar were reached, and the solitary cabin of Tennessee's Partner.

Viewed under more favorable circumstances, it would not have been a cheerful place. The unpicturesque site, the rude and unlovely outlines, the unsavory details, which distinguish the nest-building of the California miner, were all here, with the dreariness of decay superadded. A few paces from the cabin there was a rough enclosure, which, in the brief days of Tennessee's Partner's matrimonial felicity, had been used as a garden, but was now overgrown with fern. As we approached it we were surprised to find that what we had taken for a recent attempt at cultivation was the broken soil about an open grave.

The cart was halted before the enclosure; and rejecting the offers of assistance with the same air of simple self-reliance he had displayed throughout, Tennessee's Partner lifted the rough coffin on his back, and deposited it, unaided, within the shallow grave. He then nailed down the board which served as a lid; and mounting the little mound of earth beside it, took off his hat, and slowly mopped his face with his handkerchief. This the crowd felt was a preliminary to speech; and they disposed themselves variously on stumps and boulders, and sat expectant.

'When a man,' began Tennessee's Partner, slowly, 'has been running free all day, what's the natural thing for him to do? Why, to come home. And if he ain't in a condition to go home, what can his best friend do? Why, bring him home! And here's Tennessee has been running free, and we brings him home from his wandering.' He paused, and picked up a fragment of quartz, rubbed it thoughtfully on his sleeve, and went on: 'It ain't the first time that I've packed him on my back, as you see'd me now. It ain't the first time that I brought him to this yer cabin when he couldn't help himself; it ain't the first time that I and "Jinny" have waited for him on yon hill, and picked him up and so fetched him home, when he couldn't speak, and didn't know me. And now that it's the last time, why—' he paused, and rubbed the quartz gently on his sleeve—'you see it's sort of rough on his pardner. And now, gentlemen,' he added, abruptly, picking up his long-handled shovel, 'the fun'l's over; and my thanks, and Tennessee's thanks, to you for your trouble.'

Resisting any proffers of assistance, he began to fill in the grave, turning his back upon the crowd, that after a few moments' hesitation gradually withdrew. As they crossed the little ridge that hid Sandy Bar from view, some, looking back, thought they could see Tennessee's Partner, his work done, sitting upon the grave, his shovel between his knees, and his face buried in his red bandanna handkerchief. But it was argued by others that you couldn't tell his face from his handkerchief at that distance; and this point remained undecided.

In the reaction that followed the feverish excitement of that day, Tennessee's Partner was not forgotten. A secret investigation had cleared him of any complicity in Tennessee's guilt, and left only a suspicion of his general sanity. Sandy Bar made a point of calling on him, and proffering various uncouth, but well-meant kindnesses. But from that day his rude health and great strength seemed visibly to decline; and when the rainy season fairly set in, and the tiny grass-blades were beginning to peep from the rocky mound above Tennessee's grave, he took to his bed.

One night, when the pines beside the cabin were swaying in the storm, and trailing their slender fingers over the roof, and the roar and rush of the swollen river were heard below, Tennessee's Partner lifted his head from the pillow, saying, 'It is time to go for Tennessee; I must put "Jinny" in the cart'; and would have risen from his bed but for the restraint of his attendant. Struggling, he still pursued his singular fancy:

'There, now, steady, "Jinny,"—steady, old girl. How dark it is!
Look out for the ruts,—and look out for him, too, old gal.
Sometimes, you know, when he's blind drunk, he drops down
right in the trail. Keep on straight up to the pine on the top of
the hill. Thar—I told you so!—thar he is,—coming this way,
too,—all by himself, sober, and his face a-shining. Tennessee!
Pardner!'

And so they met.

THE IDYL OF RED GULCH

SANDY was very drunk. He was lying under an azalea-bush, in pretty much the same attitude in which he had fallen some hours before. How long he had been lying there he could not tell, and didn't care; how long he should lie there was a matter equally indefinite and unconsidered. A tranquil philosophy, born of his physical condition, suffused and saturated his moral being.

The spectacle of a drunken man, and of this drunken man in particular, was not, I grieve to say, of sufficient novelty in Red Gulch to attract attention. Earlier in the day some local satirist had erected a temporary tombstone at Sandy's head, bearing the inscription, 'Effects of McCorkle's whiskey,—kills at forty rods,' with a hand pointing to McCorkle's saloon. But this, I imagine, was, like most local satire, personal; and was a reflection upon the unfairness of the process rather than a commentary upon the impropriety of the result. With this facetious exception, Sandy had been undisturbed. A wandering mule, released from his pack, had cropped the scant herbage beside him, and sniffed curiously at the prostrate man; a vagabond dog, with that deep sympathy which the species have for drunken men, had licked his dusty boots, and curled himself up at his feet, and lay there, blinking one eye in the sunlight, with a simulation of dissipation that was ingenious and dog-like in its implied flattery of the unconscious man beside him.

Meanwhile the shadows of the pine-trees had slowly swung around until they crossed the road, and their trunks barred the open meadow with gigantic parallels of black and yellow. Little puffs of red dust, lifted by the plunging hoofs of passing teams, dispersed in a grimy shower upon the recumbent man. The sun sank lower and lower; and still Sandy stirred not. And then the repose of this philosopher was disturbed, as other philosophers have been, by the intrusion of an unphilosophical sex.

'Miss Mary,' as she was known to the little flock that she had just dismissed from the log school-house beyond the pines, was taking her afternoon walk. Observing an unusually fine cluster of blossoms on the azalea-bush opposite, she crossed the road to pluck it,—picking her way through the red dust, not without certain fierce little shivers of disgust, and some feline circumlocution. And then she came suddenly upon Sandy!

Of course she uttered the little *staccato** cry of her sex. But when she had paid that tribute to her physical weakness she became overbold, and halted for a moment,—at least six feet from this prostrate monster,—with her white skirts gathered in her hand, ready for flight. But neither sound nor motion came from the bush. With one little foot she then overturned the satirical head-board, and muttered 'Beasts!'—an epithet which probably, at that moment, conveniently classified in her mind the entire male population of Red Gulch. For Miss Mary, being possessed of certain rigid notions of her own, had not, perhaps, properly appreciated the demonstrative gallantry for which the Californian has been so justly celebrated by his brother Californians, and had, as a new-comer, perhaps, fairly earned the reputation of being 'stuck up.'

As she stood there she noticed, also, that the slant sunbeams were heating Sandy's head to what she judged to be an unhealthy temperature, and that his hat was lying uselessly at his side. To pick it up and to place it over his face was a work requiring some courage, particularly as his eyes were open. Yet she did it and made good her retreat. But she was somewhat concerned, on looking back, to see that the hat was removed, and that Sandy was sitting up and saying something.

The truth was, that in the calm depths of Sandy's mind he was satisfied that the rays of the sun were beneficial and healthful; that from childhood he had objected to lying down in a hat; that no people but condemned fools, past redemption, ever wore hats; and that his right to dispense with them when he pleased was inalienable. This was the statement of his inner consciousness. Unfortunately, its outward expression was vague, being limited to a repetition of the following formula,— 'Su'shine all ri'! Wasser maär, eh? Wass up, su'shine?'

Miss Mary stopped, and, taking fresh courage from her vantage of distance, asked him if there was anything that he wanted.

'Wass up? Wasser maär?' continued Sandy, in a very high key.

'Get up, you horrid man!' said Miss Mary, now thoroughly incensed; 'get up, and go home.'

Sandy staggered to his feet. He was six feet high, and Miss Mary trembled. He started forward a few paces and then stopped.

'Wass I go home for?' he suddenly asked, with great gravity.

'Go and take a bath,' replied Miss Mary, eying his grimy person with great disfavor.

To her infinite dismay, Sandy suddenly pulled off his coat and vest, threw them on the ground, kicked off his boots, and, plunging wildly forward, darted headlong over the hill, in the direction of the river.

'Goodness Heavens!—the man will be drowned!' said Miss Mary; and then, with feminine inconsistency, she ran back to the school-house, and locked herself in.

That night, while seated at supper with her hostess, the blacksmith's wife, it came to Miss Mary to ask, demurely, if her husband ever got drunk. 'Abner,' responded Mrs Stidger, reflectively, 'let's see: Abner hasn't been tight since last 'lection.' Miss Mary would have liked to ask if he preferred lying in the sun on these occasions, and if a cold bath would have hurt him; but this would have involved an explanation, which she did not then care to give. So she contented herself with opening her gray eyes widely at the red-cheeked Mrs Stidger,— a fine specimen of Southwestern efflorescence,—and then dismissed the subject altogether. The next day she wrote to her dearest friend, in Boston: 'I think I find the intoxicated portion of this community the least objectionable. I refer, my dear, to the men, of course. I do not know anything that could make the women tolerable.'

In less than a week Miss Mary had forgotten this episode, except that her afternoon walks took thereafter, almost unconsciously, another direction. She noticed, however, that every morning a fresh cluster of azalea-blossoms appeared among the flowers on her desk. This was not strange, as her little flock were aware of her fondness for flowers, and invariably kept her desk bright with anemones, syringas, and lupines; but, on questioning them, they, one and all, professed ignorance of the azaleas. A few days later, Master Johnny Stidger, whose desk was nearest to the window, was suddenly taken with spasms of apparently gratuitous laughter, that threatened the discipline of the school. All that Miss Mary could get from him was, that some one had been 'looking in the winder.' Irate and indignant, she sallied from her hive to do battle with the intruder. As she turned the corner of the school-house she came plump upon the quondam* drunkard,—now perfectly sober, and inexpressibly sheepish and guilty-looking.

These facts Miss Mary was not slow to take a feminine advantage of, in her present humor. But it was somewhat confusing to observe, also, that the beast, despite some faint signs of past dissipation, was amiable-looking,—in fact, a kind of blond Samson, whose corn-colored, silken beard apparently had never yet known the touch of barber's razor or Delilah's shears.* So that the cutting speech which quivered on her ready tongue died upon her lips, and she contented herself with receiving his stammering apology with supercilious eyelids and the gathered skirts of uncontamination. When she re-entered the school-room, her eyes fell upon the azaleas with a new sense of revelation. And then she laughed, and the little people all laughed, and they were all unconsciously very happy.

It was on a hot day—and not long after this—that two short-legged boys came to grief on the threshold of the school with a pail of water, which they had laboriously brought from the spring, and that Miss Mary compassionately seized the pail and started for the spring herself. At the foot of the hill a shadow crossed her path, and a blue-shirted arm dexterously, but gently relieved her of her burden. Miss Mary was both embarrassed and angry. 'If you carried more of that for yourself,' she said, spitefully, to the blue arm, without deigning to raise her lashes to its owner, 'you'd do better.' In the submissive silence that followed she regretted the speech, and thanked him so sweetly at the door that he stumbled. Which caused the children to laugh again,—a laugh in which Miss Mary joined, until the color came faintly into her pale cheek. The next day a barrel was mysteriously placed beside the door, and as mysteriously filled with fresh spring-water every morning.

Nor was this superior young person without other quiet attentions. 'Profane Bill,' driver of the Slumgullion Stage, widely known in the newspapers for his 'gallantry' in invariably offering the box-seat to the fair sex, had excepted Miss Mary from this attention, on the ground that he had a habit of 'cussin' on up grades,' and gave her half the coach to herself. Jack Hamlin, a gambler, having once silently ridden with her in the same coach, afterward threw a decanter at the head of a confederate for mentioning her name in a bar-room. The over-dressed mother of a pupil whose paternity was doubtful had often lingered near this astute Vestal's temple,* never daring to enter its sacred precincts, but content to worship the priestess from afar.

With such unconscious intervals the monotonous procession of blue skies, glittering sunshine, brief twilights, and starlit nights passed over Red Gulch. Miss Mary grew fond of walking in the sedate and proper woods. Perhaps she believed, with Mrs Stidger, that the balsamic odors of the firs 'did her chest good,' for certainly her slight cough was less frequent and her step was firmer; perhaps she had learned the unending lesson which the patient pines are never weary of repeating to heedful or listless ears. And so, one day, she planned a picnic on Buckeye Hill, and took the children with her. Away from the dusty road, the straggling shanties, the yellow ditches, the clamor of restless engines, the cheap finery of shop-windows, the deeper glitter of paint and colored glass, and the thin veneering which barbarism takes upon itself in such localities,—what infinite relief was theirs! The last heap of ragged rock and clay passed, the last unsightly chasm crossed,—how the waiting woods opened their long files to receive them! How the children—perhaps because they had not yet grown quite away from the breast of the bounteous Mother—threw themselves face downward on her brown bosom with uncouth caresses, filling the air with their laughter; and how Miss Mary herself—felinely fastidious and intrenched as she was in the purity of spotless skirts, collar, and cuffs—forgot all, and ran like a crested quail at the head of her brood, until, romping, laughing, and panting, with a loosened braid of brown hair, a hat hanging by a knotted ribbon from her throat, she came suddenly and violently, in the heart of the forest, upon—the luckless Sandy!

The explanations, apologies, and not overwise conversation that ensued, need not be indicated here. It would seem,

however, that Miss Mary had already established some acquaintance with this ex-drunkard. Enough that he was soon
accepted as one of the party; that the children, with that quick
intelligence which Providence gives the helpless, recognized a
friend, and played with his blond beard, and long silken
mustache, and took other liberties,—as the helpless are apt to
do. And when he had built a fire against a tree, and had shown
them other mysteries of wood-craft, their admiration knew no
bounds. At the close of two such foolish, idle, happy hours he
found himself lying at the feet of the schoolmistress, gazing
dreamily in her face, as she sat upon the sloping hillside,
weaving wreaths of laurel and syringa, in very much the same
attitude as he had lain when first they met. Nor was the
similitude greatly forced. The weakness of an easy, sensuous
nature, that had found a dreamy exaltation in liquor, it is to be
feared was now finding an equal intoxication in love.

I think that Sandy was dimly conscious of this himself. I
know that he longed to be doing something,—slaying a grizzly,
scalping a savage, or sacrificing himself in some way for the sake
of this sallow-faced, gray-eyed schoolmistress. As I should like
to present him in a heroic attitude, I stay my hand with great
difficulty at this moment, being only withheld from introducing
such an episode by a strong conviction that it does not usually
occur at such times. And I trust that my fairest reader, who
remembers that, in a real crisis, it is always some uninteresting
stranger or unromantic policeman, and not Adolphus,* who
rescues, will forgive the omission.

So they sat there, undisturbed,—the woodpeckers chattering
overhead, and the voices of the children coming pleasantly from
the hollow below. What they said matters little. What they
thought—which might have been interesting—did not tran-
spire. The woodpeckers only learned how Miss Mary was an
orphan; how she left her uncle's house, to come to California,
for the sake of health and independence; how Sandy was an
orphan, too; how he came to California for excitement; how he
had lived a wild life, and how he was trying to reform; and
other details, which, from a woodpecker's view-point, undoubtedly must have seemed stupid, and a waste of time. But
even in such trifles was the afternoon spent; and when the

children were again gathered, and Sandy, with a delicacy which the schoolmistress well understood, took leave of them quietly at the outskirts of the settlement, it had seemed the shortest day of her weary life.

As the long, dry summer withered to its roots, the school term of Red Gulch—to use a local euphuism—'dried up' also. In another day Miss Mary would be free; and for a season, at least, Red Gulch would know her no more. She was seated alone in the school-house, her cheek resting on her hand, her eyes half closed in one of those day-dreams in which Miss Mary—I fear, to the danger of school discipline—was lately in the habit of indulging. Her lap was full of mosses, ferns, and other woodland memories. She was so preoccupied with these and her own thoughts that a gentle tapping at the door passed unheard, or translated itself into the remembrance of far-off woodpeckers. When at last it asserted itself more distinctly, she started up with a flushed cheek and opened the door. On the threshold stood a woman, the self-assertion and audacity of whose dress were in singular contrast to her timid, irresolute bearing.

Miss Mary recognized at a glance the dubious mother of her anonymous pupil. Perhaps she was disappointed, perhaps she was only fastidious; but as she coldly invited her to enter, she half unconsciously settled her white cuffs and collar, and gathered closer her own chaste skirts. It was, perhaps, for this reason that the embarrassed stranger, after a moment's hesitation, left her gorgeous parasol open and sticking in the dust beside the door, and then sat down at the farther end of a long bench. Her voice was husky as she began:—

'I heerd tell that you were goin' down to the Bay to-morrow, and I couldn't let you go until I came to thank you for your kindness to my Tommy.'

Tommy, Miss Mary said, was a good boy, and deserved more than the poor attention she could give him.

'Thank you, miss; thank ye!' cried the stranger, brightening even through the color which Red Gulch knew facetiously as her 'war paint,' and striving, in her embarrassment, to drag the long bench nearer the schoolmistress. 'I thank you, miss, for that! and if I am his mother, there ain't a sweeter, dearer, better boy lives than him. And if I ain't much as says it, thar ain't a sweeter, dearer, angeler teacher lives than he's got.'

Miss Mary, sitting primly behind her desk, with a ruler over her shoulder, opened her gray eyes widely at this, but said nothing.

'It ain't for you to be complimented by the like of me, I know,' she went on, hurriedly. 'It ain't for me to be comin' here, in broad day, to do it, either; but I come to ask a favor,—not for me, miss,—not for me, but for the darling boy.'

Encouraged by a look in the young schoolmistress's eye, and putting her lilac-gloved hands together, the fingers downward, between her knees, she went on, in a low voice:—

'You see, miss, there's no one the boy has any claim on but me, and I ain't the proper person to bring him up. I thought some, last year, of sending him away to 'Frisco to school, but when they talked of bringing a schoolma'am here, I waited till I saw you, and then I knew it was all right, and I could keep my boy a little longer. And O, miss, he loves you so much; and if you could hear him talk about you, in his pretty way, and if he could ask you what I ask you now, you couldn't refuse him.

'It is natural,' she went on, rapidly, in a voice that trembled strangely between pride and humility,—'it's natural that he should take to you, miss, for his father, when I first knew him, was a gentleman,—and the boy must forget me, sooner or later,—and so I ain't a goin' to cry about that. For I come to ask you to take my Tommy,—God bless him for the bestest, sweetest boy that lives,—to—to—take him with you.'

She had risen and caught the young girl's hand in her own, and had fallen on her knees beside her.

'I've money plenty, and it's all yours and his. Put him in some good school, where you can go and see him, and help him to—to—to forget his mother. Do with him what you like. The worst you can do will be kindness to what he will learn with me. Only take him out of this wicked life, this cruel place, this home of shame and sorrow. You will; I know you will,—won't you? You will,—you must not, you cannot say no! You will make him as pure, as gentle as yourself; and when he has grown up, you will tell him his father's name,—the name that hasn't passed my lips for years,—the name of Alexander Morton, whom they call here Sandy! Miss Mary!—do not take your hand away! Miss Mary, speak to me! You will take my boy? Do not put your face from me. I know it ought not to look on such as me. Miss Mary!—my God, be merciful!—she is leaving me!'

Miss Mary had risen, and, in the gathering twilight, had felt her way to the open window. She stood there, leaning against the casement, her eyes fixed on the last rosy tints that were fading from the western sky. There was still some of its light on her pure young forehead, on her white collar, on her clasped white hands, but all fading slowly away. The suppliant had dragged herself, still on her knees, beside her.

'I know it takes time to consider. I will wait here all night; but I cannot go until you speak. Do not deny me now. You will!—I see it in your sweet face,—such a face as I have seen in my dreams. I see it in your eyes, Miss Mary!—you will take my boy!'

The last red beam crept higher, suffused Miss Mary's eyes with something of its glory, flickered, and faded, and went out. The sun had set on Red Gulch. In the twilight and silence Miss Mary's voice sounded pleasantly.

'I will take the boy. Send him to me to-night.'

The happy mother raised the hem of Miss Mary's skirts to her lips. She would have buried her hot face in its virgin folds, but she dared not. She rose to her feet.

'Does—this man—know of your intention?' asked Miss Mary, suddenly.

'No, nor cares. He has never even seen the child to know it.'

'Go to him at once,—to-night,—now! Tell him what you have done. Tell him I have taken his child, and tell him— he must never see—see—the child again. Wherever it may be, he must not come; wherever I may take it, he must not follow! There, go now, please,—I'm weary, and—have much yet to do!'

They walked together to the door. On the threshold the woman turned.

'Good night.'

She would have fallen at Miss Mary's feet. But at the same moment the young girl reached out her arms, caught the sinful woman to her own pure breast for one brief moment, and then closed and locked the door.

*

It was with a sudden sense of great responsibility that Profane Bill took the reins of the Slumgullion Stage the next morning, for the schoolmistress was one of his passengers. As he entered the high-road, in obedience to a pleasant voice from the 'inside,' he suddenly reined up his horses and respectfully waited, as 'Tommy' hopped out at the command of Miss Mary.

'Not that bush, Tommy,—the next.'

Tommy whipped out his new pocket-knife, and, cutting a branch from a tall azalea-bush, returned with it to Miss Mary.

'All right now?'

'All right.'

And the stage-door closed on the Idyl of Red Gulch.

HIGH-WATER MARK

WHEN the tide was out on the Dedlow Marsh, its extended dreariness was patent. Its spongy, low-lying surface, sluggish, inky pools, and tortuous sloughs, twisting their slimy way, eel-like, toward the open bay, were all hard facts. So were the few green tussocks, with their scant blades, their amphibious flavor, and unpleasant dampness. And if you choose to indulge your fancy,—although the flat monotony of the Dedlow Marsh was not inspiring,—the wavy line of scattered drift gave an unpleasant consciousness of the spent waters, and made the dead certainty of the returning tide a gloomy reflection, which no present sunshine could dissipate. The greener meadow-land seemed oppressed with this idea, and made no positive attempt at vegetation until the work of reclamation should be complete. In the bitter fruit of the low cranberry-bushes one might fancy he detected a naturally sweet disposition curdled and soured by an injudicious course of too much regular cold water.

The vocal expression of the Dedlow Marsh was also melancholy and depressing. The sepulchral boom of the bittern, the shriek of the curlew, the scream of passing brent, the wrangling of quarrelsome teal, the sharp, querulous protest of the startled crane, and syllabled complaint of the 'killdeer' plover were beyond the power of written expression. Nor was the aspect of these mournful fowls at all cheerful and inspiring. Certainly not the blue heron standing midleg deep in the water, obviously catching cold in a reckless disregard of wet feet and consequences; nor the mournful curlew, the dejected plover, or the low-spirited snipe, who saw fit to join him in his suicidal contemplation; nor the impassive kingfisher—an ornithological Marius*—reviewing the desolate expanse; nor the black raven that went to and fro over the face of the marsh continually, but evidently couldn't make up his mind whether the waters had subsided, and felt low-spirited in the reflection that, after all this trouble, he wouldn't be able to give a definite answer. On the contrary, it was evident at a glance that the dreary expanse of Dedlow Marsh told unpleasantly on the birds, and that the season of migration was looked forward to with a feeling of relief and satisfaction by the full-grown, and of extravagant anticipation by the callow, brood. But if Dedlow Marsh was cheerless at the slack of the low tide, you should have seen it when the tide was strong and full. When the damp air blew chilly over the cold, glittering expanse, and came to the faces of those who looked seaward like another tide; when a steel-like glint marked the low hollows and the sinuous line of slough; when the great shell-incrusted trunks of fallen trees arose again, and went forth on their dreary, purposeless wanderings, drifting hither and thither, but getting no farther toward any goal at the falling tide or the day's decline than the cursed Hebrew in the legend;* when the glossy ducks swung silently, making neither ripple nor furrow on the shimmering surface; when the fog came in with the tide and shut out the blue above, even as the green below had been obliterated; when boatmen, lost in that fog, paddling about in a hopeless way, started at what seemed the brushing of mermen's fingers on the boat's keel, or shrank from the tufts of grass spreading around like the floating hair of a corpse, and knew by these signs that they were lost upon Dedlow Marsh, and must make a night of it, and a gloomy one at that,—then you might know something of Dedlow Marsh at high water.

Let me recall a story connected with this latter view which never failed to recur to my mind in my long gunning excursions upon Dedlow Marsh. Although the event was briefly recorded in the county paper, I had the story, in all its eloquent detail, from the lips of the principal actor. I cannot hope to catch the varying emphasis and peculiar coloring of feminine delineation, for my narrator was a woman; but I'll try to give at least its substance.

She lived midway of the great slough of Dedlow Marsh and a good-sized river, which debouched four miles beyond into an estuary formed by the Pacific Ocean, on the long sandy peninsula which constituted the southwestern boundary of a noble bay. The house in which she lived was a small frame cabin raised from the marsh a few feet by stout piles, and was three miles distant from the settlements upon the river. Her husband was a logger,—a profitable business in a county where the principal occupation was the manufacture of lumber.

It was the season of early spring, when her husband left on the ebb of a high tide, with a raft of logs for the usual transportation to the lower end of the bay. As she stood by the door of the little cabin when the voyagers departed she noticed a cold look in the southeastern sky, and she remembered hearing her husband say to his companions that they must endeavor to complete their voyage before the coming of the southwesterly gale which he saw brewing. And that night it began to storm and blow harder than she had ever before experienced, and some great trees fell in the forest by the river, and the house rocked like her baby's cradle.

But however the storm might roar about the little cabin, she knew that one she trusted had driven bolt and bar with his own strong hand, and that had he feared for her he would not have left her. This, and her domestic duties, and the care of her little sickly baby, helped to keep her mind from dwelling on the weather, except, of course, to hope that he was safely harbored with the logs at Utopia in the dreary distance. But she noticed that day, when she went out to feed the chickens and look after the cow, that the tide was up to the little fence of their garden-patch, and the roar of the surf on the south beach, though miles away, she could hear distinctly. And she began to think that she would like to have some one to talk with about matters, and she believed that if it had not been so far and so stormy, and the trail so impassable, she would have taken the baby and have gone over to Ryckman's, her nearest neighbor. But then, you see, he might have returned in the storm, all wet, with no one to see to him; and it was a long exposure for baby, who was croupy and ailing.

But that night, she never could tell why, she didn't feel like sleeping or even lying down. The storm had somewhat abated, but she still 'sat and sat,' and even tried to read. I don't know whether it was a Bible or some profane magazine that this poor woman read, but most probably the latter, for the words all ran together and made such sad nonsense that she was forced at last to put the book down and turn to that dearer volume which lay before her in the cradle, with its white initial leaf as yet unsoiled, and try to look forward to its mysterious future. And, rocking the cradle, she thought of everything and everybody, but still was wide awake as ever.

It was nearly twelve o'clock when she at last laid down in her clothes. How long she slept she could not remember, but she awoke with a dreadful choking in her throat, and found herself standing, trembling all over, in the middle of the room, with her baby clasped to her breast, and she was 'saying something.' The baby cried and sobbed, and she walked up and down trying to hush it, when she heard a scratching at the door. She opened it fearfully, and was glad to see it was only old Pete, their dog, who crawled, dripping with water, into the room. She would like to have looked out, not in the faint hope of her husband's coming, but to see how things looked; but the wind shook the door so savagely that she could hardly hold it. Then she sat down a little while, and then walked up and down a little while, and then she lay down again a little while. Lying close by the wall of the little cabin, she thought she heard once or twice something scrape slowly against the clapboards, like the scraping of branches. Then there was a little gurgling sound, 'like the baby made when it was swallowing'; then something went 'click-click' and 'cluck-cluck,' so that she sat up in bed. When she did so she was attracted by something else that seemed creeping from the back door towards the centre of the room. It wasn't much wider than her little finger, but soon it swelled to the width of her hand, and began spreading all over the floor. It was water.

She ran to the front door and threw it wide open, and saw nothing but water. She ran to the back door and threw it open, and saw nothing but water. She ran to the side window, and, throwing that open, she saw nothing but water. Then she remembered hearing her husband once say that there was no danger in the tide, for that fell regularly, and people could calculate on it, and that he would rather live near the bay than the river, whose banks might overflow at any time. But was it the tide? So she ran again to the back door, and threw out a stick of wood. It drifted away towards the bay. She scooped up some of the water and put it eagerly to her lips. It was fresh and sweet. It was the river, and not the tide!

It was then—O, God be praised for his goodness! she did neither faint nor fall; it was then—blessed be the Saviour for it was his merciful hand that touched and strengthened her in this awful moment—that fear dropped from her like a garment, and her trembling ceased. It was then and thereafter that she never lost her self-command, through all the trials of that gloomy night.

She drew the bedstead towards the middle of the room, and placed a table upon it and on that she put the cradle. The water on the floor was already over her ankles, and the house once or twice moved so perceptibly, and seemed to be racked so, that the closet doors all flew open. Then she heard the same rasping and thumping against the wall, and, looking out, saw that a large uprooted tree, which had lain near the road at the upper end of the pasture, had floated down to the house. Luckily its long roots dragged in the soil and kept it from moving as rapidly as the current, for had it struck the house in its full career, even the strong nails and bolts in the piles could not have withstood the shock. The hound had leaped upon its knotty surface, and crouched near the roots shivering and whining. A ray of hope flashed across her mind. She drew a heavy blanket from the bed, and, wrapping it about the babe, waded in the deepening waters to the door. As the tree swung again, broadside on, making the little cabin creak and tremble, she leaped on to its trunk. By God's mercy she succeeded in obtaining a footing on its slippery surface, and, twining an arm about its roots, she held in the other her moaning child. Then something cracked near the front porch, and the whole front of the house she had just quitted fell forward,—just as cattle fall on their knees before they lie down,—and at the same moment the great redwood-tree swung round and drifted away with its living cargo into the black night.

For all the excitement and danger, for all her soothing of her crying babe, for all the whistling of the wind, for all the uncertainty of her situation, she still turned to look at the deserted and water-swept cabin. She remembered even then, and she wonders how foolish she was to think of it at that time, that she wished she had put on another dress and the baby's best clothes; and she kept praying that the house would be spared so that he, when he returned, would have something to come to, and it wouldn't be quite so desolate, and—how could he ever know what had become of her and baby? And at the thought she grew sick and faint. But she had something else to do besides worrying, for whenever the long roots of her ark struck an obstacle, the whole trunk made half a revolution, and twice dipped her in the black water. The hound, who kept distracting her by running up and down the tree and howling, at last fell off at one of these collisions. He swam for some time beside her, and she tried to get the poor beast upon the tree, but he 'acted silly' and wild, and at last she lost sight of him forever. Then she and her baby were left alone. The light which had burned for a few minutes in the deserted cabin was quenched suddenly. She could not then tell whither she was drifting. The outline of the white dunes on the peninsula showed dimly ahead, and she judged the tree was moving in a line with the river. It must be about slack water, and she had probably reached the eddy formed by the confluence of the tide and the overflowing waters of the river. Unless the tide fell soon, there was present danger of her drifting to its channel, and being carried out to sea or crushed in the floating drift. That peril averted, if she were carried out on the ebb toward the bay, she might hope to strike one of the wooded promontories of the peninsula, and rest till daylight. Sometimes she thought she heard voices and shouts from the river, and the bellowing of cattle and bleating of sheep. Then again it was only the ringing in her ears and throbbing of her heart. She found at about this time that she was so chilled and stiffened in her cramped position that she could scarcely move, and the baby cried so when she put it to her breast that she noticed the milk refused to flow; and she was so frightened at that, that she put her head under her shawl, and for the first time cried bitterly.

When she raised her head again, the boom of the surf was behind her, and she knew that her ark had again swung round. She dipped up the water to cool her parched throat, and found that it was salt as her tears. There was a relief, though, for by this sign she knew that she was drifting with the tide. It was then the wind went down, and the great and awful silence oppressed her. There was scarcely a ripple against the furrowed sides of the great trunk on which she rested, and around her all was black gloom and quiet. She spoke to the baby just to hear herself speak, and to know that she had not lost her voice. She thought then,—it was queer, but she could not help thinking it,—how awful must have been the night when the great ship swung over the Asiatic peak,* and the sounds of creation were blotted out from the world. She thought, too, of mariners clinging to spars, and of poor women who were lashed to rafts, and beaten to death by the cruel sea. She tried to thank God that she was thus spared, and lifted her eyes from the baby who had fallen into a fretful sleep. Suddenly, away to the southward, a great light lifted itself out of the gloom, and flashed and flickered, and flickered and flashed again. Her heart fluttered quickly against the baby's cold cheek. It was the lighthouse at the entrance of the bay. As she was yet wondering, the tree suddenly rolled a little, dragged a little, and then seemed to lie quiet and still. She put out her hand and the current gurgled against it. The tree was aground, and, by the position of the light and the noise of the surf, aground upon the Dedlow Marsh.

Had it not been for her baby, who was ailing and croupy, had it not been for the sudden drying up of that sensitive fountain, she would have felt safe and relieved. Perhaps it was this which tended to make all her impressions mournful and gloomy. As the tide rapidly fell, a great flock of black brent fluttered by her, screaming and crying. Then the plover flew up and piped mournfully, as they wheeled around the trunk, and at last fearlessly lit upon it like a gray cloud. Then the heron flew over and around her, shrieking and protesting, and at last dropped its gaunt legs only a few yards from her. But, strangest of all, a pretty white bird, larger than a dove,—like a pelican, but not a pelican,—circled around and around her. At last it lit upon a rootlet of the tree, quite over her shoulder. She put out her hand and stroked its beautiful white neck, and it never appeared to move. It stayed there so long that she thought she would lift up the baby to see it, and try to attract her attention. But when she did so, the child was so chilled and cold, and had such a blue look under the little lashes which it didn't raise at all, that she screamed aloud, and the bird flew away, and she fainted.

Well, that was the worst of it, and perhaps it was not so much, after all, to any but herself. For when she recovered her senses it was bright sunlight, and dead low water. There was a confused noise of guttural voices about her, and an old squaw, singing an Indian 'hushaby,' and rocking herself from side to side before a fire built on the marsh, before which she, the recovered wife and mother, lay weak and weary. Her first thought was for her baby, and she was about to speak, when a young squaw, who must have been a mother herself, fathomed her thought and brought her the 'mowitch,' pale but living, in such a queer little willow cradle all bound up, just like the squaw's own young one, that she laughed and cried together, and the young squaw and the old squaw showed their big white teeth and glinted their black eyes and said, 'Plenty get well, skeena mowitch,' 'wagee man come plenty soon,' and she could have kissed their brown faces in her joy. And then she found that they had been gathering berries on the marsh in their queer, comical baskets, and saw the skirt of her gown fluttering on the tree from afar, and the old squaw couldn't resist the temptation of procuring a new garment, and came down and discovered the 'wagee' woman and child. And of course she gave the garment to the old squaw, as you may imagine, and when *he* came at last and rushed up to her, looking about ten years older in his anxiety, she felt so faint again that they had to carry her to the canoe. For, you see, he knew nothing about the flood until he met the Indians at Utopia, and knew by the signs that the poor woman was his wife. And at the next high-tide he towed the tree away back home, although it wasn't worth the trouble, and built another house, using the old tree for the foundation and props, and called it after her, 'Mary's Ark!' But you may guess the next house was built above High-water mark. And that's all.

Not much, perhaps, considering the malevolent capacity of the Dedlow Marsh. But you must tramp over it at low water, or paddle over it at high tide, or get lost upon it once or twice in the fog, as I have, to understand properly Mary's adventure, or to appreciate duly the blessings of living beyond High-Water Mark.

A LONELY RIDE

As I stepped into the Slumgullion stage I saw that it was a dark night, a lonely road, and that I was the only passenger. Let me assure the reader that I have no ulterior design in making this assertion. A long course of light reading has forewarned me what every experienced intelligence must confidently look for from such a statement. The story-teller who wilfully tempts Fate by such obvious beginnings; who is to the expectant reader in danger of being robbed or half murdered, or frightened by an escaped lunatic, or introduced to his lady-love for the first time, deserves to be detected. I am relieved to say that none of these things occurred to me. The road from Wingdam to Slumgullion knew no other banditti than the regularly licensed hotel-keepers; lunatics had not yet reached such depth of imbecility as to ride of their own free-will in California stages; and my Laura,* amiable and long-suffering as she always is, could not, I fear, have borne up against these depressing circumstances long enough to have made the slightest impression on me.

I stood with my shawl and carpet-bag in hand, gazing doubtingly on the vehicle. Even in the darkness the red dust of Wingdam was visible on its roof and sides, and the red slime of Slumgullion clung tenaciously to its wheels. I opened the door; the stage creaked uneasily, and in the gloomy abyss the swaying straps beckoned me, like ghostly hands, to come in now, and have my sufferings out at once.

I must not omit to mention the occurrence of a circumstance which struck me as appalling and mysterious. A lounger on the steps of the hotel, whom I had reason to suppose was not in any way connected with the stage company, gravely descended, and, walking toward the conveyance, tried the handle of the door, opened it, expectorated in the carriage, and returned to the hotel with a serious demeanor. Hardly had he resumed his position, when another individual, equally disinterested, impassively walked down the steps, proceeded to the back of the stage, lifted it, expectorated carefully on the axle, and returned slowly and pensively to the hotel. A third spectator wearily disengaged himself from one of the Ionic columns of the portico and walked to the box, remained for a moment in serious and expectorative contemplation of the boot, and then returned to his column. There was something so weird in this baptism that I grew quite nervous.

Perhaps I was out of spirits. A number of infinitesimal annoyances, winding up with the resolute persistency of the clerk at the stage-office to enter my name misspelt on the way-bill, had not predisposed me to cheerfulness. The inmates of the Eureka House, from a social view-point, were not attractive. There was the prevailing opinion—so common to many honest people—that a serious style of deportment and conduct toward a stranger indicates high gentility and elevated station. Obeying this principle, all hilarity ceased on my entrance to supper, and general remark merged into the safer and uncompromising chronicle of several bad cases of diphtheria, then epidemic at Wingdam. When I left the dining-room, with an odd feeling that I had been supping exclusively on mustard and tea-leaves, I stopped a moment at the parlor door. A piano, harmoniously related to the dinner-bell, tinkled responsive to a diffident and uncertain touch. On the white wall the shadow of an old and sharp profile was bending over several symmetrical and shadowy curls. 'I sez to Mariar, Mariar, sez I, "Praise to the face is open disgrace." ' I heard no more. Dreading some susceptibility to sincere expression on the subject of female loveliness, I walked away, checking the compliment that otherwise might have risen unbidden to my lips, and have brought shame and sorrow to the household.

It was with the memory of these experiences resting heavily upon me, that I stood hesitatingly before the stage door. The driver, about to mount, was for a moment illuminated by the open door of the hotel. He had the wearied look which was the distinguishing expression of Wingdam. Satisfied that I was properly way-billed and receipted for, he took no further notice of me. I looked longingly at the box-seat, but he did not respond to the appeal. I flung my carpet-bag into the chasm, dived recklessly after it, and—before I was fairly seated—with a great sigh, a creaking of unwilling springs, complaining bolts,

and harshly expostulating axle, we moved away. Rather the
hotel door slipped behind, the sound of the piano sank to rest,
and the night and its shadows moved solemnly upon us.

To say it was dark expressed but faintly the pitchy obscurity
that encompassed the vehicle. The roadside trees were scarcely
distinguishable as deeper masses of shadow; I knew them only
by the peculiar sodden odor that from time to time sluggishly
flowed in at the open window as we rolled by. We proceeded
slowly; so leisurely that, leaning from the carriage, I more than
once detected the fragrant sigh of some astonished cow, whose
ruminating repose upon the highway we had ruthlessly disturbed. But in the darkness our progress, more the guidance of
some mysterious instinct than any apparent volition of our own,
gave an indefinable charm of security to our journey, that a
moment's hesitation or indecision on the part of the driver
would have destroyed.

I had indulged a hope that in the empty vehicle I might
obtain that rest so often denied me in its crowded condition. It
was a weak delusion. When I stretched out my limbs it was
only to find that the ordinary conveniences for making several
people distinctly uncomfortable were distributed throughout
my individual frame. At last, resting my arms on the straps,
by dint of much gymnastic effort I became sufficiently composed to be aware of a more refined species of torture. The
springs of the stage, rising and falling regularly, produced
a rhythmical beat, which began to painfully absorb my attention. Slowly this thumping merged into a senseless echo of
the mysterious female of the hotel parlor, and shaped itself
into this awful and benumbing axiom,—'Praise-to-the-face-is-
open-disgrace. Praise-to-the-face-is-open-disgrace.' Inequalities
of the road only quickened its utterance or drawled it to an
exasperating length.

It was of no use to seriously consider the statement. It was
of no use to except to it indignantly. It was of no use to recall
the many instances where praise to the face had redounded to
the everlasting honor of praiser and bepraised; of no use to
dwell sentimentally on modest genius and courage lifted up and
strengthened by open commendation; of no use to except to the
mysterious female,—to picture her as rearing a thin-blooded

generation on selfish and mechanically repeated axioms,—all
this failed to counteract the monotonous repetition of this
sentence. There was nothing to do but to give in,—and I was
about to accept it weakly, as we too often treat other illusions
of darkness and necessity, for the time being,—when I became
aware of some other annoyance that had been forcing itself
upon me for the last few moments. How quiet the driver was!

Was there any driver? Had I any reason to suppose that he
was not lying, gagged and bound on the roadside, and the
highwayman, with blackened face who did the thing so quietly,
driving me—whither? The thing is perfectly feasible. And what
is this fancy now being jolted out of me. A story? It's of no use
to keep it back,—particularly in this abysmal vehicle, and here
it comes: I am a Marquis,—a French Marquis; French, because
the peerage is not so well known, and the country is better
adapted to romantic incident,—a Marquis, because the demo-
cratic reader delights in the nobility. My name is something
ligny. I am coming from Paris to my country-seat at St
Germain. It is a dark night, and I fall asleep and tell my honest
coachman, André, not to disturb me, and dream of an angel.
The carriage at last stops at the chateau. It is so dark that when
I alight I do not recognize the face of the footman who holds
the carriage door. But what of that?—*peste!* * I am heavy with
sleep. The same obscurity also hides the old familiar indecen-
cies of the statues on the terrace; but there is a door, and it
opens and shuts behind me smartly. Then I find myself in a
trap, in the presence of the brigand who has quietly gagged
poor André and conducted the carriage thither. There is
nothing for me to do, as a gallant French Marquis, but to say,
'*Parbleu!*'* draw my rapier, and die valorously! I am found a
week or two after, outside a deserted *cabaret* near the barrier,
with a hole through my ruffled linen and my pockets stripped.
No; on second thoughts, I am rescued,—rescued by the angel I
have been dreaming of, who is the assumed daughter of the
brigand, but the real daughter of an intimate friend.

Looking from the window again, in the vain hope of distinguishing the driver, I found my eyes were growing accustomed
to the darkness. I could see the distant horizon, defined by
India-inky woods, relieving a lighter sky. A few stars widely

spaced in this picture glimmered sadly. I noticed again the infinite depth of patient sorrow in their serene faces; and I hope that the Vandal who first applied the flippant 'twinkle' to them may not be driven melancholy mad by their reproachful eyes. I noticed again the mystic charm of space that imparts a sense of individual solitude to each integer of the densest constellation, involving the smallest star with immeasurable loneliness. Something of this calm and solitude crept over me, and I dozed in my gloomy cavern. When I awoke the full moon was rising. Seen from my window, it had an indescribably unreal and theatrical effect. It was the full moon of Norma,—that remarkable celestial phenomenon which rises so palpably to a hushed audience and a sublime *andante* chorus, until the *Casta Diva** is sung,—the 'inconstant moon' that then and thereafter remains fixed in the heavens as though it were a part of the solar system inaugurated by Joshua.* Again the white-robed Druids filed past me, again I saw that improbable mistletoe cut from that impossible oak, and again cold chills ran down my back with the first strain of the recitative. The thumping springs essayed to beat time, and the private-box-like obscurity of the vehicle lent a cheap enchantment to the view. But it was a vast improvement upon my past experience, and I hugged the fond delusion.

My fears for the driver were dissipated with the rising moon. A familiar sound had assured me of his presence in the full possession of at least one of his most important functions. Frequent and full expectoration convinced me that his lips were as yet not sealed by the gag of highwaymen, and soothed my anxious ear. With this load lifted from my mind, and assisted by the mild presence of Diana, who left, as when she visited Endymion,* much of her splendor outside my cavern,—I looked around the empty vehicle. On the forward seat lay a woman's hair-pin. I picked it up with an interest that, however, soon abated. There was no scent of the roses to cling to it still, not even of hair-oil. No bend or twist in its rigid angles betrayed any trait of its wearer's character. I tried to think that it might have been 'Mariar's.' I tried to imagine that, confining the symmetrical curls of that girl, it might have heard the soft compliments whispered in her ears, which provoked the wrath of the aged female. But in vain. It was reticent and unswerving in its upright fidelity, and at last slipped listlessly through my fingers.

I had dozed repeatedly,—waked on the threshold of oblivion by contact with some of the angles of the coach, and feeling that I was unconsciously assuming, in imitation of a humble insect of my childish recollection, that spherical shape which could best resist those impressions, when I perceived that the moon, riding high in the heavens, had begun to separate the formless masses of the shadowy landscape. Trees isolated, in clumps and assemblages, changed places before my window. The sharp outlines of the distant hills came back, as in daylight, but little softened in the dry, cold, dewless air of a California summer night. I was wondering how late it was, and thinking that if the horses of the night* travelled as slowly as the team before us, Faustus might have been spared his agonizing prayer, when a sudden spasm of activity attacked my driver. A succession of whip-snappings, like a pack of Chinese crackers, broke from the box before me. The stage leaped forward, and when I could pick myself from under the seat, a long white building had in some mysterious way rolled before my window. It must be Slumgullion! As I descended from the stage I addressed the driver:—

'I thought you changed horses on the road?'

'So we did. Two hours ago.'

'That's odd. I didn't notice it.'

'Must have been asleep, sir. Hope you had a pleasant nap. Bully place for a nice quiet snooze,—empty stage, sir!'

THE MAN OF NO ACCOUNT

His name was Fagg,—David Fagg. He came to California in '52 with us, in the 'Skyscraper.' I don't think he did it in an adventurous way. He probably had no other place to go to. When a knot of us young fellows would recite what splendid opportunities we resigned to go, and how sorry our friends were to have us leave, and show daguerreotypes and locks of hair, and talk of Mary and Susan, the man of no account used to sit by and listen with a pained, mortified expression on his plain face, and say nothing. I think he had nothing to say. He had no associates except when we patronized him; and, in point of fact, he was a good deal of sport to us. He was always sea-sick whenever we had a capful of wind. He never got his sea-legs on either. And I never shall forget how we all laughed when Rattler took him the piece of pork on a string, and—But you know that time-honored joke. And then we had such a splendid lark with him. Miss Fanny Twinkler couldn't bear the sight of him, and we used to make Fagg think that she had taken a fancy to him, and send him little delicacies and books from the cabin. You ought to have witnessed the rich scene that took place when he came up, stammering and very sick, to thank her! Didn't she flash up grandly and beautifully and scornfully? So like 'Medora,'* Rattler said,—Rattler knew Byron by heart,—and wasn't old Fagg awfully cut up? But he got over it, and when Rattler fell sick at Valparaiso, old Fagg used to nurse him. You see he was a good sort of fellow, but he lacked manliness and spirit.

He had absolutely no idea of poetry. I've seen him sit stolidly by, mending his old clothes, when Rattler delivered that stirring apostrophe of Byron's to the ocean. He asked Rattler once, quite seriously, if he thought Byron was ever sea-sick. I don't remember Rattler's reply, but I know we all laughed very much, and I have no doubt it was something good, for Rattler was smart.

When the 'Skyscraper' arrived at San Francisco we had a grand 'feed.' We agreed to meet every year and perpetuate the occasion. Of course we didn't invite Fagg. Fagg was a steerage-passenger, and it was necessary, you see, now we were ashore, to exercise a little discretion. But Old Fagg, as we called him,—he was only about twenty-five years old, by the way,—was the source of immense amusement to us that day. It appeared that he had conceived the idea that he could walk to Sacramento, and actually started off afoot. We had a good time, and shook hands with one another all around, and so parted. Ah me! only eight years ago, and yet some of those hands then clasped in amity have been clenched at each other, or have dipped furtively in one another's pockets. I know that we didn't dine together the next year, because young Barker swore he wouldn't put his feet under the same mahogany with such a very contemptible scoundrel as that Mixer; and Nibbles, who borrowed money at Valparaiso of young Stubbs, who was then a waiter in a restaurant, didn't like to meet such people.

When I bought a number of shares in the Coyote Tunnel at Mugginsville, in '54, I thought I'd take a run up there and see it. I stopped at the Empire Hotel, and after dinner I got a horse and rode round the town and out to the claim. One of those individuals whom newspaper correspondents call 'our intelligent informant,' and to whom in all small communities the right of answering questions is tacitly yielded, was quietly pointed out to me. Habit had enabled him to work and talk at the same time, and he never pretermitted either. He gave me a history of the claim, and added: 'You see, stranger' (he addressed the bank before him), 'gold is sure to come out 'er that theer claim (he put in a comma with his pick), but the old pro–pri–e–tor (he wriggled out the word and the point of his pick) warn't of much account (a long stroke of the pick for a period). He was green, and let the boys about here jump him,'—and the rest of his sentence was confided to his hat, which he had removed to wipe his manly brow with his red bandanna.

I asked him who was the original proprietor.

'His name war Fagg.'

I went to see him. He looked a little older and plainer. He had worked hard, he said, and was getting on 'so, so.' I took quite a liking to him and patronized him to some extent. Whether I did so because I was beginning to have a distrust for such fellows as Rattler and Mixer is not necessary for me to state.

You remember how the Coyote Tunnel went in, and how awfully we shareholders were done! Well, the next thing I heard was that Rattler, who was one of the heaviest shareholders, was up at Mugginsville keeping bar for the proprietor of the Mugginsville Hotel, and that old Fagg had struck it rich, and didn't know what to do with his money. All this was told me by Mixer, who had been there, settling up matters, and likewise that Fagg was sweet upon the daughter of the proprietor of the aforesaid hotel. And so by hearsay and letter I eventually gathered that old Robins, the hotel man, was trying to get up a match between Nellie Robins and Fagg. Nellie was a pretty, plump, and foolish little thing, and would do just as her father wished. I thought it would be a good thing for Fagg if he should marry and settle down; that as a married man he might be of some account. So I ran up to Mugginsville one day to look after things.

It did me an immense deal of good to make Rattler mix my drinks for me,—Rattler! the gay, brilliant, and unconquerable Rattler, who had tried to snub me two years ago. I talked to him about old Fagg and Nellie, particularly as I thought the subject was distasteful. He never liked Fagg, and he was sure, he said, that Nellie didn't. Did Nellie like anybody else? He turned around to the mirror behind the bar and brushed up his hair! I understood the conceited wretch. I thought I'd put Fagg on his guard and get him to hurry up matters. I had a long talk with him. You could see by the way the poor fellow acted that he was badly stuck. He sighed, and promised to pluck up courage to hurry matters to a crisis. Nellie was a good girl, and I think had a sort of quiet respect for old Fagg's unobtrusiveness. But her fancy was already taken captive by Rattler's superficial qualities, which were obvious and pleasing. I don't think Nellie was any worse than you or I. We are more apt to take acquaintances at their apparent value than their intrinsic worth. It's less trouble, and, except when we want to trust them, quite as convenient. The difficulty with women is that their feelings are apt to get interested sooner than ours, and then, you know, reasoning is out of the question. This is what old Fagg would have known had he been of any account. But he wasn't. So much the worse for him.

It was a few months afterward, and I was sitting in my office when in walked old Fagg. I was surprised to see him down, but we talked over the current topics in that mechanical manner of people who know that they have something else to say, but are obliged to get at it in that formal way. After an interval Fagg in his natural manner said,—

'I'm going home!'

'Going home?'

'Yes,—that is, I think I'll take a trip to the Atlantic States. I came to see you, as you know I have some little property, and I have executed a power of attorney for you to manage my affairs. I have some papers I'd like to leave with you. Will you take charge of them?'

'Yes,' I said. 'But what of Nellie?'

His face fell. He tried to smile, and the combination resulted in one of the most startling and grotesque effects I ever beheld. At length he said,—

'I shall not marry Nellie,—that is,'—he seemed to apologize internally for the positive form of expression,—'I think that I had better not.'

'David Fagg,' I said with sudden severity, 'you're of no account!'

To my astonishment his face brightened. 'Yes,' said he, 'that's it!—I'm of no account! But I always knew it. You see I thought Rattler loved that girl as well as I did, and I knew she liked him better than she did me, and would be happier I dare say with him. But then I knew that old Robins would have preferred me to him, as I was better off,—and the girl would do as he said,—and, you see, I thought I was kinder in the way,—and so I left. But,' he continued, as I was about to interrupt him, 'for fear the old man might object to Rattler, I've lent him enough to set him up in business for himself in Dogtown. A pushing, active, brilliant fellow, you know, like Rattler can get along, and will soon be in his old position again,—and you needn't be hard on him, you know, if he doesn't. Good by.'

I was too much disgusted with his treatment of that Rattler to be at all amiable, but as his business was profitable, I promised to attend to it, and he left. A few weeks passed. The return steamer arrived, and a terrible incident occupied the papers for days afterward. People in all parts of the State conned eagerly the details of an awful shipwreck, and those who had friends aboard went away by themselves, and read the long list of the lost under their breath. I read of the gifted, the gallant, the noble, and loved ones who had perished, and among them I think I was the first to read the name of David Fagg. For the 'man of no account' had 'gone home!'

STORIES

MLISS

I

JUST where the Sierra Nevada begins to subside in gentler undulations, and the rivers grow less rapid and yellow, on the side of a great red mountain, stands 'Smith's Pocket.' Seen from the red road at sunset, in the red light and the red dust, its white houses look like the outcroppings of quartz on the mountain-side. The red stage topped with red-shirted passengers is lost to view half a dozen times in the tortuous descent, turning up unexpectedly in out-of-the-way places, and vanishing altogether within a hundred yards of the town. It is probably owing to this sudden twist in the road that the advent of a stranger at Smith's Pocket is usually attended with a peculiar circumstance. Dismounting from the vehicle at the stage-office, the too confident traveller is apt to walk straight out of town under the impression that it lies in quite another direction. It is related that one of the tunnel-men, two miles from town, met one of these self-reliant passengers with a carpet-bag, umbrella, Harper's Magazine, and other evidences of 'Civilization and Refinement,' plodding along over the road he had just ridden, vainly endeavoring to find the settlement of Smith's Pocket.

An observant traveller might have found some compensation for his disappointment in the weird aspect of that vicinity. There were huge fissures on the hillside, and displacements of the red soil, resembling more the chaos of some primary elemental upheaval than the work of man; while, half-way down, a long flume straddled its narrow body and disproportionate legs over the chasm, like an enormous fossil of some forgotten antediluvian. At every step smaller ditches crossed the road, hiding in their sallow depths unlovely streams that crept away to a clandestine union with the great yellow torrent below, and here and there were the ruins of some cabin with the chimney alone left intact and the hearthstone open to the skies.

The settlement of Smith's Pocket owed its origin to the finding of a 'pocket' on its site by a veritable Smith. Five thousand dollars were taken out of it in one half-hour by Smith. Three thousand dollars were expended by Smith and others in erecting a flume and in tunnelling. And then Smith's Pocket was found to be only a pocket, and subject like other pockets to depletion. Although Smith pierced the bowels of the great red mountain, that five thousand dollars was the first and last return of his labor. The mountain grew reticent of its golden secrets, and the flume steadily ebbed away the remainder of Smith's fortune. Then Smith went into quartz-mining; then into quartz-milling; then into hydraulics and ditching, and then by easy degrees into saloon-keeping. Presently it was whispered that Smith was drinking a great deal; then it was known that Smith was a habitual drunkard, and then people began to think, as they are apt to, that he had never been anything else. But the settlement of Smith's Pocket, like that of most discoveries, was happily not dependent on the fortune of its pioneer, and other parties projected tunnels and found pockets. So Smith's Pocket became a settlement with its two fancy stores, its two hotels, its one express-office, and its two first families. Occasionally its one long straggling street was overawed by the assumption of the latest San Francisco fashions, imported per express, exclusively to the first families; making outraged Nature, in the ragged outline of her furrowed surface, look still more homely, and putting personal insult on that greater portion of the population to whom the Sabbath, with a change of linen, brought merely the necessity of cleanliness, without the luxury of adornment. Then there was a Methodist Church, and hard by a Monte Bank, and a little beyond, on the mountain-side, a graveyard; and then a little school-house.

'The Master,' as he was known to his little flock, sat alone one night in the school-house, with some open copy-books before him, carefully making those bold and full characters which are supposed to combine the extremes of chirographical and moral excellence, and had got as far as 'Riches are deceitful,' and was elaborating the noun with an insincerity of flourish that was quite in the spirit of his text, when he heard a gentle tapping. The woodpeckers had been busy about the roof during the day, and the noise did not disturb his work. But the opening of the door, and the tapping continuing from the inside, caused him to look up. He was slightly startled by the figure of a young girl, dirty and shabbily clad. Still, her great black eyes, her coarse, uncombed, lustreless black hair falling over her sun-burned face, her red arms and feet streaked with the red soil, were all familiar to him. It was Melissa Smith,— Smith's motherless child.

'What can she want here?' thought the master. Everybody knew 'Mliss,' as she was called, throughout the length and height of Red Mountain. Everybody knew her as an incorrigible girl. Her fierce, ungovernable disposition, her mad freaks and lawless character, were in their way as proverbial as the story of her father's weaknesses, and as philosophically accepted by the townsfolk. She wrangled with and fought the school-boys with keener invective and quite as powerful arm. She followed the trails with a woodman's craft, and the master had met her before, miles away, shoeless, stockingless, and bareheaded on the mountain road. The miners' camps along the stream supplied her with subsistence during these voluntary pilgrimages, in freely offered alms. Not but that a larger protection had been previously extended to Mliss. The Rev. Joshua McSnagley, 'stated' preacher, had placed her in the hotel as servant, by way of preliminary refinement, and had introduced her to his scholars at Sunday school. But she threw plates occasionally at the landlord, and quickly retorted to the cheap witticisms of the guests, and created in the Sabbath school a sensation that was so inimical to the orthodox dulness and placidity of that institution, that, with a decent regard for the starched frocks and unblemished morals of the two pink-and-white-faced children of the first families, the reverend gentleman had her ignominiously expelled. Such were the antecedents, and such the character of Mliss, as she stood before the master. It was shown in the ragged dress, the unkempt hair, and bleeding feet, and asked his pity. It flashed from her black, fearless eyes, and commanded his respect.

'I come here to-night,' she said rapidly and boldly, keeping her hard glance on his, 'because I knew you was alone. I wouldn't come here when them gals was here. I hate 'em and they hates me. That's why. You keep school, don't you? I want to be teached!'

If to the shabbiness of her apparel and uncomeliness of her tangled hair and dirty face she had added the humility of tears, the master would have extended to her the usual moiety* of pity, and nothing more. But with the natural, though illogical instincts of his species, her boldness awakened in him something of that respect which all original natures pay unconsciously to one another in any grade. And he gazed at her the more fixedly as she went on still rapidly, her hand on that door-latch and her eyes on his:—

'My name's Mliss,—Mliss Smith! You can bet your life on that. My father's Old Smith,—Old Bummer Smith,—that's what's the matter with him. Mliss Smith,—and I'm coming to school!'

'Well?' said the master.

Accustomed to be thwarted and opposed, often wantonly and cruelly, for no other purpose than to excite the violent impulses of her nature, the master's phlegm evidently took her by surprise. She stopped; she began to twist a lock of her hair between her fingers; and the rigid line of upper lip, drawn over the wicked little teeth, relaxed and quivered slightly. Then her eyes dropped, and something like a blush struggled up to her cheek, and tried to assert itself through the splashes of redder soil, and the sunburn of years. Suddenly she threw herself forward, calling on God to strike her dead, and fell quite weak and helpless, with her face on the master's desk, crying and sobbing as if her heart would break.

The master lifted her gently and waited for the paroxysm to pass. When with face still averted, she was repeating between her sobs the *mea culpa* of childish penitence,—that 'she'd be good, she didn't mean to,' etc., it came to him to ask her why she had left Sabbath school.

Why had she left the Sabbath school?—why? O yes. What did he (McSnagley) want to tell her she was wicked for? What did he tell her that God hated her for? If God hated her, what did she want to go to Sabbath school for? *She* didn't want to be 'beholden' to anybody who hated her.

Had she told McSnagley this?

Yes, she had.

The master laughed. It was a hearty laugh, and echoed so oddly in the little school-house, and seemed so inconsistent and discordant with the sighing of the pines without, that he shortly corrected himself with a sigh. The sigh was quite as sincere in its way, however, and after a moment of serious silence he asked about her father.

Her father? What father? Whose father? What had he ever done for her? Why did the girls hate her? Come now! what made the folks say, 'Old Bummer Smith's Mliss!' when she passed? Yes; O yes. She wished he was dead,—she was dead,—everybody was dead; and her sobs broke forth anew.

The master then, leaning over her, told her as well as he could what you or I might have said after hearing such unnatural theories from childish lips; only bearing in mind perhaps better than you or I the unnatural facts of her ragged dress, her bleeding feet, and the omnipresent shadow of her drunken father. Then, raising her to her feet, he wrapped his shawl around her, and, bidding her come early in the morning, he walked with her down the road. There he bade her 'good night.' The moon shone brightly on the narrow path before them. He stood and watched the bent little figure as it staggered down the road, and waited until it had passed the little graveyard and reached the curve of the hill, where it turned and stood for a moment, a mere atom of suffering outlined against the far-off patient stars. Then he went back to his work. But the lines of the copybook thereafter faded into long parallels of never-ending road, over which childish figures seemed to pass sobbing and crying into the night. Then, the little school-house seeming lonelier than before, he shut the door and went home.

The next morning Mliss came to school. Her face had been washed, and her coarse black hair bore evidence of recent struggles with the comb, in which both had evidently suffered. The old defiant look shone occasionally in her eyes, but her manner was tamer and more subdued. Then began a series of little trials and self-sacrifices, in which master and pupil bore an equal part, and which increased the confidence and sympathy between them. Although obedient under the master's eye, at times during recess, if thwarted or stung by a fancied slight, Mliss would rage in ungovernable fury, and many a palpitating young savage, finding himself matched with his own weapons of torment, would seek the master with torn jacket and scratched face, and complaints of the dreadful Mliss. There was a serious division among the townspeople on the subject; some threatening to withdraw their children from such evil companionship, and others as warmly upholding the course of the master in his work of reclamation. Meanwhile, with a steady persistence that seemed quite astonishing to him on looking back afterward, the master drew Mliss gradually out of the shadow of her past life, as though it were but her natural progress down the narrow path on which he had set her feet the moonlit night of their first meeting. Remembering the experience of the evangelical McSnagley, he carefully avoided that Rock of Ages on which that unskilful pilot had shipwrecked her young faith. But if, in the course of her reading, she chanced to stumble upon those few words which have lifted such as she above the level of the older, the wiser, and the more prudent,—if she learned something of a faith that is symbolized by suffering, and the old light softened in her eyes, it did not take the shape of a lesson. A few of the plainer people had made up a little sum by which the ragged Mliss was enabled to assume the garments of respect and civilization; and often a rough shake of the hand, and words of homely commendation from a red-shirted and burly figure, sent a glow to the cheek of the young master, and set him to thinking if it was altogether deserved.

Three months had passed from the time of their first meeting, and the master was sitting late one evening over the moral and sententious copies, when there came a tap at the door, and again Mliss stood before him. She was neatly clad and clean-faced, and there was nothing perhaps but the long black hair and bright black eyes to remind him of his former apparition. 'Are you busy?' she asked. 'Can you come with me?'—and on his signifying his readiness, in her old wilful way she said, 'Come, then, quick!'

They passed out of the door together and into the dark road. As they entered the town the master asked her whither she was going. She replied, 'To see my father.'

It was the first time he had heard her call him by that filial title, or indeed anything more than 'Old Smith' or the 'Old Man.' It was the first time in three months that she had spoken of him at all, and the master knew she had kept resolutely aloof from him since her great change. Satisfied from her manner that it was fruitless to question her purpose, he passively followed. In out-of-the-way places, low groggeries, restaurants, and saloons; in gambling-hells and dance-houses, the master, preceded by Mliss, came and went. In the reeking smoke and blasphemous outcries of low dens, the child, holding the master's hand, stood and anxiously gazed, seemingly unconscious of all in the one absorbing nature of her pursuit. Some of the revellers, recognizing Mliss, called to the child to sing and dance for them, and would have forced liquor upon her but for the interference of the master. Others, recognizing him mutely, made way for them to pass. So an hour slipped by. Then the child whispered in his ear that there was a cabin on the other side of the creek crossed by the long flume, where she thought he still might be. Thither they crossed,—a toilsome half-hour's walk,—but in vain. They were returning by the ditch at the abutment of the flume, gazing at the lights of the town on the opposite bank, when, suddenly, sharply, a quick report rang out on the clear night air. The echoes caught it, and carried it round and round Red Mountain, and set the dogs to barking all along the streams. Lights seemed to dance and move quickly on the outskirts of the town for a few moments, the stream rippled quite audibly beside them, a few stones loosened themselves from the hillside and splashed into the stream, a heavy wind seemed to surge the branches of the funereal pines, and then the silence seemed to fall thicker, heavier, and deadlier. The master turned towards Mliss with an unconscious gesture of protection, but the child had gone. Oppressed by a strange fear, he ran quickly down the trail to the river's bed, and, jumping from boulder to boulder, reached the base of Red Mountain and the outskirts of the village. Midway of the crossing he looked up and held his breath in awe. For high above him on the narrow flume he saw the fluttering little figure of his late companion crossing swiftly in the darkness.

He climbed the bank, and, guided by a few lights moving about a central point on the mountain, soon found himself breathless among a crowd of awe-stricken and sorrowful men. Out from among them the child appeared, and, taking the master's hand, led him silently before what seemed a ragged hole in the mountain. Her face was quite white, but her excited manner gone, and her look that of one to whom some long-expected event had at last happened,—an expression that to the master in his bewilderment seemed almost like relief. The walls of the cavern were partly propped by decaying timbers. The child pointed to what appeared to be some ragged, cast-off clothes left in the hole by the late occupant. The master approached nearer with his flaming dip, and bent over them. It was Smith, already cold, with a pistol in his hand and a bullet in his heart, lying beside his empty pocket.

II

The opinion which McSnagley expressed in reference to a 'change of heart' supposed to be experienced by Mliss was more forcibly described in the gulches and tunnels. It was thought there that Mliss had 'struck a good lead.' So when there was a new grave added to the little enclosure, and at the expense of the master a little board and inscription put above it, the Red Mountain Banner came out quite handsomely, and did the fair thing to the memory of one of 'our oldest Pioneers,' alluding gracefully to that 'bane of noble intellects,' and otherwise genteelly shelving our dear brother with the past. 'He leaves an only child to mourn his loss,' says the Banner, 'who is now an exemplary scholar, thanks to the efforts of the Rev. Mr McSnagley.' The Rev. McSnagley, in fact, made a strong point of Mliss's conversion, and, indirectly attributing to the unfortunate child the suicide of her father, made affecting allusions in Sunday school to the beneficial effects of the 'silent tomb,' and in this cheerful contemplation drove most of the children into speechless horror, and caused the pink-and-white scions of the first families to howl dismally and refuse to be comforted.

The long dry summer came. As each fierce day burned itself out in little whiffs of pearl-gray smoke on the mountain summits, and the upspringing breeze scattered its red embers over the landscape, the green wave which in early spring upheaved above Smith's grave grew sere and dry and hard. In those days the master, strolling in the little churchyard of a

Sabbath afternoon, was sometimes surprised to find a few wild-flowers plucked from the damp pine-forests scattered there, and oftener rude wreaths hung upon the little pine cross. Most of these wreaths were formed of a sweet-scented grass, which the children loved to keep in their desks, intertwined with the plumes of the buckeye, the syringa, and the wood-anemone; and here and there the master noticed the dark blue cowl of the monk's-hood,* or deadly aconite. There was something in the odd association of this noxious plant with these memorials which occasioned a painful sensation to the master deeper than his esthetic sense. One day, during a long walk, in crossing a wooded ridge he came upon Mliss in the heart of the forest, perched upon a prostrate pine, on a fantastic throne formed by the hanging plumes of lifeless branches, her lap full of grasses and pine-burrs, and crooning to herself one of the negro melodies of her younger life. Recognizing him at a distance, she made room for him on her elevated throne, and with a grave assumption of hospitality and patronage that would have been ridiculous had it not been so terribly earnest, she fed him with pine-nuts and crab-apples. The master took that opportunity to point out to her the noxious and deadly qualities of the monk's-hood, whose dark blossoms he saw in her lap, and extorted from her a promise not to meddle with it as long as she remained his pupil. This done,—as the master had tested her integrity before,—he rested satisfied, and the strange feeling which had overcome him on seeing them died away.

Of the homes that were offered Mliss when her conversion became known, the master preferred that of Mrs Morpher, a womanly and kind-hearted specimen of Southwestern efflores-cence, known in her maidenhood as the 'Per-rairie Rose.' Being one of those who contend resolutely against their own natures, Mrs Morpher, by a long series of self-sacrifices and struggles, had at last subjugated her naturally careless disposition to principles of 'order,' which she considered, in common with Mr Pope, as 'Heaven's first law.' But she could not entirely govern the orbits of her satellites, however regular her own movements, and even her own 'Jeemes' sometimes collided with her. Again her old nature asserted itself in her children. Lycurgus dipped into the cupboard 'between meals,' and Aristides came home from school without shoes, leaving those important articles on the threshold, for the delight of a barefooted walk down the ditches. Octavia and Cassandra were 'keerless' of their clothes. So with but one exception, however much the 'Prairie Rose' might have trimmed and pruned and trained her own matured luxuriance, the little shoots came up defiantly wild and straggling. That one exception was Clytemnestra Morpher, aged fifteen. She was the realization of her mother's immaculate conception,—neat, orderly, and dull.

It was an amiable weakness of Mrs Morpher to imagine that 'Clytie' was a consolation and model for Mliss. Following this fallacy, Mrs Morpher threw Clytie at the head of Mliss when she was 'bad,' and set her up before the child for adoration in her penitential moments. It was not, therefore, surprising to the master to hear that Clytie was coming to school, obviously as a favor to the master and as an example for Mliss and others. For 'Clytie' was quite a young lady. Inheriting her mother's physical peculiarities, and in obedience to the climatic laws of the Red Mountain region, she was an early bloomer. The youth of Smith's Pocket, to whom this kind of flower was rare, sighed for her in April and languished in May. Enamored swains haunted the school-house at the hour of dismissal. A few were jealous of the master.

Perhaps it was this latter circumstance that opened the master's eyes to another. He could not help noticing that Clytie was romantic; that in school she required a great deal of attention; that her pens were uniformly bad and wanted fixing; that she usually accompanied the request with a certain expectation in her eye that was somewhat disproportionate to the quality of service she verbally required; that she sometimes allowed the curves of a round, plump white arm to rest on his when he was writing her copies; that she always blushed and flung back her blond curls when she did so. I don't remember whether I have stated that the master was a young man,—it's of little consequence, however; he had been severely educated in the school in which Clytie was taking her first lesson, and, on the whole, withstood the flexible curves and factitious glance like the fine young Spartan that he was. Perhaps an insufficient quality of food may have tended to this asceticism. He generally avoided

Clytie; but one evening, when she returned to the school-house after something she had forgotten, and did not find it until the master walked home with her, I hear that he endeavored to make himself particularly agreeable,—partly from the fact, I imagine, that his conduct was adding gall and bitterness to the already overcharged hearts of Clytemnestra's admirers.

The morning after this affecting episode Mliss did not come to school. Noon came, but not Mliss. Questioning Clytie on the subject, it appeared that they had left the school together, but the wilful Mliss had taken another road. The afternoon brought her not. In the evening he called on Mrs Morpher, whose motherly heart was really alarmed. Mr Morpher had spent all day in search of her, without discovering a trace that might lead to her discovery. Aristides was summoned as a probable accomplice, but that equitable infant succeeded in impressing the household with his innocence. Mrs Morpher entertained a vivid impression that the child would yet be found drowned in a ditch, or, what was almost as terrible, muddied and soiled beyond the redemption of soap and water. Sick at heart, the master returned to the school-house. As he lit his lamp and seated himself at his desk, he found a note lying before him addressed to himself, in Mliss's handwriting. It seemed to be written on a leaf torn from some old memorandum-book, and, to prevent sacrilegious trifling, had been sealed with six broken wafers. Opening it almost tenderly, the master read as follows:—

RESPECTED SIR,—When you read this, I am run away. Never to come back. *Never*, NEVER, NEVER. You can give my beeds to Mary Jennings, and my Amerika's Pride [a highly colored lithograph from a tobacco-box] to Sally Flanders. But don't you give anything to Clytie Morpher. Don't you dare to. Do you know what my oppinion is of her, it is this, she is perfekly disgustin. That is all and no more at present from

Yours respectfully,
MELISSA SMITH.

The master sat pondering on this strange epistle till the moon lifted its bright face above the distant hills, and illuminated the trail that led to the school-house, beaten quite hard with the coming and going of little feet. Then, more satisfied in mind, he tore the missive into fragments and scattered them along the road.

At sunrise the next morning he was picking his way through the palm-like fern and thick underbrush of the pine-forest, starting the hare from its form, and awakening a querulous protest from a few dissipated crows, who had evidently been making a night of it, and so came to the wooded ridge where he had once found Mliss. There he found the prostrate pine and tasselled branches, but the throne was vacant. As he drew nearer, what might have been some frightened animal started through the crackling limbs. It ran up the tossed arms of the fallen monarch, and sheltered itself in some friendly foliage. The master, reaching the old seat, found the nest still warm; looking up in the intertwining branches, he met the black eyes of the errant Mliss. They gazed at each other without speaking. She was first to break the silence.

'What do you want?' she asked curtly.

The master had decided on a course of action. 'I want some crab-apples,' he said humbly.

'Sha' n't have 'em! go away. Why don't you get 'em of Clytemnerestera?' (It seemed to be a relief to Mliss to express her contempt in additional syllables to that classical young woman's already long-drawn title.) 'O you wicked thing!'

'I am hungry, Lissy. I have eaten nothing since dinner yesterday. I am famished!' and the young man in a state of remarkable exhaustion leaned against the tree.

Melissa's heart was touched. In the bitter days of her gypsy life she had known the sensation he so artfully simulated. Overcome by his heart-broken tone, but not entirely divested of suspicion, she said,—

'Dig under the tree near the roots, and you'll find lots; but mind you don't tell,' for Mliss had *her* hoards as well as the rats and squirrels.

But the master, of course, was unable to find them; the effects of hunger probably blinding his senses. Mliss grew uneasy. At length she peered at him through the leaves in an elfish way, and questioned,—

'If I come down and give you some, you'll promise you won't touch me?'

The master promised.

'Hope you'll die if you do!'

The master accepted instant dissolution as a forfeit. Mliss slid down the tree. For a few moments nothing transpired but the munching of the pine-nuts. 'Do you feel better?' she asked, with some solicitude. The master confessed to a recuperated feeling, and then, gravely thanking her, proceeded to retrace his steps. As he expected, he had not gone far before she called him. He turned. She was standing there quite white, with tears in her widely opened orbs. The master felt that the right moment had come. Going up to her, he took both her hands, and, looking in her tearful eyes, said, gravely, 'Lissy, do you remember the first evening you came to see me?'

Lissy remembered.

'You asked me if you might come to school, for you wanted to learn something and be better, and I said—'

'Come,' responded the child, promptly.

'What would *you* say if the master now came to you and said that he was lonely without his little scholar, and that he wanted her to come and teach him to be better?'

The child hung her head for a few moments in silence. The master waited patiently. Tempted by the quiet, a hare ran close to the couple, and raising her bright eyes and velvet forepaws, sat and gazed at them. A squirrel ran half-way down the furrowed bark of the fallen tree, and there stopped.

'We are waiting, Lissy,' said the master, in a whisper, and the child smiled. Stirred by a passing breeze, the tree-tops rocked, and a long pencil of light stole through their interlaced boughs full on the doubting face and irresolute little figure. Suddenly she took the master's hand in her quick way. What she said was scarcely audible, but the master, putting the black hair back from her forehead, kissed her; and so, hand in hand, they passed out of the damp aisles and forest odors into the open sunlit road.

III

Somewhat less spiteful in her intercourse with other scholars, Mliss still retained an offensive attitude in regard to Clytemnestra. Perhaps the jealous element was not entirely lulled in her passionate little breast. Perhaps it was only that the round curves and plump outline offered more extended pinching surface. But while such ebullitions were under the master's control, her enmity occasionally took a new and irrepressible form.

The master in his first estimate of the child's character could not conceive that she had ever possessed a doll. But the master, like many other professed readers of character, was safer in *a posteriori* than *a priori* reasoning. Mliss had a doll, but then it was emphatically Mliss's doll,—a smaller copy of herself. Its unhappy existence had been a secret discovered accidentally by Mrs Morpher. It had been the old-time companion of Mliss's wanderings, and bore evident marks of suffering. Its original complexion was long since washed away by the weather and anointed by the slime of ditches. It looked very much as Mliss had in days past. Its one gown of faded stuff was dirty and ragged as hers had been. Mliss had never been known to apply to it any childish term of endearment. She never exhibited it in the presence of other children. It was put severely to bed in a hollow tree near the school-house, and only allowed exercise during Mliss's rambles. Fulfilling a stern duty to her doll, as she would to herself, it knew no luxuries.

Now Mrs Morpher, obeying a commendable impulse, bought another doll and gave it to Mliss. The child received it gravely and curiously. The master on looking at it one day fancied he saw a slight resemblance in its round red cheeks and mild blue eyes to Clytemnestra. It became evident before long that Mliss had also noticed the same resemblance. Accordingly she hammered its waxen head on the rocks when she was alone, and sometimes dragged it with a string round its neck to and from school. At other times, setting it up on her desk, she made a pin-cushion of its patient and inoffensive body. Whether this was done in revenge of what she considered a second figurative obtrusion of Clytie's excellences upon her, or whether she had an intuitive appreciation of the rites of certain other heathens, and, indulging in that 'Fetish' ceremony, imagined that the original of her wax model would pine away and finally die, is a metaphysical question I shall not now consider.

In spite of these moral vagaries, the master could not help noticing in her different tasks the working of a quick, restless, and vigorous perception. She knew neither the hesitancy nor the doubts of childhood. Her answers in class were always slightly dashed with audacity. Of course she was not infallible. But her courage and daring in passing beyond her own depth and that of the floundering little swimmers around her, in their minds outweighed all errors of judgment. Children are not better than grown people in this respect, I fancy; and whenever the little red hand flashed above her desk, there was a wondering silence, and even the master was sometimes oppressed with a doubt of his own experience and judgment.

Nevertheless, certain attributes which at first amused and entertained his fancy began to afflict him with grave doubts. He could not but see that Mliss was revengeful, irreverent, and wilful. That there was but one better quality which pertained to her semi-savage disposition,—the faculty of physical fortitude and self-sacrifice, and another, though not always an attribute of the noble savage,—Truth. Mliss was both fearless and sincere; perhaps in such a character the adjectives were synonymous.

The master had been doing some hard thinking on this subject, and had arrived at that conclusion quite common to all who think sincerely, that he was generally the slave of his own prejudices, when he determined to call on the Rev. McSnagley for advice. This decision was somewhat humiliating to his pride, as he and McSnagley were not friends. But he thought of Mliss, and the evening of their first meeting; and perhaps with a pardonable superstition that it was not chance alone that had guided her wilful feet to the school-house, and perhaps with a complacent consciousness of the rare magnanimity of the act, he choked back his dislike and went to McSnagley.

The reverend gentleman was glad to see him. Moreover, he observed that the master was looking 'peartish,' and hoped he had got over the 'neuralgy' and 'rheumatiz.' He himself had been troubled with a dumb 'ager' since last conference. But he had learned to 'rastle and pray.'

Pausing a moment to enable the master to write his certain method of curing the dumb 'ager' upon the book and volume of his brain, Mr McSnagley proceeded to inquire after Sister Morpher. 'She is an adornment to Chris*tew*anity, and has a likely growin' young family,' added Mr McSnagley; 'and there's that mannerly young gal,—so well behaved,—Miss Clytie.' In fact, Clytie's perfections seemed to affect him to such an extent that he dwelt for several minutes upon them. The master was doubly embarrassed. In the first place, there was an enforced contrast with poor Mliss in all this praise of Clytie. Secondly, there was something unpleasantly confidential in his tone of speaking of Mrs Morpher's earliest born. So that the master, after a few futile efforts to say something natural, found it convenient to recall another engagement, and left without asking the information required, but in his after reflections somewhat unjustly giving the Rev. Mr McSnagley the full benefit of having refused it.

Perhaps this rebuff placed the master and pupil once more in the close communion of old. The child seemed to notice the change in the master's manner, which had of late been constrained, and in one of their long post-prandial walks she stopped suddenly, and, mounting a stump, looked full in his face with big, searching eyes. 'You ain't mad?' said she, with an interrogative shake of the black braids. 'No.' 'Nor bothered?' 'No.' 'Nor hungry?' (Hunger was to Mliss a sickness that might attack a person at any moment.) 'No.' 'Nor thinking of her?' 'Of whom, Lissy?' 'That white girl.' (This was the latest epithet invented by Mliss, who was a very dark brunette, to express Clytemnestra.) 'No.' 'Upon your word?' (A substitute for 'Hope you'll die!' proposed by the master.) 'Yes.' 'And sacred honor?' 'Yes.' Then Mliss gave him a fierce little kiss, and, hopping down, fluttered off. For two or three days after that she condescended to appear more like other children, and be, as she expressed it, 'good.'

Two years had passed since the master's advent at Smith's Pocket, and as his salary was not large, and the prospects of Smith's Pocket eventually becoming the capital of the State not entirely definite, he contemplated a change. He had informed the school trustees privately of his intentions, but, educated young men of unblemished moral character being scarce at that time, he consented to continue his school term through the winter to early spring. None else knew of his intention except his one friend, a Dr Duchesne, a young Creole physician known

to the people of Wingdam as 'Duchesny.' He never mentioned
it to Mrs Morpher, Clytie, or any of his scholars. His reticence
was partly the result of a constitutional indisposition to fuss,
partly a desire to be spared the questions and surmises of vulgar
curiosity, and partly that he never really believed he was going
to do anything before it was done.

He did not like to think of Mliss. It was a selfish instinct,
perhaps, which made him try to fancy his feeling for the child
was foolish, romantic, and unpractical. He even tried to imagine
that she would do better under the control of an older and
sterner teacher. Then she was nearly eleven, and in a few years,
by the rules of Red Mountain, would be a woman. He had done
his duty. After Smith's death he addressed letters to Smith's
relatives, and received one answer from a sister of Melissa's
mother. Thanking the master, she stated her intention of
leaving the Atlantic States for California with her husband in a
few months. This was a slight superstructure for the airy castle
which the master pictured for Mliss's home, but it was easy to
fancy that some loving, sympathetic woman, with the claims of
kindred, might better guide her wayward nature. Yet, when the
master had read the letter, Mliss listened to it carelessly,
received it submissively, and afterwards cut figures out of it
with her scissors, supposed to represent Clytemnestra, labelled
'the white girl,' to prevent mistakes, and impaled them upon
the outer walls of the school-house.

When the summer was about spent, and the last harvest had
been gathered in the valleys, the master bethought him of
gathering in a few ripened shoots of the young idea, and of
having his Harvest-Home, or Examination. So the savans and
professionals of Smith's Pocket were gathered to witness that
time-honored custom of placing timid children in a constrained
position, and bullying them as in a witness-box. As usual in
such cases, the most audacious and self-possessed were the
lucky recipients of the honors. The reader will imagine that in
the present instance Mliss and Clytie were pre-eminent, and
divided public attention; Mliss with her clearness of material
perception and self-reliance, Clytie with her placid self-esteem
and saint-like correctness of deportment. The other little ones
were timid and blundering. Mliss's readiness and brilliancy, of

course, captivated the greatest number and provoked the greatest applause. Mliss's antecedents had unconsciously awakened the strongest sympathies of a class whose athletic forms were ranged against the walls, or whose handsome bearded faces looked in at the windows. But Mliss's popularity was overthrown by an unexpected circumstance.

McSnagley had invited himself, and had been going through the pleasing entertainment of frightening the more timid pupils by the vaguest and most ambiguous questions delivered in an impressive funereal tone; and Mliss had soared into Astronomy, and was tracking the course of our spotted ball through space, and keeping time with the music of the spheres, and defining the tethered orbits of the planets, when McSnagley impressively arose. 'Meelissy! ye were speaking of the revolutions of this yere yearth and the move-*ments* of the sun, and I think ye said it had been a doing of it since the creashun, eh?' Mliss nodded a scornful affirmative. 'Well, war that the truth?' said McSnagley, folding his arms. 'Yes,' said Mliss, shutting up her little red lips tightly. The handsome outlines at the windows peered further in the school-room, and a saintly Raphael-face, with blond beard and soft blue eyes, belonging to the biggest scamp in the diggings, turned toward the child and whispered, 'Stick to it, Mliss!' The reverend gentleman heaved a deep sigh, and cast a compassionate glance at the master, then at the children, and then rested his look on Clytie. That young woman softly elevated her round, white arm. Its seductive curves were enhanced by a gorgeous and massive specimen bracelet, the gift of one of her humblest worshippers, worn in honor of the occasion. There was a momentary silence. Clytie's round cheeks were very pink and soft. Clytie's big eyes were very bright and blue. Clytie's low-necked white book-muslin rested softly on Clytie's white, plump shoulders. Clytie looked at the master, and the master nodded. Then Clytie spoke softly:—

'Joshua commanded the sun to stand still, and it obeyed him!' There was a low hum of applause in the school-room, a triumphant expression on McSnagley's face, a grave shadow on the master's, and a comical look of disappointment reflected from the windows. Mliss skimmed rapidly over her Astronomy, and then shut the book with a loud snap. A groan burst from

McSnagley, an expression of astonishment from the school-room, a yell from the windows, as Mliss brought her red fist down on the desk, with the emphatic declaration,—

'It's a d—n lie. I don't believe it!'

IV

The long wet season had drawn near its close. Signs of spring were visible in the swelling buds and rushing torrents. The pine-forests exhaled the fresher spicery. The azaleas were already budding, the Ceanothus* getting ready its lilac livery for spring. On the green upland which climbed Red Mountain at its southern aspect the long spike of the monk's-hood shot up from its broad-leaved stool, and once more shook its dark-blue bells. Again the billow above Smith's grave was soft and green, its crest just tossed with the foam of daisies and buttercups. The little graveyard had gathered a few new dwellers in the past year, and the mounds were placed two by two by the little paling until they reached Smith's grave, and there there was but one. General superstition had shunned it, and the plot beside Smith was vacant.

There had been several placards posted about the town, intimating that, at a certain period, a celebrated dramatic company would perform, for a few days, a series of 'side-splitting' and 'screaming farces'; that, alternating pleasantly with this, there would be some melodrama and a grand divertisement, which would include singing, dancing, etc. These announcements occasioned a great fluttering among the little folk, and were the theme of much excitement and great speculation among the master's scholars. The master had promised Mliss, to whom this sort of thing was sacred and rare, that she should go, and on that momentous evening the master and Mliss 'assisted.'

The performance was the prevalent style of heavy mediocrity; the melodrama was not bad enough to laugh at nor good enough to excite. But the master, turning wearily to the child, was astonished, and felt something like self-accusation in noticing the peculiar effect upon her excitable nature. The red blood flushed in her cheeks at each stroke of her panting little heart.

Her small passionate lips were slightly parted to give vent to her hurried breath. Her widely opened lids threw up and arched her black eyebrows. She did not laugh at the dismal comicalities of the funny man, for Mliss seldom laughed. Nor was she discreetly affected to the delicate extremes of the corner of a white handkerchief, as was the tender-hearted 'Clytie,' who was talking with her 'feller' and ogling the master at the same moment. But when the performance was over, and the green curtain fell on the little stage, Mliss drew a long deep breath, and turned to the master's grave face with a half-apologetic smile and wearied gesture. Then she said, 'Now take me home!' and dropped the lids of her black eyes, as if to dwell once more in fancy on the mimic stage.

On their way to Mrs Morpher's the master thought proper to ridicule the whole performance. Now he shouldn't wonder if Mliss thought that the young lady who acted so beautifully was really in earnest, and in love with the gentleman who wore such fine clothes. Well, if she were in love with him it was a very unfortunate thing! 'Why?' said Mliss, with an upward sweep of the drooping lid. 'Oh! well, he couldn't support his wife at his present salary, and pay so much a week for his fine clothes, and then they wouldn't receive as much wages if they were married as if they were merely lovers,—that is,' added the master, 'if they are not already married to somebody else; but I think the husband of the pretty young countess takes the tickets at the door, or pulls up the curtain, or snuffs the candles, or does something equally refined and elegant. As to the young man with nice clothes, which are really nice now, and must cost at least two and a half or three dollars, not to speak of that mantle of red drugget which I happen to know the price of, for I bought some of it for my room once,—as to this young man, Lissy, he is a pretty good fellow, and if he does drink occasionally, I don't think people ought to take advantage of it and give him black eyes and throw him in the mud. Do you? I am sure he might owe me two dollars and a half a long time, before I would throw it up in his face, as the fellow did the other night at Wingdam.'

Mliss had taken his hand in both of hers and was trying to look in his eyes, which the young man kept as resolutely averted. Mliss had a faint idea of irony, indulging herself sometimes in a species of sardonic humor, which was equally visible in her actions and her speech. But the young man continued in this strain until they had reached Mrs Morpher's, and he had deposited Mliss in her maternal charge. Waiving the invitation of Mrs Morpher to refreshment and rest, and shading his eyes with his hand to keep out the blue-eyed Clytemnestra's siren glances, he excused himself, and went home.

For two or three days after the advent of the dramatic company, Mliss was late at school, and the master's usual Friday afternoon ramble was for once omitted, owing to the absence of his trustworthy guide. As he was putting away his books and preparing to leave the school-house, a small voice piped at his side, 'Please, sir?' The master turned and there stood Aristides Morpher.

'Well, my little man,' said the master, impatiently, 'what is it? quick!'

'Please, sir, me and "Kerg" thinks that Mliss is going to run away agin.'

'What's that, sir?' said the master, with that unjust testiness with which we always receive disagreeable news.

'Why, sir, she don't stay home any more, and "Kerg" and me see her talking with one of those actor fellers, and she's with him now; and please, sir, yesterday she told "Kerg" and me she could make a speech as well as Miss Cellerstina Montmoressy, and she spouted right off by heart,' and the little fellow paused in a collapsed condition.

'What actor?' asked the master.

'Him as wears the shiny hat. And hair. And gold pin. And gold chain,' said the just Aristides, putting periods for commas to eke out his breath.

The master put on his gloves and hat, feeling an unpleasant tightness in his chest and thorax, and walked out in the road. Aristides trotted along by his side, endeavoring to keep pace with his short legs to the master's strides, when the master stopped suddenly, and Aristides bumped up against him. 'Where were they talking?' asked the master, as if continuing the conversation.

'At the Arcade,' said Aristides.

When they reached the main street the master paused. 'Run down home,' said he to the boy. 'If Mliss is there, come to the Arcade and tell me. If she isn't there, stay home; run!' And off trotted the short-legged Aristides.

The Arcade was just across the way,—a long, rambling building containing a bar-room, billiard-room, and restaurant. As the young man crossed the plaza he noticed that two or three of the passers-by turned and looked after him. He looked at his clothes, took out his handkerchief and wiped his face, before he entered the bar-room. It contained the usual number of loungers, who stared at him as he entered. One of them looked at him so fixedly and with such a strange expression that the master stopped and looked again, and then saw it was only his own reflection in a large mirror. This made the master think that perhaps he was a little excited, and so he took up a copy of the Red Mountain Banner from one of the tables, and tried to recover his composure by reading the column of advertisements.

He then walked through the bar-room, through the restaurant, and into the billiard-room. The child was not there. In the latter apartment a person was standing by one of the tables with a broad-brimmed glazed hat on his head. The master recognized him as the agent of the dramatic company; he had taken a dislike to him at their first meeting, from the peculiar fashion of wearing his beard and hair. Satisfied that the object of his search was not there, he turned to the man with a glazed hat. He had noticed the master, but tried that common trick of unconsciousness, in which vulgar natures always fail. Balancing a billiard-cue in his hand, he pretended to play with a ball in the centre of the table. The master stood opposite to him until he raised his eyes; when their glances met, the master walked up to him.

He had intended to avoid a scene or quarrel, but when he began to speak, something kept rising in his throat and retarded his utterance, and his own voice frightened him, it sounded so distant, low, and resonant. 'I understand,' he began, 'that Melissa Smith, an orphan, and one of my scholars, has talked with you about adopting your profession. Is that so?'

The man with the glazed hat leaned over the table, and made an imaginary shot, that sent the ball spinning round the cushions. Then walking round the table he recovered the ball and placed it upon the spot. This duty discharged, getting ready for another shot, he said,—

'S'pose she has?'

The master choked up again, but, squeezing the cushion of the table in his gloved hand, he went on:—

'If you are a gentleman, I have only to tell you that I am her guardian, and responsible for her career. You know as well as I do the kind of life you offer her. As you may learn of any one here, I have already brought her out of an existence worse than death,—out of the streets and the contamination of vice. I am trying to do so again. Let us talk like men. She has neither father, mother, sister, or brother. Are you seeking to give her an equivalent for these?'

The man with the glazed hat examined the point of his cue, and then looked around for somebody to enjoy the joke with him.

'I know that she is a strange, wilful girl,' continued the master, 'but she is better than she was. I believe that I have some influence over her still. I beg and hope, therefore, that you will take no further steps in this matter, but as a man, as a gentleman, leave her to me. I am willing—' But here something rose again in the master's throat, and the sentence remained unfinished.

The man with the glazed hat, mistaking the master's silence, raised his head with a coarse, brutal laugh, and said in a loud voice,—

'Want her yourself, do you? That cock won't fight here, young man!'

The insult was more in the tone than the words, more in the glance than tone, and more in the man's instinctive nature than all these. The best appreciable rhetoric to this kind of animal is a blow. The master felt this, and, with his pent-up, nervous energy finding expression in the one act, he struck the brute full in his grinning face. The blow sent the glazed hat one way and the cue another, and tore the glove and skin from the master's hand from knuckle to joint. It opened up the corners of the fellow's mouth, and spoilt the peculiar shape of his beard for some time to come.

There was a shout, an imprecation, a scuffle, and the trampling of many feet. Then the crowd parted right and left, and two sharp quick reports followed each other in rapid succession. Then they closed again about his opponent, and the master was standing alone. He remembered picking bits of burning wadding from his coat-sleeve with his left hand. Some one was holding his other hand. Looking at it, he saw it was still bleeding from the blow, but his fingers were clenched around the handle of a glittering knife. He could not remember when or how he got it.

The man who was holding his hand was Mr Morpher. He hurried the master to the door, but the master held back, and tried to tell him as well as he could with his parched throat about 'Mliss.' 'It's all right, my boy,' said Mr Morpher. 'She's home!' And they passed out into the street together. As they walked along Mr Morpher said that Mliss had come running into the house a few moments before, and had dragged him out, saying that somebody was trying to kill the master at the Arcade. Wishing to be alone, the master promised Mr Morpher that he would not seek the Agent again that night, and parted from him, taking the road toward the school-house. He was surprised in nearing it to find the door open,—still more surprised to find Mliss sitting there.

The master's nature, as I have hinted before, had, like most sensitive organizations, a selfish basis. The brutal taunt thrown out by his late adversary still rankled in his heart. It was possible, he thought, that such a construction might be put upon his affection for the child, which at best was foolish and Quixotic. Besides, had she not voluntarily abnegated his authority and affection? And what had everybody else said about her? Why should he alone combat the opinion of all, and be at last obliged tacitly to confess the truth of all they had predicted? And he had been a participant in a low bar-room fight with a common boor, and risked his life, to prove what? What had he proved? Nothing? What would the people say? What would his friends say? What would McSnagley say?

In his self-accusation the last person he should have wished to meet was Mliss. He entered the door, and, going up to his desk, told the child, in a few cold words, that he was busy, and wished to be alone. As she rose he took her vacant seat, and, sitting down, buried his head in his hands. When he looked up again she was still standing there. She was looking at his face with an anxious expression.

'Did you kill him?' she asked.

'No!' said the master.

'That's what I gave you the knife for!' said the child, quickly.

'Gave me the knife?' repeated the master, in bewilderment.

'Yes, gave you the knife. I was there under the bar. Saw you hit him. Saw you both fall. He dropped his old knife. I gave it to you. Why didn't you stick him?' said Mliss rapidly, with an expressive twinkle of the black eyes and a gesture of the little red hand.

The master could only look his astonishment.

'Yes,' said Mliss. 'If you'd asked me, I'd told you I was off with the play-actors. Why was I off with the play-actors? Because you wouldn't tell me you was going away. I knew it. I heard you tell the Doctor so. I wasn't a goin' to stay here alone with those Morphers. I'd rather die first.'

With a dramatic gesture which was perfectly consistent with her character, she drew from her bosom a few limp green leaves, and, holding them out at arm's-length, said in her quick vivid way, and in the queer pronunciation of her old life, which she fell into when unduly excited,—

'That's the poison plant you said would kill me. I'll go with the play-actors, or I'll eat this and die here. I don't care which. I won't stay here, where they hate and despise me! Neither would you let me, if you didn't hate and despise me too!'

The passionate little breast heaved, and two big tears peeped over the edge of Mliss's eyelids, but she whisked them away with the corner of her apron as if they had been wasps.

'If you lock me up in jail,' said Mliss, fiercely, 'to keep me from the play-actors, I'll poison myself. Father killed himself,— why shouldn't I? You said a mouthful of that root would kill me, and I always carry it here,' and she struck her breast with her clenched fist.

The master thought of the vacant plot beside Smith's grave, and of the passionate little figure before him. Seizing her hands in his and looking full into her truthful eyes, he said,—

'Lissy, will you go with *me?*'

The child put her arms around his neck, and said joyfully, 'Yes.'

'But now—to-night?'

'To-night.'

And, hand in hand, they passed into the road,—the narrow road that had once brought her weary feet to the master's door, and which it seemed she should not tread again alone. The stars glittered brightly above them. For good or ill the lesson had been learned, and behind them the school of Red Mountain closed upon them forever.

THE RIGHT EYE OF THE COMMANDER

THE year of grace 1797 passed away on the coast of California in a southwesterly gale. The little bay of San Carlos, albeit sheltered by the headlands of the blessed Trinity, was rough and turbulent; its foam clung quivering to the seaward wall of the Mission garden; the air was filled with flying sand and spume, and as the Señor Comandante, Hermenegildo Salvatierra, looked from the deep embrasured window of the Presidio guard-room, he felt the salt breath of the distant sea buffet a color into his smoke-dried cheeks.

The Commander, I have said, was gazing thoughtfully from the window of the guard-room. He may have been reviewing the events of the year now about to pass away. But, like the garrison at the Presidio, there was little to review; the year, like its predecessors, had been uneventful,—the days had slipped by in a delicious monotony of simple duties, unbroken by incident or interruption. The regularly recurring feasts and saints' days, the half-yearly courier from San Diego, the rare transport-ship and rarer foreign vessel, were the mere details of his patriarchal life. If there was no achievement, there was certainly no failure. Abundant harvests and patient industry amply supplied the wants of Presidio and Mission. Isolated from the family of nations, the wars which shook the world concerned them not so much as the last earthquake; the struggle that emancipated their sister colonies on the other side of the continent to them had no suggestiveness. In short, it was that glorious Indian summer of California history, around which so much poetical haze still lingers,—that bland, indolent autumn of Spanish rule, so soon to be followed by the wintry storms of Mexican independence and the reviving spring of American conquest.

The Commander turned from the window and walked toward the fire that burned brightly on the deep oven-like hearth. A pile of copy-books, the work of the Presidio school, lay on the table. As he turned over the leaves with a paternal interest, and surveyed the fair round Scripture text,—the first pious pot-hooks of the pupils of San Carlos,—an audible commentary fell from his lips: ' "Abimelech took her from Abraham"—ah, little one, excellent!—"Jacob sent to see his brother"—body of Christ! that up-stroke of thine, Paquita, is marvellous; the Governor shall see it!' A film of honest pride dimmed the Commander's left eye,—the right, alas! twenty years before had been sealed by an Indian arrow. He rubbed it softly with the sleeve of his leather jacket, and continued: ' "The Ishmaelites having arrived—" '

He stopped, for there was a step in the courtyard, a foot upon the threshold, and a stranger entered. With the instinct of an old soldier, the Commander, after one glance at the intruder, turned quickly toward the wall, where his trusty Toledo* hung, or should have been hanging. But it was not there, and as he recalled that the last time he had seen that weapon it was being ridden up and down the gallery by Pepito, the infant son of Bautista, the tortilio-maker, he blushed and then contented himself with frowning upon the intruder.

But the stranger's air, though irreverent, was decidedly peaceful. He was unarmed, and wore the ordinary cape of tarpauling and sea-boots of a mariner. Except a villanous smell of codfish, there was little about him that was peculiar.

His name, as he informed the Commander, in Spanish that was more fluent than elegant or precise,—his name was Peleg Scudder. He was master of the schooner 'General Court,' of the port of Salem, in Massachusetts, on a trading-voyage to the South Seas, but now driven by stress of weather into the bay of San Carlos. He begged permission to ride out the gale under the headlands of the blessed Trinity, and no more. Water he did not need, having taken in a supply at Bodega. He knew the strict surveillance of the Spanish port regulations in regard to foreign vessels, and would do nothing against the severe discipline and good order of the settlement. There was a slight tinge of sarcasm in his tone as he glanced toward the desolate parade-ground of the Presidio and the open unguarded gate. The fact was that the sentry, Felipe Gomez, had discreetly retired to shelter at the beginning of the storm, and was then sound asleep in the corridor.

The Commander hesitated. The port regulations were severe, but he was accustomed to exercise individual authority, and beyond an old order issued ten years before, regarding the American ship 'Columbia,' there was no precedent to guide him. The storm was severe, and a sentiment of humanity urged him to grant the stranger's request. It is but just to the Commander to say, that his inability to enforce a refusal did not weigh with his decision. He would have denied with equal disregard of consequences that right to a seventy-four gun ship which he now yielded so gracefully to this Yankee trading-schooner. He stipulated only, that there should be no communication between the ship and shore. 'For yourself, Señor Captain,' he continued, 'accept my hospitality. The fort is yours as long as you shall grace it with your distinguished presence'; and with old-fashioned courtesy, he made the semblance of withdrawing from the guard-room.

Master Peleg Scudder smiled as he thought of the half-dismantled fort, the two mouldy brass cannon, cast in Manila a century previous, and the shiftless garrison. A wild thought of accepting the Commander's offer literally, conceived in the reckless spirit of a man who never let slip an offer for trade, for a moment filled his brain, but a timely reflection of the commercial unimportance of the transaction checked him. He only took a capacious quid of tobacco, as the Commander gravely drew a settle before the fire, and in honor of his guest untied the black silk handkerchief that bound his grizzled brows.

What passed between Salvatierra and his guest that night it becomes me not, as a grave chronicler of the salient points of history, to relate. I have said that Master Peleg Scudder was a fluent talker, and under the influence of divers strong waters, furnished by his host, he became still more loquacious. And think of a man with a twenty years' budget of gossip! The Commander learned, for the first time, how Great Britain lost her colonies; of the French Revolution; of the great Napoleon, whose achievements, perhaps, Peleg colored more highly than the Commander's superiors would have liked. And when Peleg turned questioner, the Commander was at his mercy. He gradually made himself master of the gossip of the Mission and Presidio, the 'small-beer' chronicles of that pastoral age, the conversion of the heathen, the Presidio schools, and even asked the Commander how he had lost his eye! It is said that at this point of the conversation Master Peleg produced from about his person divers small trinkets, kick-shaws and new-fangled trifles, and even forced some of them upon his host. It is further alleged that under the malign influence of Peleg and several glasses of *aguardiente*,* the Commander lost somewhat of his decorum, and behaved in a manner unseemly for one in his position, reciting high-flown Spanish poetry, and even piping in a thin, high voice, divers madrigals and heathen canzonets of an amorous complexion; chiefly in regard to a 'little one' who was his, the Commander's, 'soul'! These allegations, perhaps unworthy the notice of a serious chronicler, should be received with great caution, and are introduced here as simple hearsay. That the Commander, however, took a handkerchief and attempted to show his guest the mysteries of the *sembi cuacua*,* capering in an agile but indecorous manner about the apartment, has been denied. Enough for the purposes of this narrative, that at midnight Peleg assisted his host to bed with many protestations of undying friendship, and then, as the gale had abated, took his leave of the Presidio and hurried aboard the 'General Court.' When the day broke the ship was gone.

I know not if Peleg kept his word with his host. It is said that the holy fathers at the Mission that night heard a loud chanting in the plaza, as of the heathens singing psalms through their noses; that for many days after an odor of salt codfish prevailed in the settlement; that a dozen hard nutmegs, which were unfit for spice or seed, were found in the possession of the wife of the baker, and that several bushels of shoe-pegs, which bore a pleasing resemblance to oats, but were quite inadequate to the purposes of provender, were discovered in the stable of the blacksmith. But when the reader reflects upon the sacredness of a Yankee trader's word, the stringent discipline of the Spanish port regulations, and the proverbial indisposition of my countrymen to impose upon the confidence of a simple people, he will at once reject this part of the story.

A roll of drums, ushering in the year 1798, awoke the Commander. The sun was shining brightly, and the storm had ceased. He sat up in bed, and through the force of habit rubbed his left eye. As the remembrance of the previous night came back to him, he jumped from his couch and ran to the window. There was no ship in the bay. A sudden thought seemed to strike him, and he rubbed both of his eyes. Not content with this, he consulted the metallic mirror which hung beside his crucifix. There was no mistake; the Commander had a visible second eye,—a right one,—as good, save for the purposes of vision, as the left.

Whatever might have been the true secret of this transformation, but one opinion prevailed at San Carlos. It was one of those rare miracles vouchsafed a pious Catholic community as an evidence to the heathen, through the intercession of the blessed San Carlos himself. That their beloved Commander, the temporal defender of the Faith, should be the recipient of this miraculous manifestation was most fit and seemly. The Commander himself was reticent; he could not tell a falsehood,—he dared not tell the truth. After all, if the good folk of San Carlos believed that the powers of his right eye were actually restored, was it wise and discreet for him to undeceive them? For the first time in his life the Commander thought of policy,—for the first time he quoted that text which has been the lure of so many well-meaning but easy Christians, of being 'all things to all men.' Infeliz Hermenegildo Salvatierra!

For by degrees an ominous whisper crept through the little settlement. The Right Eye of the Commander, although miraculous, seemed to exercise a baleful effect upon the beholder. No one could look at it without winking. It was cold, hard, relentless and unflinching. More than that, it seemed to be endowed with a dreadful prescience,—a faculty of seeing through and into the inarticulate thoughts of those it looked upon. The soldiers of the garrison obeyed the eye rather than the voice of their commander, and answered his glance rather than his lips in questioning. The servants could not evade the ever-watchful, but cold attention that seemed to pursue them. The children of the Presidio School smirched their copy-books under the awful supervision, and poor Paquita, the prize pupil, failed utterly in that marvellous up-stroke when her patron stood beside her. Gradually distrust, suspicion, self-accusation, and timidity took the place of trust, confidence, and security throughout San Carlos. Whenever the Right Eye of the Commander fell, a shadow fell with it.

Nor was Salvatierra entirely free from the baleful influence of his miraculous acquisition. Unconscious of its effect upon others, he only saw in their actions evidence of certain things that the crafty Peleg had hinted on that eventful New Year's eve. His most trusty retainers stammered, blushed, and faltered before him. Self-accusations, confessions of minor faults and delinquencies, or extravagant excuses and apologies met his mildest inquiries. The very children that he loved—his pet pupil, Paquita—seemed to be conscious of some hidden sin. The result of this constant irritation showed itself more plainly. For the first half-year the Commander's voice and eye were at variance. He was still kind, tender, and thoughtful in speech. Gradually, however, his voice took upon itself the hardness of his glance and its sceptical, impassive quality, and as the year again neared its close it was plain that the Commander had fitted himself to the eye, and not the eye to the Commander.

It may be surmised that these changes did not escape the watchful solicitude of the Fathers. Indeed, the few who were first to ascribe the right eye of Salvatierra to miraculous origin and the special grace of the blessed San Carlos, now talked openly of witchcraft and the agency of Luzbel, the evil one. It would have fared ill with Hermenegildo Salvatierra had he been aught but Commander or amenable to local authority. But the reverend father, Friar Manuel de Cortes, had no power over the political executive, and all attempts at spiritual advice failed signally. He retired baffled and confused from his first interview with the Commander, who seemed now to take a grim satisfaction in the fateful power of his glance. The holy father contradicted himself, exposed the fallacies of his own arguments, and even, it is asserted, committed himself to several undoubted heresies. When the Commander stood up at mass, if the officiating priest caught that sceptical and searching eye, the service was inevitably ruined. Even the power of the Holy Church seemed to be lost, and the last hold upon the affections of the people and the good order of the settlement departed from San Carlos.

As the long dry summer passed, the low hills that surrounded the white walls of the Presidio grew more and more to resemble in hue the leathern jacket of the Commander, and Nature herself seemed to have borrowed his dry, hard glare. The earth was cracked and seamed with drought; a blight had fallen upon the orchards and vineyards, and the rain, long delayed and ardently prayed for, came not. The sky was as tearless as the right eye of the Commander. Murmurs of discontent, insubordination, and plotting among the Indians reached his ears; he only set his teeth the more firmly, tightened the knot of his black silk handkerchief, and looked up his Toledo.

The last day of the year 1798 found the Commander sitting, at the hour of evening prayers, alone in the guard-room. He no longer attended the services of the Holy Church, but crept away at such times to some solitary spot, where he spent the interval in silent meditation. The firelight played upon the low beams and rafters, but left the bowed figure of Salvatierra in darkness. Sitting thus, he felt a small hand touch his arm, and, looking down, saw the figure of Paquita, his little Indian pupil, at his knee. 'Ah, littlest of all,' said the Commander, with something of his old tenderness, lingering over the endearing diminutives of his native speech,—'sweet one, what doest thou here? Art thou not afraid of him whom every one shuns and fears?'

'No,' said the little Indian, readily, 'not in the dark. I hear your voice,—the old voice; I feel your touch,—the old touch; but I see not your eye, Señor Comandante. That only I fear,—and that, O Señor, O my father,' said the child, lifting her little arms towards his,—'that I know is not thine own!'

The Commander shuddered and turned away. Then, recovering himself, he kissed Paquita gravely on the forehead and bade her retire. A few hours later, when silence had fallen upon the Presidio, he sought his own couch and slept peacefully.

At about the middle watch of the night a dusky figure crept through the low embrasure of the Commander's apartment. Other figures were flitting through the parade-ground, which the Commander might have seen had he not slept so quietly. The intruder stepped noiselessly to the couch and listened to the sleeper's deep-drawn inspiration. Something glittered in the firelight as the savage lifted his arm; another moment and the sore perplexities of Hermenegildo Salvatierra would have been over, when suddenly the savage started and fell back in a paroxysm of terror. The Commander slept peacefully, but his right eye, widely opened, fixed and unaltered, glared coldly on the would-be assassin. The man fell to the earth in a fit, and the noise awoke the sleeper.

To rise to his feet, grasp his sword, and deal blows thick and fast upon the mutinous savages who now thronged the room, was the work of a moment. Help opportunely arrived, and the undisciplined Indians were speedily driven beyond the walls, but in the scuffle the Commander received a blow upon his right eye, and, lifting his hand to that mysterious organ, it was gone. Never again was it found, and never again, for bale or bliss, did it adorn the right orbit of the Commander.

With it passed away the spell that had fallen upon San Carlos. The rain returned to invigorate the languid soil, harmony was restored between priest and soldier, the green grass presently waved over the sere hillsides, the children flocked again to the side of their martial preceptor, a *Te Deum** was sung in the Mission Church, and pastoral content once more smiled upon the gentle valleys of San Carlos. And far southward crept the 'General Court' with its master, Peleg Scudder, trafficking in beads and peltries with the Indians, and offering glass eyes, wooden legs, and other Boston notions to the chiefs.

NOTES BY FLOOD AND FIELD

I. IN THE FIELD

IT was near the close of an October day that I began to be disagreeably conscious of the Sacramento Valley. I had been riding since sunrise, and my course through the depressing monotony of the long level landscape affected me more like a dull dyspeptic dream than a business journey, performed under that sincerest of natural phenomena,—a California sky. The recurring stretches of brown and baked fields, the gaping fissures in the dusty trail, the hard outline of the distant hills, and the herds of slowly moving cattle, seemed like features of some glittering stereoscopic picture that never changed. Active exercise might have removed this feeling, but my horse by some subtle instinct had long since given up all ambitious effort, and had lapsed into a dogged trot.

It was autumn, but not the season suggested to the Atlantic reader under that title. The sharply defined boundaries of the wet and dry seasons were prefigured in the clear outlines of the distant hills. In the dry atmosphere the decay of vegetation was too rapid for the slow hectic which overtakes an Eastern landscape, or else Nature was too practical for such thin disguises. She merely turned the Hippocratic face* to the spectator, with the old diagnosis of Death in her sharp, contracted features.

In the contemplation of such a prospect there was little to excite any but a morbid fancy. There were no clouds in the flinty blue heavens, and the setting of the sun was accompanied with as little ostentation as was consistent with the dryly practical atmosphere. Darkness soon followed, with a rising wind, which increased as the shadows deepened on the plain. The fringe of alder by the watercourse began to loom up as I urged my horse forward. A half-hour's active spurring brought me to a *corral*, and a little beyond a house, so low and broad it seemed at first sight to be half buried in the earth.

My second impression was that it had grown out of the soil, like some monstrous vegetable, its dreary proportions were so in keeping with the vast prospect. There were no recesses along its roughly boarded walls for vagrant and unprofitable shadows to lurk in the daily sunshine. No projection for the wind by night to grow musical over, to wail, whistle, or whisper to; only a long wooden shelf containing a chilly-looking tin basin, and a bar of soap. Its uncurtained windows were red with the sinking sun, as though bloodshot and inflamed from a too long unlidded existence. The tracks of cattle led to its front door, firmly closed against the rattling wind.

To avoid being confounded with this familiar element, I walked to the rear of the house, which was connected with a smaller building by a slight platform. A grizzled, hard-faced old man was standing there, and met my salutation with a look of inquiry, and, without speaking, led the way to the principal room. As I entered, four young men, who were reclining by the fire, slightly altered their attitudes of perfect repose, but beyond that betrayed neither curiosity nor interest. A hound started from a dark corner with a growl, but was immediately kicked by the old man into obscurity, and silenced again. I can't tell why, but I instantly received the impression that for a long time the group by the fire had not uttered a word or moved a muscle. Taking a seat, I briefly stated my business.

Was a United States surveyor. Had come on account of the Espíritu Santo Rancho. Wanted to correct the exterior boundaries of township lines, so as to connect with the near exteriors of private grants. There had been some intervention to the old survey by a Mr Tryan who had pre-empted adjacent—'settled land warrants,' interrupted the old man. 'Ah, yes! Land Warrants,—and then this was Mr Tryan?'

I had spoken mechanically, for I was preoccupied in connecting other public lines with private surveys, as I looked in his face. It was certainly a hard face, and reminded me of the singular effect of that mining operation known as 'ground sluicing'; the harder lines of underlying character were exposed, and what were once plastic curves and soft outlines were obliterated by some powerful agency.

There was a dryness in his voice not unlike the prevailing atmosphere of the valley, as he launched into an *ex parte** statement of the contest, with a fluency, which, like the wind without, showed frequent and unrestrained expression. He told me—what I had already learned—that the boundary line of the old Spanish grant was a creek, described in the loose phraseology of the *deseño** as beginning in the *valda* or skirt of the hill, its precise location long the subject of litigation. I listened and answered with little interest, for my mind was still distracted by the wind which swept violently by the house, as well as by his odd face, which was again reflected in the resemblance that the silent group by the fire bore toward him. He was still talking, and the wind was yet blowing, when my confused attention was aroused by a remark addressed to the recumbent figures.

'Now, then, which on ye'll see the stranger up the creek to Altascar's, to-morrow?'

There was a general movement of opposition in the group, but no decided answer.

'Kin you go, Kerg?'

'Who's to look up stock in Strarberry per-ar-ie?'

This seemed to imply a negative, and the old man turned to another hopeful, who was pulling the fur from a mangy bear-skin on which he was lying, with an expression as though it were somebody's hair.

'Well, Tom, wot's to hinder you from goin'?'

'Mam's goin' to Brown's store at sun-up, and I s'pose I've got to pack her and the baby agin.'

I think the expression of scorn this unfortunate youth exhibited for the filial duty into which he had been evidently beguiled, was one of the finest things I had ever seen.

'Wise?'

Wise deigned no verbal reply, but figuratively thrust a worn and patched boot into the discourse. The old man flushed quickly.

'I told ye to get Brown to give you a pair the last time you war down the river.'

'Said he wouldn't without'en order. Said it was like pulling gum-teeth to get the money from you even then.'

There was a grim smile at this local hit at the old man's parsimony, and Wise, who was clearly the privileged wit of the family, sank back in honorable retirement.

'Well, Joe, ef your boots are new, and you aren't pestered with wimmin and children, p'r'aps you'll go,' said Tryan, with a nervous twitching, intended for a smile, about a mouth not remarkably mirthful.

Tom lifted a pair of bushy eyebrows, and said shortly,—

'Got no saddle.'

'Wot's gone of your saddle?'

'Kerg, there,'—indicating his brother with a look such as Cain might have worn at the sacrifice.

'You lie!' returned Kerg, cheerfully.

Tryan sprang to his feet, seizing the chair, flourishing it around his head and gazing furiously in the hard young faces which fearlessly met his own. But it was only for a moment; his arm soon dropped by his side, and a look of hopeless fatality crossed his face. He allowed me to take the chair from his hand, and I was trying to pacify him by the assurance that I required no guide, when the irrepressible Wise again lifted his voice:—

'Theer's George comin'! why don't ye ask him? He'll go and introduce you to Don Fernandy's darter, too, ef you ain't peratickler.'

The laugh which followed this joke, which evidently had some domestic allusion (the general tendency of rural pleasantry), was followed by a light step on the platform, and the young man entered. Seeing a stranger present, he stopped and colored; made a shy salute and colored again, and then, drawing a box from the corner, sat down, his hands clasped lightly together and his very handsome bright blue eyes turned frankly on mine.

Perhaps I was in a condition to receive the romantic impression he made upon me, and I took it upon myself to ask his company as guide, and he cheerfully assented. But some domestic duty called him presently away.

The fire gleamed brightly on the hearth, and, no longer resisting the prevailing influence, I silently watched the spirting flame, listening to the wind which continually shook the tenement. Besides the one chair which had acquired a new importance in my eyes, I presently discovered a crazy table in one corner, with an ink-bottle and pen; the latter in that greasy state of decomposition peculiar to country taverns and farm-houses. A goodly array of rifles and double-barrelled guns stocked the corner; half a dozen saddles and blankets lay near, with a mild flavor of the horse about them. Some deer and bear skins completed the inventory. As I sat there, with the silent group around me, the shadowy gloom within and the dominant wind without, I found it difficult to believe I had ever known a different existence. My profession had often led me to wilder scenes, but rarely among those whose unrestrained habits and easy unconsciousness made me feel so lonely and uncomfort-able. I shrank closer to myself, not without grave doubts—which I think occur naturally to people in like situations—that this was the general rule of humanity, and I was a solitary and somewhat gratuitous exception.

It was a relief when a laconic announcement of supper by a weak-eyed girl caused a general movement in the family. We walked across the dark platform, which led to another low-ceiled room. Its entire length was occupied by a table, at the farther end of which a weak-eyed woman was already taking her repast, as she, at the same time, gave nourishment to a weak-eyed baby. As the formalities of introduction had been dis-pensed with, and as she took no notice of me, I was enabled to slip into a seat without discomposing or interrupting her. Tryan extemporized a grace, and the attention of the family became absorbed in bacon, potatoes, and dried apples.

The meal was a sincere one. Gentle gurglings at the upper end of the table often betrayed the presence of the 'wellspring of pleasure.' The conversation generally referred to the labors of the day, and comparing notes as to the whereabouts of missing stock. Yet the supper was such a vast improvement upon the previous intellectual feast, that when a chance allusion of mine to the business of my visit brought out the elder Tryan, the interest grew quite exciting. I remember he inveighed bitterly against the system of ranch-holding by the 'greasers,' as he was pleased to term the native Californians. As the same ideas have been sometimes advanced under more pretentious circumstances, they may be worthy of record.

'Look at 'em holdin' the finest grazin' land that ever lay outer doors? Whar's the papers for it? Was it grants? Mighty fine grants,—most of 'em made arter the 'Merrikans got possession. More fools the 'Merrikans for lettin' 'em hold 'em. Wat paid for 'em? 'Merrikan blood and money.

'Didn't they oughter have suthin out of their native country? Wot for? Did they ever improve? Got a lot of yaller-skinned diggers, not so sensible as niggers to look arter stock, and they a sittin' home and smokin'. With their gold and silver candle-sticks, and missions, and crucifixens, priests and graven idols, and sich? Them sort things wurent allowed in Mizzoori.'

At the mention of improvements, I involuntarily lifted my eyes, and met the half-laughing, half-embarrassed look of George. The act did not escape detection, and I had at once the satisfaction of seeing that the rest of the family had formed an offensive alliance against us.

'It was agin Nater, and agin God,' added Tryan. 'God never intended gold in the rocks to be made into heathen candlesticks and crucifixens. That's why he sent 'Merrikins here. Nater never intended such a climate for lazy lopers. She never gin six months' sunshine to be slept and smoked away.'

How long he continued, and with what further illustration I could not say, for I took an early opportunity to escape to the sitting-room. I was soon followed by George, who called me to an open door leading to a smaller room, and pointed to a bed.

'You'd better sleep there to-night,' he said; 'you'll be more comfortable, and I'll call you early.'

I thanked him, and would have asked him several questions which were then troubling me, but he shyly slipped to the door and vanished.

A shadow seemed to fall on the room when he had gone. The 'boys' returned, one by one, and shuffled to their old places. A larger log was thrown on the fire, and the huge chimney glowed like a furnace, but it did not seem to melt or subdue a single line of the hard faces that it lit. In half an hour later, the furs which had served as chairs by day undertook the nightly office of mattresses, and each received its owner's full-length figure. Mr Tryan had not returned, and I missed George. I sat there, until, wakeful and nervous, I saw the fire fall and shadows mount the wall. There was no sound but the rushing of the wind and the snoring of the sleepers. At last, feeling the place insupportable, I seized my hat and, opening the door, ran out briskly into the night.

The acceleration of my torpid pulse in the keen fight with the wind, whose violence was almost equal to that of a tornado, and the familiar faces of the bright stars above me, I felt as a blessed relief. I ran not knowing whither, and when I halted, the square outline of the house was lost in the alder-bushes. An uninterrupted plain stretched before me, like a vast sea beaten flat by the force of the gale. As I kept on I noticed a slight elevation toward the horizon, and presently my progress was impeded by the ascent of an Indian mound. It struck me forcibly as resembling an island in the sea. Its height gave me a better view of the expanding plain. But even here I found no rest. The ridiculous interpretation Tryan had given the climate was somehow sung in my ears, and echoed in my throbbing pulse, as, guided by the star, I sought the house again.

But I felt fresher and more natural as I stepped upon the platform. The door of the lower building was open, and the old man was sitting beside the table, thumbing the leaves of a Bible with a look in his face as though he were hunting up prophecies against the 'Greaser.' I turned to enter, but my attention was attracted by a blanketed figure lying beside the house, on the platform. The broad chest heaving with healthy slumber, and the open, honest face were familiar. It was George, who had given up his bed to the stranger among his people. I was about to wake him, but he lay so peaceful and quiet, I felt awed and hushed. And I went to bed with a pleasant impression of his handsome face and tranquil figure soothing me to sleep.

I was awakened the next morning from a sense of lulled repose and grateful silence by the cheery voice of George, who stood beside my bed, ostentatiously twirling a 'riata,'* as if to recall the duties of the day to my sleep-bewildered eyes. I looked around me. The wind had been magically laid, and the sun shone warmly through the windows. A dash of cold water, with an extra chill on from the tin basin, helped to brighten me. It was still early, but the family had already breakfasted and dispersed, and a wagon winding far in the distance showed that the unfortunate Tom had already 'packed' his relatives away. I felt more cheerful,—there are few troubles Youth cannot distance with the start of a good night's rest. After a substantial breakfast, prepared by George, in a few moments we were mounted and dashing down the plain.

We followed the line of alder that defined the creek, now dry and baked with summer's heat, but which in winter, George told me, overflowed its banks. I still retain a vivid impression of that morning's ride, the far-off mountains, like *silhouettes*, against the steel-blue sky, the crisp dry air, and the expanding track before me, animated often by the well-knit figure of George Tryan, musical with jingling spurs, and picturesque with flying 'riata.' He rode a powerful native roan, wild-eyed, untiring in stride and unbroken in nature. Alas! the curves of beauty were concealed by the cumbrous *machillas** of the Spanish saddle, which levels all equine distinctions. The single rein lay loosely on the cruel bit that can gripe, and, if need be, crush the jaw it controls.

Again the illimitable freedom of the valley rises before me, as we again bear down into sunlit space. Can this be 'Chu-Chu,' staid and respectable filly of American pedigree,—'Chu-Chu,' forgetful of plank-roads and cobble-stones, wild with excitement, twinkling her small white feet beneath me? George laughs out of a cloud of dust, 'Give her her head; don't you see she likes it?' and 'Chu-Chu' seems to like it, and, whether bitten by native tarantula into native barbarism or emulous of the roan, 'blood' asserts itself, and in a moment the peaceful servitude of years is beaten out in the music of her clattering hoofs. The creek widens to a deep gully. We dive into it and up on the opposite side, carrying a moving cloud of impalpable powder with us. Cattle are scattered over the plain, grazing quietly, or banded together in vast restless herds. George makes a wide, indefinite sweep with the 'riata,' as if to include them all in his *vaquero's** loop, and says, 'Ours!'

'About how many, George?'

'Don't know.'

'How many?'

'Well, p'r'aps three thousand head,' says George, reflecting. 'We don't know, takes five men to look 'em up and keep run.'

'What are they worth?'

'About thirty dollars a head.'

I make a rapid calculation, and look my astonishment at the laughing George. Perhaps a recollection of the domestic economy of the Tryan household is expressed in that look, for George averts his eye and says, apologetically,—

'I 've tried to get the old man to sell and build, but you know he says it ain't no use to settle down, just yet. We must keep movin'. In fact, he built the shanty for that purpose, lest titles should fall through, and we'd have to get up and move stakes further down.'

Suddenly his quick eye detects some unusual sight in a herd we are passing, and with an exclamation he puts his roan into the centre of the mass. I follow, or rather 'Chu-Chu' darts after the roan, and in a few moments we are in the midst of apparently inextricable horns and hoofs. 'Toro!' shouts George, with vaquero enthusiasm, and the band opens a way for the swinging 'riata.' I can feel their steaming breaths, and their spume is cast on 'Chu-Chu's' quivering flank.

Wild, devilish-looking beasts are they; not such shapes as Jove might have chosen to woo a goddess, nor such as peacefully range the downs of Devon, but lean and hungry Cassius-like bovines,* economically got up to meet the exigencies of a six months' rainless climate, and accustomed to wrestle with the distracting wind and the blinding dust.

'That's not our brand,' says George; 'they're strange stock,' and he points to what my scientific eye recognizes as the astrological sign of Venus deeply seared in the brown flanks of the bull he is chasing. But the herd are closing round us with low mutterings, and George has again recourse to the authoritative 'Toro,' and with swinging 'riata' divides the 'bossy bucklers' on either side. When we are free, and breathing somewhat more easily, I venture to ask George if they ever attack any one.

'Never horsemen,—sometimes footmen. Not through rage, you know, but curiosity. They think a man and his horse are one, and if they meet a chap afoot, they run him down and trample him under hoof, in the pursuit of knowledge. But,' adds George, 'here's the lower bench of the foothills, and here's Altascar's corral, and that white building you see yonder is the *casa*.'*

A whitewashed wall enclosed a court containing another adobe building, baked with the solar beams of many summers. Leaving our horses in the charge of a few peons in the courtyard, who were basking lazily in the sun, we entered a low doorway, where a deep shadow and an agreeable coolness fell upon us, as sudden and grateful as a plunge in cool water, from its contrast with the external glare and heat. In the centre of a low-ceiled apartment sat an old man with a black silk handkerchief tied about his head; the few gray hairs that escaped from its folds relieving his gamboge-colored face. The odor of cigarritos was as incense added to the cathedral gloom of the building.

As Señor Altascar rose with well-bred gravity to receive us, George advanced with such a heightened color, and such a blending of tenderness and respect in his manner, that I was touched to the heart by so much devotion in the careless youth. In fact, my eyes were still dazzled by the effect of the outer sunshine, and at first I did not see the white teeth and black eyes of Pepita, who slipped into the corridor as we entered.

It was no pleasant matter to disclose particulars of business which would deprive the old Señor of the greater part of that land we had just ridden over, and I did it with great embarrassment. But he listened calmly,—not a muscle of his dark face stirring,—and the smoke curling placidly from his lips showed his regular respiration. When I had finished, he offered quietly to accompany us to the line of demarcation. George had meanwhile disappeared, but a suspicious conversation in broken Spanish and English, in the corridor, betrayed his vicinity. When he returned again, a little absent-minded, the old man, by far the coolest and most self-possessed of the party, extinguished his black silk cap beneath that stiff, uncomely *sombrero* which all native Californians affect. A *serapa* thrown over his shoulders hinted that he was waiting. Horses are always ready saddled in Spanish ranchos, and in half an hour from the time of our arrival we were again 'loping' in the staring sunlight.

But not as cheerfully as before. George and myself were weighed down by restraint, and Altascar was gravely quiet. To break the silence, and by way of a consolatory essay, I hinted to him that there might be further intervention or appeal, but the proffered oil and wine were returned with a careless shrug of the shoulders and a sententious '*Que bueno?* *—Your courts are always just.'

The Indian mound of the previous night's discovery was a bearing monument of the new line, and there we halted. We were surprised to find the old man Tryan waiting us. For the first time during our interview the old Spaniard seemed moved, and the blood rose in his yellow cheek. I was anxious to close the scene, and pointed out the corner boundaries as clearly as my recollection served.

'The deputies will be here to-morrow to run the lines from this initial point, and there will be no further trouble, I believe, gentlemen.'

Señor Altascar had dismounted and was gathering a few tufts of dried grass in his hands. George and I exchanged glances. He presently arose from his stooping posture, and, advancing to within a few paces of Joseph Tryan, said, in a voice broken with passion,—

'And I, Fernando Jesus Maria Altascar, put you in possession of my land in the fashion of my country.'

He threw a sod to each of the cardinal points.

'I don't know your courts, your judges, or your *corregidores.** Take the *llano!**—and take this with it. May the drought seize your cattle till their tongues hang down as long as those of your lying lawyers! May it be the curse and torment of your old age, as you and yours have made it of mine!'

We stepped between the principal actors in this scene, which only the passion of Altascar made tragical, but Tryan, with a humility but ill concealing his triumph, interrupted:—

'Let him curse on. He'll find 'em coming home to him sooner than the cattle he has lost through his sloth and pride. The Lord is on the side of the just, as well as agin all slanderers and revilers.'

Altascar but half guessed the meaning of the Missourian, yet sufficiently to drive from his mind all but the extravagant power of his native invective.

'Stealer of the Sacrament! Open not!—open not, I say, your lying, Judas lips to me! Ah! half-breed, with the soul of a cayote!—Car-r-r-ramba!'

With his passion reverberating among the consonants like distant thunder, he laid his hand upon the mane of his horse as though it had been the gray locks of his adversary, swung himself into the saddle and galloped away.

George turned to me:—

'Will you go back with us to-night?'

I thought of the cheerless walls, the silent figures by the fire, and the roaring wind, and hesitated.

'Well then, good by.'

'Good by, George.'

Another wring of the hands, and we parted. I had not ridden far, when I turned and looked back. The wind had risen early that afternoon, and was already sweeping across the plain. A cloud of dust travelled before it, and a picturesque figure occasionally emerging therefrom was my last indistinct impression of George Tryan.

II. IN THE FLOOD

Three months after the survey of the Espíritu Santo Rancho, I was again in the valley of the Sacramento. But a general and terrible visitation had erased the memory of that event as completely as I supposed it had obliterated the boundary monuments I had planted. The great flood of 1861–62 was at its height, when, obeying some indefinite yearning, I took my carpet-bag and embarked for the inundated valley.

There was nothing to be seen from the bright cabin windows of the 'Golden City' but night deepening over the water. The only sound was the pattering rain, and that had grown monotonous for the past two weeks, and did not disturb the national gravity of my countrymen as they silently sat around the cabin stove. Some on errands of relief to friends and relatives wore anxious faces, and conversed soberly on the one absorbing topic. Others, like myself, attracted by curiosity, listened eagerly to newer details. But with that human disposition to seize upon any circumstance that might give chance event the exaggerated importance of instinct, I was half conscious of something more than curiosity as an impelling motive.

The dripping of rain, the low gurgle of water, and a leaden sky greeted us the next morning as we lay beside the half-submerged levee of Sacramento. Here, however, the novelty of boats to convey us to the hotels was an appeal that was irresistible. I resigned myself to a dripping rubber-cased mariner called 'Joe,' and, wrapping myself in a shining cloak of the like material, about as suggestive of warmth as court-plaster might have been, took my seat in the stern-sheets of his boat. It was no slight inward struggle to part from the steamer, that to most of the passengers was the only visible connecting link between us and the dry and habitable earth, but we pulled away and entered the city, stemming a rapid current as we shot the levee.

We glided up the long level of K Street,—once a cheerful, busy thoroughfare, now distressing in its silent desolation. The turbid water which seemed to meet the horizon edge before us flowed at right angles in sluggish rivers through the streets. Nature had revenged herself on the local taste by disarraying the regular rectangles by huddling houses on street corners, where they presented abrupt gables to the current, or by capsizing them in compact ruin. Crafts of all kinds were gliding in and out of low-arched doorways. The water was over the top of the fences surrounding well-kept gardens, in the first stories of hotels and private dwellings, trailing its slime on velvet carpets as well as roughly boarded floors. And a silence quite as suggestive as the visible desolation was in the voiceless streets that no longer echoed to carriage-wheel or footfall. The low ripple of water, the occasional splash of oars, or the warning cry of boatmen were the few signs of life and habitation.

With such scenes before my eyes and such sounds in my ears, as I lie lazily in the boat, is mingled the song of my gondolier who sings to the music of his oars. It is not quite as romantic as his brother of the Lido* might improvise, but my Yankee 'Giuseppe' has the advantage of earnestness and energy, and gives a graphic description of the terrors of the past week and of noble deeds of self-sacrifice and devotion, occasionally pointing out a balcony from which some California Bianca* or Laura had been snatched, half clothed and famished. Giuseppe is otherwise peculiar, and refuses the proffered fare, for—am I not a citizen of San Francisco, which was first to respond to the suffering cry of Sacramento? and is not he, Giuseppe, a member of the Howard Society?* No! Giuseppe is poor, but cannot take my money. Still, if I must spend it, there is the Howard Society, and the women and children without food and clothes at the Agricultural Hall.

I thank the generous gondolier, and we go to the Hall,—a dismal, bleak place, ghastly with the memories of last year's opulence and plenty, and here Giuseppe's fare is swelled by the stranger's mite. But here Giuseppe tells me of the 'Relief Boat' which leaves for the flooded district in the interior, and here, profiting by the lesson he has taught me, I make the resolve to turn my curiosity to the account of others, and am accepted of those who go forth to succor and help the afflicted. Giuseppe takes charge of my carpet-bag, and does not part from me until I stand on the slippery deck of 'Relief Boat No. 3.'

An hour later I am in the pilot-house, looking down upon what was once the channel of a peaceful river. But its banks are only defined by tossing tufts of willow washed by the long swell that breaks over a vast inland sea. Stretches of 'tule' land fertilized by its once regular channel and dotted by flourishing ranchos are now cleanly erased. The cultivated profile of the old landscape had faded. Dotted lines in symmetrical perspective mark orchards that are buried and chilled in the turbid flood. The roofs of a few farm-houses are visible, and here and there the smoke curling from chimneys of half-submerged tenements show an undaunted life within. Cattle and sheep are gathered on Indian mounds waiting the fate of their companions whose carcasses drift by us, or swing in eddies with the wrecks of barns and out-houses. Wagons are stranded everywhere where the tide could carry them. As I wipe the moistened glass, I see nothing but water, pattering on the deck from the lowering clouds, dashing against the window, dripping from the willows, hissing by the wheels, everywhere washing, coiling, sapping, hurrying in rapids, or swelling at last into deeper and vaster lakes, awful in their suggestive quiet and concealment.

As day fades into night the monotony of this strange prospect grows oppressive. I seek the engine-room, and in the company of some of the few half-drowned sufferers we have already picked up from temporary rafts, I forget the general aspect of desolation in their individual misery. Later we meet the San Francisco packet, and transfer a number of our passengers. From them we learn how inward-bound vessels report to having struck the well-defined channel of the Sacramento, fifty miles beyond the bar. There is a voluntary contribution taken among the generous travellers for the use of our afflicted, and we part company with a hearty 'God speed' on either side. But our signal-lights are not far distant before a familiar sound comes back to us,—an indomitable Yankee cheer,—which scatters the gloom.

Our course is altered, and we are steaming over the obliterated banks far in the interior. Once or twice black objects loom up near us,—the wrecks of houses floating by. There is a slight rift in the sky towards the north, and a few bearing stars to guide us over the waste. As we penetrate into shallower water, it is deemed advisable to divide our party into smaller boats, and diverge over the submerged prairie. I borrow a pea-coat of one of the crew, and in that practical disguise am doubtfully permitted to pass into one of the boats. We give way northerly. It is quite dark yet, although the rift of cloud has widened.

It must have been about three o'clock, and we were lying upon our oars in an eddy formed by a clump of cottonwood, and the light of the steamer is a solitary, bright star in the distance, when the silence is broken by the 'bow oar':—

'Light ahead.'

All eyes are turned in that direction. In a few seconds a twinkling light appears, shines steadily, and again disappears as if by the shifting position of some black object apparently drifting close upon us.

'Stern, all; a steamer!'

'Hold hard there! Steamer be d—d!' is the reply of the coxswain. 'It's a house, and a big one too.'

It is a big one, looming in the starlight like a huge fragment of the darkness. The light comes from a single candle, which shines through a window as the great shape swings by. Some recollection is drifting back to me with it, as I listen with beating heart.

'There's some one in it, by Heavens! Give way, boys,—lay her alongside. Handsomely, now! The door's fastened; try the window; no! here's another!'

In another moment we are trampling in the water, which washes the floor to the depth of several inches. It is a large room, at the further end of which an old man is sitting wrapped in a blanket, holding a candle in one hand, and apparently absorbed in the book he holds with the other. I spring toward him with an exclamation:—

'Joseph Tryan!'

He does not move. We gather closer to him, and I lay my hand gently on his shoulder, and say:—

'Look up, old man, look up! Your wife and children, where are they? The boys,—George! Are they here? are they safe?'

He raises his head slowly, and turns his eyes to mine, and we involuntarily recoil before his look. It is a calm and quiet glance, free from fear, anger, or pain; but it somehow sends the blood curdling through our veins. He bowed his head over his book again, taking no further notice of us. The men look at me compassionately, and hold their peace. I make one more effort:—

'Joseph Tryan, don't you know me? the surveyor who surveyed your ranch,—the Espíritu Santo? Look up, old man!'

He shuddered and wrapped himself closer in his blanket. Presently he repeated to himself, 'The surveyor who surveyed your ranch,—Espíritu Santo,' over and over again, as though it were a lesson he was trying to fix in his memory.

I was turning sadly to the boatmen, when he suddenly caught me fearfully by the hand and said,—

'Hush!'

We were silent.

'Listen!' He puts his arm around my neck and whispers in my ear, 'I'm a *moving off!*'

'Moving off?'

'Hush! Don't speak so loud. Moving off. Ah! wot's that? Don't you hear?—there! listen!'

We listen, and hear the water gurgle and click beneath the floor.

'It's them wot he sent!—Old Altascar sent. They've been here all night. I heard 'em first in the creek, when they came to tell the old man to move farther off. They came nearer and nearer. They whispered under the door, and I saw their eyes on the step,—their cruel, hard eyes. Ah, why don't they quit?'

I tell the men to search the room and see if they can find any further traces of the family, while Tryan resumes his old attitude. It is so much like the figure I remember on the breezy night that a superstitious feeling is fast overcoming me. When they have returned, I tell them briefly what I know of him, and the old man murmurs again,—

'Why don't they quit, then? They have the stock,—all gone—gone, gone for the hides and hoofs,' and he groans bitterly.

'There are other boats below us. The shanty cannot have drifted far, and perhaps the family are safe by this time,' says the coxswain, hopefully.

We lift the old man up, for he is quite helpless, and carry him to the boat. He is still grasping the Bible in his right hand, though its strengthening grace is blank to his vacant eye, and he cowers in the stern as we pull slowly to the steamer, while a pale gleam in the sky shows the coming day.

I was weary with excitement, and when we reached the steamer, and I had seen Joseph Tryan comfortably bestowed, I wrapped myself in a blanket near the boiler and presently fell asleep. But even then the figure of the old man often started before me, and a sense of uneasiness about George made a strong undercurrent to my drifting dreams. I was awakened at about eight o'clock in the morning by the engineer, who told me one of the old man's sons had been picked up and was now on board.

'Is it George Tryan?' I ask quickly.

'Don't know; but he's a sweet one, whoever he is,' adds the engineer, with a smile at some luscious remembrance. 'You'll find him for'ard.'

I hurry to the bow of the boat, and find, not George, but the irrepressible Wise, sitting on a coil of rope, a little dirtier and rather more dilapidated than I can remember having seen him.

He is examining, with apparent admiration, some rough, dry clothes that have been put out for his disposal. I cannot help thinking that circumstances have somewhat exalted his usual cheerfulness. He puts me at my ease by at once addressing me:—

'These are high old times, ain't they? I say, what do you reckon's become o' them thar bound'ry moniments you stuck? Ah!'

The pause which succeeds this outburst is the effect of a spasm of admiration at a pair of high boots, which, by great exertion, he has at last pulled on his feet.

'So you've picked up the ole man in the shanty, clean crazy? He must have been soft to have stuck there instead o' leavin' with the old woman. Didn't know me from Adam; took me for George!'

At this affecting instance of paternal forgetfulness, Wise was evidently divided between amusement and chagrin. I took advantage of the contending emotions to ask about George.

'Don't know whar he is! If he'd tended stock instead of running about the prairie, packin' off wimmin and children, he might have saved suthin. He lost every hoof and hide, I'll bet a cookey! Say you,' to a passing boatman, 'when are you goin' to give us some grub? I'm hungry 'nough to skin and eat a hoss. Reckon I'll turn butcher when things is dried up, and save hides, horns, and taller.'

I could not but admire this indomitable energy, which under softer climatic influences might have borne such goodly fruit.

'Have you any idea what you'll do, Wise?' I ask.

'Thar ain't much to do now,' says the practical young man. 'I'll have to lay over a spell, I reckon, till things comes straight. The land ain't worth much now, and won't be, I dessay, for some time. Wonder whar the ole man'll drive stakes next.'

'I meant as to your father and George, Wise.'

'O, the ole man and I'll go on to "Miles's," whar Tom packed the old woman and babies last week. George'll turn up some-whar atween this and Altascar's, ef he ain't thar now.'

I ask how the Altascars have suffered.

'Well, I reckon he ain't lost much in stock. I shouldn't wonder if George helped him drive 'em up the foot-hills. And his "casa" 's built too high. O, thar ain't any water thar, you bet. Ah,' says Wise, with reflective admiration, 'those greasers ain't the darned fools people thinks 'em. I'll bet thar ain't one swamped out in all 'er Californy.' But the appearance of 'grub,' cut this rhapsody short.

'I shall keep on a little farther,' I say, 'and try to find George.'

Wise stared a moment at this eccentricity until a new light dawned upon him.

'I don't think you'll save much. What's the percentage,—workin' on shares, eh!'

I answer that I am only curious, which I feel lessens his opinion of me, and with a sadder feeling than his assurance of George's safety might warrant, I walked away.

From others whom we picked up from time to time we heard of George's self-sacrificing devotion, with the praises of the many he had helped and rescued. But I did not feel disposed to return until I had seen him, and soon prepared myself to take a boat to the lower 'valda'* of the foot-hills, and visit Altascar. I soon perfected my arrangements, bade farewell to Wise, and took a last look at the old man, who was sitting by the furnace-fires quite passive and composed. Then our boat-head swung round, pulled by sturdy and willing hands.

It was again raining, and a disagreeable wind had risen. Our course lay nearly west, and we soon knew by the strong current that we were in the creek of the Espíritu Santo. From time to time the wrecks of barns were seen, and we passed many half-submerged willows hung with farming implements.

We emerge at last into a broad silent sea. It is the 'llano de Espíritu Santo.' As the wind whistles by me, piling the shallower fresh water into mimic waves, I go back, in fancy, to the long ride of October over that boundless plain, and recall the sharp outlines of the distant hills which are now lost in the lowering clouds. The men are rowing silently, and I find my mind, released from its tension, growing benumbed and depressed as then. The water, too, is getting more shallow as we leave the banks of the creek, and with my hand dipped listlessly over the thwarts, I detect the tops of chimisal,* which shows the tide to have somewhat fallen. There is a black mound, bearing to the north of the line of alder, making an adverse current, which, as we sweep to the right to avoid, I recognize. We pull close alongside and I call to the men to stop.

There was a stake driven near its summit with the initials, 'L. E. S. I.' Tied half-way down was a curiously worked 'riata.' It was George's. It had been cut with some sharp instrument, and the loose gravelly soil of the mound was deeply dented with horse's hoofs. The stake was covered with horse-hairs. It was a record, but no clew.

The wind had grown more violent, as we still fought our way forward, resting and rowing by turns, and oftener 'poling' the shallower surface, but the old 'valda,' or bench, is still distant. My recollection of the old survey enables me to guess the relative position of the meanderings of the creek, and an occasional simple professional experiment to determine the distance gives my crew the fullest faith in my ability. Night overtakes us in our impeded progress. Our condition looks more dangerous than it really is, but I urge the men, many of whom are still new in this mode of navigation, to greater exertion by assurance of perfect safety and speedy relief ahead. We go on in this way until about eight o'clock, and ground by the willows. We have a muddy walk for a few hundred yards before we strike a dry trail, and simultaneously the white walls of Altascar's appear like a snow-bank before us. Lights are moving in the courtyard; but otherwise the old tomb-like repose characterizes the building.

One of the peons recognized me as I entered the court, and Altascar met me on the corridor.

I was too weak to do more than beg his hospitality for the men who had dragged wearily with me. He looked at my hand, which still unconsciously held the broken 'riata.' I began, wearily, to tell him about George and my fears, but with a gentler courtesy than was even his wont, he gravely laid his hand on my shoulder.

'*Poco a poco** Señor,—not now. You are tired, you have hunger, you have cold. Necessary it is you should have peace.'

He took us into a small room and poured out some French cognac, which he gave to the men that had accompanied me. They drank and threw themselves before the fire in the larger room. The repose of the building was intensified that night, and I even fancied that the footsteps on the corridor were lighter and softer. The old Spaniard's habitual gravity was deeper; we might have been shut out from the world as well as the whistling storm, behind those ancient walls with their time-worn inheritor.

Before I could repeat my inquiry he retired. In a few minutes two smoking dishes of 'chupa'* with coffee were placed before us, and my men ate ravenously. I drank the coffee, but my excitement and weariness kept down the instincts of hunger.

I was sitting sadly by the fire when he re-entered.

'You have eat?'

I said, 'Yes,' to please him.

'*Bueno*, eat when you can,—food and appetite are not always.'

He said this with that Sancho-like* simplicity with which most of his countrymen utter a proverb, as though it were an experience rather than a legend, and, taking the 'riata' from the floor, held it almost tenderly before him.

'It was made by me, Señor.'

'I kept it as a clew to him, Don Altascar,' I said. 'If I could find him—'

'He is here.'

'Here! and'—but I could not say, 'well!' I understood the gravity of the old man's face, the hushed footfalls, the tomb-like repose of the building in an electric flash of consciousness; I held the clew to the broken riata at last. Altascar took my hand, and we crossed the corridor to a sombre apartment. A few tall candles were burning in sconces before the window.

In an alcove there was a deep bed with its counterpane, pillows, and sheets heavily edged with lace, in all that splendid luxury which the humblest of these strange people lavish upon this single item of their household. I stepped beside it and saw George lying, as I had seen him once before, peacefully at rest. But a greater sacrifice than that he had known was here, and his generous heart was stilled forever.

'He was honest and brave,' said the old man, and turned away.

There was another figure in the room; a heavy shawl drawn over her graceful outline, and her long black hair hiding the hands that buried her downcast face. I did not seem to notice her, and, retiring presently, left the loving and loved together.

When we were again beside the crackling fire, in the shifting shadows of the great chamber, Altascar told me how he had that morning met the horse of George Tryan swimming on the prairie; how that, farther on, he found him lying, quite cold and dead, with no marks or bruises on his person; that he had probably become exhausted in fording the creek, and that he had as probably reached the mound only to die for want of that help he had so freely given to others; that, as a last act, he had freed his horse. These incidents were corroborated by many who collected in the great chamber that evening,—women and children,—most of them succored through the devoted energies of him who lay cold and lifeless above.

He was buried in the Indian mound,—the single spot of strange perennial greenness, which the poor aborigines had raised above the dusty plain. A little slab of sandstone with the initials 'G. T.' is his monument, and one of the bearings of the initial corner of the new survey of the 'Espíritu Santo Rancho.'

BOHEMIAN PAPERS

THE MISSION DOLORES

THE Mission Dolores is destined to be 'The Last Sigh' of the native Californian. When the last 'Greaser' shall indolently give way to the bustling Yankee, I can imagine he will, like the Moorish King,* ascend one of the Mission hills to take his last lingering look at the hilled city. For a long time he will cling tenaciously to Pacific Street. He will delve in the rocky fastnesses of Telegraph Hill until progress shall remove it. He will haunt Vallejo Street, and those back slums which so vividly typify the degradation of a people; but he will eventually make way for improvement. The Mission will be last to drop from his nerveless fingers.

As I stand here this pleasant afternoon, looking up at the old chapel,—its ragged senility contrasting with the smart spring sunshine, its two gouty pillars with the plaster dropping away like tattered bandages, its rayless windows, its crumbling entrances, the leper spots on its whitewashed wall eating through the dark adobe,—I give the poor old mendicant but a few years longer to sit by the highway and ask alms in the names of the blessed saints. Already the vicinity is haunted with the shadow of its dissolution. The shriek of the locomotive discords with the Angelus bell. An Episcopal church, of a green Gothic type, with massive buttresses of Oregon pine, even now mocks its hoary age with imitation and supplants it with a sham. Vain, alas! were those rural accessories, the nurseries and market-gardens, that once gathered about its walls and resisted civic encroachment. They, too, are passing away. Even those queer little adobe buildings with tiled roofs like longitudinal slips of cinnamon, and walled enclosures sacredly guarding a few bullock horns and strips of hide. I look in vain for the half-reclaimed Mexican, whose respectability stopped at his waist, and whose red sash under his vest was the utter undoing of his black broadcloth. I miss, too, those black-haired women, with swaying unstable busts, whose dresses were always unseasonable in texture and pattern; whose wearing of a shawl was a terrible awakening from the poetic dream of the Spanish mantilla. Traces of another nationality are visible. The railroad 'navvy' has builded his shanty near the chapel, and smokes his pipe in the Posada. Gutturals have taken the place of linguals and sibilants; I miss the half-chanted, half-drawled cadences that used to mingle with the cheery 'All aboard' of the stage-driver, in those good old days when the stages ran hourly to the Mission, and a trip thither was an excursion. At the very gates of the temple, in the place of those 'who sell doves for sacrifice,' a vender of mechanical spiders has halted with his unhallowed wares. Even the old Padre—last type of the Missionary, and descendant of the good Junipero*—I cannot find to-day; in his stead a light-haired Celt is reading a lesson from a Vulgate* that is wonderfully replete with double r's. Gentle priest, in thy R-isons,* let the stranger and heretic be remembered.

I open a little gate and enter the Mission Churchyard. There is no change here, though perhaps the graves lie closer together. A willow-tree, growing beside the deep, brown wall, has burst into tufted plumes in the fulness of spring. The tall grass-blades over each mound show a strange quickening of the soil below. It is pleasanter here than on the bleak mountain seaward, where distracting winds continually bring the strife and turmoil of the ocean. The Mission hills lovingly embrace the little cemetery, whose decorative taste is less ostentatious. The foreign flavor is strong; here are never-failing garlands of *immortelles*,* with their sepulchral spicery; here are little cheap medallions of pewter, with the adornment of three black tears, that would look like the three of clubs, but that the simple humility of the inscription counterbalances all sense of the ridiculous. Here are children's graves with guardian angels of great specific gravity; but here, too, are the little one's toys in a glass case beside them. Here is the average quantity of execrable original verses; but one stanza—over a sailor's grave— is striking, for it expresses a hope of salvation through the 'Lord High Admiral Christ'! Over the foreign graves there is a notable lack of scriptural quotation, and an increase, if I may say it, of humanity and tenderness. I cannot help thinking that too many of my countrymen are influenced by a morbid desire to make a practical point of this occasion, and are too apt hastily to crowd a whole life of omission into the culminating act. But when I see the gray *immortelles* crowning a tombstone, I know I shall find the mysteries of the resurrection shown rather in symbols, and only the love taught in His new commandment left for the graphic touch. But 'they manage these things better in France.'

During my purposeless ramble the sun has been steadily climbing the brown wall of the church, and the air seems to grow cold and raw. The bright green dies out of the grass, and the rich bronze comes down from the wall. The willow-tree seems half inclined to doff its plumes, and wears the dejected air of a broken faith and violated trust. The spice of the *immortelles* mixes with the incense that steals through the open window. Within, the barbaric gilt and crimson look cold and cheap in this searching air; by this light the church certainly is old and ugly. I cannot help wondering whether the old Fathers, if they ever revisit the scene of their former labors, in their larger comprehensions, view with regret the impending change, or mourn over the day when the Mission Dolores shall appropriately come to grief.

JOHN CHINAMAN

THE expression of the Chinese face in the aggregate is neither cheerful nor happy. In an acquaintance of half a dozen years, I can only recall one or two exceptions to this rule. There is an abiding consciousness of degradation,—a secret pain or self-humiliation visible in the lines of the mouth and eye. Whether it is only a modification of Turkish gravity, or whether it is the dread Valley of the Shadow of the Drug through which they are continually straying, I cannot say. They seldom smile, and their laughter is of such an extraordinary and sardonic nature— so purely a mechanical spasm, quite independent of any mirthful attribute—that to this day I am doubtful whether I ever saw a Chinaman laugh. A theatrical representation by natives, one might think, would have set my mind at ease on this point; but it did not. Indeed, a new difficulty presented itself,—the impossibility of determining whether the performance was a tragedy or farce. I thought I detected the low comedian in an active youth who turned two somersaults, and knocked everybody down on entering the stage. But, unfortunately, even this classic resemblance to the legitimate farce of our civilization was deceptive. Another brocaded actor, who represented the hero of the play, turned three somersaults, and not only upset my theory and his fellow-actors at the same time, but apparently run a-muck behind the scenes for some time afterward. I looked around at the glinting white teeth to observe the effect of these two palpable hits. They were received with equal acclamation, and apparently equal facial spasms. One or two beheadings which enlivened the play produced the same sardonic effect, and left upon my mind a painful anxiety to know what was the serious business of life in China. It was noticeable, however, that my unrestrained laughter had a discordant effect, and that triangular eyes sometimes turned ominously toward the 'Fanqui devil'; but as I retired discreetly before the play was finished, there were no serious results. I have only given the above as an instance of the impossibility of deciding upon the outward and superficial expression of

Chinese mirth. Of its inner and deeper existence I have some private doubts. An audience that will view with a serious aspect the hero, after a frightful and agonizing death, get up and quietly walk off the stage, cannot be said to have remarkable perceptions of the ludicrous.

I have often been struck with the delicate pliability of the Chinese expression and taste, that might suggest a broader and deeper criticism than is becoming these pages. A Chinaman will adopt the American costume, and wear it with a taste of color and detail that will surpass those 'native, and to the manner born.' To look at a Chinese slipper, one might imagine it impossible to shape the original foot to anything less cumbrous and roomy, yet a neater-fitting boot than that belonging to the Americanized Chinaman is rarely seen on this side of the Continent. When the loose sack or paletot* takes the place of his brocade blouse, it is worn with a refinement and grace that might bring a jealous pang to the exquisite of our more refined civilization. Pantaloons fall easily and naturally over legs that have known unlimited freedom and bagginess, and even garrote collars meet correctly around sun-tanned throats. The new expression seldom overflows in gaudy cravats. I will back my Americanized Chinaman against any neophyte of European birth in the choice of that article. While in our own State, the Greaser resists one by one the garments of the Northern invader, and even wears the livery of his conqueror with a wild and buttonless freedom, the Chinaman, abused and degraded as he is, changes by correctly graded transition to the garments of Christian civilization. There is but one article of European wear that he avoids. These Bohemian eyes have never yet been pained by the spectacle of a tall hat on the head of an intelligent Chinaman.

My acquaintance with John has been made up of weekly interviews, involving the adjustment of the washing accounts, so that I have not been able to study his character from a social view-point or observe him in the privacy of the domestic circle. I have gathered enough to justify me in believing him to be generally honest, faithful, simple, and painstaking. Of his simplicity let me record an instance where a sad and civil young Chinaman brought me certain shirts with most of the buttons missing and others hanging on delusively by a single thread. In a moment of unguarded irony I informed him that unity would at least have been preserved if the buttons were removed altogether. He smiled sadly and went away. I thought I had hurt his feelings, until the next week when he brought me my shirts with a look of intelligence, and the buttons carefully and totally erased. At another time, to guard against his general disposition to carry off anything as soiled clothes that he thought could hold water, I requested him to always wait until he saw me. Coming home late one evening, I found the household in great consternation, over an immovable Celestial who had remained seated on the front door-step during the day, sad and submissive, firm but also patient, and only betraying any animation or token of his mission when he saw me coming. This same Chinaman evinced some evidences of regard for a little girl in the family, who in her turn reposed such faith in his intellectual qualities as to present him with a preternaturally uninteresting Sunday-school book, her own property. This book John made a point of carrying ostentatiously with him in his weekly visits. It appeared usually on the top of the clean clothes, and was sometimes painfully clasped outside of the big bundle of solid linen. Whether John believed he unconsciously imbibed some spiritual life through its pasteboard cover, as the Prince in the Arabian Nights imbibed the medicine through the handle of the mallet, or whether he wished to exhibit a due sense of gratitude, or whether he hadn't any pockets, I have never been able to ascertain. In his turn he would sometimes cut marvellous imitation roses from carrots for his little friend. I am inclined to think that the few roses strewn in John's path were such scentless imitations. The thorns only were real. From the persecutions of the young and old of a certain class, his life was a torment. I don't know what was the exact philosophy that Confucius taught, but it is to be hoped that poor John in his persecution is still able to detect the conscious hate and fear with which inferiority always regards the possibility of even-handed justice, and which is the key-note to the vulgar clamor about servile and degraded races.

FROM A BACK WINDOW

I REMEMBER that long ago, as a sanguine and trustful child, I became possessed of a highly colored lithograph, representing a fair Circassian* sitting by a window. The price I paid for this work of art may have been extravagant, even in youth's fluctuating slate-pencil currency; but the secret joy I felt in its possession knew no pecuniary equivalent. It was not alone that Nature in Circassia lavished alike upon the cheek of beauty and the vegetable kingdom that most expensive of colors,—Lake;* nor was it that the rose which bloomed beside the fair Circassian's window had no visible stem, and was directly grafted upon a marble balcony; but it was because it embodied an idea. That idea was a hinting of my Fate. I felt that somewhere a young and fair Circassian was sitting by a window looking out for me. The idea of resisting such an array of charms and color never occurred to me, and to my honor be it recorded, that during the feverish period of adolescence I never thought of averting my destiny. But as vacation and holiday came and went, and as my picture at first grew blurred, and then faded quite away between the Eastern and Western continents in my atlas, so its charm seemed mysteriously to pass away. When I became convinced that few females, of Circassian or other origin, sat pensively resting their chins on their henna-tinged nails, at their parlor windows, I turned my attention to back windows. Although the fair Circassian has not yet burst upon me with open shutters, some peculiarities not unworthy of note have fallen under my observation. This knowledge has not been gained without sacrifice. I have made myself familiar with back windows and their prospects, in the weak disguise of seeking lodgings, heedless of the suspicious glances of landladies and their evident reluctance to show them. I have caught cold by long exposure to draughts. I have become estranged from friends by unconsciously walking to their back windows during a visit, when the weekly linen hung upon the line, or where Miss Fanny (ostensibly indisposed) actually assisted in the laundry, and Master Bobby, in scant attire, disported himself on the area railings. But I have thought of Galileo, and the invariable experience of all seekers and discoverers of truth has sustained me.

Show me the back windows of a man's dwelling, and I will tell you his character. The rear of a house only is sincere. The attitude of deception kept up at the front windows leaves the back area defenceless. The world enters at the front door, but nature comes out at the back passage. That glossy, well-brushed individual, who lets himself in with a latch-key at the front door at night, is a very different being from the slipshod wretch who growls of mornings for hot water at the door of the kitchen. The same with Madame whose contour of figure grows angular, whose face grows pallid, whose hair comes down, and who looks some ten years older through the sincere medium of a back window. No wonder that intimate friends fail to recognize each other in this *dos à dos** position. You may imagine yourself familiar with the silver door-plate and bow-windows of the mansion where dwells your Saccharissa;* you may even fancy you recognize her graceful figure between the lace curtains of the upper chamber which you fondly imagine to be hers; but you shall dwell for months in the rear of her dwelling and within whispering distance of her bower, and never know it. You shall see her with a handkerchief tied round her head in confidential discussion with the butcher, and know her not. You shall hear her voice in shrill expostulation with her younger brother, and it shall awaken no familiar response.

I am writing at a back window. As I prefer the warmth of my coal-fire to the foggy freshness of the afternoon breeze that rattles the leafless shrubs in the garden below me, I have my window-sash closed; consequently, I miss much of the shrilly altercation that has been going on in the kitchen of No. 7 just opposite. I have heard fragments of an entertaining style of dialogue usually known as 'chaffing,' which has just taken place between Biddy in No. 9 and the butcher who brings the dinner. I have been pitying the chilled aspect of a poor canary, put out to taste the fresh air, from the window of No. 5. I have been watching—and envying, I fear—the real enjoyment of two children raking over an old dust-heap in the alley, containing the waste and *débris* of all the back yards in the neighborhood.

What a wealth of soda-water bottles and old iron they have acquired! But I am waiting for an even more familiar prospect from my back window. I know that later in the afternoon, when the evening paper comes, a thickset, gray-haired man will appear in his shirt-sleeves at the back door of No. 9, and, seating himself on the door-step, begin to read. He lives in a pretentious house, and I hear he is a rich man. But there is such humility in his attitude, and such evidence of gratitude at being allowed to sit outside of his own house and read his paper in his shirt-sleeves, that I can picture his domestic history pretty clearly. Perhaps he is following some old habit of humbler days. Perhaps he has entered into an agreement with his wife not to indulge his disgraceful habit in-doors. He does not look like a man who could be coaxed into a dressing-gown. In front of his own palatial residence, I know him to be a quiet and respectable middle-aged business-man, but it is from my back window that my heart warms toward him in his shirt-sleeved simplicity. So I sit and watch him in the twilight as he reads gravely, and wonder sometimes, when he looks up, squares his chest, and folds his paper thoughtfully over his knee, whether he doesn't fancy he hears the letting down of bars, or the tinkling of bells, as the cows come home and stand lowing for him at the gate.

BOONDER

I NEVER knew how the subject of this memoir came to attach himself so closely to the affections of my family. He was not a prepossessing dog. He was not a dog of even average birth and breeding. His pedigree was involved in the deepest obscurity. He may have had brothers and sisters, but in the whole range of my canine acquaintance (a pretty extensive one), I never detected any of Boonder's peculiarities in any other of his species. His body was long, and his forelegs and hind-legs were very wide apart, as though Nature originally intended to put an extra pair between them, but had unwisely allowed herself to be persuaded out of it. This peculiarity was annoying on cold nights, as it always prolonged the interval of keeping the door open for Boonder's ingress long enough to allow two or three dogs of a reasonable length to enter. Boonder's feet were decided; his toes turned out considerably, and in repose his favorite attitude was the first position of dancing. Add to a pair of bright eyes ears that seemed to belong to some other dog, and a symmetrically pointed nose that fitted all apertures like a pass-key, and you have Boonder as we knew him.

I am inclined to think that his popularity was mainly owing to his quiet impudence. His advent in the family was that of an old member, who had been absent for a short time, but had returned to familiar haunts and associations. In a Pythagorean point of view this might have been the case, but I cannot recall any deceased member of the family who was in life partial to bone-burying (though it might be *post mortem* a consistent amusement), and this was Boonder's great weakness. He was at first discovered coiled up on a rug in an upper chamber, and was the least disconcerted of the entire household. From that moment Boonder became one of its recognized members, and privileges, often denied the most intelligent and valuable of his species, were quietly taken by him and submitted to by us. Thus, if he were found coiled up in a clothes-basket, or any article of clothing assumed locomotion on its own account, we only said, 'O, it's Boonder,' with a feeling of relief that it was nothing worse.

I have spoken of his fondness for bone-burying. It could not be called an economical faculty, for he invariably forgot the locality of his treasure, and covered the garden with purposeless holes; but although the violets and daisies were not improved by Boonder's gardening, no one ever thought of punishing him. He became a synonyme for Fate; a Boonder to be grumbled at, to be accepted philosophically,—but never to be averted. But although he was not an intelligent dog, nor an ornamental dog, he possessed some gentlemanly instincts. When he performed his only feat,—begging upon his hind legs (and looking remarkably like a penguin),—ignorant strangers would offer him crackers or cake, which he didn't like, as a reward of merit. Boonder always made a great show of accepting the proffered dainties, and even made hypocritical contortions as if swallowing, but always deposited the morsel when he was unobserved in the first convenient receptacle,—usually the visitor's overshoes.

In matters that did not involve courtesy, Boonder was sincere in his likes and dislikes. He was instinctively opposed to the railroad. When the track was laid through our street, Boonder maintained a defiant attitude toward every rail as it went down, and resisted the cars shortly after to the fullest extent of his lungs. I have a vivid recollection of seeing him, on the day of the trial trip, come down the street in front of the car, barking himself out of all shape, and thrown back several feet by the recoil of each bark. But Boonder was not the only one who has resisted innovations, or has lived to see the innovation prosper and even crush—But I am anticipating. Boonder had previously resisted the gas, but although he spent one whole day in angry altercation with the workmen,—leaving his bones unburied and bleaching in the sun,—somehow the gas went in. The Spring Valley water was likewise unsuccessfully opposed, and the grading of an adjoining lot was for a long time a personal matter between Boonder and the contractor.

These peculiarities seemed to evince some decided character and embody some idea. A prolonged debate in the family upon this topic resulted in an addition to his name,—we called him

'Boonder the Conservative,' with a faint acknowledgment of his fateful power. But, although Boonder had his own way, his path was not entirely of roses. Thorns sometimes pricked his sensibilities. When certain minor chords were struck on the piano, Boonder was always painfully affected and howled a remonstrance. If he were removed for company's sake to the back yard, at the recurrence of the provocation, he would go his whole length (which was something) to improvise a howl that should reach the performer. But we got accustomed to Boonder, and as we were fond of music the playing went on.

One morning Boonder left the house in good spirits with his regular bone in his mouth, and apparently the usual intention of burying it. The next day he was picked up lifeless on the track,—run over apparently by the first car that went out of the depot.

SELECTED STORIES
AND WRITINGS

BROWN OF CALAVERAS

A SUBDUED tone of conversation, and the absence of cigar-smoke and boot-heels at the windows of the Wingdam stage-coach, made it evident that one of the inside passengers was a woman. A disposition on the part of loungers at the stations to congregate before the window, and some concern in regard to the appearance of coats, hats, and collars, further indicated that she was lovely. All of which Mr Jack Hamlin, on the box-seat, noted with the smile of cynical philosophy. Not that he depreciated the sex, but that he recognized therein a deceitful element, the pursuit of which sometimes drew mankind away from the equally uncertain blandishments of poker,—of which it may be remarked that Mr Hamlin was a professional exponent.

So that, when he placed his narrow boot on the wheel and leaped down, he did not even glance at the window from which a green veil was fluttering, but lounged up and down with that listless and grave indifference of his class, which was, perhaps, the next thing to good-breeding. With his closely buttoned figure and self-contained air he was a marked contrast to the other passengers, with their feverish restlessness, and boisterous emotion; and even Bill Masters, a graduate of Harvard, with his slovenly dress, his overflowing vitality, his intense appreciation of lawlessness and barbarism, and his mouth filled with crackers and cheese, I fear cut but an unromantic figure beside this lonely calculator of chances, with his pale Greek face and Homeric gravity.

The driver called 'All aboard!' and Mr Hamlin returned to the coach. His foot was upon the wheel, and his face raised to the level of the open window, when, at the same moment, what appeared to him to be the finest eyes in the world suddenly met his. He quietly dropped down again, addressed a few words to one of the inside passengers, effected an exchange of seats, and as quietly took his place inside. Mr Hamlin never allowed his philosophy to interfere with decisive and prompt action.

I fear that this irruption of Jack cast some restraint upon the other passengers,—particularly those who were making themselves most agreeable to the lady. One of them leaned forward, and apparently conveyed to her information regarding Mr Hamlin's profession in a single epithet. Whether Mr Hamlin heard it, or whether he recognized in the informant a distinguished jurist, from whom, but a few evenings before, he had won several thousand dollars, I cannot say. His colorless face betrayed no sign; his black eyes, quietly observant, glanced indifferently past the legal gentleman, and rested on the much more pleasing features of his neighbor. An Indian stoicism—said to be an inheritance from his maternal ancestor—stood him in good service, until the rolling wheels rattled upon the river-gravel at Scott's Ferry, and the stage drew up at the International Hotel for dinner. The legal gentleman and a member of Congress leaped out, and stood ready to assist the descending goddess, while Colonel Starbottle, of Siskiyou, took charge of her parasol and shawl. In this multiplicity of attention there was a momentary confusion and delay. Jack Hamlin quietly opened the *opposite* door of the coach, took the lady's hand,—with that decision and positiveness which a hesitating and undecided sex know how to admire,—and in an instant had dexterously and gracefully swung her to the ground, and again lifted her to the platform. An audible chuckle on the box, I fear, came from that other cynic, 'Yuba Bill,' the driver. 'Look keerfully arter that baggage, Kernel,' said the expressman, with affected concern, as he looked after Colonel Starbottle, gloomily bringing up the rear of the triumphant procession to the waiting-room.

Mr Hamlin did not stay for dinner. His horse was already saddled, and awaiting him. He dashed over the ford, up the gravelly hill, and out into the dusty perspective of the Wingdam road, like one leaving an unpleasant fancy behind him. The inmates of dusty cabins by the roadside shaded their eyes with their hands, and looked after him, recognizing the man by his horse, and speculating what 'was up with Comanche Jack.' Yet much of this interest centred in the horse, in a community where the time made by 'French Pete's' mare, in his run from the Sheriff of Calaveras, eclipsed all concern in the ultimate fate of that worthy.

The sweating flanks of his gray at length recalled him to himself. He checked his speed, and, turning into a by-road, sometimes used as a cut-off, trotted leisurely along, the reins hanging listlessly from his fingers. As he rode on, the character of the landscape changed, and became more pastoral. Openings in groves of pine and sycamore disclosed some rude attempts at cultivation,—a flowering vine trailed over the porch of one cabin, and a woman rocked her cradled babe under the roses of another. A little farther on Mr Hamlin came upon some barelegged children, wading in the willowy creek, and so wrought upon them with a badinage peculiar to himself, that they were emboldened to climb up his horse's legs and over his saddle, until he was fain to develop an exaggerated ferocity of demeanor, and to escape, leaving behind some kisses and coin. And then, advancing deeper into the woods, where all signs of habitation failed, he began to sing,—uplifting a tenor so singularly sweet, and shaded by a pathos so subduing and tender, that I wot the robins and linnets stopped to listen. Mr Hamlin's voice was not cultivated; the subject of his song was some sentimental lunacy, borrowed from the negro minstrels; but there thrilled through all some occult quality of tone and expression that was unspeakably touching. Indeed, it was a wonderful sight to see this sentimental blackleg, with a pack of cards in his pocket and a revolver at his back, sending his voice before him through the dim woods with a plaint about his 'Nelly's grave,' in a way that overflowed the eyes of the listener. A sparrow-hawk, fresh from his sixth victim, possibly recognizing in Mr Hamlin a kindred spirit, stared at him in surprise, and was fain to confess the superiority of man. With a superior predatory capacity, *he* couldn't sing.

But Mr Hamlin presently found himself again on the high-road, and at his former pace. Ditches and banks of gravel, denuded hillsides, stumps, and decayed trunks of trees, took the place of woodland and ravine, and indicated his approach to civilization. Then a church-steeple came in sight, and he knew that he had reached home. In a few moments he was clattering down the single narrow street, that lost itself in a chaotic ruin of races, ditches, and tailings at the foot of the hill, and dismounted before the gilded windows of the 'Magnolia' saloon. Passing through the long bar-room, he pushed open a green-baize door, entered a dark passage, opened another door with a pass-key, and found himself in a dimly lighted room, whose furniture, though elegant and costly for the locality, showed signs of abuse. The inlaid centre-table was overlaid with stained disks that were not contemplated in the original design. The embroidered arm-chairs were discolored, and the green velvet lounge, on which Mr Hamlin threw himself, was soiled at the foot with the red soil of Wingdam.

Mr Hamlin did not sing in his cage. He lay still, looking at a highly colored painting above him, representing a young creature of opulent charms. It occurred to him then, for the first time, that he had never seen exactly that kind of a woman, and that, if he should, he would not, probably, fall in love with her. Perhaps he was thinking of another style of beauty. But just then some one knocked at the door. Without rising, he pulled a cord that apparently shot back a bolt, for the door swung open, and a man entered.

The new-comer was broad-shouldered and robust,—a vigor not borne out in the face, which, though handsome, was singularly weak, and disfigured by dissipation. He appeared to be also under the influence of liquor, for he started on seeing Mr Hamlin, and said, 'I thought Kate was here'; stammered, and seemed confused and embarrassed.

Mr Hamlin smiled the smile which he had before worn on the Wingdam coach, and sat up, quite refreshed and ready for business.

'You didn't come up on the stage,' continued the new-comer, 'did you?'

'No,' replied Hamlin; 'I left it at Scott's Ferry. It isn't due for half an hour yet. But how's luck, Brown?'

'D—— bad,' said Brown, his face suddenly assuming an expression of weak despair; 'I'm cleaned out again, Jack,' he continued, in a whining tone, that formed a pitiable contrast to his bulky figure, 'can't you help me with a hundred till to-morrow's clean-up? You see I've got to send money home to the old woman, and—you've won twenty times that amount from me.'

The conclusion was, perhaps, not entirely logical, but Jack overlooked it, and handed the sum to his visitor. 'The old woman business is about played out, Brown,' he added, by way of commentary; 'why don't you say you want to buck agin' faro? You know you ain't married!'

'Fact, sir,' said Brown, with a sudden gravity, as if the mere contact of the gold with the palm of the hand had imparted some dignity to his frame. 'I've got a wife—a d—— good one, too, if I do say it—in the States. It's three year since I've seen her, and a year since I've writ to her. When things is about straight, and we get down to the lead, I'm going to send for her.'

'And Kate?' queried Mr Hamlin, with his previous smile.

Mr Brown, of Calaveras, essayed an archness of glance, to cover his confusion, which his weak face and whiskey-muddled intellect but poorly carried out, and said,—

'D—— it, Jack, a man must have a little liberty, you know. But come, what do you say to a little game? Give us a show to double this hundred.'

Jack Hamlin looked curiously at his fatuous friend. Perhaps he knew that the man was predestined to lose the money, and preferred that it should flow back into his own coffers rather than any other. He nodded his head, and drew his chair toward the table. At the same moment there came a rap upon the door.

'It's Kate,' said Mr Brown.

Mr Hamlin shot back the bolt, and the door opened. But, for the first time in his life, he staggered to his feet, utterly unnerved and abashed, and for the first time in his life the hot blood crimsoned his colorless cheeks to his forehead. For before him stood the lady he had lifted from the Wingdam coach, whom Brown—dropping his cards with a hysterical laugh—greeted as

'My old woman, by thunder!'

They say that Mrs Brown burst into tears, and reproaches of her husband. I saw her, in 1857, at Marysville, and disbelieve the story. And the Wingdam Chronicle, of the next week, under the head of 'Touching Reunion,' said: 'One of those beautiful and touching incidents, peculiar to California life, occurred last week in our city. The wife of one of Wingdam's eminent pioneers, tired of the effete civilization of the East and its inhospitable climate, resolved to join her noble husband upon these golden shores. Without informing him of her intention, she undertook the long journey, and arrived last week. The joy of the husband may be easier imagined than described. The meeting is said to have been indescribably affecting. We trust her example may be followed.'

Whether owing to Mrs Brown's influence, or to some more successful speculations, Mr Brown's financial fortune from that day steadily improved. He bought out his partners in the 'Nip and Tuck' lead, with money which was said to have been won at poker, a week or two after his wife's arrival, but which rumor, adopting Mrs Brown's theory that Brown had forsworn the gaming-table, declared to have been furnished by Mr Jack Hamlin. He built and furnished the 'Wingdam House,' which pretty Mrs Brown's great popularity kept overflowing with guests. He was elected to the Assembly, and gave largess to churches. A street in Wingdam was named in his honor.

Yet it was noted that in proportion as he waxed wealthy and fortunate, he grew pale, thin, and anxious. As his wife's popularity increased, he became fretful and impatient. The most uxorious of husbands, he was absurdly jealous. If he did not interfere with his wife's social liberty, it was because it was maliciously whispered that his first and only attempt was met by an outburst from Mrs Brown that terrified him into silence. Much of this kind of gossip came from those of her own sex whom she had supplanted in the chivalrous attentions of Wingdam, which, like most popular chivalry, was devoted to an admiration of power, whether of masculine force or feminine beauty. It should be remembered, too, in her extenuation, that, since her arrival, she had been the unconscious priestess of a mythological worship, perhaps not more ennobling to her womanhood than that which distinguished an older Greek democracy. I think that Brown was dimly conscious of this. But his only confidant was Jack Hamlin, whose *infelix** reputation naturally precluded any open intimacy with the family, and whose visits were infrequent.

It was midsummer, and a moonlit night; and Mrs Brown, very rosy, large-eyed, and pretty, sat upon the piazza, enjoying the fresh incense of the mountain breeze, and, it is to be feared, another incense which was not so fresh, nor quite as innocent.

Beside her sat Colonel Starbottle and Judge Boompointer, and a later addition to her court, in the shape of a foreign tourist. She was in good spirits.

'What do you see down the road?' inquired the gallant Colonel, who had been conscious, for the last few minutes, that Mrs Brown's attention was diverted.

'Dust,' said Mrs Brown, with a sigh. 'Only Sister Anne's "flock of sheep." '*

The Colonel, whose literary recollections did not extend farther back than last week's paper, took a more practical view. 'It ain't sheep,' he continued; 'it's a horseman. Judge, ain't that Jack Hamlin's gray?'

But the Judge didn't know; and, as Mrs Brown suggested the air was growing too cold for further investigations, they retired to the parlor.

Mr Brown was in the stable, where he generally retired after dinner. Perhaps it was to show his contempt for his wife's companions; perhaps, like other weak natures, he found pleasure in the exercise of absolute power over inferior animals. He had a certain gratification in the training of a chestnut mare, whom he could beat or caress as pleased him, which he couldn't do with Mrs Brown. It was here that he recognized a certain gray horse which had just come in, and, looking a little farther on, found his rider. Brown's greeting was cordial and hearty; Mr Hamlin's somewhat restrained. But at Brown's urgent request, he followed him up the back stairs to a narrow corridor, and thence to a small room looking out upon the stable-yard. It was plainly furnished with a bed, a table, a few chairs, and a rack for guns and whips.

'This yer's my home, Jack,' said Brown, with a sigh, as he threw himself upon the bed, and motioned his companion to a chair. 'Her room's t'other end of the hall. It's more'n six months since we've lived together, or met, except at meals. It's mighty rough papers on the head of the house, ain't it?' he said, with a forced laugh. 'But I'm glad to see you, Jack, d—— glad,' and he reached from the bed, and again shook the unresponsive hand of Jack Hamlin.

'I brought ye up here, for I didn't want to talk in the stable; though, for the matter of that, it's all round town. Don't strike a light. We can talk here in the moonshine. Put up your feet on that winder, and sit here beside me. Thar's whiskey in that jug.'

Mr Hamlin did not avail himself of the information. Brown, of Calaveras, turned his face to the wall, and continued:—

'If I didn't love the woman, Jack, I wouldn't mind. But it's loving her, and seeing her, day arter day, goin' on at this rate, and no one to put down the brake; that's what gits me! But I'm glad to see ye, Jack, d—— glad.'

In the darkness he groped about until he had found and wrung his companion's hand again. He would have detained it, but Jack slipped it into the buttoned breast of his coat, and asked, listlessly, 'How long has this been going on?'

'Ever since she came here; ever since the day she walked into the Magnolia. I was a fool then; Jack, I'm a fool now; but I didn't know how much I loved her till then. And she hasn't been the same woman since.

'But that ain't all, Jack; and it's what I wanted to see you about, and I'm glad you've come. It ain't that she doesn't love me any more; it ain't that she fools with every chap that comes along, for, perhaps, I staked her love and lost it, as I did everything else at the Magnolia; and, perhaps, foolin' is nateral to some women, and thar ain't no great harm done, 'cept to the fools. But, Jack, I think,—I think she loves somebody else. Don't move, Jack; don't move; if your pistol hurts ye, take it off.

'It's been more'n six months now that she's seemed unhappy and lonesome, and kinder nervous and scared like. And sometimes I've ketched her lookin' at me sort of timid and pitying. And she writes to somebody. And for the last week she's been gathering her own things,—trinkets, and furbelows, and jew'lry,—and, Jack, I think she's goin' off. I could stand all but that. To have her steal away like a thief—' He put his face downward to the pillow, and for a few moments there was no sound but the ticking of a clock on the mantel. Mr Hamlin lit a cigar, and moved to the open window. The moon no longer shone into the room, and the bed and its occupant were in shadow. 'What shall I do, Jack?' said the voice from the darkness.

The answer came promptly and clearly from the window-side,—'Spot the man, and kill him on sight.'

'But, Jack?'

'He's took the risk!'

'But will that bring *her* back?'

Jack did not reply, but moved from the window towards the door.

'Don't go yet, Jack; light the candle, and sit by the table. It's a comfort to see ye, if nothin' else.'

Jack hesitated, and then complied. He drew a pack of cards from his pocket and shuffled them, glancing at the bed. But Brown's face was turned to the wall. When Mr Hamlin had shuffled the cards, he cut them, and dealt one card on the opposite side of the table and towards the bed, and another on his side of the table for himself. The first was a deuce; his own card, a king. He then shuffled and cut again. This time 'dummy' had a queen, and himself a four-spot. Jack brightened up for the third deal. It brought his adversary a deuce, and himself a king again. 'Two out of three,' said Jack, audibly.

'What's that, Jack?' said Brown.

'Nothing.'

Then Jack tried his hand with dice; but he always threw sixes, and his imaginary opponent aces. The force of habit is sometimes confusing.

Meanwhile, some magnetic influence in Mr Hamlin's presence, or the anodyne of liquor, or both, brought surcease of sorrow, and Brown slept. Mr Hamlin moved his chair to the window, and looked out on the town of Wingdam, now sleeping peacefully,—its harsh outlines softened and subdued, its glaring colors mellowed and sobered in the moonlight that flowed over all. In the hush he could hear the gurgling of water in the ditches, and the sighing of the pines beyond the hill. Then he looked up at the firmament, and as he did so a star shot across the twinkling field. Presently another, and then another. The phenomenon suggested to Mr Hamlin a fresh augury. If in another fifteen minutes another star should fall—He sat there, watch in hand, for twice that time, but the phenomenon was not repeated.

The clock struck two, and Brown still slept. Mr Hamlin approached the table, and took from his pocket a letter, which he read by the flickering candle-light. It contained only a single line, written in pencil, in a woman's hand,—

'Be at the corral, with the buggy, at three.'

The sleeper moved uneasily, and then awoke. 'Are you there, Jack?'

'Yes.'

'Don't go yet. I dreamed just now, Jack,—dreamed of old times. I thought that Sue and me was being married agin, and that the parson, Jack, was—who do you think?—you!'

The gambler laughed, and seated himself on the bed,—the paper still in his hand.

'It's a good sign, ain't it?' queried Brown.

'I reckon. Say, old man, hadn't you better get up?'

The 'old man,' thus affectionately appealed to, rose, with the assistance of Hamlin's outstretched hand.

'Smoke?'

Brown mechanically took the proffered cigar.

'Light?'

Jack had twisted the letter into a spiral, lit it, and held it for his companion. He continued to hold it until it was consumed, and dropped the fragment—a fiery star—from the open window. He watched it as it fell, and then returned to his friend.

'Old man,' he said, placing his hands upon Brown's shoulders, 'in ten minutes I'll be on the road, and gone like that spark. We won't see each other agin; but, before I go, take a fool's advice: sell out all you've got, take your wife with you, and quit the country. It ain't no place for you, nor her. Tell her she must go; make her go, if she won't. Don't whine because you can't be a saint, and she ain't an angel. Be a man,—and treat her like a woman. Don't be a d—— fool. Good by.'

He tore himself from Brown's grasp, and leaped down the stairs like a deer. At the stable-door he collared the half-sleeping hostler, and backed him against the wall. 'Saddle my horse in two minutes, or I'll—' The ellipsis was frightfully suggestive.

'The missis said you was to have the buggy,' stammered the man.

'D——n the buggy!'

The horse was saddled as fast as the nervous hands of the astounded hostler could manipulate buckle and strap.

'Is anything up, Mr Hamlin?' said the man, who, like all his class, admired the *élan* of his fiery patron, and was really concerned in his welfare.

'Stand aside!'

The man fell back. With an oath, a bound, and clatter, Jack was into the road. In another moment, to the man's half-awakened eyes, he was but a moving cloud of dust in the distance, towards which a star just loosed from its brethren was trailing a stream of fire.

But early that morning the dwellers by the Wingdam turn-pike, miles away, heard a voice, pure as a sky-lark's, singing afield. They who were asleep turned over on their rude couches to dream of youth and love and olden days. Hard-faced men and anxious gold-seekers, already at work, ceased their labors and leaned upon their picks, to listen to a romantic vagabond ambling away against the rosy sunrise.

MRS SKAGGS'S HUSBANDS

I. WEST

THE sun was rising in the foothills. But for an hour the black mass of Sierra eastward of Angel's had been outlined with fire, and the conventional morning had come two hours before with the down coach from Placerville. The dry, cold, dewless California night still lingered in the long cañons and folded skirts of Table Mountain. Even on the mountain road the air was still sharp, and that urgent necessity for something to keep out the chill, which sent the barkeeper sleepily among his bottles and wineglasses at the station, obtained all along the road.

Perhaps it might be said that the first stir of life was in the bar-rooms. A few birds twittered in the sycamores at the roadside, but long before that glasses had clicked and bottles gurgled in the saloon of the Mansion House. This was still lit by a dissipated looking hanging-lamp, which was evidently the worse for having been up all night, and bore a singular resemblance to a faded reveler of Angel's, who even then sputtered and flickered in *his* socket in an armchair below it,—a resemblance so plain that when the first level sunbeam pierced the window-pane, the barkeeper, moved by a sentiment of consistency and compassion, put them both out together.

Then the sun came up haughtily. When it had passed the eastern ridge it began, after its habit, to lord it over Angel's, sending the thermometer up twenty degrees in as many minutes, driving the mules to the sparse shade of corrals and fences, making the red dust incandescent, and renewing its old imperious aggression on the spiked bosses of the convex shield of pines that defended Table Mountain. Thither by nine o'clock all coolness had retreated, and the 'outsides' of the up stage plunged their hot faces in its aromatic shadows as in water.

It was the custom of the driver of the Wingdam coach to whip up his horses and enter Angel's at that remarkable pace which the woodcuts in the hotel bar-room represented to credulous humanity as the usual rate of speed of that conveyance. At such times the habitual expression of disdainful reticence and lazy official severity which he wore on the box became intensified as the loungers gathered about the vehicle, and only the boldest ventured to address him. It was the Hon. Judge Beeswinger, Member of Assembly, who to-day presumed, perhaps rashly, on the strength of his official position.

'Any political news from below, Bill?' he asked, as the latter slowly descended from his lofty perch, without, however, any perceptible coming down of mien or manner.

'Not much,' said Bill, with deliberate gravity. 'The President o' the United States hez n't bin hisself sens you refoosed that seat in the Cabinet. The ginral feelin' in perlitical circles is one o' regret.'

Irony, even of this outrageous quality, was too common in Angel's to excite either a smile or a frown. Bill slowly entered the bar-room during a dry, dead silence, in which only a faint spirit of emulation survived.

'Ye didn't bring up that agint o' Rothschild's this trip?' asked the barkeeper slowly, by way of vague contribution to the prevailing tone of conversation.

'No,' responded Bill, with thoughtful exactitude. 'He said he couldn't look inter that claim o' Johnson's without first consultin' the Bank o' England.'

The Mr Johnson here alluded to being present as the faded reveler the barkeeper had lately put out, and as the alleged claim notoriously possessed no attractions whatever to capitalists, expectation naturally looked to him for some response to this evident challenge. He did so by simply stating that he would 'take sugar' in his, and by walking unsteadily towards the bar, as if accepting a festive invitation. To the credit of Bill be it recorded that he did not attempt to correct the mistake, but gravely touched glasses with him, and after saying 'Here's another nail in your coffin,'—a cheerful sentiment, to which 'And the hair all off your head' was playfully added by the others,—he threw off his liquor with a single dexterous movement of head and elbow, and stood refreshed.

'Hello, old major!' said Bill, suddenly setting down his glass. 'Are *you* there?'

It was a boy, who, becoming bashfully conscious that this epithet was addressed to him, retreated sideways to the doorway, where he stood beating his hat against the doorpost with an assumption of indifference that his downcast but mirthful dark eyes and reddening cheek scarcely bore out. Perhaps it was owing to his size, perhaps it was to a certain cherubic outline of face and figure, perhaps to a peculiar trustfulness of expression, that he did not look half his age, which was really fourteen.

Everybody in Angel's knew the boy. Either under the venerable title bestowed by Bill, or as 'Tom Islington,' after his adopted father, his was a familiar presence in the settlement, and the theme of much local criticism and comment. His waywardness, indolence, and unaccountable amiability—a quality at once suspicious and gratuitous in a pioneer community like Angel's—had often been the subject of fierce discussion. A large and reputable majority believed him destined for the gallows; a minority not quite so reputable enjoyed his presence without troubling themselves much about his future; to one or two the evil predictions of the majority possessed neither novelty nor terror.

'Anything for me, Bill?' asked the boy half mechanically, with the air of repeating some jocular formulary perfectly understood by Bill.

'Anythin' for you!' echoed Bill, with an overacted severity equally well understood by Tommy,—'anythin' for you? No! And it's my opinion there won't be anythin' for you ez long ez you hang around bar-rooms and spend your valooable time with loafers and bummers. Git!'

The reproof was accompanied by a suitable exaggeration of gesture (Bill had seized a decanter), before which the boy retreated still good-humoredly. Bill followed him to the door. 'Dern my skin, if he hezn't gone off with that bummer Johnson,' he added, as he looked down the road.

'What's he expectin', Bill?' asked the barkeeper.

'A letter from his aunt. Reckon he'll hev to take it out in expectin'. Likely they're glad to get shut o' him.'

'He's leadin' a shiftless, idle life here,' interposed the Member of Assembly.

'Well,' said Bill, who never allowed any one but himself to abuse his protégé, 'seein' he ain't expectin' no offis from the hands of an enlightened constitooency, it *is* rayther a shiftless life.' After delivering this Parthian arrow with a gratuitous twanging of the bow to indicate its offensive personality, Bill winked at the barkeeper, slowly resumed a pair of immense, bulgy buckskin gloves, which gave his fingers the appearance of being painfully sore and bandaged, strode to the door without looking at anybody, called out, 'All aboard,' with a perfunctory air of supreme indifference whether the invitation was heeded, remounted his box, and drove stolidly away.

Perhaps it was well that he did so, for the conversation at once assumed a disrespectful attitude toward Tom and his relatives. It was more than intimated that Tom's alleged aunt was none other than Tom's real mother, while it was also asserted that Tom's alleged uncle did not himself participate in this intimate relationship to the boy to an extent which the fastidious taste of Angel's deemed moral and necessary. Popular opinion also believed that Islington, the adopted father, who received a certain stipend ostensibly for the boy's support, retained it as a reward for his reticence regarding these facts. 'He ain't ruinin' hisself by wastin' it on Tom,' said the barkeeper, who possibly possessed positive knowledge of much of Islington's disbursements. But at this point exhausted nature languished among some of the debaters, and he turned from the frivolity of conversation to his severer professional duties.

It was also well that Bill's momentary attitude of didactic propriety was not further excited by the subsequent conduct of his protégé. For by this time Tom, half supporting the unstable Johnson, who developed a tendency to occasionally dash across the glaring road, but checked himself midway each time, reached the corral which adjoined the Mansion House. At its farther extremity was a pump and horse-trough. Here, without a word being spoken, but evidently in obedience to some habitual custom, Tom led his companion. With the boy's assistance, Johnson removed his coat and neckcloth, turned back the collar of his shirt, and gravely placed his head beneath the pump-spout. With equal gravity and deliberation, Tom took his place at the handle. For a few moments only the splashing of water and regular strokes of the pump broke the solemnly ludicrous silence. Then there was a pause in which Johnson put his hands to his dripping head, felt it critically as if it belonged to somebody else, and raised his eyes to his companion. 'That ought to fetch *it*,' said Tom, in answer to the look. 'Ef it don't,' replied Johnson doggedly, with an air of relieving himself of all further responsibility in the matter, 'it's got to, thet's all!'

If 'it' referred to some change in the physiognomy of Johnson, 'it' had probably been 'fetched' by the process just indicated. The head that went under the pump was large, and clothed with bushy, uncertain-colored hair; the face was flushed, puffy, and expressionless, the eyes injected and full. The head that came out from under the pump was of smaller size and different shape, the hair straight, dark, and sleek, the face pale and hollow-cheeked, the eyes bright and restless. In the haggard, nervous ascetic that rose from the horse-trough there was very little trace of the Bacchus* that had bowed there a moment before. Familiar as Tom must have been with the spectacle, he could not help looking inquiringly at the trough, as if expecting to see some traces of the previous Johnson in its shallow depths.

A narrow strip of willow, alder, and buckeye—a mere dusty, raveled fringe of the green mantle that swept the high shoulders of Table Mountain—lapped the edge of the corral. The silent pair were quick to avail themselves of even its scant shelter from the overpowering sun. They had not proceeded far, before Johnson, who was walking quite rapidly in advance, suddenly brought himself up, and turned to his companion with an interrogative 'Eh?'

'I didn't speak,' said Tommy quietly.

'Who said you spoke?' said Johnson, with a quick look of cunning. 'In course you didn't speak, and I didn't speak neither. Nobody spoke. Wot makes you think you spoke?' he continued, peering curiously into Tommy's eyes.

The smile which habitually shone there quickly vanished as the boy stepped quietly to his companion's side, and took his arm without a word.

'In course you didn't speak, Tommy,' said Johnson deprecatingly. 'You ain't a boy to go for to play an ole soaker like me.

That's wot I like you for. Thet's wot I seed in you from the first. I sez, "Thet 'ere boy ain't going to play you, Johnson! You can go your whole pile on him, when you can't trust even a barkeep'." Thet's wot I said. Eh?'

This time Tommy prudently took no notice of the interrogation, and Johnson went on: 'Ef I was to ask you another question, you wouldn't go to play me neither—would you, Tommy?'

'No,' said the boy.

'Ef I was to ask you,' continued Johnson, without heeding the reply, but with a growing anxiety of eye and a nervous twitching of his lips,—'ef I was to ask you, fur instance, ef that was a jackass rabbit that jest passed,—eh?—you'd say it was or was not, ez the case may be. You wouldn't play the ole man on thet?'

'No,' said Tommy quietly, 'it *was* a jackass rabbit.'

'Ef I was to ask you,' continued Johnson, 'ef it wore, say, fur instance, a green hat with yaller ribbons, you wouldn't play me, and say it did, onless'—he added, with intensified cunning—'onless it *did?*'

'No,' said Tommy, 'of course I wouldn't; but then, you see, *it did.*'

'It did?'

'It did!' repeated Tommy stoutly; 'a green hat with yellow ribbons—and—and—a red rosette.'

'I didn't get to see the ros-ette,' said Johnson, with slow and conscientious deliberation, yet with an evident sense of relief; 'but that ain't sayin' it wa'n't there, you know. Eh?'

Tommy glanced quietly at his companion. There were great beads of perspiration on his ashen-gray forehead, and on the ends of his lank hair; the hand which twitched spasmodically in his was cold and clammy, the other, which was free, had a vague, purposeless, jerky activity, as if attached to some deranged mechanism. Without any apparent concern in these phenomena, Tommy halted, and, seating himself on a log, motioned his companion to a place beside him. Johnson obeyed without a word. Slight as was the act, perhaps no other incident of their singular companionship indicated as completely the dominance of this careless, half-effeminate, but self-possessed boy over this doggedly self-willed, abnormally excited man.

'It ain't the square thing,' said Johnson, after a pause, with a laugh that was neither mirthful nor musical, and frightened away a lizard that had been regarding the pair with breathless suspense,—'it ain't the square thing for jackass rabbits to wear hats, Tommy,—is it, eh?'

'Well,' said Tommy, with unmoved composure, 'sometimes they do and sometimes they don't. Animals are mighty queer.' And here Tommy went off in an animated, but, I regret to say, utterly untruthful and untrustworthy account of the habits of California fauna, until he was interrupted by Johnson.

'And snakes, eh, Tommy?' said the man, with an abstracted air, gazing intently on the ground before him.

'And snakes,' said Tommy, 'but they don't bite,—at least not that kind you see. There!—don't move, Uncle Ben, don't move; they're gone now. And it's about time you took your dose.'

Johnson had hurriedly risen as if to leap upon the log, but Tommy had as quickly caught his arm with one hand while he drew a bottle from his pocket with the other. Johnson paused and eyed the bottle. 'Ef you say so, my boy,' he faltered, as his fingers closed nervously around it; 'say "when," then.' He raised the bottle to his lips and took a long draught, the boy regarding him critically. 'When,' said Tommy suddenly. Johnson started, flushed, and returned the bottle quickly. But the color that had risen to his cheek stayed there, his eye grew less restless, and as they moved away again the hand that rested on Tommy's shoulder was steadier.

Their way lay along the flank of Table Mountain,—a wandering trail through a tangled solitude that might have seemed virgin and unbroken but for a few oyster-cans, yeast-powder tins, and empty bottles that had been apparently stranded by the 'first low wash' of pioneer waves. On the ragged trunk of an enormous pine hung a few tufts of gray hair caught from a passing grizzly, but in strange juxtaposition at its foot lay an empty bottle of incomparable bitters,—the *chef d'œuvre** of a hygienic civilization, and blazoned with the arms of an all-healing republic. The head of a rattlesnake peered from a case that had contained tobacco, which was still brightly placarded with the high-colored effigy of a popular danseuse. And a little beyond this the soil was broken and fissured, there was a confused mass of roughly hewn timber, a straggling line of sluicing, a heap of gravel and dirt, a rude cabin, and the claim of Johnson.

Except for the rudest purposes of shelter from rain and cold, the cabin possessed but little advantage over the simple savagery of surrounding nature. It had all the practical directness of the habitation of some animal, without its comfort or picturesque quality; the very birds that haunted it for food must have felt their own superiority as architects. It was inconceivably dirty, even with its scant capacity for accretion; it was singularly stale, even in its newness and freshness of material. Unspeakably dreary as it was in shadow, the sunlight visited it in a blind, aching, purposeless way, as if despairing of mellowing its outlines or of even tanning it into color.

The claim worked by Johnson in his intervals of sobriety was represented by half a dozen rude openings in the mountainside, with the heaped-up débris of rock and gravel before the mouth of each. They gave very little evidence of engineering skill or constructive purpose, or indeed showed anything but the vague, successively abandoned essays of their projector. To-day they served another purpose, for as the sun had heated the little cabin almost to the point of combustion, curling up the long dry shingles, and starting aromatic tears from the green pine beams, Tommy led Johnson into one of the larger openings, and with a sense of satisfaction threw himself panting upon its rocky floor. Here and there the grateful dampness was condensed in quiet pools of water, or in a monotonous and soothing drip from the rocks above. Without lay the staring sunlight—colorless, clarified, intense.

For a few moments they lay resting on their elbows in blissful contemplation of the heat they had escaped. 'Wot do you say,' said Johnson slowly, without looking at his companion, but abstractedly addressing himself to the landscape beyond,—'wot do you say to two straight games fur one thousand dollars?'

'Make it five thousand,' replied Tommy reflectively also to the landscape, 'and I'm in.'

'Wot do I owe you now?' said Johnson, after a lengthened silence.

'One hundred and seventy-five thousand two hundred and fifty dollars,' replied Tommy with business-like gravity.

'Well,' said Johnson after a deliberation commensurate with the magnitude of the transaction, 'ef you win, call it a hundred and eighty thousand, round. War's the keerds?'

They were in an old tin box in a crevice of a rock above his head. They were greasy and worn with service. Johnson dealt, albeit his right hand was still uncertain,—hovering, after dropping the cards, aimlessly about Tommy, and being only recalled by a strong nervous effort. Yet, notwithstanding this incapacity for even honest manipulation, Mr Johnson covertly turned a knave from the bottom of the pack with such shameless inefficiency and gratuitous unskillfulness, that even Tommy was obliged to cough and look elsewhere to hide his embarrassment. Possibly for this reason the young gentleman was himself constrained, by way of correction, to add a valuable card to his own hand, over and above the number he legitimately held.

Nevertheless the game was unexciting and dragged listlessly. Johnson won. He recorded the fact and the amount with a stub of pencil and shaking fingers in wandering hieroglyphics all over a pocket diary. Then there was a long pause, when Johnson slowly drew something from his pocket and held it up before his companion. It was apparently a dull red stone.

'Ef,' said Johnson slowly, with his old look of simple cunning,—'ef you happened to pick up sich a rock ez that, Tommy, what might you say it was?'

'Don't know,' said Tommy.

'Mightn't you say,' continued Johnson cautiously, 'that it was gold or silver?'

'Neither,' said Tommy promptly.

'Mightn't you say it was quicksilver? Mightn't you say that ef thar was a friend o' yourn ez knew war to go and turn out ten ton of it a day, and every ton worth two thousand dollars, that he had a soft thing, a very soft thing,—allowin', Tommy, that you used sich language, which you don't?'

'But,' said the boy, coming to the point with great directness, '*do* you know where to get it? have you struck it, Uncle Ben?'

Johnson looked carefully round. 'I hev, Tommy. Listen. I know whar thar's cartloads of it. But thar's only one other specimen—the mate to this yer—thet's above ground, and thet's in 'Frisco. Thar's an agint comin' up in a day or two to look into it. I sent for him. Eh?'

His bright, restless eyes were concentrated on Tommy's face now, but the boy showed neither surprise not interest. Least of all did he betray any recollection of Bill's ironical and gratuitous corroboration of this part of the story.

'Nobody knows it,' continued Johnson in a nervous whisper,—'nobody knows it but you and the agint in 'Frisco. The boys workin' round yar passes by and sees the old man grubbin' away, and no signs o' color, not even rotten quartz; the boys loafin' round the Mansion House sees the old man lyin' round free in bar-rooms, and they laughs and sez, "Played out," and spects nothin'. Maybe ye think they spects suthin' now, eh?' queried Johnson suddenly, with a sharp look of suspicion.

Tommy looked up, shook his head, threw a stone at a passing rabbit, but did not reply.

'When I fust set eyes on you, Tommy,' continued Johnson, apparently reassured, 'the fust day you kem and pumped for me, an entire stranger, and hevin' no call to do it, I sez, "Johnson, Johnson," sez I, "yer's a boy you kin trust. Yer's a boy that won't play you; yer's a chap that's white and square,'— white and square, Tommy: them's the very words I used.'

He paused for a moment, and then went on in a confidential whisper, ' "You want capital, Johnson," sez I, "to develop your resources, and you want a pardner. Capital you can send for, but your pardner, Johnson,—your pardner is right yer. And his name, it is Tommy Islington." Them's the very words I used.'

He stopped and chafed his clammy hands upon his knees. 'It's six months ago sens I made you my pardner. Thar ain't a lick I've struck sens then, Tommy, thar ain't a han'ful o' yearth I've washed, thar ain't a shovelful o' rock I've turned over, but I tho't o' you. "Share, and share alike," sez I. When I wrote to my agint, I wrote ekal for my pardner, Tommy Islington, he hevin' no call to know ef the same was man or boy.'

He had moved nearer the boy, and would perhaps have laid his hand caressingly upon him, but even in his manifest affection there was a singular element of awed restraint and even fear,—a suggestion of something withheld even his fullest confidences, a hopeless perception of some vague barrier that never could be surmounted. He may have been at times dimly conscious that, in the eyes which Tommy raised to his, there was thorough intellectual appreciation, critical good-humor, even feminine softness, but nothing more. His nervousness somewhat heightened by his embarrassment, he went on with an attempt at calmness which his twitching white lips and unsteady fingers made pathetically grotesque. 'Thar's a bill o' sale in my bunk, made out accordin' to law, of an ekal ondivided half of the claim, and the consideration is two hundred and fifty thousand dollars—gambling debts—gambling debts from me to you, Tommy, you understand?'—nothing could exceed the intense cunning of his eye at this moment—'and then thar's a will.'

'A will?' said Tommy in amused surprise.

Johnson looked frightened.

'Eh?' he said hurriedly, 'wot will? Who said anythin' 'bout a will, Tommy?'

'Nobody,' replied Tommy with unblushing calm.

Johnson passed his hand over his cold forehead, wrung the damp ends of his hair with his fingers, and went on: 'Times when I'm took bad ez I was to-day, the boys about yer sez—you sez, maybe, Tommy—it's whiskey. It ain't, Tommy. It's pizen—quicksilver pizen. That's what's the matter with me. I'm salivated! Salivated with merkery.

'I've heerd o' it before,' continued Johnson, appealing to the boy, 'and ez a boy o' permiskus reading, I reckon you hev too. Them men as works in cinnabar sooner or later gets salivated. It's bound to fetch 'em some time. Salivated by merkery.'

'What are you goin' to do for it?' asked Tommy.

'When the agint comes up, and I begins to realize on this yer mine,' said Johnson contemplatively, 'I goes to New York. I sez to the barkeep' o' the hotel, "Show me the biggest doctor here." He shows me. I sez to him, "Salivated by merkery—a year's standin'—how much?" He sez, "Five thousand dollars, and take two o' these pills at bedtime, and an ekil number o' powders at meals, and come back in a week." And I goes back in a week, cured, and signs a certifikit to that effect.'

Encouraged by a look of interest in Tommy's eye, he went on.

'So I gets cured. I goes to the barkeep', and I sez, "Show me the biggest, fashionblest house thet's for sale yer." And he sez, "The biggest nat'rally b'longs to John Jacob Astor."* And I sez, "Show him," and he shows him. And I sez, "Wot might you ask for this yer house?" And he looks at me scornful, and sez, "Go 'way, old man; you must be sick." And I fetches him one over the left eye and he apologizes, and I gives him his own price for the house. I stocks that house with mahogany furniture and pervisions, and thar we lives,—you and me, Tommy, you and me!'

The sun no longer shone upon the hillside. The shadows of the pines were beginning to creep over Johnson's claim, and the air within the cavern was growing chill. In the gathering darkness his eyes shone brightly as he went on: 'Then thar comes a day when we gives a big spread. We invites gov'ners, members o' Congress, gentlemen o' fashion, and the like. And among 'em I invites a Man as holds his head very high, a Man I once knew; but he doesn't know I knows him, and he doesn't remember me. And he comes and he sits opposite me, and I watches him. And he's very airy, this Man, and very chipper, and he wipes his mouth with a white hankercher, and he smiles, and he ketches my eye. And he sez, "A glass o' wine with you, Mr Johnson;" and he fills his glass and I fills mine, and we rises. And I heaves that wine, glass and all, right into his damned grinnin' face. And he jumps for me—for he is very game this Man, very game—but some on 'em grabs him, and he sez, "Who be you?" And I sez, "Skaggs! Damn you, Skaggs! Look at me! Gimme back my wife and child, gimme back the money you stole, gimme back the good name you took away, gimme back the health you ruined, gimme back the last twelve years! Give 'em to me, damn you, quick, before I cuts your heart out!" And naterally, Tommy, he can't do it. And so I cuts his heart out, my boy; I cuts his heart out.'

The purely animal fury of his eye suddenly changed again to cunning. 'You think they hangs me for it, Tommy, but they don't. Not much, Tommy. I goes to the biggest lawyer there, and I says to him, "Salivated by merkery—you hear me—salivated by merkery." And he winks at me, and he goes to the judge, and he sez, "This yer unfortnet man isn't responsible—

he's been salivated by merkery." And he brings witnesses; you comes, Tommy, and you sez ez how you've seen me took bad afore; and the doctor, he comes, and he sez as how he's seen me frightful; and the jury, without leavin' their seats, brings in a verdict o' justifiable insanity,—salivated by merkery.'

In the excitement of his climax he had risen to his feet, but would have fallen had not Tommy caught him and led him into the open air. In this sharper light there was an odd change visible in his yellow-white face,—a change which caused Tommy to hurriedly support him, half leading, half dragging him toward the little cabin. When they had reached it, Tommy placed him on a rude 'bunk,' or shelf, and stood for a moment in anxious contemplation of the tremor-stricken man before him. Then he said rapidly, 'Listen, Uncle Ben. I'm goin' to town—to town, you understand—for the doctor. You're not to get up or move on any account until I return. Do you hear?' Johnson nodded violently. 'I'll be back in two hours.' In another moment he was gone.

For an hour Johnson kept his word. Then he suddenly sat up, and began to gaze fixedly at a corner of the cabin. From gazing at it he began to smile, from smiling at it he began to talk, from talking at it he began to scream, from screaming he passed to cursing and sobbing wildly. Then he lay quiet again.

He was so still that to merely human eyes he might have seemed asleep or dead. But a squirrel, that, emboldened by the stillness, had entered from the roof, stopped short upon a beam above the bunk, for he saw that the man's foot was slowly and cautiously moving towards the floor, and that the man's eyes were as intent and watchful as his own. Presently, still without a sound, both feet were upon the floor. And then the bunk creaked, and the squirrel whisked into the eaves of the roof. When he peered forth again, everything was quiet, and the man was gone.

An hour later two muleteers on the Placerville Road passed a man with disheveled hair, glaring, bloodshot eyes, and clothes torn with bramble and stained with the red dust of the mountain. They pursued him, when he turned fiercely on the foremost, wrested a pistol from his grasp, and broke away. Later still, when the sun had dropped behind Payne's Ridge, the underbrush on Deadwood Slope crackled with a stealthy but continuous tread. It must have been an animal whose dimly outlined bulk, in the gathering darkness, showed here and there in vague but incessant motion; it could be nothing but an animal whose utterance was at once so incoherent, monotonous, and unremitting. Yet, when the sound came nearer, and the chaparral was parted, it seemed to be a man, and that man Johnson.

Above the baying of phantasmal hounds that pressed him hard and drove him on, with never rest or mercy; above the lashing of a spectral whip that curled about his limbs, sang in his ears, and continually stung him forward; above the outcries of the unclean shapes that thronged about him,—he could still distinguish one real sound, the rush and sweep of hurrying waters. The Stanislaus River! A thousand feet below him drove its yellowing current. Through all the vacillations of his unseated mind he had clung to one idea—to reach the river, to lave in it, to swim it if need be, but to put it forever between him and the harrying shapes, to drown forever in its turbid depths the thronging spectres, to wash away in its yellow flood all stains and color of the past. And now he was leaping from boulder to boulder, from blackened stump to stump, from gnarled bush to bush, caught for a moment and withheld by clinging vines, or plunging downward into dusty hollows, until, rolling, dropping, sliding, and stumbling, he reached the river-bank, whereon he fell, rose, staggered forward, and fell again with outstretched arms upon a rock that breasted the swift current. And there he lay as dead.

A few stars came out hesitatingly above Deadwood Slope. A cold wind that had sprung up with the going down of the sun fanned them into momentary brightness, swept the heated flanks of the mountain, and ruffled the river. Where the fallen man lay there was a sharp curve in the stream, so that in the gathering shadows the rushing water seemed to leap out of the darkness and to vanish again. Decayed driftwood, trunks of trees, fragments of broken sluicing—the wash and waste of many a mile—swept into sight a moment, and were gone. All of decay, wreck, and foulness gathered in the long circuit of mining-camp and settlement, all the dregs and refuse of a crude and wanton civilization, reappeared for an instant, and then were hurried away in the darkness and lost. No wonder that, as the wind ruffled the yellow waters, the waves seemed to lift their unclean hands toward the rock whereon the fallen man lay, as if eager to snatch him from it, too, and hurry him toward the sea.

It was very still. In the clear air a horn blown a mile away was heard distinctly. The jingling of a spur and a laugh on the highway over Payne's Ridge sounded clearly across the river. The rattling of harness and hoofs foretold for many minutes the approach of the Wingdam coach, that at last, with flashing lights, passed within a few feet of the rock. Then for an hour all again was quiet. Presently the moon, round and full, lifted herself above the serried ridge and looked down upon the river. At first the bared peak of Deadwood Hill gleamed white and skull-like. Then the shadows of Payne's Ridge cast on the slope slowly sank away, leaving the unshapely stumps, the dusty fissures, and clinging outcrop of Deadwood Slope to stand out in black and silver. Still stealing softly downward, the moonlight touched the bank and the rock, and then glittered brightly on the river. The rock was bare and the man was gone, but the river still hurried swiftly to the sea.

'Is there anything for me?' asked Tommy Islington, as, a week after, the stage drew up at the Mansion House, and Bill slowly entered the bar-room. Bill did not reply, but, turning to a stranger who had entered with him, indicated with a jerk of his finger the boy. The stranger turned with an air half of business, half of curiosity, and looked critically at Tommy. 'Is there anything for me?' repeated Tommy, a little confused at the silence and scrutiny. Bill walked deliberately to the bar, and, placing his back against it, faced Tommy with a look of demure enjoyment.

'Ef,' he remarked slowly,—'ef a hundred thousand dollars down and half a million in perspektive is ennything, Major, THERE IS!'

II. EAST

It was characteristic of Angel's that the disappearance of Johnson, and the fact that he had left his entire property to

Tommy, thrilled the community but slightly in comparison with the astounding discovery that he had anything to leave. The finding of a cinnabar lode at Angel's absorbed all collateral facts or subsequent details. Prospectors from adjoining camps thronged the settlement; the hillside for a mile on either side of Johnson's claim was staked out and pre-empted; trade received a sudden stimulus; and, in the excited rhetoric of the 'Weekly Record,' 'a new era had broken upon Angel's.' 'On Thursday last,' added that paper, 'over five hundred dollars were taken in over the bar of the Mansion House.'

Of the fate of Johnson there was little doubt. He had been last seen lying on a boulder on the river-bank by outside passengers of the Wingdam night coach, and when Finn of Robinson's Ferry admitted to have fired three shots from a revolver at a dark object struggling in the water near the ferry, which he 'suspicioned' to be a bear, the question seemed to be settled. Whatever might have been the fallibility of his judgment, of the accuracy of his aim there could be no doubt. The general belief that Johnson, after possessing himself of the muleteer's pistol, could have run amuck gave a certain retributive justice to this story, which rendered it acceptable to the camp.

It was also characteristic of Angel's that no feeling of envy or opposition to the good fortune of Tommy Islington prevailed there. That he was thoroughly cognizant, from the first, of Johnson's discovery, that his attentions to him were interested, calculating, and speculative, was, however, the general belief of the majority,—a belief that, singularly enough, awakened the first feelings of genuine respect for Tommy ever shown by the camp. 'He ain't no fool; Yuba Bill seed thet from the first,' said the barkeeper. It was Yuba Bill who applied for the guardianship of Tommy after his accession to Johnson's claim, and on whose bonds the richest men of Calaveras were represented. It was Yuba Bill, also, when Tommy was sent East to finish his education, who accompanied him to San Francisco, and, before parting with his charge on the steamer's deck, drew him aside, and said, 'Ef at enny time you want enny money, Tommy, over and 'bove your 'lowance, you kin write; but ef you'll take my advice,' he added, with a sudden huskiness mitigating the severity of his voice, 'you'll forget every derned ole spavined, string-halted bummer, as you ever met or knew at Angel's,—ev'ry one, Tommy,—ev'ry one! And so—boy—take care of yourself—and—and God bless ye, and pertikerly d—n me for a first-class A 1 fool.' It was Yuba Bill, also, after this speech, who glared savagely around, walked down the crowded gangplank with a rigid and aggressive shoulder, picked a quarrel with his cabman, and, after bundling that functionary into his own vehicle, took the reins himself, and drove furiously to his hotel. 'It cost me,' said Bill, recounting the occurrence somewhat later at Angel's,—'it cost me a matter o' twenty dollars afore the jedge the next mornin'; but you kin bet high thet I taught them 'Frisco chaps suthin' new about drivin'. I didn't make it lively in Montgomery Street for about ten minutes—oh no!'

And so by degrees the two original locators of the great Cinnabar Lode faded from the memory of Angel's, and Calaveras knew them no more. In five years their very names had been forgotten; in seven the name of the town was changed; in ten the town itself was transported bodily to the hillside, and the chimney of the Union Smelting Works by night flickered like a corpse-light over the site of Johnson's cabin, and by day poisoned the pure spices of the pines. Even the Mansion House was dismantled, and the Wingdam stage deserted the highway for a shorter cut by Quicksilver City. Only the bared crest of Deadwood Hill, as of old, sharply cut the clear blue sky, and at its base, as of old, the Stanislaus River, unwearied and unresting, babbled, whispered, and hurried away to the sea.

A midsummer's day was breaking lazily on the Atlantic. There was not wind enough to move the vapors in the foggy offing, but when the vague distance heaved against a violet sky there were dull red streaks that, growing brighter, presently painted out the stars. Soon the brown rocks of Greyport appeared faintly suffused, and then the whole ashen line of dead coast was kindled, and the lighthouse beacons went out one by one. And then a hundred sail, before invisible, started out of the vapory horizon, and pressed toward the shore. It was morning, indeed, and some of the best society in Greyport, having been up all night, were thinking it was time to go to bed.

For as the sky flashed brighter it fired the clustering red roofs of a picturesque house by the sands that had all that night, from open lattice and illuminated balcony, given light and music to the shore. It glittered on the broad crystal spaces of a great conservatory that looked upon an exquisite lawn, where all night long the blended odors of sea and shore had swooned under the summer moon. But it wrought confusion among the colored lamps on the long veranda, and startled a group of ladies and gentlemen who had stepped from the drawing-room window to gaze upon it. It was so searching and sincere in its way, that, as the carriage of the fairest Miss Gillyflower rolled away, that peerless young woman, catching sight of her face in the oval mirror, instantly pulled down the blinds, and, nestling the whitest shoulders in Greyport against the crimson cushions, went to sleep.

'How haggard everybody is! Rose, dear, you look almost intellectual,' said Blanche Masterman.

'I hope not,' said Rose simply. 'Sunrises are very trying. Look how that pink regularly puts out Mrs Brown-Robinson, hair and all!'

'The angels,' said the Count de Nugat, with a polite gesture toward the sky, 'must have find these celestial combinations very bad for the toilette.'

'They're safe in white,—except when they sit for their pictures in Venice,' said Blanche. 'How fresh Mr Islington looks! It's really uncomplimentary to us.'

'I suppose the sun recognizes in me no rival,' said the young man demurely. 'But,' he added, 'I have lived much in the open air and require very little sleep.'

'How delightful!' said Mrs Brown-Robinson in a low, enthusiastic voice, and a manner that held the glowing sentiment of sixteen and the practical experiences of thirty-two in dangerous combination;—'how perfectly delightful! What sunrises you must have seen, and in such wild, romantic places! How I envy you! My nephew was a classmate of yours, and has often repeated to me those charming stories you tell of your adventures. Won't you tell some now? Do! How you must tire of us and this artificial life here, so frightfully artificial, you know' (in a confidential whisper); 'and then to think of the days when you roamed the great West with the Indians, and the bisons, and the grizzly bears! Of course, you have seen grizzly bears and bisons?'

'Of course he has, dear,' said Blanche a little pettishly, throwing a cloak over her shoulders, and seizing her chaperon by the arm; 'his earliest infancy was soothed by bisons, and he proudly points to the grizzly bear as the playmate of his youth. Come with me, and I'll tell you all about it. How good it is of you,' she added, *sotto voce*, to Islington as he stood by the carriage,—'how perfectly good it is of you to be like those animals you tell us of, and not know your full power. Think, with your experiences and our credulity, what stories you *might* tell! And you are going to walk? Good-night, then.' A slim, gloved hand was frankly extended from the window, and the next moment the carriage rolled away.

'Isn't Islington throwing away a chance there?' said Captain Merwin on the veranda.

'Perhaps he couldn't stand my lovely aunt's superadded presence. But then, he's the guest of Blanche's father, and I daresay they see enough of each other as it is.'

'But isn't it a rather dangerous situation?'

'For him, perhaps; although he's awfully old, and very queer. For her, with an experience that takes in all the available men in both hemispheres, ending with Nugat over there, I should say a man more or less wouldn't affect her much, anyway. Of course,' he laughed, 'these are the accents of bitterness. But that was last year.'

Perhaps Islington did not overhear the speaker; perhaps, if he did, the criticism was not new. He turned carelessly away, and sauntered out on the road to the sea. Thence he strolled along the sands toward the cliffs, where, meeting an impediment in the shape of a garden wall, he leaped it with a certain agile, boyish ease and experience, and struck across an open lawn toward the rocks again. The best society of Greyport were not early risers, and the spectacle of a trespasser in an evening dress excited only the criticism of grooms hanging about the stables, or cleanly housemaids on the broad verandas that in Greyport architecture dutifully gave upon the sea. Only once, as he entered the boundaries of Cliffwood Lodge, the famous seat of

Renwyck Masterman, was he aware of suspicious scrutiny; but a slouching figure that vanished quickly in the lodge offered no opposition to his progress. Avoiding the pathway to the lodge, Islington kept along the rocks until, reaching a little promontory and rustic pavilion, he sat down and gazed upon the sea.

And presently an infinite peace stole upon him. Except where the waves lapped lazily the crags below, the vast expanse beyond seemed unbroken by ripple, heaving only in broad ponderable sheets, and rhythmically, as if still in sleep. The air was filled with a luminous haze that caught and held the direct sunbeams. In the deep calm that lay upon the sea, it seemed to Islington that all the tenderness of culture, magic of wealth, and spell of refinement that for years had wrought upon that favored shore had extended its gracious influence even here. What a pampered and caressed old ocean it was; cajoled, flattered, and fêted where it lay! An odd recollection of the turbid Stanislaus hurrying by the ascetic pines, of the grim outlines of Deadwood Hill, swam before his eyes, and made the yellow green of the velvet lawn and graceful foliage seem almost tropical by contrast. And, looking up, a few yards distant he beheld a tall slip of a girl gazing upon the sea—Blanche Masterman.

She had plucked somewhere a large fan-shaped leaf, which she held parasol-wise, shading the blonde masses of her hair, and hiding her gray eyes. She had changed her festal dress, with its amplitude of flounce and train, for a closely fitting, half-antique habit whose scant outlines would have been trying to limbs less shapely, but which prettily accented the graceful curves and sweeping lines of this Greyport goddess. As Islington rose, she came toward him with a frankly outstretched hand and unconstrained manner. Had she observed him first? I don't know.

They sat down together on a rustic seat, Miss Blanche facing the sea and shading her eyes with the leaf.

'I don't really know how long I have been sitting here,' said Islington, 'or whether I have not been actually asleep and dreaming. It seemed too lovely a morning to go to bed. But you?'

From behind the leaf, it appeared that Miss Blanche, on retiring, had been pursued by a hideous four-winged insect which defied the efforts of herself and maid to dislodge. Odin, the Spitz dog, had insisted upon scratching at the door. And it made her eyes red to sleep in the morning. And she had an early call to make. And the sea looked lovely.

'I'm glad to find you here, whatever be the cause,' said Islington, with his old directness. 'To-day, as you know, is my last day in Greyport, and it is much pleasanter to say good-by under this blue sky than even beneath your father's wonderful frescoes yonder. I want to remember you, too, as part of this pleasant prospect which belongs to us all, rather than recall you in anybody's particular setting.'

'I know,' said Blanche, with equal directness, 'that houses are one of the defects of our civilization; but I don't think I ever heard the idea as elegantly expressed before. Where do you go?'

'I don't know yet. I have several plans. I may go to South America and become president of one of the republics,—I am not particular which. I am rich, but in that part of America which lies outside of Greyport it is necessary for every man to have some work. My friends think I should have some great aim in life, with a capital A. But I was born a vagabond, and a vagabond I shall probably die.'

'I don't know anybody in South America,' said Blanche languidly. 'There were two girls here last season, but they didn't wear stays in the house, and their white frocks never were properly done up. If you go to South America, you must write to me.'

'I will. Can you tell me the name of this flower which I found in your greenhouse? It looks much like a California blossom.'

'Perhaps it is. Father bought it of a half-crazy old man who came here one day. Do you know him?'

Islington laughed. 'I am afraid not. But let me present this in a less business-like fashion.'

'Thank you. Remind me to give you one in return before you go,—or will you choose yourself?'

They had both risen as by a common instinct.

'Good-by.'

The cool, flower-like hand lay in his for an instant.

'Will you oblige me by putting aside that leaf a moment before I go?'

'But my eyes are red, and I look like a perfect fright.'

Yet, after a long pause, the leaf fluttered down, and a pair of very beautiful but withal very clear and critical eyes met his. Islington was constrained to look away. When he turned again she was gone.

'Mr. Hislington,—sir!'

It was Chalker, the English groom, out of breath with running.

'Seein' you alone, sir—beg your pardon, sir—but there's a person'—

'A person! what the devil do you mean? Speak English—no, damn it, I mean don't,' said Islington snappishly.

'I said a person, sir. Beg pardon—no offense—but not a gent, sir. In the lib'ry.'

A little amused even through the utter dissatisfaction with himself and vague loneliness that had suddenly come upon him, Islington, as he walked toward the lodge, asked, 'Why isn't he a gent?'

'No gent—beggin' your pardin, sir—'ud guy a man in sarvis, sir. Takes me 'ands so, sir, as I sits in the rumble at the gate, and puts 'em downd so, sir, and sez, "Put 'em in your pocket, young man,—or is it a road agint you expects to see, that you 'olds hup your 'ands, hand crosses 'em like to that?" sez he. "'Old 'ard," sez he, "on the short curves, or you'll bust your precious crust," sez he. And hasks for you, sir. This way, sir.'

They entered the lodge. Islington hurried down the long Gothic hall and opened the library door.

In an armchair, in the centre of the room, a man sat apparently contemplating a large, stiff, yellow hat with an enormous brim, that was placed on the floor before him. His hands rested lightly between his knees, but one foot was drawn up at the side of his chair in a peculiar manner. In the first glance that Islington gave, the attitude in some odd, irreconcilable way suggested a brake. In another moment he dashed across the room, and, holding out both hands, cried, 'Yuba Bill!'

The man rose, caught Islington by the shoulders, wheeled him round, hugged him, felt of his ribs like a good-natured ogre, shook his hands violently, laughed, and then said somewhat ruefully, 'And however did you know me?'

Seeing that Yuba Bill evidently regarded himself as in some elaborate disguise, Islington laughed, and suggested that it must have been instinct.

'And you?' said Bill, holding him at arm's length and surveying him critically,—'you!—toe think—toe think—a little cuss no higher nor a trace, a boy as I've flicked outer the road with a whip time in agin, a boy ez never hed much clothes to speak of, turned into a sport!'

Islington remembered, with a thrill of ludicrous terror, that he still wore his evening dress.

'Turned,' continued Yuba Bill severely,—'turned into a restyourant waiter,—a garsong! Eh, Alfonse, bring me a patty de foy grass and an omelet, demme!'

'Dear old chap!' said Islington, laughing, and trying to put his hand over Bill's bearded mouth, 'but you—*you* don't look exactly like yourself! You're not well, Bill.' And indeed, as he turned toward the light, Bill's eyes appeared cavernous, and his hair and beard thickly streaked with gray.

'Maybe it's this yer harness,' said Bill a little anxiously. 'When I hitches on this yer curb' (he indicated a massive gold watch-chain with enormous links), 'and mounts this "morning star" ' (he pointed to a very large solitaire pin which had the appearance of blistering his whole shirt-front), 'it kinder weighs heavy on me, Tommy. Otherwise I'm all right, my boy—all right.' But he evaded Islington's keen eye and turned from the light.

'You have something to tell me, Bill,' said Islington suddenly and with almost brusque directness; 'out with it.'

Bill did not speak, but moved uneasily toward his hat.

'You didn't come three thousand miles, without a word of warning, to talk to me of old times,' said Islington more kindly, 'glad as I would have been to see you. It isn't your way, Bill, and you know it. We shall not be disturbed here,' he added, in reply to an inquiring glance that Bill directed to the door, 'and I am ready to hear you.'

'Firstly, then,' said Bill, drawing his chair nearer Islington, 'answer me one question, Tommy, fair and square, and up and down.'

'Go on,' said Islington with a slight smile.

'Ef I should say to you, Tommy—say to you to-day, right here, you must come with me—you must leave this place for a month, a year, two years, maybe, perhaps for ever—is there anything that 'ud keep you—anything, my boy, ez you couldn't leave?'

'No,' said Tommy quietly; 'I am only visiting here. I thought of leaving Greyport to-day.'

'But if I should say to you, Tommy, come with me on a *pasear* * to Chiny, to Japan, to South Ameriky, p'r'aps, could you go?'

'Yes,' said Islington after a slight pause.

'Thar isn't ennything,' said Bill, drawing a little closer, and lowering his voice confidentially,—'ennything in the way of a young woman—you understand, Tommy—ez would keep you? They're mighty sweet about here; and whether a man is young or old, Tommy, there's always some woman as is brake or whip to him!'

In a certain excited bitterness that characterized the delivery of this abstract truth, Bill did not see that the young man's face flushed slightly as he answered 'No.'

'Then listen. It's seven years ago, Tommy, thet I was working one o' the Pioneer coaches over from Gold Hill. Ez I stood in front o' the stage-office, the sheriff o' the county comes to me, and he sez, "Bill," sez he, "I've got a looney chap, as I'm in charge of, taking 'im down to the 'sylum in Stockton. He'z quiet and peaceable, but the insides don't like to ride with him. Hev you enny objection to give him a lift on the box beside you?" I sez, "No; put him up." When I came to go and get up on that box beside him, that man, Tommy—that man sittin' there, quiet and peaceable, was—Johnson!

'He didn't know me, my boy,' Yuba Bill continued, rising and putting his hands on Tommy's shoulders,—'he didn't know me. He didn't know nothing about you, nor Angel's, nor the quicksilver lode, nor even his own name. He said his name was Skaggs, but I knowed it was Johnson. Thar was times, Tommy, you might have knocked me off that box with a feather; thar was times when if the twenty-seven passengers o' that stage hed found theirselves swimming in the American River five hundred feet below the road, I never could have explained it satisfactorily to the company,—never.

'The sheriff said,' Bill continued hastily, as if to preclude any interruption from the young man,—'the sheriff said he had been brought into Murphy's Camp three years before, dripping with water, and sufferin' from perkussion of the brain, and had been cared for generally by the boys 'round. When I told the sheriff I knowed 'im, I got him to leave him in my care; and I took him to 'Frisco, Tommy, to 'Frisco, and I put him in charge o' the best doctors there, and paid his board myself. There was nothin' he didn't have ez he wanted. Don't look that way, my dear boy, for God's sake don't!'

'O Bill!' said Islington, rising and staggering to the window, 'why did you keep this from me?'

'Why?' said Bill, turning on him savagely,—'why? because I wa'n't a fool. Thar was you, winnin' your way in college; thar was *you*, risin' in the world, and of some account to it. Yer was an old bummer, ez good ez dead to it—a man ez oughter been dead afore! a man ez never denied it! But you allus liked him better nor me,' said Bill bitterly.

'Forgive me, Bill,' said the young man, seizing both his hands. 'I know you did it for the best; but go on.'

'Thar ain't much more to tell, nor much use to tell it, as I can see,' said Bill moodily. 'He never could be cured, the doctors said, for he had what they called monomania—was always talking about his wife and darter that somebody had stole away years ago, and plannin' revenge on that somebody. And six months ago he was missed. I tracked him to Carson, to Salt Lake City, to Omaha, to Chicago, to New York,—and here!'

'Here!' echoed Islington.

'Here! And that's what brings me here to-day. Whether he's crazy or well, whether he's huntin' you or lookin' up that other man, you must get away from here. You mustn't see him. You and me, Tommy, will go away on a cruise. In three or four years he'll be dead or missing, and then we'll come back. Come.' And he rose to his feet.

'Bill,' said Islington, rising also, and taking the hand of his friend with the same quiet obstinacy that in the old days had endeared him to Bill, 'wherever he is, here or elsewhere, sane or crazy, I shall seek and find him. Every dollar that I have shall be his, every dollar that I have spent shall be returned to him.

I am young yet, thank God, and can work; and if there is a way out of this miserable business, I shall find it.'

'I knew,' said Bill with a surliness that ill concealed his evident admiration of the calm figure before him—'I knew the partikler style of d——n fool that you was, and expected no better. Good-by, then—God Almighty! who's that?'

He was on his way to the open French window, but had started back, his face quite white and bloodless, and his eyes staring. Islington ran to the window and looked out. A white skirt vanished around the corner of the veranda. When he returned, Bill had dropped into a chair.

'It must have been Miss Masterman, I think; but what's the matter?'

'Nothing,' said Bill faintly; 'have you got any whiskey handy?'

Islington brought a decanter and, pouring out some spirits, handed the glass to Bill. Bill drained it, and then said, 'Who is Miss Masterman?'

'Mr Masterman's daughter; that is, an adopted daughter, I believe.'

'Wot name?'

'I really don't know,' said Islington pettishly, more vexed than he cared to own at this questioning.

Yuba Bill rose and walked to the window, closed it, walked back again to the door, glanced at Islington, hesitated, and then returned to his chair.

'I didn't tell you I was married—did I?' he said suddenly, looking up in Islington's face with an unsuccessful attempt at a reckless laugh.

'No,' said Islington, more pained at the manner than the words.

'Fact,' said Yuba Bill. 'Three years ago it was, Tommy,—three years ago!'

He looked so hard at Islington that, feeling he was expected to say something, he asked vaguely, 'Whom did you marry?'

'Thet's it!' said Yuba Bill; 'I can't ezactly say; partikly, though a she-devil! generally, the wife of half a dozen other men.'

Accustomed, apparently, to have his conjugal infelicities a theme of mirth among men, and seeing no trace of amusement on Islington's grave face, his dogged, reckless manner softened, and, drawing his chair closer to Islington, he went on: 'It all began outer this: we was coming down Watson's grade one night pretty free, when the expressman turns to me and says, "There's a row inside, and you'd better pull up!" I pulls up, and out hops, first a woman, and then two or three chaps swearin' and cursin', and tryin' to drag some one arter them. Then it 'peared, Tommy, thet it was this woman's drunken husband they was going to put out for abusin' her and strikin' her in the coach; and if it hadn't been for me, my boy, they'd have left that chap thar in the road. But I fixes matters up by putting her alongside o' me on the box, and we drove on. She was very white, Tommy,—for the matter o' that, she was always one o' these very white women, that never got red in the face,—but she never cried a whimper. Most women would have cried. It was queer, but she never cried. I thought so at the time.

'She was very tall, with a lot o' light hair meandering down the back of her head, as long as a deerskin whiplash, and about the color. She hed eyes thet'd bore ye through at fifty yards, and pooty hands and feet. And when she kinder got out o' that stiff, narvous state she was in, and warmed up a little, and got chipper, by G—d, sir, she was handsome,—she was that!'

A little flushed and embarrassed at his own enthusiasm, he stopped, and then said carelessly, 'They got off at Murphy's.'

'Well,' said Islington.

'Well, I used to see her often arter thet, and when she was alone she allus took the box-seat. She kinder confided her troubles to me, how her husband got drunk and abused her; and I didn't see much o' him, for he was away in 'Frisco arter thet. But it was all square, Tommy,—all square 'twixt me and her.

'I got a-going there a good deal, and then one day I sez to myself, "Bill, this won't do," and I got changed to another route. Did you ever know Jackson Filltree, Tommy?' said Bill, breaking off suddenly.

'No.'

'Might have heerd of him, p'r'aps?'

'No,' said Islington impatiently.

'Jackson Filltree ran the express from White's out to Summit, 'cross the North Fork of the Yuba. One day he sez to me,

"Bill, that's a mighty bad ford at the North Fork." I sez, "I believe you, Jackson." "It'll git me some day, Bill, sure," sez he. I sez, "Why don't you take the lower ford?" "I don't know," sez he, "but I can't." So ever after, when I met him, he sez, "That North Fork ain't got me yet." One day I was in Sacramento, and up comes Filltree. He sez, "I've sold out the express business on account of the North Fork, but it's bound to get me yet, Bill, sure;" and he laughs. Two weeks after they finds his body below the ford, whar he tried to cross, comin' down from the summit way. Folks said it was foolishness; Tommy, I sez it was Fate! The second day arter I was changed to the Placerville route, thet woman comes outer the hotel above the stage-office. Her husband, she said, was lying sick in Placerville; that's what she said; but it was Fate, Tommy, Fate. Three months afterward, her husband takes an overdose of morphine for delirium tremens, and dies. There's folks ez sez she gave it to him, but it's Fate. A year after that I married her,—Fate, Tommy, Fate!

'I lived with her jest three months,' he went on, after a long breath,—'three months! It ain't much time for a happy man. I've seen a good deal o' hard life in my day, but there was days in that three months longer than any day in my life,—days, Tommy, when it was a toss-up whether I should kill her or she me. But thar, I'm done. You are a young man, Tommy, and I ain't goin' to tell things thet, old as I am, three years ago I couldn't have believed.'

When at last, with his grim face turned toward the window, he sat silently with his clenched hands on his knees before him, Islington asked where his wife was now.

'Ask me no more, my boy,—no more. I've said my say.' With a gesture as of throwing down a pair of reins before him, he rose, and walked to the window.

'You kin understand, Tommy, why a little trip around the world 'ud do me good. Ef you can't go with me, well and good. But go I must.'

'Not before luncheon, I hope,' said a very sweet voice, as Blanche Masterman suddenly stood before them. 'Father would never forgive me if in his absence I permitted one of Mr Islington's friends to go in this way. You will stay, won't you?

Do! And you will give me your arm now; and when Mr Islington has done staring, he will follow us into the dining-room and introduce you.'

'I have quite fallen in love with your friend,' said Miss Blanche, as they stood in the drawing-room looking at the figure of Bill, strolling, with his short pipe in his mouth, through the distant shrubbery. 'He asks very queer questions, though. He wanted to know my mother's maiden name.'

'He is an honest fellow,' said Islington gravely.

'You are very much subdued. You don't thank me, I daresay, for keeping you and your friend here; but you couldn't go, you know, until father returned.'

Islington smiled, but not very gayly.

'And then I think it much better for us to part here under these frescoes, don't you? Good-by.'

She extended her long, slim hand.

'Out in the sunlight there, when my eyes were red, you were very anxious to look at me,' she added in a dangerous voice.

Islington raised his sad eyes to hers. Something glittering upon her own sweet lashes trembled and fell.

'Blanche!'

She was rosy enough now, and would have withdrawn her hand, but Islington detained it. She was not quite certain but that her waist was also in jeopardy. Yet she could not help saying, 'Are you sure that there isn't anything in the way of a young woman that would keep you?'

'Blanche!' said Islington in reproachful horror.

'If gentlemen will roar out their secrets before an open window, with a young woman lying on a sofa on the veranda, reading a stupid French novel, they must not be surprised if she gives more attention to them than to her book.'

'Then you know all, Blanche?'

'I know,' said Blanche, 'let's see—I know the partikler style of—ahem!—fool you was, and expected no better. Good-by.' And, gliding like a lovely and innocent milk snake out of his grasp, she slipped away.

*

To the pleasant ripple of waves, the sound of music and light voices, the yellow midsummer moon again rose over Greyport. It looked upon formless masses of rock and shrubbery, wide spaces of lawn and beach, and a shimmering expanse of water. It singled out particular objects,—a white sail in shore, a crystal globe upon the lawn, and flashed upon something held between the teeth of a crouching figure scaling the low wall of Cliffwood Lodge. Then, as a man and woman passed out from under the shadows of the foliage into the open moonlight of the garden path, the figure leaped from the wall, and stood erect and waiting in the shadow.

It was the figure of an old man, with rolling eyes, his trembling hand grasping a long, keen knife,—a figure more pitiable than pitiless, more pathetic than terrible. But the next moment the knife was stricken from his hand, and he struggled in the firm grasp of another figure that apparently sprang from the wall beside him.

'D—n you, Masterman!' cried the old man hoarsely; 'give me fair play, and I'll kill you yet!'

'Which my name is Yuba Bill,' said Bill quietly, 'and it's time this d—n fooling was stopped.'

The old man glared in Bill's face savagely. 'I know you. You're one of Masterman's friends,—d—n you,—let me go till I cut his heart out,—let me go! Where is my Mary?—where is my wife?—there she is! there!—there!—there! Mary!' He would have screamed, but Bill placed his powerful hand upon his mouth as he turned in the direction of the old man's glance. Distinct in the moonlight the figures of Islington and Blanche, arm in arm, stood out upon the garden path.

'Give me my wife!' muttered the old man hoarsely between Bill's fingers. 'Where is she?'

A sudden fury passed over Yuba Bill's face. 'Where is your wife?' he echoed, pressing the old man back against the garden wall, and holding him there as in a vise. 'Where is your wife?' he repeated, thrusting his grim sardonic jaw and savage eyes into the old man's frightened face. 'Where is Jack Adam's wife? Where is MY wife? Where is the she-devil that drove one man mad, that sent another to hell by his own hand, that eternally broke and ruined me? Where! Where! Do you ask where? In jail in Sacramento,—in jail, do you hear?—in jail for murder, Johnson,—murder!'

The old man gasped, stiffened, and then, relaxing, suddenly slipped, a mere inanimate mass, at Yuba Bill's feet. With a sudden revulsion of feeling, Yuba Bill dropped at his side, and, lifting him tenderly in his arms, whispered, 'Look up, old man, Johnson! look up, for God's sake!—it's me,—Yuba Bill! and yonder is your daughter, and—Tommy—don't you know—Tommy, little Tommy Islington?'

Johnson's eyes slowly opened. He whispered, 'Tommy! yes, Tommy! Sit by me, Tommy. But don't sit so near the bank. Don't you see how the river is rising and beckoning to me—hissing, and boilin' over the rocks? It's gittin' higher!—hold me, Tommy,—hold me, and don't let me go yet. We'll live to cut his heart out, Tommy,—we'll live—we'll'—

His head sank, and the rushing river, invisible to all eyes save his, leaped toward him out of the darkness, and bore him away, no longer to the darkness, but through it to the distant, peaceful, shining sea.

WAN LEE, THE PAGAN

As I opened Hop Sing's letter there fluttered to the ground a square strip of yellow paper covered with hieroglyphics, which at first glance I innocently took to be the label from a pack of Chinese fire-crackers. But the same envelope also contained a smaller strip of rice paper, with two Chinese characters traced in India ink, that I at once knew to be Hop Sing's visiting card. The whole, as afterwards literally translated, ran as follows:—

To the stranger the gates of my house are not closed; the rice-jar is on the left, and the sweetmeats on the right, as you enter.
Two sayings of the Master:
Hospitality is the virtue of the son and the wisdom of the ancestor.
The superior man is light-hearted after the crop-gathering; he makes a festival.
When the stranger is in your melon patch observe him not too closely; inattention is often the highest form of civility.
Happiness, Peace, and Prosperity.   HOP SING.

Admirable, certainly, as was this morality and proverbial wisdom, and although this last axiom was very characteristic of my friend Hop Sing, who was that most sombre of all humorists, a Chinese philosopher, I must confess that, even after a very free translation, I was at a loss to make any immediate application of the message. Luckily I discovered a third inclosure in the shape of a little note in English and Hop Sing's own commercial hand. It ran thus:—

The pleasure of your company is requested at No.—Sacramento Street, on Friday evening at eight o'clock. A cup of tea at nine—sharp.
HOP SING.

This explained all. It meant a visit to Hop Sing's warehouse, the opening and exhibition of some rare Chinese novelties and curios, a chat in the back office, a cup of tea of a perfection unknown beyond these sacred precincts, cigars, and a visit to the Chinese Theatre or Temple. This was in fact the favorite programme of Hop Sing when he exercised his functions of hospitality as the chief factor or superintendent of the Ning Foo Company.

At eight o'clock on Friday evening I entered the warehouse of Hop Sing. There was that deliciously commingled mysterious foreign odor that I had so often noticed; there was the old array of uncouth-looking objects, the long procession of jars and crockery, the same singular blending of the grotesque and the mathematically neat and exact, the same endless suggestions of frivolity and fragility, the same want of harmony in colors that were each, in themselves, beautiful and rare. Kites in the shape of enormous dragons and gigantic butterflies; kites so ingeniously arranged as to utter at intervals, when facing the wind, the cry of a hawk; kites so large as to be beyond any boy's power of restraint—so large that you understood why kite-flying in China was an amusement for adults; gods of china and bronze so gratuitously ugly as to be beyond any human interest or sympathy from their very impossibility; jars of sweetmeats covered all over with moral sentiments from Confucius; hats that looked like baskets, and baskets that looked like hats; silk so light that I hesitate to record the incredible number of square yards that you might pass through the ring on your little finger—these and a great many other indescribable objects were all familiar to me. I pushed my way through the dimly lighted warehouse until I reached the back office or parlor, where I found Hop Sing waiting to receive me.

Before I describe him I want the average reader to discharge from his mind any idea of a Chinaman that he may have gathered from the pantomime. He did not wear beautifully scalloped drawers fringed with little bells—I never met a Chinaman who did; he did not habitually carry his forefinger extended before him at right angles with his body, nor did I ever hear him utter the mysterious sentence, 'Ching a ring a ring chaw,' nor dance under any provocation. He was, on the whole, a rather grave, decorous, handsome gentleman. His complexion, which extended all over his head except where his long pig-tail grew, was like a very nice piece of glazed brown paper-muslin. His eyes were black and bright, and his eyelids set at an angle of 15°; his nose straight and delicately formed, his mouth small, and his teeth white and clean. He wore a dark blue silk blouse, and in the streets on cold days a short jacket of Astrakhan fur.* He wore also a pair of drawers of blue brocade gathered tightly over his calves and ankles, offering a general sort of suggestion that he had forgotten his trousers that morning, but that, so gentlemanly were his manners, his friends had forborne to mention the fact to him. His manner was urbane, although quite serious. He spoke French and English fluently. In brief, I doubt if you could have found the equal of this Pagan shopkeeper among the Christian traders of San Francisco.

There were a few others present: a Judge of the Federal Court, an editor, a high government official, and a prominent merchant. After we had drunk our tea, and tasted a few sweetmeats from a mysterious jar, that looked as if it might contain a preserved mouse among its other nondescript treasures, Hop Sing arose, and gravely beckoning us to follow him, began to descend to the basement. When we got there, we were amazed at finding it brilliantly lighted, and that a number of chairs were arranged in a half-circle on the asphalt pavement. When he had courteously seated us, he said,—

'I have invited you to witness a performance which I can at least promise you no other foreigners but yourselves have ever seen. Wang, the court juggler, arrived here yesterday morning. He has never given a performance outside of the palace before. I have asked him to entertain my friends this evening. He requires no theatre, stage, accessories, or any confederate— nothing more than you see here. Will you be pleased to examine the ground yourselves, gentlemen.'

Of course we examined the premises. It was the ordinary basement or cellar of the San Francisco storehouse, cemented to keep out the damp. We poked our sticks into the pavement and rapped on the walls to satisfy our polite host, but for no other purpose. We were quite content to be the victims of any clever deception. For myself, I knew I was ready to be deluded to any extent, and if I had been offered an explanation of what followed, I should have probably declined it.

Although I am satisfied that Wang's general performance was the first of that kind ever given on American soil, it has probably since become so familiar to many of my readers that I shall not bore them with it here. He began by setting to flight, with the aid of his fan, the usual number of butterflies made before our eyes of little bits of tissue-paper, and kept them in the air during the remainder of the performance. I have a vivid recollection of the judge trying to catch one that had lit on his knee, and of its evading him with the pertinacity of a living insect. And even at this time Wang, still plying his fan, was taking chickens out of hats, making oranges disappear, pulling endless yards of silk from his sleeve, apparently filling the whole area of the basement with goods that appeared mysteriously from the ground, from his own sleeves, from nowhere! He swallowed knives to the ruin of his digestion for years to come; he dislocated every limb of his body; he reclined in the air, apparently upon nothing. But his crowning performance, which I have never yet seen repeated, was the most weird, mysterious, and astounding. It is my apology for this long introduction, my sole excuse for writing this article, the genesis of this veracious history.

He cleared the ground of its encumbering articles for a space of about fifteen feet square, and then invited us all to walk forward and again examine it. We did so gravely; there was nothing but the cemented pavement below to be seen or felt. He then asked for the loan of a handkerchief, and, as I chanced to be nearest him, I offered mine. He took it and spread it open upon the floor. Over this he spread a large square of silk, and over this again a large shawl nearly covering the space he had cleared. He then took a position at one of the points of this rectangle, and began a monotonous chant, rocking his body to and fro in time with the somewhat lugubrious air.

We sat still and waited. Above the chant we could hear the striking of the city clocks, and the occasional rattle of a cart in the street overhead. The absolute watchfulness and expectation, the dim, mysterious half-light of the cellar, falling in a gruesome way upon the misshapen bulk of a Chinese deity in the background, a faint smell of opium smoke mingling with spice, and the dreadful uncertainty of what we were really waiting for, sent an uncomfortable thrill down our backs, and made us look at each other with a forced and unnatural smile. This feeling was heightened when Hop Sing slowly rose, and, without a word, pointed with his finger to the centre of the shawl.

There was something beneath the shawl! Surely—and something that was not there before. At first a mere suggestion in relief, a faint outline, but growing more and more distinct and visible every moment. The chant still continued, the perspiration began to roll from the singer's face, gradually the hidden object took upon itself a shape and bulk that raised the shawl in its centre some five or six inches. It was now unmistakably the outline of a small but perfect human figure, with extended arms and legs. One or two of us turned pale; there was a feeling of general uneasiness, until the editor broke the silence by a gibe that, poor as it was, was received with spontaneous enthusiasm. Then the chant suddenly ceased, Wang arose, and, with a quick, dexterous movement, stripped both shawl and silk away, and discovered, sleeping peacefully upon my handkerchief, a tiny Chinese baby!

The applause and uproar which followed this revelation ought to have satisfied Wang, even if his audience was a small one; it was loud enough to awaken the baby—a pretty little boy about a year old, looking like a Cupid cut out of sandalwood. He was whisked away almost as mysteriously as he appeared. When Hop Sing returned my handkerchief to me with a bow, I asked if the juggler was the father of the baby. 'No sabe!'* said the imperturbable Hop Sing, taking refuge in that Spanish form of noncommittalism so common in California.

'But does he have a new baby for every performance?' I asked.

'Perhaps; who knows?'

'But what will become of this one?'

'Whatever you choose, gentlemen,' replied Hop Sing, with a courteous inclination; 'it was born here—you are its godfathers.'

There were two characteristic peculiarities of any Californian assemblage in 1856: it was quick to take a hint, and generous to the point of prodigality in its response to any charitable appeal. No matter how sordid or avaricious the individual, he could not resist the infection of sympathy. I doubled the points of my handkerchief into a bag, dropped a coin into it, and, without a word, passed it to the judge. He quietly added a twenty-dollar gold-piece, and passed it to the next; when it was returned to me it contained over a hundred dollars. I knotted the money in the handkerchief, and gave it to Hop Sing.

'For the baby, from its godfathers.'

'But what name?' said the judge. There was a running fire of 'Erebus,' 'Nox,' 'Plutus,' 'Terra Cotta,' 'Antæus,' etc., etc. Finally the question was referred to our host.

'Why not keep his own name,' he said quietly,—'Wan Lee?' And he did.

And thus was Wan Lee, on the night of Friday the 5th of March, 1856, born into this veracious chronicle.

The last form of the 'Northern Star' for the 19th of July, 1865,—the only daily paper published in Klamath County,— had just gone to press, and at three A.M. I was putting aside my proofs and manuscripts, preparatory to going home, when I discovered a letter lying under some sheets of paper which I must have overlooked. The envelope was considerably soiled, it had no postmark, but I had no difficulty in recognizing the hand of my friend Hop Sing. I opened it hurriedly, and read as follows:—

My DEAR SIR,—I do not know whether the bearer will suit you, but unless the office of 'devil' in your newspaper is a purely technical one, I think he has all the qualities required. He is very quick, active, and intelligent; understands English better than he speaks it, and makes up for any defect by his habits of observation and imitation. You have only to show him how to do a thing once, and he will repeat it, whether it is an offense or a virtue. But you certainly know him already; you are one of his godfathers, for is he not Wan Lee, the reputed son of Wang the conjurer, to whose performances I had the honor to introduce you? But perhaps you have forgotten it.

I shall send him with a gang of coolies to Stockton, thence by express to your town. If you can use him there, you will do me a favor, and probably save his life, which is at present in great peril from the hands of the younger members of your Christian and highly civilized race who attend the enlightened schools in San Francisco.

He has acquired some singular habits and customs from his experience of Wang's profession, which he followed for some years, until he became too large to go in a hat, or be produced from his father's sleeve. The money you left with me has been expended on his education; he has gone through the Tri-literal Classics, but, I think, without much benefit. He knows but little of Confucius,* and absolutely nothing of Mencius.* Owing to the negligence of his father, he associated, perhaps, too much with American children.

I should have answered your letter before, by post, but I thought that Wan Lee himself would be a better messenger for this.

Yours respectfully,

HOP SING.

And this was the long-delayed answer to my letter to Hop Sing. But where was 'the bearer'? How was the letter delivered? I summoned hastily the foreman, printers, and office boy, but without eliciting anything; no one had seen the letter delivered, nor knew anything of the bearer. A few days later I had a visit from my laundryman, Ah Ri.

'You wantee debbil? All lightee; me catchee him.'

He returned in a few moments with a bright-looking Chinese boy, about ten years old, with whose appearance and general intelligence I was so greatly impressed that I engaged him on the spot. When the business was concluded, I asked his name.

'Wan Lee,' said the boy.

'What! Are you the boy sent out by Hop Sing? What the devil do you mean by not coming here before, and how did you deliver that letter?'

Wan Lee looked at me and laughed. 'Me pitchee in top side window.'

I did not understand. He looked for a moment perplexed, and then, snatching the letter out of my hand, ran down the stairs. After a moment's pause, to my great astonishment, the letter came flying in at the window, circled twice around the room, and then dropped gently like a bird upon my table. Before I had got over my surprise Wan Lee reappeared, smiled, looked at the letter and then at me, said, 'So, John,' and then remained gravely silent. I said nothing further, but it was understood that this was his first official act.

His next performance, I grieve to say, was not attended with equal success. One of our regular paper-carriers fell sick, and, at a pinch, Wan Lee was ordered to fill his place. To prevent mistakes he was shown over the route the previous evening, and supplied at about daylight with the usual number of subscribers' copies. He returned after an hour, in good spirits and without the papers. He had delivered them all he said.

Unfortunately for Wan Lee, at about eight o'clock indignant subscribers began to arrive at the office. They had received their copies; but how? In the form of hard-pressed cannon-balls, delivered by a single shot and a mere *tour de force* through the glass of bedroom windows. They had received them full in the face, like a baseball, if they happened to be up and stirring; they had received them in quarter sheets, tucked in at separate windows; they had found them in the chimney, pinned against the door, shot through attic windows, delivered in long slips through convenient keyholes, stuffed into ventilators, and occupying the same can with the morning's milk. One subscriber, who waited for some time at the office door, to have a personal interview with Wan Lee (then comfortably locked in my bedroom), told me, with tears of rage in his eyes, that he had been awakened at five o'clock by a most hideous yelling below his windows; that on rising, in great agitation, he was startled by the sudden appearance of the 'Northern Star,' rolled hard and bent into the form of a boomerang or East Indian club, that sailed into the window, described a number of fiendish circles in the room, knocked over the light, slapped the baby's face, 'took' him (the subscriber) 'in the jaw,' and then returned out of the window, and dropped helplessly in the area. During the rest of the day wads and strips of soiled paper, purporting to be copies of the 'Northern Star' of that morning's issue, were brought indignantly to the office. An admirable editorial on 'The Resources of Humboldt County,' which I had constructed the evening before, and which, I have reason to believe, might have changed the whole balance of trade during the ensuing year, and left San Francisco bankrupt at her wharves, was in this way lost to the public.

It was deemed advisable for the next three weeks to keep Wan Lee closely confined to the printing-office and the purely mechanical part of the business. Here he developed a surprising quickness and adaptability, winning even the favor and good will of the printers and foreman, who at first looked upon his introduction into the secrets of their trade as fraught with the gravest political significance. He learned to set type readily and neatly, his wonderful skill in manipulation aiding him in the mere mechanical act, and his ignorance of the language confining him simply to the mechanical effort—confirming the printer's axiom that the printer who considers or follows the ideas of his copy makes a poor compositor. He would set up deliberately long diatribes against himself, composed by his fellow printers, and hung on his hook as copy, and even such short sentences as 'Wan Lee is the devil's own imp,' 'Wan Lee is a Mongolian rascal,' and bring the proof to me with happiness beaming from every tooth and satisfaction shining in his huckleberry eyes.

It was not long, however, before he learned to retaliate on his mischievous persecutors. I remember one instance in which his reprisal came very near involving me in a serious misunderstanding. Our foreman's name was Webster, and Wan Lee presently learned to know and recognize the individual and combined letters of his name. It was during a political campaign, and the eloquent and fiery Colonel Starbottle of Siskiyou had delivered an effective speech, which was reported especially for the 'Northern Star.' In a very sublime peroration Colonel Starbottle had said, 'In the language of the godlike Webster,* I repeat'—and here followed the quotation, which I have forgotten. Now, it chanced that Wan Lee, looking over the galley after it had been revised, saw the name of his chief persecutor, and, of course, imagined the quotation his. After the form was locked up, Wan Lee took advantage of Webster's absence to remove the quotation, and substitute a thin piece of lead, of the same size as the type, engraved with Chinese characters, making a sentence which, I had reason to believe, was an utter and abject confession of the incapacity and offensiveness of the Webster family generally, and exceedingly eulogistic of Wan Lee himself personally.

The next morning's paper contained Colonel Starbottle's speech in full, in which it appeared that the 'godlike' Webster had on one occasion uttered his thoughts in excellent but perfectly enigmatical Chinese. The rage of Colonel Starbottle knew no bounds. I have a vivid recollection of that admirable man walking into my office and demanding a retraction of the statement.

'But, my dear sir,' I asked, 'are you willing to deny, over your own signature, that Webster ever uttered such a sentence? Dare you deny that, with Mr Webster's well-known attainments, a knowledge of Chinese might not have been among the number?

Are you willing to submit a translation suitable to the capacity of our readers, and deny, upon your honor as a gentleman, that the late Mr Webster ever uttered such a sentiment? If you are, sir, I am willing to publish your denial.'

The Colonel was not, and left, highly indignant.

Webster, the foreman, took it more coolly. Happily he was unaware that for two days after, Chinamen from the laundries, from the gulches, from the kitchens, looked in the front office door with faces beaming with sardonic delight; that three hundred extra copies of the 'Star' were ordered for the wash-houses on the river. He only knew that during the day Wan Lee occasionally went off into convulsive spasms, and that he was obliged to kick him into consciousness again. A week after the occurrence I called Wan Lee into my office.

'Wan,' I said gravely, 'I should like you to give me, for my own personal satisfaction, a translation of that Chinese sentence which my gifted countryman, the late godlike Webster, uttered upon a public occasion.' Wan Lee looked at me intently, and then the slightest possible twinkle crept into his black eyes. Then he replied, with equal gravity,—

'Mishtel Webstel,—he say: "China boy makee me belly much foolee. China boy makee me heap sick." ' Which I have reason to think was true.

But I fear I am giving but one side, and not the best, of Wan Lee's character. As he imparted it to me, his had been a hard life. He had known scarcely any childhood—he had no recollection of a father or mother. The conjurer Wang had brought him up. He had spent the first seven years of his life in appearing from baskets, in dropping out of hats, in climbing ladders, in putting his little limbs out of joint in posturing. He had lived in an atmosphere of trickery and deception; he had learned to look upon mankind as dupes of their senses; in fine, if he had thought at all, he would have been a skeptic; if he had been a little older, he would have been a cynic; if he had been older still, he would have been a philosopher. As it was, he was a little imp! A good-natured imp it was, too,—an imp whose moral nature had never been awakened, an imp up for a holiday, and willing to try virtue as a diversion. I don't know that he had any spiritual nature; he was very superstitious; he carried about with him a hideous little porcelain god, which he was in the habit of alternately reviling and propitiating. He was too intelligent for the commoner Chinese vices of stealing or gratuitous lying. Whatever discipline he practiced was taught by his intellect.

I am inclined to think that his feelings were not altogether unimpressible,—although it was almost impossible to extract an expression from him,—and I conscientiously believe he became attached to those that were good to him. What he might have become under more favorable conditions than the bondsman of an overworked, underpaid literary man, I don't know; I only know that the scant, irregular, impulsive kindnesses that I showed him were gratefully received. He was very loyal and patient—two qualities rare in the average American servant. He was like Malvolio,* 'sad and civil' with me; only once, and then under great provocation, do I remember of his exhibiting any impatience. It was my habit, after leaving the office at night, to take him with me to my rooms, as the bearer of any supplemental or happy afterthought in the editorial way, that might occur to me before the paper went to press. One night I had been scribbling away past the usual hour of dismissing Wan Lee, and had become quite oblivious of his presence in a chair near my door, when suddenly I became aware of a voice saying, in plaintive accents, something that sounded like 'Chy Lee.'

I faced around sternly.

'What did you say?'

'Me say, "Chy Lee." '

'Well?' I said impatiently.

'You sabe, "How do, John"?'

'Yes.'

'You sabe, "So long, John"?'

'Yes.'

'Well, "Chy Lee" allee same!'

I understood him quite plainly. It appeared that 'Chy Lee' was a form of 'good-night,' and that Wan Lee was anxious to go home. But an instinct of mischief which I fear I possessed in common with him, impelled me to act as if oblivious of the hint. I muttered something about not understanding him, and again bent over my work. In a few minutes I heard his wooden shoes pattering pathetically over the floor. I looked up. He was standing near the door.

'You no sabe, "Chy Lee"?'

'No,' I said sternly.

'You sabe muchee big foolee!—allee same!'

And with this audacity upon his lips he fled. The next morning, however, he was as meek and patient as before, and I did not recall his offense. As a probable peace-offering, he blacked all my boots,—a duty never required of him,—including a pair of buff deerskin slippers and an immense pair of horseman's jack-boots, on which he indulged his remorse for two hours.

I have spoken of his honesty as being a quality of his intellect rather than his principle, but I recall about this time two exceptions to the rule. I was anxious to get some fresh eggs, as a change to the heavy diet of a mining town, and knowing that Wan Lee's countrymen were great poultry-raisers, I applied to him. He furnished me with them regularly every morning, but refused to take any pay, saying that the man did not sell them,—a remarkable instance of self-abnegation, as eggs were then worth half a dollar apiece. One morning, my neighbor, Foster, dropped in upon me at breakfast, and took occasion to bewail his own ill fortune, as his hens had lately stopped laying, or wandered off in the bush. Wan Lee, who was present during our colloquy, preserved his characteristic sad taciturnity. When my neighbor had gone, he turned to me with a slight chuckle—'Flostel's hens—Wan Lee's hens—allee same!' His other offense was more serious and ambitious. It was a season of great irregularities in the mails, and Wan Lee had heard me deplore the delay in the delivery of my letters and newspapers. On arriving at my office one day, I was amazed to find my table covered with letters, evidently just from the post-office, but unfortunately not one addressed to me. I turned to Wan Lee, who was surveying them with a calm satisfaction, and demanded an explanation. To my horror he pointed to an empty mail-bag in the corner, and said, 'Postman he say, "No lettee, John—no lettee, John." Postman plentee lie! Postman no good. Me catchee lettee last night—allee same!' Luckily it was still early; the mails had not been distributed; I had a hurried interview with the postmaster, and Wan Lee's bold attempt at robbing the U.S. Mail was finally condoned, by the purchase of a new mail-bag, and the whole affair thus kept a secret.

If my liking for my little pagan page had not been sufficient, my duty to Hop Sing was enough to cause me to take Wan Lee with me when I returned to San Francisco, after my two years' experience with the 'Northern Star.' I do not think he contemplated the change with pleasure. I attributed his feelings to a nervous dread of crowded public streets—when he had to go across town for me on an errand, he always made a long circuit of the outskirts; to his dislike for the discipline of the Chinese and English school to which I proposed to send him; to his fondness for the free, vagrant life of the mines; to sheer willfulness! That it might have been a superstitious premonition did not occur to me until long after.

Nevertheless it really seemed as if the opportunity I had long looked for and confidently expected had come,—the opportunity of placing Wan Lee under gently restraining influences, of subjecting him to a life and experience that would draw out of him what good my superficial care and ill-regulated kindness could not reach. Wan Lee was placed at the school of a Chinese missionary,—an intelligent and kind-hearted clergyman, who had shown great interest in the boy, and who, better than all, had a wonderful faith in him. A home was found for him in the family of a widow, who had a bright and interesting daughter about two years younger than Wan Lee. It was this bright, cheery, innocent, and artless child that touched and reached a depth in the boy's nature that hitherto had been unsuspected— that awakened a moral susceptibility which had lain for years insensible alike to the teachings of society or the ethics of the theologian.

These few brief months, bright with a promise that we never saw fulfilled, must have been happy ones to Wan Lee. He worshiped his little friend with something of the same superstition, but without any of the caprice, that he bestowed upon his porcelain Pagan god. It was his delight to walk behind her to school, carrying her books,—a service always fraught with danger to him from the little hands of his Caucasian Christian brothers. He made her the most marvelous toys; he would cut out of carrots and turnips the most astonishing roses and tulips; he made lifelike chickens out of melon-seeds; he constructed fans and kites, and was singularly proficient in the making of dolls' paper dresses. On the other hand she played and sang to him; taught him a thousand little prettinesses and refinements only known to girls; gave him a yellow ribbon for his pigtail, as best suiting his complexion; read to him; showed him wherein he was original and valuable; took him to Sunday-school with her, against the precedents of the school, and, small-womanlike, triumphed. I wish I could add here, that she effected his conversion, and made him give up his porcelain idol, but I am telling a true story, and this little girl was quite content to fill him with her own Christian goodness, without letting him know that he was changed. So they got along very well together—this little Christian girl, with her shining cross hanging around her plump, white, little neck, and this dark little Pagan, with his hideous porcelain god hidden away in his blouse.

There were two days of that eventful year which will long be remembered in San Francisco,—two days when a mob of her citizens set upon and killed unarmed, defenseless foreigners, because they were foreigners and of another race, religion, and color, and worked for what wages they could get. There were some public men so timid that, seeing this, they thought that the end of the world had come; there were some eminent statesmen, whose names I am ashamed to write here, who began to think that the passage in the Constitution which guarantees civil and religious liberty to every citizen or foreigner was a mistake. But there were also some men who were not so easily frightened, and in twenty-four hours we had things so arranged that the timid men could wring their hands in safety, and the eminent statesmen utter their doubts without hurting anybody or anything. And in the midst of this I got a note from Hop Sing, asking me to come to him immediately.

I found his warehouse closed and strongly guarded by the police against any possible attack of the rioters. Hop Sing admitted me through a barred grating with his usual imperturbable calm, but, as it seemed to me, with more than his usual seriousness. Without a word he took my hand and led me to the rear of the room, and thence downstairs into the basement. It was dimly lighted, but there was something lying on the floor covered by a shawl. As I approached, he drew the shawl away with a sudden gesture, and revealed Wan Lee, the Pagan, lying there dead!

Dead, my reverend friends, dead! Stoned to death in the streets of San Francisco, in the year of grace, eighteen hundred and sixty-nine, by a mob of half-grown boys and Christian school-children!

As I put my hand reverently upon his breast, I felt something crumbling beneath his blouse. I looked inquiringly at Hop Sing. He put his hand between the folds of silk, and drew out something with the first bitter smile I had ever seen on the face of that Pagan gentleman.

It was Wan Lee's porcelain god, crushed by a stone from the hands of those Christian iconoclasts!

A PASSAGE IN THE LIFE OF
MR JOHN OAKHURST

HE always thought it must have been Fate. Certainly nothing could have been more inconsistent with his habits than to have been in the Plaza at seven o'clock of that midsummer morning. The sight of his colorless face in Sacramento was rare at that season, and indeed at any season, anywhere, publicly, before two o'clock in the afternoon. Looking back upon it in after years, in the light of a chanceful life, he determined, with the characteristic philosophy of his profession, that it must have been Fate.

Yet it is my duty, as a strict chronicler of facts, to state that Mr Oakhurst's presence there that morning was due to a very simple cause. At exactly half past six, the bank being then a winner to the amount of twenty thousand dollars, he had risen from the faro-table, relinquished his seat to an accomplished assistant, and withdrawn quietly, without attracting a glance from the silent, anxious faces bowed over the table. But when he entered his luxurious sleeping-room, across the passageway, he was a little shocked at finding the sun streaming through an inadvertently opened window. Something in the rare beauty of the morning, perhaps something in the novelty of the idea, struck him as he was about to close the blinds, and he hesitated. Then, taking his hat from the table, he stepped down a private staircase into the street.

The people who were abroad at that early hour were of a class quite unknown to Mr Oakhurst. There were milkmen and hucksters delivering their wares, small tradespeople opening their shops, housemaids sweeping doorsteps, and occasionally a child. These Mr Oakhurst regarded with a certain cold curiosity, perhaps quite free from the cynical disfavor with which he generally looked upon the more pretentious of his race whom he was in the habit of meeting. Indeed, I think he was not altogether displeased with the admiring glances which these humble women threw after his handsome face and figure, conspicuous even in a country of fine-looking men. While it is very probable that this wicked vagabond, in the pride of his social isolation, would have been coldly indifferent to the advances of a fine lady, a little girl who ran admiringly by his side in a ragged dress had the power to call a faint flush into his colorless cheek. He dismissed her at last, but not until she had found out—what sooner or later her large-hearted and discriminating sex inevitably did—that he was exceedingly free and open-handed with his money, and also—what perhaps none other of her sex ever did—that the bold black eyes of this fine gentleman were in reality of a brownish and even tender gray.

There was a small garden before a white cottage in a side-street that attracted Mr Oakhurst's attention. It was filled with roses, heliotrope, and verbena,—flowers familiar enough to him in the expensive and more portable form of bouquets, but, as it seemed to him then, never before so notably lovely. Perhaps it was because the dew was yet fresh upon them, perhaps it was because they were unplucked, but Mr Oakhurst admired them, not as a possible future tribute to the fascinating and accomplished Miss Ethelinda, then performing at the Varieties, for Mr Oakhurst's especial benefit, as she had often assured him; nor yet as a *douceur* * to the enthralling Miss Montmorrissy, with whom Mr Oakhurst expected to sup that evening, but simply for himself, and mayhap for the flowers' sake. Howbeit, he passed on, and so out into the open plaza, where, finding a bench under a cottonwood-tree, he first dusted the seat with his handkerchief, and then sat down.

It was a fine morning. The air was so still and calm that a sigh from the sycamores seemed like the deep-drawn breath of the just awakening tree, and the faint rustle of its boughs as the outstretching of cramped and reviving limbs. Far away the Sierras stood out against a sky so remote as to be of no positive color,—so remote that even the sun despaired of ever reaching it, and so expended its strength recklessly on the whole landscape, until it fairly glittered in a white and vivid contrast. With a very rare impulse, Mr Oakhurst took off his hat, and half reclined on the bench, with his face to the sky. Certain birds who had taken a critical attitude on a spray above him apparently began an animated discussion regarding his possible malevolent intentions. One or two, emboldened by the silence, hopped on the ground at his feet, until the sound of wheels on the gravel walk frightened them away.

Looking up, he saw a man coming slowly towards him, wheeling a nondescript vehicle in which a woman was partly sitting, partly reclining. Without knowing why, Mr Oakhurst instantly conceived that the carriage was the invention and workmanship of the man, partly from its oddity, partly from the strong, mechanical hand that grasped it, and partly from a certain pride and visible consciousness in the manner in which the man handled it. Then Mr Oakhurst saw something more,— the man's face was familiar. With that regal faculty of not forgetting a face that had ever given him professional audience, he instantly classified it under the following mental formula: 'At 'Frisco, Polka Saloon. Lost his week's wages. I reckon seventy dollars—on red. Never came again.' There was, however, no trace of this in the calm eyes and unmoved face that he turned upon the stranger, who, on the contrary, blushed, looked embarrassed, hesitated, and then stopped with an involuntary motion that brought the carriage and its fair occupant face to face with Mr Oakhurst.

I should hardly do justice to the position she will occupy in this veracious chronicle by describing the lady now—if, indeed, I am able to do it at all. Certainly, the popular estimate was conflicting. The late Colonel Starbottle—to whose large experience of a charming sex I have before been indebted for many valuable suggestions—had, I regret to say, depreciated her fascinations. 'A yellow-faced cripple, by dash—a sick woman, with mahogany eyes. One of your blanked spiritual creatures, with no flesh on her bones.' On the other hand, however, she enjoyed later much complimentary disparagement from her own sex. Miss Celestina Howard, second leader in the ballet at the Varieties, had, with great alliterative directness, in after years, denominated her as an 'aquiline asp.' Mlle Brimborion remembered that she had always warned 'Mr Jack' that this woman would 'empoison' him. But Mr Oakhurst, whose impressions are perhaps the most important, only saw a pale, thin, deep-eyed woman, raised above the level of her companion by the refinement of long suffering and isolation, and a certain shy virginity of manner. There was a suggestion of physical purity in the folds of her fresh-looking robe, and a certain picturesque tastefulness in the details, that, without knowing why, made him think that the robe was her invention and handiwork, even as the carriage she occupied was evidently the work of her companion. Her own hand, a trifle too thin, but well-shaped, subtle-fingered, and gentlewomanly, rested on the side of the carriage, the counterpart of the strong mechanical grasp of her companion's.

There was some obstruction to the progress of the vehicle, and Mr Oakhurst stepped forward to assist. While the wheel was being lifted over the curbstone, it was necessary that she should hold his arm, and for a moment her thin hand rested there, light and cold as a snowflake, and then—as it seemed to him—like a snowflake melted away. Then there was a pause, and then conversation—the lady joining occasionally and shyly.

It appeared that they were man and wife. That for the past two years she had been a great invalid, and had lost the use of her lower limbs from rheumatism. That until lately she had been confined to her bed, until her husband—who was a master carpenter—had bethought himself to make her this carriage. He took her out regularly for an airing before going to work, because it was his only time, and—they attracted less attention. They had tried many doctors, but without avail. They had been advised to go to the Sulphur Springs, but it was expensive. Mr Decker, the husband, had once saved eighty dollars for that purpose, but while in San Francisco had his pocket picked—Mr Decker was so senseless. (The intelligent reader need not be told that it is the lady who is speaking.) They had never been able to make up the sum again, and they had given up the idea. It was a dreadful thing to have one's pocket picked. Did he not think so?

Her husband's face was crimson, but Mr Oakhurst's countenance was quite calm and unmoved, as he gravely agreed with her, and walked by her side until they passed the little garden that he had admired. Here Mr Oakhurst commanded a halt, and, going to the door, astounded the proprietor by a preposterously extravagant offer for a choice of the flowers. Presently he returned to the carriage with his arms full of roses, heliotrope, and verbena, and cast them in the lap of the invalid.

While she was bending over them with childish delight, Mr Oakhurst took the opportunity of drawing her husband aside.

'Perhaps,' he said in a low voice, and a manner quite free from any personal annoyance,—'perhaps it's just as well that you lied to her as you did. You can say now that the pickpocket was arrested the other day, and you got your money back.' Mr Oakhurst quietly slipped four twenty-dollar gold-pieces into the broad hand of the bewildered Mr Decker. 'Say that—or anything you like—but the truth. Promise me you won't say that!'

The man promised. Mr Oakhurst quietly returned to the front of the little carriage. The sick woman was still eagerly occupied with the flowers, and as she raised her eyes to his, her faded cheek seemed to have caught some color from the roses, and her eyes some of their dewy freshness. But at that instant Mr Oakhurst lifted his hat, and before she could thank him was gone.

I grieve to say that Mr Decker shamelessly broke his promise. That night, in the very goodness of his heart and uxorious self-abnegation, he, like all devoted husbands, not only offered himself, but his friend and benefactor, as a sacrifice on the family altar. It is only fair, however, to add that he spoke with great fervor of the generosity of Mr Oakhurst, and dealt with an enthusiasm quite common with his class on the mysterious fame and prodigal vices of the gambler.

'And now, Elsie, dear, say that you'll forgive me,' said Mr Decker, dropping on one knee beside his wife's couch. 'I did it for the best. It was for you, dearey, that I put that money on them cards that night in 'Frisco. I thought to win a heap,—enough to take you away, and enough left to get you a new dress.'

Mrs Decker smiled and pressed her husband's hand. 'I do forgive you, Joe, dear,' she said, still smiling, with eyes abstractedly fixed on the ceiling; 'and you ought to be whipped for deceiving me so, you bad boy, and making me make such a speech. There, say no more about it. If you'll be very good hereafter, and will just now hand me that cluster of roses, I'll forgive you.' She took the branch in her fingers, lifted the roses to her face, and presently said, behind their leaves,—

'Joe!'

'What is it, lovey?'

'Do you think that this Mr—what do you call him?—Jack Oakhurst would have given that money back to you if I hadn't made that speech?'

'Yes.'

'If he hadn't seen me at all?'

Mr Decker looked up. His wife had managed in some way to cover up her whole face with the roses, except her eyes, which were dangerously bright.

'No; it was you, Elsie—it was all along of seeing you that made him do it.'

'A poor sick woman like me?'

'A sweet, little, lovely, pooty Elsie—Joe's own little wifey! How could he help it?'

Mrs Decker fondly cast one arm around her husband's neck, still keeping the roses to her face with the other. From behind them she began to murmur gently and idiotically, 'Dear, ole square Joey. Elsie's oney booful big bear.' But, really, I do not see that my duty as a chronicler of facts compels me to continue this little lady's speech any further, and out of respect to the unmarried reader I stop.

Nevertheless, the next morning Mrs Decker betrayed some slight and apparently uncalled-for irritability on reaching the plaza, and presently desired her husband to wheel her back home. Moreover, she was very much astonished at meeting Mr Oakhurst just as they were returning, and even doubted if it were he, and questioned her husband as to his identity with the stranger of yesterday as he approached. Her manner to Mr Oakhurst, also, was quite in contrast with her husband's frank welcome. Mr Oakhurst instantly detected it. 'Her husband has told her all, and she dislikes me,' he said to himself, with that fatal appreciation of the half-truths of a woman's motives that causes the wisest masculine critic to stumble. He lingered only long enough to take the business address of the husband, and then, lifting his hat gravely, without looking at the lady, went his way. It struck the honest master carpenter as one of the charming anomalies of his wife's character that, although the meeting was evidently very much constrained and unpleasant, instantly afterward his wife's spirits began to rise. 'You was hard on him—a leetle hard, wasn't you, Elsie?' said Mr Decker deprecatingly. 'I'm afraid he may think I've broke my promise.' 'Ah, indeed,' said the lady indifferently. Mr Decker instantly stepped round to the front of the vehicle. 'You look like an A I first-class lady riding down Broadway in her own carriage, Elsie,' said he; 'I never seed you lookin' so peart and sassy before.'

A few days later the proprietor of the San Isabel Sulphur Springs received the following note in Mr Oakhurst's well-known dainty hand:—

DEAR STEVE,—I've been thinking over your proposition to buy Nichols's quarter interest and have concluded to go in. But I don't see how the thing will pay until you have more accommodation down there, and for the best class—I mean *my* customers. What we want is an extension to the main building, and two or three cottages put up. I send down a builder to take hold of the job at once. He takes his sick wife with him, and you are to look after them as you would for one of us.

I may run down there myself, after the races, just to look after things; but I sha'n't set upon any game this season.

Yours always,
JOHN OAKHURST.

It was only the last sentence of this letter that provoked criticism. 'I can understand,' said Mr Hamlin, a professional brother, to whom Mr Oakhurst's letter was shown,—'I can understand why Jack goes in heavy and builds, for it's a sure spec, and is bound to be a mighty soft thing in time, if he comes here regularly. But why in blank he don't set up a bank this season and take the chance of getting some of the money back that he puts into circulation in building, is what gets me. I wonder now,' he mused deeply, 'what *is* his little game.'

The season had been a prosperous one to Mr Oakhurst, and proportionally disastrous to several members of the Legislature, judges, colonels, and others who had enjoyed but briefly the pleasure of Mr Oakhurst's midnight society. And yet Sacramento had become very dull to him. He had lately formed a habit of early morning walks,—so unusual and startling to his friends, both male and female, as to occasion the intensest curiosity. Two or three of the latter set spies upon his track, but the inquisition resulted only in the discovery that Mr Oakhurst walked to the plaza, sat down upon one particular bench for a few moments, and then returned without seeing anybody, and the theory that there was a woman in the case was abandoned. A few superstitious gentlemen of his own profession believed that he did it for 'luck.' Some others, more practical, declared that he went out to 'study points.'

After the races at Marysville, Mr Oakhurst went to San Francisco; from that place he returned to Marysville, but a few days after was seen at San José, Santa Cruz, and Oakland. Those who met him declared that his manner was restless and feverish, and quite unlike his ordinary calmness and phlegm. Colonel Starbottle pointed out the fact that at San Francisco, at the Club, Jack had declined to deal. 'Hand shaky, sir—depend upon it; don't stimulate enough—blank him!'

From San José he started to go to Oregon by land with a rather expensive outfit of horses and camp equipage, but on reaching Stockton he suddenly diverged, and four hours later found him, with a single horse, entering the cañon of the San Isabel Warm Sulphur Springs.

It was a pretty triangular valley lying at the foot of three sloping mountains, dark with pines and fantastic with madroño and manzanita. Nestling against the mountain-side, the straggling buildings and long piazza of the hotel glittered through the leaves; and here and there shone a white toy-like cottage. Mr Oakhurst was not an admirer of nature, but he felt something of the same novel satisfaction in the view that he experienced in his first morning walk in Sacramento. And now carriages began to pass him on the road filled with gayly dressed women, and the cold California outlines of the landscape began to take upon themselves somewhat of a human warmth and color. And then the long hotel piazza came in view, efflorescent with the full-toileted fair. Mr Oakhurst, a good rider after the California fashion, did not check his speed as he approached his destination, but charged the hotel at a gallop, threw his horse on his haunches within a foot of the piazza, and then quietly emerged from the cloud of dust that veiled his dismounting.

Whatever feverish excitement might have raged within, all his habitual calm returned as he stepped upon the piazza. With the instinct of long habit he turned and faced the battery of eyes with the same cold indifference with which he had for years encountered the half-hidden sneers of men and the half-frightened admiration of women. Only one person stepped forward to welcome him. Oddly enough, it was Dick Hamilton, perhaps the only one present who, by birth, education, and position, might have satisfied the most fastidious social critic. Happily for Mr Oakhurst's reputation, he was also a very rich banker and social leader. 'Do you know who that is you spoke to?' asked young Parker, with an alarmed expression. 'Yes,' replied Hamilton, with characteristic effrontery; 'the man you lost a thousand dollars to last week. *I* only know him *socially*.' 'But isn't he a gambler?' queried the youngest Miss Smith. 'He is,' replied Hamilton; 'but I wish, my dear young lady, that we all played as open and honest a game as our friend yonder, and were as willing as he is to abide by its fortunes.'

But Mr Oakhurst was happily out of hearing of this colloquy, and was even then lounging listlessly, yet watchfully, along the upper hall. Suddenly he heard a light footstep behind him, and then his name called in a familiar voice that drew the blood quickly to his heart. He turned, and she stood before him.

But how transformed! If I have hesitated to describe the hollow-eyed cripple,—the quaintly dressed artisan's wife, a few pages ago,—what shall I do with this graceful, shapely, elegantly attired gentlewoman into whom she has been merged within these two months? In good faith, she was very pretty. You and I, my dear madam, would have been quick to see that those charming dimples were misplaced for true beauty, and too fixed in their quality for honest mirthfulness; that the delicate lines around those aquiline nostrils were cruel and selfish; that the sweet, virginal surprise of those lovely eyes was as apt to be opened on her plate as upon the gallant speeches of her dinner partner; that her sympathetic color came and went more with her own spirits than yours. But you and I are not in love with her, dear madam, and Mr Oakhurst is. And even in the folds of her Parisian gown, I am afraid this poor fellow saw the same subtle strokes of purity that he had seen in her homespun robe.

And then there was the delightful revelation that she could walk, and that she had dear little feet of her own in the tiniest slippers of her French shoemaker, with such preposterous blue bows, and Chappell's own stamp, Rue de something or other, Paris, on the narrow sole.

He ran towards her with a heightened color and outstretched hands. But she whipped her own behind her, glanced rapidly up and down the long hall, and stood looking at him with a half-audacious, half-mischievous admiration in utter contrast to her old reserve.

'I've a great mind not to shake hands with you at all. You passed me just now on the piazza without speaking, and I ran after you, as I suppose many another poor woman has done.'

Mr Oakhurst stammered that she was so changed.

'The more reason why you should know me. Who changed me? You. You have re-created me. You found a helpless, crippled, sick, poverty-stricken woman, with one dress to her back, and that her own make, and you gave her life, health, strength, and fortune. You did, and you know it, sir. How do you like your work?' She caught the side seams of her gown in either hand and dropped him a playful courtesy. Then, with a sudden, relenting gesture, she gave him both her hands.

Outrageous as this speech was, and unfeminine, as I trust every fair reader will deem it, I fear it pleased Mr Oakhurst. Not but that he was accustomed to a certain frank female admiration; but then it was of the *coulisses** and not of the cloister, with which he always persisted in associating Mrs Decker. To be addressed in this way by an invalid Puritan, a sick saint, with the austerity of suffering still clothing her,—a woman who had a Bible on the dressing-table, who went to church three times a day, and was devoted to her husband, completely bowled him over. He still held her hands as she went on,—

'Why didn't you come before? What were you doing in Marysville, in San José, in Oakland? You see I have followed you. I saw you as you came down the cañon, and knew you at once. I saw your letter to Joseph, and knew you were coming. Why didn't you write to me? You will some time! Good-evening, Mr Hamilton.'

She had withdrawn her hands, but not until Hamilton, ascending the staircase, was nearly abreast of them. He raised his hat to her with well-bred composure, nodded familiarly to Oakhurst, and passed on. When he had gone Mrs Decker lifted her eyes to Mr Oakhurst. 'Some day I shall ask a great favor of you!'

Mr Oakhurst begged that it should be now. 'No, not until you know me better. Then, some day, I shall want you to—kill that man!'

She laughed, such a pleasant little ringing laugh, such a display of dimples,—albeit a little fixed in the corners of her mouth,—such an innocent light in her brown eyes, and such a lovely color in her cheeks, that Mr Oakhurst—who seldom laughed—was fain to laugh too. It was as if a lamb had proposed to a fox a foray into a neighboring sheepfold.

A few evenings after this, Mrs Decker arose from a charmed circle of her admirers on the hotel piazza, excused herself for a few moments, laughingly declined an escort, and ran over to her little cottage—one of her husband's creation—across the road. Perhaps from the sudden and unwonted exercise in her still convalescent state, she breathed hurriedly and feverishly as she entered her boudoir, and once or twice placed her hand upon her breast. She was startled on turning up the light to find her husband lying on the sofa.

'You look hot and excited, Elsie, love,' said Mr Decker; 'you ain't took worse, are you?'

Mrs Decker's face had paled, but now flushed again. 'No,' she said, 'only a little pain here,' as she again placed her hand upon her corsage.

'Can I do anything for you?' said Mr Decker, rising with affectionate concern.

'Run over to the hotel and get me some brandy, quick!'

Mr Decker ran. Mrs Decker closed and bolted the door, and then putting her hand to her bosom, drew out the pain. It was folded foursquare, and was, I grieve to say, in Mr Oakhurst's handwriting.

She devoured it with burning eyes and cheeks until there came a step upon the porch. Then she hurriedly replaced it in her bosom and unbolted the door. Her husband entered; she raised the spirits to her lips and declared herself better.

'Are you going over there again to-night?' asked Mr Decker submissively.

'No,' said Mrs Decker, with her eyes fixed dreamily on the floor.

'I wouldn't if I was you,' said Mr Decker with a sigh of relief. After a pause he took a seat on the sofa, and drawing his wife to his side, said, 'Do you know what I was thinking of when you came in, Elsie?' Mrs Decker ran her fingers through his stiff black hair, and couldn't imagine.

'I was thinking of old times, Elsie; I was thinking of the days when I built that kerridge for you, Elsie—when I used to take you out to ride, and was both hoss and driver! We was poor then, and you was sick, Elsie, but we was happy. We've got money now, and a house, and you're quite another woman. I may say, dear, that you're a *new* woman. And that's where the trouble comes in. I could build you a kerridge, Elsie; I could build you a house, Elsie—but there I stopped. I couldn't build up *you*. You're strong and pretty, Elsie, and fresh and new. But somehow, Elsie, you ain't no work of mine!'

He paused. With one hand laid gently on his forehead and the other pressed upon her bosom as if to feel certain of the presence of her pain, she said sweetly and soothingly:—

'But it was your work, dear.'

Mr Decker shook his head sorrowfully. 'No, Elsie, not mine. I had the chance to do it once and I let it go. It's done now; but not by me.'

Mrs Decker raised her surprised, innocent eyes to his. He kissed her tenderly, and then went on in a more cheerful voice.

'That ain't all I was thinking of, Elsie. I was thinking that maybe you give too much of your company to that Mr Hamilton. Not that there's any wrong in it, to you or him. But it might make people talk. You're the only one here, Elsie,' said the master carpenter, looking fondly at his wife, 'who isn't talked about; whose work ain't inspected or condemned.'

Mrs Decker was glad he had spoken about it. She had thought so, too, but she could not well be uncivil to Mr Hamilton, who was a fine gentleman, without making a powerful enemy. 'And he's always treated me as if I was a born lady in his own circle,' added the little woman, with a certain pride that made her husband fondly smile. 'But I have thought of a plan. He will not stay here if I should go away. If, for instance, I went to San Francisco to visit ma for a few days, he would be gone before I should return.'

Mr Decker was delighted. 'By all means,' he said; 'go to-morrow. Jack Oakhurst is going down, and I 'll put you in his charge.'

Mrs Decker did not think it was prudent. 'Mr Oakhurst is our friend, Joseph, but you know his reputation.' In fact, she did not know that she ought to go now, knowing that he was going the same day; but with a kiss Mr Decker overcame her scruples. She yielded gracefully. Few women, in fact, knew how to give up a point as charmingly as she.

She stayed a week in San Francisco. When she returned she was a trifle thinner and paler than she had been. This she explained as the result of perhaps too active exercise and excitement. 'I was out of doors nearly all the time, as ma will tell you,' she said to her husband, 'and always alone. I am getting quite independent now,' she added gayly. 'I don't want any escort—I believe, Joey dear, I could get along even without you—I'm so brave!'

But her visit, apparently, had not been productive of her impelling design. Mr Hamilton had not gone, but had remained, and called upon them that very evening. 'I've thought of a plan, Joey, dear,' said Mrs Decker when he had departed. 'Poor Mr Oakhurst has a miserable room at the hotel—suppose you ask him when he returns from San Francisco to stop with us. He can have our spare room. I don't think,' she added archly, 'that Mr Hamilton will call often.' Her husband laughed, intimated that she was a little coquette, pinched her cheek, and complied. 'The queer thing about a woman,' he said afterwards confidentially to Mr Oakhurst, 'is, that without having any plan of her own, she 'll take anybody's and build a house on it entirely different to suit herself. And dern my skin, if you'll be able to say whether or not you didn't give the scale and measurements yourself. That's what gets me.'

The next week Mr Oakhurst was installed in the Deckers' cottage. The business relations of her husband and himself were known to all, and her own reputation was above suspicion. Indeed, few women were more popular. She was domestic, she was prudent, she was pious. In a country of great feminine freedom and latitude, she never rode or walked with anybody but her husband; in an epoch of slang and ambiguous expression, she was always precise and formal in her speech; in the midst of a fashion of ostentatious decoration she never wore a diamond, nor a single valuable jewel. She never permitted an indecorum in public; she never countenanced the familiarities of California society. She declaimed against the prevailing tone of infidelity and skepticism in religion. Few people who were present will ever forget the dignified yet stately manner with which she rebuked Mr Hamilton in the public parlor for entering upon the discussion of a work on materialism, lately published; and some among them, also, will not forget the expression of amused surprise on Mr Hamilton's face, that gradually changed to sardonic gravity as he courteously waived his point. Certainly, not Mr Oakhurst, who from that moment began to be uneasily impatient of his friend, and even—if such a term could be applied to any moral quality in Mr Oakhurst—to fear him.

For, during this time, Mr Oakhurst had begun to show symptoms of a change in his usual habits. He was seldom, if ever, seen in his old haunts, in a bar-room, or with his old associates. Pink and white notes, in distracted handwriting, accumulated on the dressing-table in his rooms at Sacramento. It was given out in San Francisco that he had some organic disease of the heart, for which his physician had prescribed perfect rest. He read more, he took long walks, he sold his fast horses, he went to church.

I have a very vivid recollection of his first appearance there. He did not accompany the Deckers, nor did he go into their pew, but came in as the service commenced, and took a seat quietly in one of the back pews. By some mysterious instinct his presence became presently known to the congregation, some of whom so far forgot themselves, in their curiosity, as to face around and apparently address their responses to him. Before the service was over it was pretty well understood that 'miserable sinners' meant Mr Oakhurst. Nor did this mysterious influence fail to affect the officiating clergyman, who introduced an allusion to Mr Oakhurst's calling and habits in a sermon on the architecture of Solomon's Temple, and in a manner so pointed and yet labored as to cause the youngest of us to flame with indignation. Happily, however, it was lost upon Jack; I do not think he even heard it. His handsome, colorless face—albeit a trifle worn and thoughtful—was inscrutable. Only once, during the singing of a hymn, at a certain note in the contralto's voice, there crept into his dark eyes a look of wistful tenderness, so yearning and yet so hopeless that those who were watching him felt their own glisten. Yet I retain a very vivid remembrance of his standing up to receive the benediction, with the suggestion, in his manner and tightly buttoned coat, of taking the fire of his adversary at ten paces. After church he disappeared as quietly as he had entered, and fortunately escaped hearing the comments on his rash act. His appearance was generally considered as an impertinence—attributable only to some wanton fancy—or possibly a bet. One or two thought that the sexton was exceedingly remiss in not turning him out after discovering who he was; and a prominent pewholder remarked that if he couldn't take his wife and daughters to that church without exposing them to such an influence, he would try to find some church where he could. Another traced Mr Oakhurst's presence to certain Broad Church radical tendencies, which he regretted to say he had lately noted in their pastor. Deacon Sawyer, whose delicately organized, sickly wife had already borne him eleven children, and died in an ambitious attempt to complete the dozen, avowed that the presence of a person of Mr Oakhurst's various and indiscriminate gallantries was an insult to the memory of the deceased that, as a man, he could not brook.

It was about this time that Mr Oakhurst, contrasting himself with a conventional world in which he had hitherto rarely mingled, became aware that there was something in his face, figure, and carriage quite unlike other men,—something that if it did not betray his former career, at least showed an individuality and originality that was suspicious. In this belief he shaved off his long, silken mustache, and religiously brushed out his clustering curls every morning. He even went so far as to affect a negligence of dress, and hid his small, slim, arched feet in the largest and heaviest walking-shoes. There is a story told that he went to his tailor in Sacramento, and asked him to make him a suit of clothes like everybody else. The tailor, familiar with Mr Oakhurst's fastidiousness, did not know what he meant. 'I mean,' said Mr Oakhurst savagely, 'something *respectable*,—something that doesn't exactly fit me, you know.' But however Mr Oakhurst might hide his shapely limbs in homespun and home-made garments, there was something in his carriage, something in the pose of his beautiful head, something in the strong and fine manliness of his presence, something in the perfect and utter discipline and control of his muscles, something in the high repose of his nature—a repose not so much a matter of intellectual ruling as of his very nature—that go where he would, and with whom, he was always a notable man in ten thousand. Perhaps this was never so clearly intimated to Mr Oakhurst as when, emboldened by Mr Hamilton's advice and assistance and his predilections, he became a San Francisco broker. Even before objection was made to his presence in the Board—the objection, I remember, was urged very eloquently by Watt Sanders, who was supposed to be the inventor of the 'freezing-out' system of disposing of poor stockholders, and who also enjoyed the reputation of having been the impelling cause of Briggs of Tuolumne's ruin and suicide—even before this formal protest of respectability against lawlessness, the aquiline suggestions of Mr Oakhurst's mien and countenance not only prematurely fluttered the pigeons, but absolutely occasioned much uneasiness among the fish-hawks, who circled below him with their booty. 'Dash me! but he's as likely to go after us as anybody,' said Joe Fielding.

It wanted but a few days before the close of the brief summer season at San Isabel Warm Springs. Already there had been some migration of the more fashionable, and there was an uncomfortable suggestion of dregs and lees in the social life that remained. Mr Oakhurst was moody; it was hinted that even the secure reputation of Mrs Decker could no longer protect her from the gossip which his presence excited. It is but fair to her to say that during the last few weeks of this trying ordeal she looked like a sweet, pale martyr, and conducted herself toward her traducers with the gentle, forgiving manner of one who relied not upon the idle homage of the crowd, but upon the security of a principle that was dearer than popular favor. 'They talk about myself and Mr Oakhurst, my dear,' she said to a friend, 'but Heaven and my husband can best answer their calumny. It never shall be said that my husband ever turned his back upon a friend in the moment of his adversity because the position was changed, because his friend was poor and he was rich.' This was the first intimation to the public that Jack had lost money, although it was known generally that the Deckers had lately bought some valuable property in San Francisco.

A few evenings after this an incident occurred which seemed to unpleasantly discord with the general social harmony that had always existed at San Isabel. It was at dinner, and Mr Oakhurst and Mr Hamilton, who sat together at a separate table, were observed to rise in some agitation. When they reached the hall, by a common instinct they stepped into a little breakfast-room which was vacant, and closed the door. Then Mr Hamilton turned, with a half-amused, half-serious smile, toward his friend, and said,—

'If we are to quarrel, Jack Oakhurst,—you and I,—in the name of all that is ridiculous, don't let it be about a'—

I do not know what was the epithet intended. It was either unspoken or lost. For at that very instant Mr Oakhurst raised a wine-glass and dashed its contents into Hamilton's face.

As they faced each other the men seemed to have changed natures. Mr Oakhurst was trembling with excitement, and the wine-glass that he returned to the table shivered between his fingers. Mr Hamilton stood there, grayish white, erect, and dripping. After a pause he said coldly,—

'So be it. But remember! our quarrel commences here. If I fall by your hand, you shall not use it to clear her character; if you fall by mine, you shall not be called a martyr. I am sorry it has come to this, but amen!—the sooner now the better.'

He turned proudly, dropped his lids over his cold steel-blue eyes, as if sheathing a rapier, bowed, and passed coldly out.

They met twelve hours later in a little hollow two miles from the hotel, on the Stockton road. As Mr Oakhurst received his pistol from Colonel Starbottle's hands he said to him in a low voice, 'Whatever turns up or down I shall not return to the hotel. You will find some directions in my room. Go there'— but his voice suddenly faltered, and he turned his glistening eyes away, to his second's intense astonishment. 'I've been out a dozen times with Jack Oakhurst,' said Colonel Starbottle afterwards, 'and I never saw him anyways cut before. Blank me if I didn't think he was losing his sand, till he walked to position.'

The two reports were almost simultaneous. Mr Oakhurst's right arm dropped suddenly to his side, and his pistol would have fallen from his paralyzed fingers, but the discipline of trained nerve and muscle prevailed, and he kept his grasp until he had shifted it to the other hand, without changing his position. Then there was a silence that seemed interminable, a gathering of two or three dark figures where a smoke curl still lazily floated, and then the hurried, husky, panting voice of Colonel Starbottle in his ear, 'He's hit hard—through the lungs—you must run for it!'

Jack turned his dark, questioning eyes upon his second, but did not seem to listen; rather seemed to hear some other voice, remoter in the distance. He hesitated, and then made a step forward in the direction of the distant group. Then he paused again as the figures separated, and the surgeon came hastily toward him.

'He would like to speak with you a moment,' said the man. 'You have little time to lose, I know; but,' he added in a lower voice, 'it is my duty to tell you he has still less.'

A look of despair so hopeless in its intensity swept over Mr Oakhurst's usually impassive face that the surgeon started. 'You are hit,' he said, glancing at Jack's helpless arm.

'Nothing—a mere scratch,' said Jack hastily. Then he added, with a bitter laugh, 'I'm not in luck to-day. But come! We'll see what he wants.'

His long feverish stride outstripped the surgeon's, and in another moment he stood where the dying man lay—like most dying men—the one calm, composed, central figure of an anxious group. Mr Oakhurst's face was less calm as he dropped on one knee beside him and took his hand. 'I want to speak with this gentleman alone,' said Hamilton, with something of his old imperious manner, as he turned to those about him. When they drew back, he looked up in Oakhurst's face.

'I've something to tell you, Jack.'

His own face was white, but not so white as that which Mr Oakhurst bent over him—a face so ghastly, with haunting doubts and a hopeless presentiment of coming evil, a face so piteous in its infinite weariness and envy of death, that the dying man was touched, even in the languor of dissolution, with a pang of compassion, and the cynical smile faded from his lips.

'Forgive me, Jack,' he whispered more feebly, 'for what I have to say. I don't say it in anger, but only because it must be said. I could not do my duty to you—I could not die contented until you knew it all. It's a miserable business at best, all around. But it can't be helped now. Only I ought to have fallen by Decker's pistol and not yours.'

A flush like fire came into Jack's cheek, and he would have risen, but Hamilton held him fast.

'Listen! in my pocket you will find two letters. Take them—there! You will know the handwriting. But promise you will not read them until you are in a place of safety. Promise me!'

Jack did not speak, but held the letters between his fingers as if they had been burning coals.

'Promise me,' said Hamilton faintly.

'Why?' asked Oakhurst, dropping his friend's hand coldly.

'Because,' said the dying man with a bitter smile,—'because—when you have read them—you—will—go back—to capture—and death!'

They were his last words. He pressed Jack's hand faintly. Then his grasp relaxed, and he fell back a corpse.

It was nearly ten o'clock at night, and Mrs Decker reclined languidly upon the sofa with a novel in her hand, while her husband discussed the politics of the country in the bar-room of the hotel. It was a warm night, and the French window looking out upon a little balcony was partly open. Suddenly she heard a foot upon the balcony, and she raised her eyes from the book with a slight start. The next moment the window was hurriedly thrust wide and a man entered.

Mrs Decker rose to her feet with a little cry of alarm.

'For Heaven's sake, Jack, are you mad? He has only gone for a little while—he may return at any moment. Come an hour later—to-morrow—any time when I can get rid of him—but go, now, dear, at once.'

Mr Oakhurst walked toward the door, bolted it, and then faced her without a word. His face was haggard, his coat-sleeve hung loosely over an arm that was bandaged and bloody.

Nevertheless, her voice did not falter as she turned again toward him. 'What has happened, Jack? Why are you here?'

He opened his coat, and threw two letters in her lap.

'To return your lover's letters—to kill you—and then myself,' he said in a voice so low as to be almost inaudible.

Among the many virtues of this admirable woman was invincible courage. She did not faint, she did not cry out. She sat quietly down again, folded her hands in her lap, and said calmly,—

'And why should you not?'

Had she recoiled, had she shown any fear or contrition, had she essayed an explanation or apology, Mr Oakhurst would have looked upon it as an evidence of guilt. But there is no quality that courage recognizes so quickly as courage, there is no condition that desperation bows before but desperation; and Mr Oakhurst's power of analysis was not so keen as to prevent him from confounding her courage with a moral quality. Even in his fury he could not help admiring this dauntless invalid.

'Why should you not?' she repeated with a smile. 'You gave me life, health, and happiness, Jack. You gave me your love. Why should you not take what you have given? Go on. I am ready.'

She held out her hands with that same infinite grace of yielding with which she had taken his own on the first day of their meeting at the hotel. Jack raised his head, looked at her for one wild moment, dropped upon his knees beside her, and raised the folds of her dress to his feverish lips. But she was too clever not to instantly see her victory; she was too much of a woman, with all her cleverness, to refrain from pressing that victory home. At the same moment, as with the impulse of an outraged and wounded woman, she rose, and with an imperious gesture pointed to the window. Mr Oakhurst rose in his turn, cast one glance upon her, and without another word passed out of her presence forever.

When he had gone, she closed the window and bolted it, and going to the chimneypiece placed the letters, one by one, in the flame of the candle until they were consumed. I would not have the reader think that during this painful operation she was unmoved. Her hand trembled and—not being a brute—for some minutes (perhaps longer) she felt very badly, and the corners of her sensitive mouth were depressed. When her husband arrived it was with a genuine joy that she ran to him, and nestled against his broad breast with a feeling of security that thrilled the honest fellow to the core.

'But I've heard dreadful news to-night, Elsie,' said Mr Decker, after a few endearments were exchanged.

'Don't tell me anything dreadful, dear; I'm not well to-night,' she pleaded sweetly.

'But it's about Mr Oakhurst and Hamilton.'

'Please!' Mr Decker could not resist the petitionary grace of those white hands and that sensitive mouth, and took her to his arms. Suddenly he said, 'What's that?'

He was pointing to the bosom of her white dress. Where Mr Oakhurst had touched her there was a spot of blood.

It was nothing; she had slightly cut her hand in closing the window; it shut so hard! If Mr Decker had remembered to close and bolt the shutter before he went out, he might have saved her this. There was such a genuine irritability and force in this remark that Mr Decker was quite overcome by remorse. But Mrs Decker forgave him with that graciousness which I have before pointed out in these pages, and with the halo of that forgiveness and marital confidence still lingering above the pair, with the reader's permission we will leave them and return to Mr Oakhurst.

But not for two weeks. At the end of that time he walked into his rooms in Sacramento, and in his old manner took his seat at the faro-table.

'How's your arm, Jack?' asked an incautious player.

There was a smile followed the question, which, however, ceased as Jack looked up quietly at the speaker.

'It bothers my dealing a little, but I can shoot as well with my left.'

The game was continued in that decorous silence which usually distinguished the table at which Mr John Oakhurst presided.

A PROTEGEE OF JACK HAMLIN'S

I

THE steamer Silveropolis was sharply and steadily cleaving the broad, placid shallows of the Sacramento River. A large wave like an eagre,* diverging from its bow, was extending to either bank, swamping the tules* and threatening to submerge the lower levees. The great boat itself—a vast but delicate structure of airy stories, hanging galleries, fragile colonnades, gilded cornices, and resplendent frescoes—was throbbing throughout its whole perilous length with the pulse of high pressure and the strong monotonous beat of a powerful piston. Floods of foam pouring from the high paddle-boxes on either side and reuniting in the wake of the boat left behind a track of dazzling whiteness, over which trailed two dense black banners flung from its lofty smokestacks.

Mr Jack Hamlin had quietly emerged from his stateroom on deck and was looking over the guards. His hands were resting lightly on his hips over the delicate curves of his white waistcoat, and he was whistling softly, possibly some air to which he had made certain card-playing passengers dance the night before. He was in comfortable case, and his soft brown eyes under their long lashes were veiled with gentle tolerance of all things. He glanced lazily along the empty hurricane deck forward; he glanced lazily down to the saloon deck below him. Far out against the guards below him leaned a young girl. Mr Hamlin knitted his brows slightly.

He remembered her at once. She had come on board that morning with one Ned Stratton, a brother gambler, but neither a favorite nor intimate of Jack's. From certain indications in the pair, Jack had inferred that she was some foolish or reckless creature whom 'Ed' had 'got on a string,' and was spiriting away from her friends and family. With the abstract morality of this situation Jack was not in the least concerned. For himself he did not indulge in that sort of game; the inexperience and vacillations of innocence were apt to be bothersome, and besides, a certain modest doubt of his own competency to make an original selection had always made him prefer to confine his gallantries to the wives of men of greater judgment than himself who had. But it suddenly occurred to him that he had seen Stratton quickly slip off the boat at the last landing stage. Ah! that was it; he had cast away and deserted her. It was an old story. Jack smiled. But he was not greatly amused with Stratton.

She was very pale, and seemed to be clinging to the network railing, as if to support herself, although she was gazing fixedly at the yellow glancing current below, which seemed to be sucked down and swallowed in the paddle-box as the boat swept on. It certainly was a fascinating sight—this sloping rapid, hurrying on to bury itself under the crushing wheels. For a brief moment Jack saw how they would seize anything floating on that ghastly incline, whirl it round in one awful revolution of the beating paddles, and then bury it, broken and shattered out of all recognition, deep in the muddy undercurrent of the stream behind them.

She moved away presently with an odd, stiff step, chafing her gloved hands together as if they had become stiffened, too, in her rigid grasp of the railing. Jack leisurely watched her as she moved along the narrow strip of deck. She was not at all to his taste,—a rather plump girl with a rustic manner and a great deal of brown hair under her straw hat. She might have looked better had she not been so haggard. When she reached the door of the saloon she paused, and then, turning suddenly, began to walk quickly back again. As she neared the spot where she had been standing her pace slackened, and when she reached the railing she seemed to relapse against it in her former helpless fashion. Jack became lazily interested. Suddenly she lifted her head and cast a quick glance around and above her. In that momentary lifting of her face Jack saw her expression. Whatever it was, his own changed instantly; the next moment there was a crash on the lower deck. It was Jack who had swung himself over the rail and dropped ten feet, to her side. But not before she had placed one foot in the meshes of the netting and had gripped the railing for a spring.

The noise of Jack's fall might have seemed to her bewildered fancy as a part of her frantic act, for she fell forward vacantly on the railing. But by this time Jack had grasped her arm as if to help himself to his feet.

'I might have killed myself by that foolin', mightn't I?' he said cheerfully.

The sound of a voice so near her seemed to recall to her dazed sense the uncompleted action his fall had arrested. She made a convulsive bound towards the railing, but Jack held her fast.

'Don't,' he said in a low voice,—'don't, it won't pay. It's the sickest game that ever was played by man or woman. Come here!'

He drew her towards an empty state room whose door was swinging on its hinges a few feet from them. She was trembling violently; he half led, half pushed her into the room, closed the door, and stood with his back against it as she dropped into a chair. She looked at him vacantly; the agitation she was undergoing inwardly had left her no sense of outward perception.

'You know Stratton would be awfully riled,' continued Jack easily. 'He's just stepped out to see a friend and got left by the fool boat. He'll be along by the next steamer, and you're bound to meet him in Sacramento.'

Her staring eyes seemed suddenly to grasp his meaning. But to his surprise she burst out with a certain hysterical desperation, 'No! no! Never! *never* again! Let me pass! I must go,' and struggled to regain the door. Jack, albeit singularly relieved to know that she shared his private sentiments regarding Stratton, nevertheless resisted her. Whereat she suddenly turned white, reeled back, and sank in a dead faint in the chair.

The gambler turned, drew the key from the inside of the door, passed out, locking it behind him, and walked leisurely into the main saloon.

'Mrs Johnson,' he said gravely, addressing the stewardess, a tall mulatto, with his usual winsome supremacy over dependents and children, 'you'll oblige me if you'll corral a few smelling salts, vinaigrettes, hairpins, and violet powder, and unload them in deck stateroom No. 257. There's a lady'—

'A lady, Marse Hamlin?' interrupted the mulatto, with an archly significant flash of her white teeth.

'A lady,' continued Jack with unabashed gravity, 'in a sort of conniption fit. A relative of mine; in fact, a niece, my only sister's child. Hadn't seen each other for ten years, and it was too much for her.'

The woman glanced at him with a mingling of incredulous belief but delighted obedience, hurriedly gathered a few articles from her cabin, and followed him to No. 257. The young girl was still unconscious. The stewardess applied a few restoratives with the skill of long experience, and the young girl opened her eyes. They turned vacantly from the stewardess to Jack with a look of half recognition and half frightened inquiry.

'Yes,' said Jack, addressing the eyes, although ostentatiously speaking to Mrs Johnson, 'she'd only just come by steamer to 'Frisco and wasn't expecting to see me, and we dropped right into each other here on the boat. And I haven't seen her since she was so high. Sister Mary ought to have warned me by letter; but she was always a slouch at letter-writing. There, that'll do, Mrs Johnson. She's coming round; I reckon I can manage the rest. But you go now and tell the purser I want one of those inside staterooms for my niece,—*my niece*, you hear,—so that you can be near her and look after her.'

As the stewardess turned obediently away the young girl attempted to rise, but Jack checked her.

'No,' he said, almost brusquely; 'you and I have some talking to do before she gets back, and we've no time for foolin'. You heard what I told her just now! Well, it's got to be as I said, you sabe.* As long as you're on this boat you're my niece, and my sister Mary's child. As I haven't got any sister Mary, you don't run any risk of falling foul of her, and you ain't taking any one's place. That settles that. Now, do you or do you not want to see that man again? Say yes, and if he's anywhere above ground I'll yank him over to you as soon as we touch shore.' He had no idea of interfering with his colleague's amours, but he had determined to make Stratton pay for the bother their slovenly sequence had caused him. Yet he was relieved and astonished by her frantic gesture of indignation and abhorrence. 'No?' he repeated grimly. 'Well, that settles that. Now, look here; quick, before she comes—do you want to go back home to your friends?'

But here occurred what he had dreaded most and probably thought he had escaped. She had stared at him, at the stewardess, at the walls, with abstracted, vacant, and bewildered, but always undimmed and unmoistened eyes. A sudden convulsion shook her whole frame, her blank expression broke like a shattered mirror, she threw her hands over her eyes and fell forward with her face to the back of her chair in an outburst of tears.

Alas for Jack! with the breaking up of those sealed fountains came her speech also, at first disconnected and incoherent, and then despairing and passionate. No! she had no longer friends or home! She had lost and disgraced them! She had disgraced *herself!* There was no home for her but the grave. Why had Jack snatched her from it? Then bit by bit, she yielded up her story,—a story decidedly commonplace to Jack, uninteresting, and even irritating to his fastidiousness. She was a schoolgirl (not even a convent girl, but the inmate of a Presbyterian female academy at Napa. Jack shuddered as he remembered to have once seen certain of the pupils walking with a teacher), and she lived with her married sister. She had seen Stratton while going to and fro on the San Francisco boat; she had exchanged notes with him, had met him secretly, and finally consented to elope with him to Sacramento, only to discover when the boat had left the wharf the real nature of his intentions. Jack listened with infinite weariness and inward chafing. He had read all this before in cheap novelettes, in the police reports, in the Sunday papers; he had heard a street preacher declaim against it, and warn young women of the serpent-like wiles of tempters of the Stratton variety. But even now Jack failed to recognize Stratton as a serpent, or indeed anything but a blundering cheat and clown, who had left his dirty 'prentice work on his (Jack's) hands. But the girl was helpless and, it seemed, homeless, all through a certain desperation of feeling which, in spite of her tears, he could not but respect. That momentary shadow of death had exalted her. He stroked his mustache, pulled down his white waistcoat, and let her cry, without saying anything. He did not know that this most objectionable phase of her misery was her salvation and his own.

But the stewardess would return in a moment.

'You'd better tell me what to call you,' he said quietly. 'I ought to know my niece's first name.'

The girl caught her breath, and between two sobs said, 'Sophonisba.'

Jack winced. It seemed only to need this last sentimental touch to complete the idiotic situation.

'I'll call you Sophy,' he said hurriedly and with an effort. 'And now look here! You are going in that cabin with Mrs Johnson where she can look after you, but I can't. So I'll have to take your word, for I'm not going to give you away before Mrs Johnson, that you won't try that foolishness—you know what I mean—before I see you again. Can I trust you?'

With her head still bowed over the chair back, she murmured slowly somewhere from under her disheveled hair: 'Yes.'

'Honest Injin?' adjured Jack gravely.

'Yes.'

The shuffling step of the stewardess was heard slowly approaching.

'Yes,' continued Jack abruptly, slightly lifting his voice, as Mrs Johnson opened the door,—'yes, if you'd only had some of those spearmint drops of your aunt Rachel's that she always gave you when these fits came on you'd have been all right inside of five minutes. Aunty was no slouch of a doctor, was she? Dear me, it only seems yesterday since I saw her. You were just playing round her knee like a kitten on the back porch. How time does fly! But here's Mrs Johnson coming to take you in. Now rouse up, Sophy, and just hook yourself on to Mrs Johnson on that side, and we'll toddle along.'

The young girl put back her heavy hair, and with her face still averted submitted to be helped to her feet by the kindly stewardess. Perhaps something homely sympathetic and nurse-like in the touch of the mulatto gave her assurance and confidence, for her head lapsed quite naturally against the woman's shoulder, and her face was partly hidden as she moved slowly along the deck. Jack accompanied them to the saloon and the inner stateroom door. A few passengers gathered curiously near, as much attracted by the unusual presence of Jack Hamlin in such a procession as by the girl herself.

'You'll look after her specially, Mrs Johnson,' said Jack, in unusually deliberate terms. 'She's been a good deal petted at home, and my sister perhaps has rather spoilt her. She's pretty much of a child still, and you'll have to humor her. Sophy,' he continued, with ostentatious playfulness, directing his voice into the dim recesses of the stateroom, 'you'll just think Mrs Johnson's your old nurse, won't you? Think it's old Katy, hey?'

To his great consternation the girl approached tremblingly from the inner shadow. The faintest and saddest of smiles for a moment played around the corners of her drawn mouth and tear-dimmed eyes as she held out her hand and said:—

'God bless you for being so kind.'

Jack shuddered and glanced quickly round. But luckily no one heard this crushing sentimentalism, and the next moment the door closed upon her and Mrs Johnson.

It was past midnight, and the moon was riding high over the narrowing yellow river, when Jack again stepped out on deck. He had just left the captain's cabin, and a small social game with the officers, which had served to some extent to vaguely relieve his irritation and their pockets. He had presumably quite forgotten the incident of the afternoon, as he looked about him, and complacently took in the quiet beauty of the night.

The low banks on either side offered no break to the uninterrupted level of the landscape, through which the river seemed to wind only as a race track for the rushing boat. Every fibre of her vast but fragile bulk quivered under the goad of her powerful engines. There was no other movement but hers, no other sound but this monstrous beat and panting; the whole tranquil landscape seemed to breathe and pulsate with her; dwellers in the tules, miles away, heard and felt her as she passed, and it seemed to Jack, leaning over the railing, as if the whole river swept like a sluice through her paddle-boxes.

Jack had quite unconsciously lounged before that part of the railing where the young girl had leaned a few hours ago. As he looked down upon the streaming yellow mill-race below him he noticed—what neither he nor the girl had probably noticed before—that a space of the top bar of the railing was hinged, and could be lifted by withdrawing a small bolt, thus giving easy access to the guards. He was still looking at it, whistling softly, when footsteps approached.

'Jack,' said a lazy voice, 'how's sister Mary?'

'It's a long time since you've seen her only child, Jack, ain't it?' said a second voice; 'and yet it sort o' seems to me somehow that I've seen her before.'

Jack recognized the voice of two of his late companions at the card-table. His whistling ceased; so also dropped every trace of color and expression from his handsome face. But he did not turn, and remained quietly gazing at the water.

'Aunt Rachel, too, must be getting on in years, Jack,' continued the first speaker, halting behind Jack.

'And Mrs Johnson does not look so much like Sophy's old nurse as she used to,' remarked the second, following his example. Still Jack remained unmoved.

'You don't seem to be interested, Jack,' continued the first speaker. 'What are you looking at?'

Without turning his head the gambler replied, 'Looking at the boat; she's booming along, just chawing up and spitting out the river, ain't she? Look at that sweep of water going under her paddle-wheels,' he continued, unbolting the rail and lifting it to allow the two men to peer curiously over the guards as he pointed to the murderous incline beneath them; 'a man wouldn't stand much show who got dropped into it. How these paddles would just snatch him bald-headed, pick him up, and slosh him round and round, and then sling him out down there in such a shape that his own father wouldn't know him.'

'Yes,' said the first speaker, with an ostentatious little laugh, 'but all that ain't telling us how sister Mary is.'

'No,' said the gambler, slipping into the opening with a white and rigid face in which nothing seemed living but the eyes,— 'no; but it's telling you how two d—d fools who didn't know when to shut their mouths might get them shut once and forever. It's telling you what might happen to two men who tried to "play" a man who didn't care to be "played,"—a man who didn't care much what he did, when he did it, or how he did it, but would do what he'd set out to do—even if in doing it he went to hell with the men he sent there.'

He had stepped out on the guards, beside the two men, closing the rail behind him. He had placed his hands on their shoulders; they had both gripped his arms; yet, viewed from the deck above, they seemed at that moment an amicable, even fraternal group, albeit the faces of the three were dead white in the moonlight.

'I don't think I'm so very much interested in sister Mary,' said the first speaker quietly, after a pause.

'And I don't seem to think so much of aunt Rachel as I did,' said his companion.

'I thought you wouldn't,' said Jack, coolly reopening the rail and stepping back again. 'It all depends upon the way you look at those things. Good-night.'

'Good-night.'

The three men paused, shook each other's hands silently, and separated, Jack sauntering slowly back to his stateroom.

II

The educational establishment of Mrs Mix and Madame Bance, situated in the best quarter of Sacramento and patronized by the highest state officials and members of the clergy, was a pretty if not an imposing edifice. Although surrounded by a high white picket-fence and entered through a heavily boarded gate, its balconies festooned with jasmine and roses, and its spotlessly draped windows as often graced with fresh, flower-like faces, were still plainly and provokingly visible above the ostentatious spikes of the pickets. Nevertheless, Mr Jack Hamlin, who had six months before placed his niece, Miss Sophonisba Brown, under its protecting care, felt a degree of uneasiness, even bordering on timidity, which was new to that usually self-confident man. Remembering how his first appearance had fluttered this dovecote and awakened a severe suspicion in the minds of the two principals, he had discarded his usual fashionable attire and elegantly fitting garments for a rough homespun suit, supposed to represent a homely agriculturist, but which had the effect of transforming him into an adorable Strephon,* infinitely more dangerous in his rustic shepherd-like simplicity. He had also shaved off his silken

mustache for the same prudential reasons, but had only succeeded in uncovering the delicate lines of his handsome mouth,
and so absurdly reducing his apparent years that his avuncular
pretensions seemed more preposterous than ever; and when he
had rung the bell and was admitted by a severe Irish waiting-
maid, his momentary hesitation and half-humorous diffidence
had such an unexpected effect upon her, that it seemed
doubtful if he would be allowed to pass beyond the vestibule.

'Shure, miss,' she said in a whisper to an under teacher,
'there 's wan at the dhure who calls himself "Mister" Hamlin,
but av it is not a young lady maskeradin' in her brother's
clothes oim very much mistaken; and av it's a boy, one of the
pupil's brothers, shure ye might put a dhress on him when you
take the others out for a walk, and he'd pass for the beauty of
the whole school.'

Meantime the unconscious subject of this criticism was
pacing somewhat uneasily up and down the formal reception
room into which he had been finally ushered. Its farther end
was filled by an enormous parlor organ, a number of music
books, and a cheerfully variegated globe. A large presentation
Bible, an equally massive illustrated volume on the Holy Land,
a few landscapes in cold, bluish milk and water colors, and rigid
heads in crayons—the work of pupils—were presumably ornamental. An imposing mahogany sofa and what seemed to be
a disproportionate excess of chairs somewhat coldly furnished
the room. Jack had reluctantly made up his mind that, if Sophy
was accompanied by any one, he would be obliged to kiss her
to keep up his assumed relationship. As she entered the room
with Miss Mix, Jack advanced and soberly saluted her on the
cheek. But so positive and apparent was the gallantry of his
presence, and perhaps so suggestive of some pastoral flirtation,
that Miss Mix, to Jack's surprise, winced perceptibly and
became stony. But he was still more surprised that the young
lady herself shrank half uneasily from his lips, and uttered a
slight exclamation. It was a new experience to Mr Hamlin.

But this somewhat mollified Miss Mix, and she slightly
relaxed her austerity. She was glad to be able to give the best
accounts of Miss Brown, not only as regarded her studies, but
as to her conduct and deportment. Really, with the present

freedom of manners and laxity of home discipline in California, it was gratifying to meet a young lady who seemed to value the importance of a proper decorum and behavior, especially towards the opposite sex. Mr Hamlin, although her guardian, was perhaps too young to understand and appreciate this. To this inexperience she must also attribute the indiscretion of his calling during school hours and without preliminary warning. She trusted, however, that this informality could be overlooked after consultation with Madame Bance, but in the mean time, perhaps for half an hour, she must withdraw Miss Brown and return with her to the class. Mr Hamlin could wait in this public room, reserved especially for visitors, until they returned. Or, if he cared to accompany one of the teachers in a formal inspection of the school, she added doubtfully, with a glance at Jack's distracting attractions, she would submit this also to Madame Bance.

'Thank you, thank you,' returned Jack hurriedly, as a depressing vision of the fifty or sixty scholars rose before his eyes, 'but I 'd rather not. I mean, you know, I 'd just as lief stay here *alone*. I wouldn't have called anyway, don't you see, only I had a day off,—and—and—I wanted to talk with my niece on family matters.'

He did not say that he had received a somewhat distressful letter from her asking him to come; a new instinct made him cautious.

Considerably relieved by Jack's unexpected abstention, which seemed to spare her pupils the distraction of his graces, Miss Mix smiled more amicably and retired with her charge. In the single glance he had exchanged with Sophy he saw that, although resigned and apparently self-controlled, she still appeared thoughtful and melancholy. She had improved in appearance and seemed more refined and less rustic in her school dress, but he was conscious of the same distinct separation of her personality (which was uninteresting to him) from the sentiment that had impelled him to visit her. She was possibly still hankering after that fellow Stratton, in spite of her protestations to the contrary; perhaps she wanted to go back to her sister, although she had declared she would die first, and had always refused to disclose her real name or give any clue by which he could have traced her relations. She would cry, of course; he almost hoped that she would not return alone; he half regretted he had come. She still held him only by a single quality of her nature,—the desperation she had shown on the boat; that was something he understood and respected.

He walked discontentedly to the window and looked out; he walked discontentedly to the end of the room and stopped before the organ. It was a fine instrument; he could see that with an admiring and experienced eye. He was alone in the room; in fact, quite alone in that part of the house which was separated from the class-rooms. He would disturb no one by trying it. And if he did, what then? He smiled a little recklessly, slowly pulled off his gloves, and sat down before it.

He played cautiously at first, with the soft pedal down. The instrument had never known a strong masculine hand before, having been fumbled and friveled over by softly incompetent, feminine fingers. But presently it began to thrill under the passionate hand of its lover, and carried away by his one innocent weakness, Jack was launched upon a sea of musical reminiscences. Scraps of church music, Puritan psalms of his boyhood; dying strains from sad, forgotten operas, fragments of oratorios and symphonies, but chiefly phrases from old masses heard at the missions of San Pedro and Santa Isabel, swelled up from his loving and masterful fingers. He had finished an Agnus Dei; the formal room was pulsating with divine aspiration; the rascal's hands were resting listlessly on the keys, his brown lashes lifted, in an effort of memory, tenderly towards the ceiling.

Suddenly, a subdued murmur of applause and a slight rustle behind him recalled him to himself again. He wheeled his chair quickly round. The two principals of the school and half a dozen teachers were standing gravely behind him, and at the open door a dozen curled and frizzled youthful heads peered in eagerly, but half restrained by their teachers. The relaxed features and apologetic attitude of Madame Bance and Miss Mix showed that Mr Hamlin had unconsciously achieved a triumph.

He might not have been as pleased to know that his extraordinary performance had solved a difficulty, effaced his other graces, and enabled them to place him on the moral pedestal of a mere musician, to whom these eccentricities were allowable and privileged. He shared the admiration extended by the young ladies to their music teacher, which was always understood to be a sexless enthusiasm and a contagious juvenile disorder. It was also a fine advertisement for the organ. Madame Bance smiled blandly, improved the occasion by thanking Mr Hamlin for having given the scholars a gratuitous lesson on the capabilities of the instrument, and was glad to be able to give Miss Brown a half-holiday to spend with her accomplished relative. Miss Brown was even now upstairs, putting on her hat and mantle. Jack was relieved. Sophy would not attempt to cry on the street.

Nevertheless, when they reached it and the gate closed behind them, he again became uneasy. The girl's clouded face and melancholy manner were not promising. It also occurred to him that he might meet some one who knew him and thus compromise her. This was to be avoided at all hazards. He began with forced gayety:—

'Well, now, where shall we go?'

She slightly raised her tear-dimmed eyes.

'Where you please—I don't care.'

'There isn't any show going on here, is there?'

He had a vague idea of a circus or menagerie—himself behind her in the shadow of the box.

'I don't know of any.'

'Or any restaurant—or cake shop?'·

'There's a place where the girls go to get candy on Main Street. Some of them are there now.'

Jack shuddered; this was not to be thought of.

'But where do you walk?'

'Up and down Main Street.'

'Where everybody can see you?' said Jack, scandalized.

The girl nodded.

They walked on in silence for a few moments. Then a bright idea struck Mr Hamlin. He suddenly remembered that in one of his many fits of impulsive generosity and largess he had given to an old negro retainer—whose wife had nursed him through a dangerous illness—a house and lot on the river bank.

He had been told that they had opened a small laundry or wash-house. It occurred to him that a stroll there and a call upon 'Uncle Hannibal and Aunt Chloe' combined the propriety and respectability due to the young person he was with, and the requisite secrecy and absence of publicity due to himself. He at once suggested it.

'You see she was a mighty good woman, and you ought to know her, for she was my old nurse'—

The girl glanced at him with a sudden impatience.

'Honest Injin,' said Jack solemnly; 'she did nurse me through my last cough. I ain't playing old family gags on you now.'

'Oh, dear,' burst out the girl impulsively, 'I do wish you wouldn't ever play them again. I wish you wouldn't pretend to be my uncle; I wish you wouldn't make me pass for your niece. It isn't right. It's all wrong. Oh, don't you know it's all wrong, and can't come right any way? It's just killing me. I can't stand it. I'd rather you'd say what I am and how I came to you and how you pitied me.'

They had luckily entered a narrow side street, and the sobs which shook the young girl's frame were unnoticed. For a few moments Jack felt a horrible conviction stealing over him, that in his present attitude towards her he was not unlike that hound Stratton, and that, however innocent his own intent, there was a sickening resemblance to the situation on the boat in the base advantage he had taken of her friendlessness. He had never told her that he was a gambler like Stratton, and that his peculiar infelix reputation among women made it impossible for him to assist her, except by stealth or the deception he had practiced, without compromising her. He who had for years faced the sneers and half-frightened opposition of the world dared not tell the truth to this girl, from whom he expected nothing and who did not interest him. He felt he was almost slinking at her side. At last he said desperately:—

'But I snatched them bald-headed at the organ, Sophy, didn't I?'

'Oh, yes,' said the girl, 'you played beautifully and grandly. It was so good of you, too. For I think, somehow, Madame Bance had been a little suspicious of you, but that settled it.

Everybody thought it was fine, and some thought it was your profession. Perhaps,' she added timidly, 'it is.'

'I play a good deal, I reckon,' said Jack, with a grim humor which did not, however, amuse him.

'I wish *I* could, and make money by it,' said the girl eagerly. Jack winced, but she did not notice it as she went on hurriedly: 'That's what I wanted to talk to you about. I want to leave the school and make my own living. Anywhere where people won't know me and where I can be alone and work. I shall die here among these girls—with all their talk of their friends and their—sisters,—and their questions about you.'

'Tell 'em to dry up,' said Jack indignantly. 'Take 'em to the cake shop and load 'em up with candy and ice cream. That'll stop their mouths. You've got money,—you got my last remittance, didn't you?' he repeated quickly. 'If you didn't, here's'—his hand was already in his pocket when she stopped him with a despairing gesture.

'Yes, yes, I got it all. I haven't touched it. I don't want it. For I can't live on you. Don't you understand,—I want to work. Listen,—I can draw and paint. Madame Bance says I do it well; my drawing-master says I might in time take portraits and get paid for it. And even now I can retouch photographs and make colored miniatures from them. And,' she stopped and glanced at Jack half timidly, 'I've—done some already.'

A glow of surprised relief suffused the gambler. Not so much at this astonishing revelation as at the change it seemed to effect in her. Her pale blue eyes, made paler by tears, cleared and brightened under their swollen lids like wiped steel; the lines of her depressed mouth straightened and became firm. Her voice had lost its hopeless monotone.

'There's a shop in the next street,—a photographer's,—where they have one of mine in their windows,' she went on, reassured by Jack's unaffected interest. 'It's only round the corner, if you care to see.'

Jack assented; a few paces farther brought them to the corner of a narrow street, where they presently turned into a broader thoroughfare and stopped before the window of a photographer. Sophy pointed to an oval frame, containing a portrait painted on porcelain. Mr Hamlin was startled. Inexperienced as he was, a certain artistic inclination told him it was good, although it is to be feared he would have been astonished even if it had been worse. The mere fact that this headstrong country girl, who had run away with a cur like Stratton, should be able to do anything else took him by surprise.

'I got ten dollars for that,' she said hesitatingly, 'and I could have got more for a larger one, but I had to do that in my room, during recreation hours. If I had more time and a place where I could work'—she stopped timidly and looked tentatively at Jack. But he was already indulging in a characteristically reckless idea of coming back after he had left Sophy, buying the miniature at an extravagant price, and ordering half a dozen more at extraordinary figures. Here, however, two passers-by, stopping ostensibly to look in the window, but really attracted by the picturesque spectacle of the handsome young rustic and his schoolgirl companion, gave Jack such a fright that he hurried Sophy away again into the side street.

'There's nothing mean about that picture business,' he said cheerfully; 'it looks like a square kind of game,' and relapsed into thoughtful silence.

At which Sophy, the ice of restraint broken, again burst into passionate appeal. If she could only go away somewhere—where she saw no one but the people who would buy her work, who knew nothing of her past nor cared to know who were her relations! She would work hard; she knew she could support herself in time. She would keep the name he had given her,—it was not distinctive enough to challenge any inquiry,—but nothing more. She need not assume to be his niece; he would always be her kind friend, to whom she owed everything, even her miserable life. She trusted still to his honor never to seek to know her real name, nor ever to speak to her of that man if he ever met him. It would do no good to her or to them; it might drive her, for she was not yet quite sure of herself, to do that which she had promised him never to do again.

There was no threat, impatience, or acting in her voice, but he recognized the same dull desperation he had once heard in it, and her eyes, which a moment before were quick and mobile, had become fixed and set. He had no idea of trying to penetrate the foolish secret of her name and relations; he had never had the slightest curiosity, but it struck him now that Stratton might at any time force it upon him. The only way that he could prevent it was to let it be known that, for unexpressed reasons, he would shoot Stratton 'on sight.' This would naturally restrict any verbal communication between them. Jack's ideas of morality were vague, but his convictions on points of honor were singularly direct and positive.

III

Meantime Hamlin and Sophy were passing the outskirts of the town; the open lots and cleared spaces were giving way to grassy stretches, willow copses, and groups of cottonwood and sycamore; and beyond the level of yellowing tules appeared the fringed and raised banks of the river. Half tropical looking cottages with deep verandas—the homes of early Southern pioneers—took the place of incomplete blocks of modern houses, monotonously alike. In these sylvan surroundings Mr Hamlin's picturesque rusticity looked less incongruous and more Arcadian;* the young girl had lost some of her restraint with her confidences, and lounging together side by side, without the least consciousness of any sentiment in their words or actions, they nevertheless contrived to impress the spectator with the idea that they were a charming pair of pastoral lovers. So strong was this impression that, as they approached aunt Chloe's laundry, a pretty rose-covered cottage with an enormous whitewashed barn-like extension in the rear, the black proprietress herself, standing at the door, called her husband to come and look at them, and flashed her white teeth in such unqualified commendation and patronage that Mr Hamlin, withdrawing himself from Sophy's side, instantly charged down upon them.

'If you don't slide the lid back over that grinning box of dominoes of yours and take it inside, I'll just carry Hannibal off with me,' he said in a quick whisper, with a half-wicked, half-mischievous glitter in his brown eyes. 'That young lady's— *a lady*—do you understand? No riffraff friend of mine, but a regular *nun*—a saint—do you hear? So you just stand back and let her take a good look round, and rest herself, until she wants you.' 'Two black idiots, Miss Brown,' he continued cheerfully in a higher voice of explanation, as Sophy approached, 'who think because one of 'em used to shave me and the other saved my life they've got a right to stand at their humble cottage door and frighten horses!'

So great was Mr Hamlin's ascendency over his former servants that even this ingenious pleasantry was received with every sign of affection and appreciation of the humorist, and of the profound respect for his companion. Aunt Chloe showed them effusively into her parlor, a small but scrupulously neat and sweet-smelling apartment, inordinately furnished with a huge mahogany centre-table and chairs, and the most fragile and meretricious china and glass ornaments on the mantel. But the three jasmine-edged lattice windows opened upon a homely garden of old-fashioned herbs and flowers, and their fragrance filled the room. The cleanest and starchiest of curtains, the most dazzling and whitest of tidies and chair-covers, bespoke the adjacent laundry; indeed, the whole cottage seemed to exhale the odors of lavender soap and freshly ironed linen. Yet the cottage was large for the couple and their assistants..

'Dar was two front rooms on de next flo' dat dey never used,' explained Aunt Chloe; 'friends allowed dat dey could let 'em to white folks, but dey had always been done kep' for Marse Hamlin, ef he ever wanted to be wid his old niggers again.'

Jack looked up quickly with a brightened face, made a sign to Hannibal, and the two left the room together.

When he came through the passage a few moments later, there was a sound of laughter in the parlor. He recognized the full, round, lazy, chuckle of Aunt Chloe, but there was a higher girlish ripple that he did not know. He had never heard Sophy laugh before. Nor, when he entered, had he ever seen her so animated. She was helping Chloe set the table, to that lady's intense delight at 'Missy's' girlish housewifery. She was picking the berries fresh from the garden, buttering the Sally Lunn,* making the tea, and arranging the details of the repast with apparently no trace of her former discontent and unhappiness in either face or manner. He dropped quietly into a chair by the window, and, with the homely scents of the garden mixing with the honest odors of Aunt Chloe's cookery, watched her with an amusement that was as pleasant and grateful as it was strange and unprecedented.

'Now, den,' said Aunt Chloe to her husband, as she put the finishing touch to the repast in a plate of doughnuts as exquisitely brown and shining as Jack's eyes were at that moment, 'Hannibal, you just come away, and let dem two white quality chillens have dey tea. Dey's done starved, shuah.' And with an approving nod to Jack, she bundled her husband from the room.

The door closed; the young girl began to pour out the tea, but Jack remained in his seat by the window. It was a singular sensation which he did not care to disturb. It was no new thing for Mr Hamlin to find himself at a tête-à-tête repast with the admiring and complaisant fair; there was a cabinet particulier in a certain San Francisco restaurant which had listened to their various vanities and professions of undying faith; he might have recalled certain festal rendezvous with a widow whose piety and impeccable reputation made it a moral duty for her to come to him only in disguise; it was but a few days before that he had been let privately into the palatial mansion of a high official for a midnight supper with a foolish wife. It was not strange, therefore, that he should be alone here, secretly, with a member of that indirect, loving sex. But that he should be sitting there in a cheap negro laundry with absolutely no sentiment of any kind towards the heavy-haired, freckled-faced country schoolgirl opposite him, from whom he sought and expected nothing, and *enjoying* it without scorn of himself or his companion, to use his own expression, 'got him.' Presently he rose and sauntered to the table with shining eyes.

'Well, what do you think of Aunt Chloe's shebang?' he asked smilingly.

'Oh, it's so sweet and clean and homelike,' said the girl quickly.

At any other time he would have winced at the last adjective. It struck him now as exactly the word.

'Would you like to live here, if you could?'

Her face brightened. She put the teapot down and gazed fixedly at Jack.

'Because you can. Look here. I spoke to Hannibal about it. You can have the two front rooms if you want to. One of 'em is big enough and light enough for a studio to do your work in. You tell that nigger what you want to put in 'em, and he's got my orders to do it. I told him about your painting; said you were the daughter of an old friend, you know. Hold on, Sophy; d—n it all, I've got to do a little gilt-edged lying; but I let you out of the niece business this time. Yes, from this moment I'm no longer your uncle. I renounce the relationship. It's hard,' continued the rascal, 'after all these years and considering sister Mary's feelings; but, as you seem to wish it, it must be done.'

Sophy's steel-blue eyes softened. She slid her long brown hand across the table and grasped Jack's. He returned the pressure quickly and fraternally, even to that half-shamed half-hurried evasion of emotion peculiar to all brothers. This was also a new sensation; but he liked it.

'You are too—too good, Mr Hamlin,' she said quietly.

'Yes,' said Jack cheerfully, 'that's what's the matter with me. It isn't natural, and if I keep it up too long it brings on my cough.'

Nevertheless, they were happy in a boy and girl fashion, eating heartily, and, I fear, not always decorously; scrambling somewhat for the strawberries, and smacking their lips over the Sally Lunn. Meantime, it was arranged that Mr Hamlin should inform Miss Mix that Sophy would leave school at the end of the term, only a few days hence, and then transfer herself to lodgings with some old family servants, where she could more easily pursue her studies in her own profession. She need not make her place of abode a secret, neither need she court publicity. She would write to Jack regularly, informing him of her progress, and he would visit her whenever he could. Jack assented gravely to the further proposition that he was to keep a strict account of all the moneys he advanced her, and that she was to repay him out of the proceeds of her first pictures. He had promised also, with a slight mental reservation, not to buy them all himself, but to trust to her success with the public. They were never to talk of what had happened before; she was to begin life anew. Of such were their confidences, spoken often together at the same moment, and with their mouths full. Only one thing troubled Jack: he had not yet told her frankly who he was and what was his reputation. He had hitherto carelessly supposed she would learn it, and in truth had cared little if she did; but it was evident from her conversation that day that by some miracle she was still in ignorance. Unable to tell her himself, he had charged Hannibal to break it to her casually after he was gone.

'You can let me down easy if you like, but you'd better make a square deal of it while you're about it. And,' Jack had added cheerfully, 'if she thinks after that she'd better drop me entirely, you just say that if she wishes to *stay*, you'll see that I don't ever come here again. And you keep your word about it too, you black nigger, or I'll be the first to thrash you.'

Nevertheless, when Hannibal and Aunt Chloe returned to clear away the repast, they were a harmonious party; albeit Mr Hamlin seemed more content to watch them silently from his chair by the window, a cigar between his lips, and the pleasant distraction of the homely scents and sounds of the garden in his senses. Allusion having been made again to the morning performance of the organ, he was implored by Hannibal to diversify his talent by exercising it on an old guitar which had passed into that retainer's possession with certain clothes of his master's when they separated. Mr Hamlin accepted it dubiously; it had twanged under his volatile fingers in more pretentious but less innocent halls. But presently he raised his tenor voice and soft brown lashes to the humble ceiling and sang.

'Way down upon the Swanee River,'

discoursed Jack plaintively,—

'Far, far away,
Thar's whar my heart is turning ever,
Thar's whar the old folks stay.'

The two dusky scions of an emotional race, that had been wont to sweeten its toils and condone its wrongs with music, sat wrapt and silent, swaying with Jack's voice until they could burst in upon the chorus. The jasmine vines trilled softly with the afternoon breeze; a slender yellow-hammer, perhaps emulous of Jack, swung himself from an outer spray and peered curiously into the room; and a few neighbors, gathering at their doors and windows, remarked that 'after all, when it came to real singing, no one could beat those d—d niggers.'

The sun was slowly sinking in the rolling gold of the river when Jack and Sophy started leisurely back through the broken shafts of light, and across the far-stretching shadows of the cottonwoods. In the midst of a lazy silence they were presently conscious of a distant monotonous throb, the booming of the up boat on the river. The sound came nearer—passed them, the boat itself hidden by the trees; but a trailing cloud of smoke above cast a momentary shadow upon their path. The girl looked up at Jack with a troubled face. Mr Hamlin smiled reassuringly; but in that instant he had made up his mind that it was his moral duty to kill Mr Edward Stratton.

IV

For the next two months Mr Hamlin was professionally engaged in San Francisco and Marysville, and the transfer of Sophy from the school to her new home was effected without his supervision. From letters received by him during that interval, it seemed that the young girl had entered energetically upon her new career, and that her artistic efforts were crowned with success. There were a few Indian-ink sketches, studies made at school and expanded in her own 'studio,' which were eagerly bought as soon as exhibited in the photographer's window,—notably by a florid and inartistic bookkeeper, an old negro woman, a slangy stable boy, a gorgeously dressed and painted female, and the bearded second officer of a river steamboat, without hesitation and without comment. This, as Mr Hamlin intelligently pointed out in a letter to Sophy, showed a general and diversified appreciation on the part of the public. Indeed, it emboldened her, in the retouching of photographs, to offer sittings to the subjects, and to undertake even large crayon copies, which had resulted in her getting so many orders that she was no longer obliged to sell her drawings, but restricted herself solely to profitable portraiture. The studio became known; even its quaint surroundings added to the popular interest, and the originality and independence of the young painter helped her to a genuine success. All this she wrote to Jack. Meantime Hannibal had assured him that he had carried out his instructions by informing 'Missy' of his old master's real occupation and reputation, but that the young lady hadn't 'took no notice.' Certainly there was no allusion to it in her letters, nor any indication in her manner. Mr Hamlin was greatly, and it seemed to him properly, relieved. And he looked forward with considerable satisfaction to an early visit to old Hannibal's laundry.

It must be confessed, also, that another matter, a simple affair of gallantry, was giving him an equally unusual, unexpected, and absurd annoyance, which he had never before permitted to such trivialities. In a recent visit to a fashionable watering-place he had attracted the attention of what appeared to be a respectable, matter-of-fact woman, the wife of a recently elected rural senator. She was, however, singularly beautiful, and as singularly cold. It was perhaps this quality, and her evident annoyance at some unreasoning prepossession which Jack's fascinations exercised upon her, that heightened that reckless desire for risk and excitement which really made up the greater part of his gallantry. Nevertheless, as was his habit, he had treated her always with a charming unconsciousness of his own attentions, and a frankness that seemed inconsistent with any insidious approach. In fact, Mr Hamlin seldom made love to anybody, but permitted it to be made to him with good-humored deprecation and cheerful skepticism. He had once, quite accidentally, while riding, come upon her when she had strayed from her own riding party, and had behaved with such unexpected circumspection and propriety, not to mention a certain thoughtful abstraction,—it was the day he had received Sophy's letter,—that she was constrained to make the first advances. This led to a later innocent rendezvous, in which Mrs Camperly was impelled to confide to Mr Hamlin the fact that her husband had really never understood her. Jack listened with an understanding and sympathy quickened by long experience of such confessions. If anything had ever kept him from marriage it was this evident incompatibility of the conjugal relations with a just conception of the feminine soul and its aspirations.

And so eventually this yearning for sympathy dragged Mrs Camperly's clean skirts and rustic purity after Jack's heels into various places and various situations not so clean, rural, or innocent; made her miserably unhappy in his absence, and still more miserably happy in his presence; impelled her to lie, cheat, and bear false witness; forced her to listen with mingled shame and admiration to narrow criticism of his faults, from natures so palpably inferior to his own that her moral sense was confused and shaken; gave her two distinct lives, but so unreal and feverish that, with a recklessness equal to his own, she was at last ready to merge them both into his. For the first time in his life Mr Hamlin found himself bored at the beginning of an affair, actually hesitated, and suddenly disappeared from San Francisco.

He turned up a few days later at Aunt Chloe's door, with various packages of presents and quite the air of a returning father of a family, to the intense delight of that lady and to Sophy's proud gratification. For he was lost in a profuse, boyish admiration of her pretty studio, and in wholesome reverence for her art and her astounding progress. They were also amused at his awe and evident alarm at the portraits of two ladies, her latest sitters, that were still on the easels, and, in consideration of his half-assumed, half-real bashfulness, they turned their faces to the wall. Then his quick, observant eye detected a photograph of himself on the mantel.

'What's that?' he asked suddenly.

Sophy and Aunt Chloe exchanged meaning glances. Sophy had, as a surprise to Jack, just completed a handsome crayon portrait of himself from an old photograph furnished by Hannibal, and the picture was at that moment in the window of her former patron,—the photographer.

'Oh, dat! Miss Sophy jus' put it dar fo' de lady sitters to look at to gib 'em a pleasant 'spresshion,' said Aunt Chloe, chuckling.

Mr Hamlin did not laugh, but quietly slipped the photograph into his pocket. Yet, perhaps, it had not been recognized.

Then Sophy proposed to have luncheon in the studio; it was quite 'Bohemian' and fashionable, and many artists did it. But to her great surprise Jack gravely objected, preferring the little parlor of Aunt Chloe, the vine-fringed windows, and the heavy respectable furniture. He thought it was profaning the studio, and then—anybody might come in. This unusual circumspection amused them, and was believed to be part of the boyish awe with which Jack regarded the models, the draperies, and the studies on the walls. Certain it was that he was much more at his ease in the parlor, and when he and Sophy were once more alone at their meal, although he ate nothing, he had regained all his old naïveté. Presently he leaned forward and placed his hand fraternally on her arm. Sophy looked up with an equally frank smile.

'You know I promised to let bygones be bygones, eh? Well, I intended it, and more,—I intended to make 'em so. I told you I'd never speak to you again of that man who tried to run you off, and I intended that no one else should. Well, as he was the only one who could talk—that meant him. But the cards are out of my hands; the game's been played without me. For he's dead!'

The girl started. Mr Hamlin's hand passed caressingly twice or thrice along her sleeve with a peculiar gentleness that seemed to magnetize her.

'Dead,' he repeated slowly. 'Shot in San Diego by another man, but not by me. I had him tracked as far as that, and had my eyes on him, but it wasn't my deal. But there,' he added, giving her magnetized arm a gentle and final tap as if to awaken it, 'he's dead, and so is the whole story. And now we'll drop it forever.'

The girl's downcast eyes were fixed on the table.

'But there's my sister,' she murmured.

'Did she know you went with him?' asked Jack.

'No; but she knows I ran away.'

'Well, you ran away from home to study how to be an artist, don't you see? Some day she'll find out you *are one;* that settles the whole thing.'

They were both quite cheerful again when Aunt Chloe returned to clear the table, especially Jack, who was in the best spirits, with preternaturally bright eyes and a somewhat rare color on his cheeks. Aunt Chloe, who had noticed that his breathing was hurried at times, watched him narrowly, and when later he slipped from the room, followed him into the passage. He was leaning against the wall. In an instant the negress was at his side.

'De Lawdy Gawd, Marse Jack, not *agin?*'

He took his handkerchief, slightly streaked with blood, from his lips and said faintly, 'Yes, it came on—on the boat; but I thought the d—d thing was over. Get me out of this, quick, to some hotel, before she knows it. You can tell her I was called away. Say that'—but his breath failed him, and when Aunt Chloe caught him like a child in her strong arms he could make no resistance.

In another hour he was unconscious, with two doctors at his bedside, in the little room that had been occupied by Sophy. It was a sharp attack, but prompt attendance and skillful nursing availed; he rallied the next day, but it would be weeks, the doctors said, before he could be removed in safety. Sophy was transferred to the parlor, but spent most of her time at Jack's bedside with Aunt Chloe, or in the studio with the door open between it and the bedroom. In spite of his enforced idleness and weakness, it was again a singularly pleasant experience to Jack; it amused him to sometimes see Sophy at her work through the open door, and when sitters came,—for he had insisted on her continuing her duties as before, keeping his invalid presence in the house a secret,—he had all the satisfaction of a mischievous boy in rehearsing to Sophy such of the conversation as could be overheard through the closed door, and speculating on the possible wonder and chagrin of the sitters had they discovered him. Even when he was convalescent and strong enough to be helped into the parlor and garden, he preferred to remain propped up in Sophy's little bedroom. It was evident, however, that this predilection was connected with no suggestion nor reminiscence of Sophy herself. It was true that he had once asked her if it didn't make her 'feel like home.' The decided negative from Sophy seemed to mildly surprise him. 'That's odd,' he said; 'now all these fixings and things,' pointing to the flowers in a vase, the little hanging shelf of books, the knickknacks on the mantel-shelf, and the few feminine ornaments that still remained, 'look rather like home to me.'

So the days slipped by, and although Mr Hamlin was soon able to walk short distances, leaning on Sophy's arm, in the evening twilight, along the river bank, he was still missed from the haunts of dissipated men. A good many people wondered, and others, chiefly of the more irrepressible sex, were singularly concerned. Apparently one of these, one sultry afternoon, stopped before the shadowed window of a photographer's; she was a handsome, well-dressed woman, yet bearing a certain country-like simplicity that was unlike the restless smartness of the more urban promenaders who passed her. Nevertheless she had halted before Mr Hamlin's picture, which Sophy had not yet dared to bring home and present to him, and was gazing at it with rapt and breathless attention. Suddenly she shook down her veil and entered the shop. Could the proprietor kindly tell her if that portrait was the work of a local artist?

The proprietor was both proud and pleased to say that *it was!* It was the work of a Miss Brown, a young girl student; in fact, a mere schoolgirl, one might say. He could show her others of her pictures.

Thanks. But could he tell her if this portrait was from life?

No doubt; the young lady had a studio, and he himself had sent her sitters.

And perhaps this was the portrait of one that he had sent her?

No; but she was very popular and becoming quite the fashion. Very probably this gentleman, who, he understood, was quite a public character, had heard of her, and selected her on that account.

The lady's face flushed slightly. The photographer continued. The picture was not for sale; it was only there on exhibition; in fact it was to be returned to-morrow.

To the sitter?

He couldn't say. It was to go back to the studio. Perhaps the sitter would be there.

And this studio? Could she have its address?

The man wrote a few lines on his card. Perhaps the lady would be kind enough to say that he had sent her. The lady, thanking him, partly lifted her veil to show a charming smile, and gracefully withdrew. The photographer was pleased. Miss

Brown had evidently got another sitter, and, from that momentary glimpse of her face, it would be a picture as beautiful and attractive as the man's. But what was the odd idea that struck him? She certainly reminded him of some one! There was the same heavy hair, only this lady's was golden, and she was older and more mature. And he remained for a moment with knitted brows musing over his counter.

Meantime the fair stranger was making her way towards the river suburb. When she reached Aunt Chloe's cottage, she paused, with the unfamiliar curiosity of a new-comer, over its quaint and incongruous exterior. She hesitated a moment also when Aunt Chloe appeared in the doorway, and, with a puzzled survey of her features, went upstairs to announce a visitor. There was the sound of hurried shutting of doors, of the moving of furniture, quick footsteps across the floor, and then a girlish laugh that startled her. She ascended the stairs breathlessly to Aunt Chloe's summons, found the negress on the landing, and knocked at a door which bore a card marked 'Studio.' The door opened; she entered; there were two sudden outcries that might have come from one voice.

'Sophonisba!'

'Marianne!'

'Hush.'

The woman had seized Sophy by the wrist and dragged her to the window. There was a haggard look of desperation in her face akin to that which Hamlin had once seen in her sister's eyes on the boat, as she said huskily: 'I did not know *you* were here. I came to see the woman who had painted Mr Hamlin's portrait. I did not know it was *you*. Listen! Quick! answer me one question. Tell me—I implore you—for the sake of the mother who bore us both!—tell me—is this the man for whom you left home?'

'No! No! A hundred times no!'

Then there was a silence. Mr Hamlin from the bedroom heard no more.

An hour later, when the two women opened the studio door, pale but composed, they were met by the anxious and tearful face of Aunt Chloe.

'Lawdy Gawd, Missy,—but dey done gone!—bofe of 'em!'

'Who is gone?' demanded Sophy, as the woman beside her trembled and grew paler still.

'Marse Jack and dat fool nigger, Hannibal.'

'Mr Hamlin gone?' repeated Sophy incredulously. 'When? Where?'

'Jess now—on de down boat. Sudden business. Didn't like to disturb yo' and yo' friend. Said he'd write.'

'But he was ill—almost helpless,' gasped Sophy.

'Dat's why he took dat old nigger. Lawdy, Missy, bress yo' heart. Dey both knows aich udder, shuah! It's all right. Dar now, dar dey are; listen.'

She held up her hand. A slow pulsation, that might have been the dull, labored beating of their own hearts, was making itself felt throughout the little cottage. It came nearer,—a deep regular inspiration that seemed slowly to fill and possess the whole tranquil summer twilight. It was nearer still—was abreast of the house—passed—grew fainter—and at last died away like a deep-drawn sigh. It was the down boat, that was now separating Mr Hamlin and his protégée, even as it had once brought them together.

THE ARGONAUTS OF '49

As so much of my writing has dealt with the Argonauts of '49,* I propose, by way of introduction, to discourse briefly on an episode of American life as quaint and typical as that of the Greek adventurers whose name I have borrowed. It is a crusade without a cross, an exodus without a prophet. It is not a pretty story; I do not know that it is even instructive. It is of a life of which, perhaps, the best that can be said is that it exists no longer.

Let me first give an idea of the country which these people re-created, and the civilization they displaced. For more than three hundred years California was of all Christian countries the least known. The glow and glamour of Spanish tradition and discovery hung about it. There was an English map in which it was set down as an island. There was the Rio de Los Reyes*—a kind of gorgeous Mississippi—leading directly to the heart of the Continent, which De Fonte claimed to have discovered. There was the Anian passage—a prophetic forecast of the Pacific Railroad—through which Maldonado* declared that he sailed to the North Atlantic. Another Spanish discoverer brought his mendacious personality directly from the Pacific, by way of Columbia River, to Lake Ontario; on which, I am rejoiced to say, he found a Yankee vessel from Boston, whose captain informed him that *he* had come up from the Atlantic only a few days before him! Along the long line of iron-bound coast* the old freebooters chased the timid Philippine galleons, and in its largest bay, beside the present gateway of the West,—San Francisco,—Sir Francis Drake* lay for two weeks and scraped the barnacles from his adventurous keels. It is only within the past twenty-five years, that a company of gold-diggers, turning up the ocean sands near Port Umpqua, came upon some large cakes of wax deeply imbedded in the broken and fire-scarred ribs of a wreck of ancient date. The Californian heart was at once fired at the discovery, and in a few weeks a hundred men or more were digging, burrowing, and scraping for the lost treasure of the Philippine galleon. At last they found—what think you?—a few cutlasses with an English stamp upon their blades. The enterprising and gallant—and slightly piratical—Sir Francis Drake had been there before them!

Yet they were peaceful, pastoral days for California. Through the great central valley the Sacramento poured an unstained current into a majestic bay, ruffled by no keels and fretted by no wharves. The Angelus bell rung at San Bernardino, and, taken up by every Mission tower along the darkening coast, called the good people to prayer and sleep before nine o'clock every night. Leagues of wild oats, progenitors of those great wheat fields that now drug the markets, hung their idle heads on the hillsides; vast herds of untamed cattle, whose hides and horns alone made the scant commerce of those days, wandered over the illimitable plains, knowing no human figure but that of the yearly riding vaquero on his unbroken mustang, which they regarded as the early aborigines did the Spanish cavalry, as one individual creation. Around the white walls of the Mission buildings were clustered the huts of the Indian neophytes, who dressed neatly, but not expensively, in mud. Presidios garrisoned by a dozen raw militiamen kept the secular order, and in the scattered pueblos rustic alcaldes dispensed, like Sancho Panza, proverbial wisdom and practical equity to the bucolic litigants. In looking over some Spanish law papers, one day, I came upon a remarkable instance of the sagacity of Alcalde Felipe Gomez of Santa Barbara. An injured wife accused her husband of serenading the wife of another. The faithless husband and his too seductive guitar were both produced in court. 'Play,' said the alcalde to the gay Lothario.* The unfortunate man was obliged to repeat his amorous performance of the preceding night. 'I find nothing here,' said the excellent alcalde after a moment's pause, 'but an infamous voice and an execrable style. I dismiss the complaint of the Señora, but I shall hold the Señor on the charge of vilely disturbing the peace of Santa Barbara.'

They were happy, tranquil days. The proprietors of the old ranchos ruled in a patriarchal style, and lived to a patriarchal age. On a soil half tropical in its character, in a climate wholly original in its practical conditions, a soft-handed Latin race slept and smoked the half year's sunshine away, and believed that they had discovered a new Spain! They awoke from their dream only to find themselves strangers on their own soil, foreigners in their own country, ignorant even of the treasure they had been sent to guard. A political and social earthquake, more powerful than any physical convulsions they had ever known, shook the foundation of the land, and in the disrupted strata and rent fissures the treasure suddenly glittered before their eyes.

Though the change came upon them suddenly, it had been prefigured by a chain of circumstances whose logical links future historians will not overlook. It was not the finding of a few grains of gold by a day laborer at Sutter's Mill,* but that for years before the way had been slowly opened and the doors unlocked to the people who were to profit by this discovery. The real pioneers of the lawless, irreligious band whose story I am repeating were the oldest and youngest religions known. Do Americans ever think that they owe their right to California to the Catholic Church and the Mormon brotherhood? Yet Father Junipero Serra ringing his bell in the heathen wilderness of Upper California, and Brigham Young* leading his half famished legions from Nauvoo to Salt Lake, were the two great commanders of the Argonauts of '49. All that western emigration which, prior to the gold discovery, penetrated the Oregon and California valleys and half Americanized the Coast, would have perished by the way, but for the providentially created oasis of Salt Lake City. The halting trains of alkali-poisoned oxen, the footsore and despairing teamsters, gathered rest and succor from the Mormon settlement. The British frigate* that sailed into the port of Monterey a day or two late, saw the American flag that had, under this providence, crossed the continent, flying from the Cross of the Cathedral! A day sooner, and this story might have been an English record.

Were our friends, the Argonauts, at all affected by these coincidences? I think not. They had that lordly contempt for a southern, soft-tongued race which belonged to their Anglo-Saxon lineage. They were given to no superstitious romance, exalted by no special mission, stimulated by no high ambition; they were skeptical of even the existence of the golden fleece until they saw it. Equal to their fate, they accepted with a kind of heathen philosophy whatever it might bring. 'If there isn't any gold, what are you going to do with these sluice-boxes?' said a newly arrived emigrant to his friend. 'They will make first-class coffins,' answered the friend, with the simple directness of a man who has calculated all his chances. If they did not burn their vessels behind them, like Pizarro,* they at least left the good ship Argo dismantled and rotting at their Colchian wharf.* Sailors were shipped only for the outward voyage; nobody expected to *return*, even those who anticipated failure. Fertile in expedients, they twisted their failures into a certain sort of success. Until recently, there stood in San Francisco a house of the early days whose foundations were built entirely of plug tobacco in boxes. The consignee had found a glut in the tobacco market, but lumber for foundations was at a tremendous premium! An Argonaut just arriving was amazed at recognizing in the boatman who pulled him ashore, and who charged him the modest sum of fifty dollars for the performance, a brother classmate of Oxford. 'Were you not,' he asked eagerly, 'senior wrangler in '43?' 'Yes,' said the other significantly, 'but I also pulled stroke oar against Cambridge.' If the special training of years sometimes failed to procure pecuniary recognition, an idle accomplishment, sometimes even a physical peculiarity, succeeded. At my first breakfast in a restaurant on Long Wharf, I was haunted during the meal by a shadowy resemblance which the waiter who took my order bore to a gentleman to whom in my boyhood I had looked up as a mirror of elegance, urbanity, and social accomplishment. Fearful lest I should insult the waiter—who carried a revolver—by this reminiscence, I said nothing to him; but a later inquiry of the proprietor proved that my suspicions were correct. 'He's mighty handy,' said the man, 'and kin talk elegant to a customer as is waiting for his cakes, and make him kinder forget he ain't sarved.' With an earnest desire to restore my old friend to his former position, I asked if it would not be possible to fill his place. 'I'm afraid not,' said the proprietor with a sudden suspicion, and he added significantly, 'I don't think you'd suit.' It was this wonderful adaptability, perhaps influenced by a climate that produced fruit out of season, that helped the Argonauts to success, or mitigated their defeats. A now distinguished lawyer, remarkable for his Herculean build, found himself on landing without a cent—rather let me say without twenty dollars—to pay the porterage of his trunk to the hotel. Shouldering it, he was staggering from the landing, when a stranger stepped towards him, remarking he had not 'half a load,' quietly added his own valise to the lawyer's burden, and handing him ten dollars and his address, departed before the legal gentleman could recover from his astonishment. The valise, however, was punctually delivered, and the lawyer often congratulated himself on the comparative ease with which he won his first fee.

Much of the easy adaptability was due to the character of the people. What that character was, perhaps it would not be well to say. At least I should prefer to defer criticism until I could add to the calmness the safe distance of the historian. You will find some of their peculiarities described in the frank autobiographies of those two gentlemen* who executed a little commission for Macbeth in which Banquo was concerned. In distant parts of the continent they had left families, creditors, and in some instances even officers of justice, perplexed and lamenting. There were husbands who had deserted their own wives,—and in some extreme cases even the wives of others,— for this haven of refuge. Nor was it possible to tell from their superficial exterior, or even their daily walk and action, whether they were or were not named in the counts of this general indictment. Some of the best men had the worst antecedents, some of the worst rejoiced in a spotless puritan pedigree. 'The boys seem to have taken a fresh deal all round,' said Mr John Oakhurst one day to me, with the easy confidence of a man who was conscious of his ability to win my money, 'and there is no knowing whether a man will turn up knave or king.' It is relevant to this anecdote that Mr John Oakhurst himself came of a family whose ancestors regarded games of chance as sinful, because they were trifling and amusing, but who had never conceived they might be made the instruments of successful speculation and even tragic earnestness. 'To think,' said Mr Oakhurst, as he rose from a ten minutes' sitting with a gain of five thousand dollars,—'to think there's folks as believes that keerds is a waste of time.'

Such were the character and the antecedents of the men who gave the dominant and picturesque coloring to the life of that period. Doubtless the papers of the ancient Argo showed a cleaner bill of moral health, but doubtless no type of adventure more distinct or original. I would not have it inferred that there was not a class, respectable in numbers as in morals, among and yet distinct from these. But they have no place here save as a background to the salient outlines and deeply etched figures of the Argonauts. Character ruled, and the strongest was not always the best. Let me bring them a little nearer. Let me sketch two pictures of them: one in their gathered concourse in their city by the sea, one in their lonely scattered cabins in the camps of the Sierras.

It is the memorable winter of '52, a typical Californian winter—unlike anything known to most of my readers; a winter from whose snowy nest in the Sierras the fluttering, new-fledged Spring freed itself without a struggle. It is a season of falling rains and springing grasses, of long nights of shower, and days of cloud and sunshine. There are hours when the quickening earth seems to throb beneath one's feet, and the blue eyes of heaven to twinkle through its misty lashes. High up in the Sierras, unsunned depths of snow form the vast reservoirs that later will flood the plains, causing the homesick wanderers on the lowlands to look with awe upon a broad expanse of overflow, a lake that might have buried the State of Massachusetts in its yellow depths. The hillsides are gay with flowers, and, as in the old fairy story, every utterance of the kindly Spring falls from her lips to the ground in rubies and emeralds. And yet it is called 'a hard season,' and flour is fifty dollars a barrel. In San Francisco it has been raining steadily for two weeks. The streets are almost impassable with mud, and over some of the more dangerous depths planks are thrown. There are few street lamps, but the shops are still lighted, and the streets are full of long-bearded, long-booted men, eager for some new excitement, their only idea of recreation from the feverish struggle of the day. Perhaps it is a passing carriage—a phenomenal carriage, one of the half dozen known in the city—that becoming helplessly mired is instantly surrounded by a score of willing hands whose owners are only too happy to be rewarded by a glimpse of a female face through the window, even though that face be haggard, painted, or gratuitously plain. Perhaps it is in the little theatre, where the cry of a baby in the audience brings down a tumultuous encore from the whole house. Perhaps it is in the gilded drinking saloon, into which some one rushes with arms extended at right angles, and conveys in that one pantomimic action the signal of the semaphore telegraph on Telegraph Hill* that a sidewheel steamer has arrived, and that there are 'letters from home.' Perhaps it is the long queue that afterwards winds and stretches from the Post Office half a mile away. Perhaps it is the eager men who, following it rapidly down, bid fifty, a hundred, two hundred, three hundred, and five hundred dollars for favored places in the line. Perhaps it is the haggard man who nervously tears open his letter and after a moment's breathless pause faints and falls senseless beside his comrades. Or perhaps it is a row and a shot in the streets, but in '52 this was hardly an excitement.

The gambling-saloon is always the central point of interest. There are four of them,—the largest public buildings in the city,—thronged and crowded all night. They are approached by no mysterious passage or guarded entrance, but are frankly open to the street, with the further invitation of gilding, lights, warmth, and music. Strange to say, there is a quaint decorum about them. They are the quietest halls in San Francisco. There is no drunkenness, no quarreling, scarcely any exultation or disappointment. Men who have already staked their health and fortune in this emigration are but little affected by the lesser stake on red or black, or the turn of a card. Business men who have gambled all day in their legitimate enterprise find nothing to excite them unduly here. In the intervals of music, a thoughtful calm pervades the vast assembly; people move around noiselessly from table to table, as if Fortune were nervous as well as fickle; a cane falling upon the floor causes every one to look up, a loud laugh or exclamation excites a stare of virtuous indignation. The most respectable citizens, though they might not play, are to be seen here of an evening. Old friends, who perhaps parted at the church door in the States, meet here without fear and without reproach. Even among the players are represented all classes and conditions of men. One night at a faro table a player suddenly slipped from his seat to the floor, a dead man. Three doctors, also players, after a brief examination, pronounced it disease of the heart. The coroner, sitting at the right of the dealer, instantly impaneled the rest of the players, who, laying down their cards, briefly gave a verdict in accordance with the facts, and went on with their game!

I do not mean to say that, under this surface calm, there was not often the intensest feeling. There was a Western man, who, having made a few thousands in the mines, came to San Francisco to take the Eastern steamer home. The night before he was to sail, he entered the Arcade saloon, and seating himself at a table in sheer listlessness, staked a twenty-dollar gold piece on the game. He won. He won again without removing his stake. It was, in short, that old story told so often—how in two hours he won a fortune, how an hour later he rose from the table a ruined man. Well—the steamer sailed without him. He was a simple man, knowing little of the world, and his sudden fortune and equally sudden reverse almost crazed him. He dared not write to the wife who awaited him; he had not pluck enough to return to the mines and build his fortune up anew. A fatal fascination held him to the spot. He took some humble occupation in the city, and regularly lost his scant earnings where his wealth had gone before. His ragged figure and haggard face appeared as regularly as the dealer at the table. So, a year passed. But if he had forgotten the waiting wife, she had not forgotten him. With infinite toil she at last procured a passage to San Francisco, and was landed with her child penniless upon its wharf. In her sore extremity she told her story to a passing stranger—the last man, perhaps, to have met—Mr John Oakhurst, a gambler! He took her to a hotel, and quietly provided for her immediate wants. Two or three evenings after this, the Western man, still playing at the same table, won some trifling stake three times in succession, as if Fortune were about to revisit him. At this moment, Mr Oakhurst clapped him on the shoulder. 'I will give you,' he said, quietly, 'three thousand dollars for your next play.' The man hesitated. 'Your wife is at the door,' continued Mr Oakhurst *sotto voce*. 'Will you take it? Quick!' The man accepted. But the spirit of the gambler was strong within him, and as Mr Oakhurst perhaps fully expected, he waited to see the result of the play. Mr Oakhurst lost! With a look of gratitude the man turned to Oakhurst and seizing the three thousand dollars hurried away, as if fearful he might change his mind. 'That was a bad spurt of yours, Jack,' said a friend innocently, not observing the smile that had passed between the dealer and Jack. 'Yes,' said Jack coolly, 'but I got tired of seein'' that chap around.' 'But,' said his friend in alarm, 'you don't mean to say that you'—and he hesitated. 'I mean to say, my dear boy,' said Jack, 'that this yer little deal was a put-up job betwixt the dealer and me. It's the first time,' he added seriously, with an oath which I think the recording angel instantly passed to Jack's credit, 'it's the first time as I ever played a game that wasn't *on the square*.'

The social life of that day was peculiar. Gentlemen made New Year's calls in long boots and red flannel shirts. In later days the wife of an old pioneer used to show a chair with a hole through its cushion made by a gentleman caller who, sitting down suddenly in bashful confusion, had exploded his revolver. The best-dressed men were gamblers; the best-dressed ladies had no right to that title. At balls and parties dancing was tabooed, owing to the unhappy complications which arose from the disproportionate number of partners to the few ladies that were present. The ingenious device of going through a quadrille with a different partner for each figure sprang from the fertile brain of a sorely beset San Francisco belle. The wife of an army officer told me that she never thought of returning home with the same escort, and not unfrequently was accompanied with what she called a 'full platoon.' 'I never knew before,' she said, 'what they meant by "the pleasure of *your company*." ' In the multiplicity of such attentions surely there was safety.

Such was the urban life of the Argonauts—its salient peculiarities softened and subdued by the constant accession of strangers from the East and the departure of its own citizens for the interior. As each succeeding ocean steamer brought fresh faces from the East, a corresponding change took place in the type and in the manners and morals. When fine clothes appeared upon the streets and men swore less frequently, people began to put locks on their doors and portable property was no longer out at night. As fine houses were built, real estate rose, and the dwellers in the old tents were pushed from the contiguity of their richer brothers. San Francisco saw herself naked, and was ashamed. The old Argonautic brotherhood, with its fierce sincerity, its terrible directness, its pathetic simplicity, was broken up. Some of the members were content to remain in a Circean* palace of material and sensuous delight, but the type was transferred to the mountains, and thither I propose to lead you.

It is a country unlike any other. Nature here is as rude, as inchoate, as unfinished, as the life. The people seem to have come here a thousand years too soon, and before the great hostess was ready to receive them. The forests, vast, silent, damp with their undergrowth of gigantic ferns, recall a remote carboniferous epoch. The trees are monstrous, sombre, and monotonously alike. Everything is new, crude, and strange. The grass blades are enormous and far apart, there is no carpet to the soil; even the few Alpine flowers are odorless and bizarre. There is nothing soft, tender, or pastoral in the landscape. Nature affects the heroics rather than the bucolics. Theocritus* himself could scarcely have given melody to the utterance of these Ætnean herdsmen, with their brierwood pipes, and their revolvers slung at their backs. There are vast spaces of rock and cliff, long intervals of ravine and cañon, and sudden and awful lapses of precipice. The lights and shadows are Rembrandtish,* and against this background the faintest outline of a human figure stands out starkly.

They lived at first in tents, and then in cabins. The climate was gracious, and except for the rudest purposes of shelter from the winter rains, they could have slept out of doors the year round, as many preferred to do. As they grew more ambitious, perhaps a small plot of ground was inclosed and cultivated; but for the first few years they looked upon themselves as tenants at will, and were afraid of putting down anything they could not take away. Chimneys to their cabins were for a long time avoided as having this objectionable feature. Even at this day, deserted mining-camps are marked by the solitary adobe chimneys still left standing where the frame of the original cabin was moved to some newer location. Their housekeeping was of the rudest kind. For many months the frying-pan formed their only available cooking-utensil. It was lashed to the wandering miner's back, like the troubadour's guitar. He fried his bread, his beans, his bacon, and occasionally stewed his coffee, in this single vessel. But that Nature worked for him with a balsamic air and breezy tonics, he would have succumbed. Happily his meals were few and infrequent; happily the inventions of his mother East were equal to his needs. His progressive track through these mountain solitudes was marked with tin cans bearing the inscriptions: 'Cove Oysters,' 'Shaker Sweet Corn,' 'Yeast Powder,' 'Boston Crackers,' and the like. But in the hour of adversity and the moment of perplexity, his main reliance was beans! It was the sole legacy of the Spanish California. The conqueror and the conquered fraternized over their *frijoles*.

The Argonaut's dress was peculiar. He was ready if not skillful with his needle, and was fond of patching his clothes until the original material disappeared beneath a cloud of amendments. The flour-sack was his main dependence. When its contents had sustained and comforted the inner man, the husk clothed the outer one. Two gentlemen of respectability in earlier days lost their identity in the labels somewhat conspicuously borne on the seats of their trousers, and were known to the camp in all seriousness as 'Genesee Mills' and 'Eagle Brand.' In the Southern mines a quantity of seamen's clothing, condemned by the Navy Department and sold at auction, was bought up, and for a year afterwards the sombre woodland shades of Stanislaus and Merced* were lightened by the white ducks and blue and white shirts of sailor landsmen. It was odd that the only picturesque bit of color in their dress was accidental, and owing to a careless, lazy custom. Their handkerchiefs of coarse blue, green, or yellow bandanna were for greater convenience in hot weather knotted at the ends and thrown shawlwise around the shoulders. Against a background of olive foliage, the effect was always striking and kaleidoscopic. The soft felt, broad-brimmed hat, since known as the California hat, was their only head-covering. A tall hat on anybody but a clergyman or a gambler would have justified a blow.

They were singularly handsome, to a man. Not solely in the muscular development and antique grace acquired through open-air exercise and unrestrained freedom of limb, but often in color, expression, and even softness of outline. They were mainly young men, whose beards were virgin, soft, silken, and curling. They had not always time to cut their hair, and this often swept their shoulders with the lovelocks of Charles II.* There were faces that made one think of Delaroche's Saviour.* There were dashing figures, bold-eyed, jauntily insolent, and cavalierly reckless, that would have delighted Meissonier.* Add to this the foreign element of Chilian and Mexican, and you have a combination of form and light and color unknown to any other modern English-speaking community. At sunset on the red mountain road, a Mexican pack-train perhaps slowly winds its way toward the plain. Each animal wears a gayly colored blanket beneath its pack saddle; the leading mule is musical with bells, and brightly caparisoned; the muleteers wear the national dress, with striped *serape* of red and black, deerskin trousers open from the knee, and fringes with bullion buttons, and have on each heel a silver spur with rowels three inches in diameter. If they were thus picturesque in external magnificence, no less romantic were they in expression and character. Their hospitality was barbaric, their generosity spontaneous. Their appreciation of merit always took the form of pecuniary testimonials, whether it was a church and parsonage given to a favorite preacher, or the Danaë-like shower of gold* they rained upon the pretty peerson of a popular actress. No mendicant had to beg; a sympathizing bystander took up a subscription in his hat. Their generosity was emulative and cumulative. During the great War of the Rebellion, the millions gathered in the Treasury of the Sanitary Commission had their source in a San Francisco bar-room. 'It's mighty rough on those chaps who are wounded,' said a casual drinker, 'and I'm sorry for them.' 'How much are you sorry?' asked a gambler. 'Five hundred dollars,' said the first speaker aggressively. 'I'll see that five hundred dollars, and go a thousand better!' said the gambler, putting down the money. In half an hour fifteen thousand dollars was telegraphed to Washington from San Francisco, and this great national charity—open to North and South alike, afterwards reinforced by three millions of California gold—sprang into life.

In their apparently thoughtless free-handedness there was often a vein of practical sagacity. It is a well-known fact that after the great fire in Sacramento, the first subscription to the rebuilding of the Methodist Church came from the hands of a noted gambler. The good pastor, while accepting the gift, could not help asking the giver why he did not keep the money to build another gambling-house. 'It would be making things a little *monotonous* out yer, ole man,' responded the gambler gravely, 'and it's variety that's wanted for a big town.'

They were splendidly loyal in their friendships. Perhaps the absence of female society and domestic ties turned the current of their tenderness and sentiment towards each other. To be a man's 'partner' signified something more than a common pecuniary or business interest; it was to be his friend through good or ill report, in adversity or fortune, to cleave to him and none other—to be ever jealous of him! There were Argonauts who were more faithful to their partners than, I fear, they had ever been to their wives; there were partners whom even the grave could not divide—who remained solitary and loyal to a dead man's memory. To insult a man's partner was to insult him; to step between two partners in a quarrel was attended with the same danger and uncertainty that involves the peace-maker in a conjugal dispute. The heroic possibilities of a Damon and a Pythias* were always present; there were men who had fulfilled all those conditions, and better still without a knowledge or belief that they were classical, with no mythology to lean their backs against, and hardly a conscious appreciation of a later faith that is symbolized by sacrifice. In these unions there were the same odd combinations often seen in the marital relations: a tall and a short man, a delicate sickly youth and a middle-aged man of powerful frame, a grave reticent nature and a spontaneous exuberant one. Yet in spite of these incongruities there was always the same blind unreasoning fidelity to each other. It is true that their zeal sometimes outran their discretion. There is a story extant that a San Francisco stranger, indulging in some free criticism of religious denominations, suddenly found himself sprawling upon the floor with an irate

Kentuckian, revolver in hand, standing over him. When an explanation was demanded by the crowd, the Kentuckian pensively returned his revolver to his belt. 'Well, *I* ain't got anythin' agin the stranger, but he said somethin' a minit ago agin Quakers, and I want him to understand that my *pardner* is a Quaker, and—a *peaceful man!*'

I should like to give some pictures of their domestic life, but the women were few and the family hearthstones and domestic altars still fewer. Of housewifely virtues the utmost was made; the model spouse invariably kept a boarding-house, and served her husband's guests. In rare cases, the woman who was a crown to her husband took in washing also.

There was a woman of this class who lived in a little mining-camp in the Sierras. Her husband was a Texan—a good-humored giant, who had won the respect of the camp probably quite as much by his amiable weakness as by his great physical power. She was an Eastern woman; had been, I think, a schoolmistress, and had lived in cities up to the time of her marriage and emigration. She was not, perhaps, personally attractive; she was plain and worn beyond her years, and her few personal accomplishments—a slight knowledge of French and Italian, music, the Latin classification of plants, natural philosophy and Blair's Rhetoric—did not tell upon the masculine inhabitants of Ringtail Cañon. Yet she was universally loved, and Aunt Ruth, as she was called, or 'Old Ma'am Richards,' was lifted into an idealization of the aunt, mother, or sister of every miner in the camp. She reciprocated in a thousand kindly ways, mending the clothes, ministering to the sick, and even answering the long home letters of the men.

Presently she fell ill. Nobody knew exactly what was the matter with her, but she pined slowly away. When the burthen of her household tasks was lifted from her shoulders, she took to long walks, wandering over the hills, and was often seen upon the highest ridge at sunset, looking toward the east. Here at last she was found senseless,—the result, it was said, of over exertion, and she was warned to keep her house. So she kept her house, and even went so far as to keep her bed. One day, to everybody's astonishment, she died. 'Do you know what they say Ma'am Richards died of?' said Yuba Bill to his partner.

'The doctor says she died of *nostalgia*,' said Bill. 'What blank thing is nostalgia?' asked the other. 'Well, it's a kind o' longin' to go to heaven!' Perhaps he was right.

As a general thing the Argonauts were not burthened with sentiment, and were utterly free from its more dangerous ally, sentimentalism. They took a sardonic delight in stripping all meretricious finery from their speech; they had a sarcastic fashion of eliminating everything but the facts from poetic or imaginative narrative. With all that terrible directness of statement which was habitual to them, when they indulged in innuendo it was significantly cruel and striking. In the early days, Lynch law punished horse-stealing with death. A man one day was arrested and tried for this offense. After hearing the evidence, the jury duly retired to consult upon their verdict. For some reason—perhaps from an insufficiency of proof, perhaps from motives of humanity, perhaps because the census was already showing an alarming decrease in the male population—the jury showed signs of hesitation. The crowd outside became impatient. After waiting an hour, the ringleader put his head into the room and asked if the jury had settled upon a verdict. 'No,' said the foreman. 'Well,' answered the leader, 'take your own time, gentlemen; only remember that we're waitin' for this yer room to lay out the corpse in!'

Their humor was frequent, although never exuberant or spontaneous, and always contained a certain percentage of rude justice or morality under its sardonic exterior. The only ethical teaching of those days was through a joke or a sarcasm. While camps were moved by an epigram, the rude equity of Judge Lynch was swayed by a witticism. Even their pathos, which was more or less dramatic, partook of this quality. The odd expression, the quaint fancy, or even the grotesque gesture that rippled the surface consciousness with a smile, a moment later touched the depths of the heart with a sense of infinite sadness. They indulged sparingly in poetry and illustration, using only its rude, inchoate form of slang. Unlike the meaningless cues and catch-words of an older civilization, their slang was the condensed epigrammatic illustration of some fact, fancy, or perception. Generally it had some significant local derivation. The half-yearly drought brought forward the popular adjuration 'dry up' to express the natural climax of evaporated fluency. 'Played out' was a reminiscence of the gambling-table, and expressed that hopeless condition of affairs when even the operations of chance are suspended. To 'take stock' in any statement, theory, or suggestion indicates a pecuniary degree of trustful credulity. One can hardly call that slang, even though it came from a gambler's lips, which gives such a vivid condensation of death and the reckoning hereafter as was conveyed in the expression, 'handing in your checks.' In those days the slang was universal; there was no occasion to which it seemed inconsistent. Thomas Starr King* once told me that, after delivering a certain controversial sermon, he overheard the following dialogue between a parishioner and his friend. 'Well,' said the enthusiastic parishioner, referring to the sermon, 'what do you think of King now?' 'Think of him?' responded the friend, 'why, he took every trick!'

Sometimes, through the national habit of amusing exaggeration or equally grotesque understatement, certain words acquired a new significance. I remember the first night I spent in Virginia City was at a new hotel which had been but recently opened. After I had got comfortably to bed, I was aroused by the noise of scuffling and shouting below, punctuated by occasional pistol shots. In the morning I made my way to the bar-room, and found the landlord behind his counter with a bruised eye, a piece of court plaster extending from his cheek to his forehead, yet withal a pleasant smile upon his face. Taking my cue from this I said to him: 'Well, landlord, you had rather a lively time here last night.' 'Yes,' he replied, pleasantly. 'It *was* rather a lively time!' 'Do you often have such lively times in Virginia City?' I added, emboldened by his cheerfulness. 'Well, no,' he said, reflectively; 'the fact is we've only just opened yer, and last night was about the first time that the boys seemed to be gettin' really *acquainted!*'

The man who objected to join in a bear hunt because 'he hadn't lost any bears lately,' and the man who replied to the tourist's question 'if they grew any corn in that locality' by saying 'not a d—d bit, in fact scarcely any,' offered easy examples of this characteristic anticlimax and exaggeration. Often a flavor of gentle philosophy mingled with it. 'In course

I'd rather not drive a mule team,' said a teamster to me. 'In course I'd rather run a bank or be President: but when you've lived as long as I have, stranger, you'll find that in this yer world a man don't always get his "drathers." ' Often a man's trade or occupation lent a graphic power to his speech. On one occasion an engineer was relating to me the particulars of a fellow workman's death by consumption. 'Poor Jim,' he said, 'he got to running slower and slower, until one day—he stopped on his centre!' What a picture of the helpless hitch in this weary human machine! Sometimes the expression was borrowed from another's profession. At one time there was a difficulty in a surveyor's camp between the surveyor and a Chinaman. 'If I was you,' said a sympathizing teamster to the surveyor, 'I'd jest take that chap and theodolite* him out o' camp.' Sometimes the slang was a mere echo of the formulas of some popular excitement or movement. During a camp-meeting in the mountains, a teamster who had been swearing at his cattle was rebuked for his impiety by a young woman who had just returned from the meeting. 'Why, Miss,' said the astonished teamster, 'you don't call that swearing, do you? Why, you ought to hear Bill Jones exhort the impenitent mule!'

But can we entirely forgive the Argonaut for making his slang gratuitously permanent, for foisting upon posterity, who may forget these extenuating circumstances, such titles as 'One Horse Gulch,' 'Poker Flat,' 'Greaser Cañon,' 'Fiddletown,' 'Murderer's Bar,' and 'Dead Broke'? The map of California is still ghastly with this unhallowed christening. A tourist may well hesitate to write 'Dead Broke,' at the top of his letter, and any stranger would be justified in declining an invitation to 'Murderer's Bar.' It seemed as if the early Californian took a sardonic delight in the contrast which these names offered to the euphony of the old Spanish titles. It is fortunate that with few exceptions the counties of the State still bear the soft Castilian labials and gentle vowels. Tuolumne, Tulare, Yolo, Calaveras, Sonoma, Tehema, Siskyou, and Mendocino, to say nothing of the glorious company of the Apostles who perpetually praise California through the Spanish Catholic calendar. Yet wherever a saint dropped a blessing, some sinner afterwards squatted with an epithet. Extremes often meet. The omnibuses in San Francisco used to run from Happy Valley to the Mission Dolores. You had to go to Blaises first before you could get to Purissima. Yet I think the ferocious directness of these titles was preferable to the pinchbeck elegance of 'Copperopolis,' 'Argentinia,' the polyglot monstrosities of 'Oroville,' of 'Placerville,' or the remarkable sentiment of 'Romeosburgh' and 'Julietstown.' Sometimes the national tendency to abbreviation was singularly shown. 'Jamestown,' near Sonora, was always known as 'Jimtown,' and 'Moquelumne Hill,' after first suffering phonetic torture by being spelt with a 'k,' was finally drawn and quartered and now appears on the stage-coach as 'Mok Hill.' There were some names that defied all conjecture. The Pioneer coaches changed horses at a place called 'Paradox.' Why Paradox? No one could tell.

I wish I could say that the Spaniard fared any better than his language at the hands of the Argonauts. He was called a 'Greaser,' an unctuous reminiscence of the Mexican war, and applied erroneously to the Spanish Californian, who was *not* a Mexican. The pure blood of Castile ran in his veins. He held his lands sometimes by royal patent of Charles V.* He was grave, simple, and confiding. He accepted the Argonaut's irony as sincere, he permitted him to squat on his lands, he allowed him to marry his daughter. He found himself, in a few years, laughed at, landless, and alone. In his sore extremity he entered into a defensive alliance with some of his persecutors, and avenged himself after an extraordinary fashion. In all matters relating to early land grants he was the evergreen witness; his was the only available memory, his the only legal testimony, on the Coast. Perhaps strengthened by this repeated exercise, his memory became one of the most extraordinary, his testimony the most complete and corroborative, known to human experience. He recalled conversations, official orders, and precedents of fifty years ago as if they were matters of yesterday. He produced grants, *deseños*, signatures, and letters with promptitude and despatch. He evolved evidence from his inner consciousness, and in less than three years Spanish land titles were lost in hopeless confusion and a cloud of witnesses. The wily Argonauts cursed the aptness of their pupil.

Socially he clung to his old customs. He had his regular *fandango*,* strummed his guitar, and danced the *semi-cuaca*. He had his regular Sunday bull-fights after Mass. But the wily Argonaut introduced 'breakdowns' in the *fandango*, substituted the banjo for the guitar, and Bourbon whiskey for *aguardiente*. He even went so far as to interfere with the bull-fights, not so much from a sense of moral ethics as with a view to giving the bulls a show. On one or two occasions he substituted a grizzly bear, who not only instantly cleared the arena, but playfully wiped out the first two rows of benches beyond. He learned horsemanship from the Spaniard and—ran off his cattle.

Yet, before taking leave of the Spanish American, it is well to recall a single figure. It is that of the earliest pioneer known to Californian history. He comes to us toiling over a southern plain—an old man, weak, emaciated, friendless, and alone. He has left his weary muleteers and acolytes a league behind him, and has wandered on without scrip* or wallet, bearing only a crucifix and a bell. It is a characteristic plain, one that tourists do not usually penetrate: scorched yet bleak, windswept, blasted and baked to its very foundations, and cracked into gaping chasms. As the pitiless sun goes down, the old man staggers forward and falls utterly exhausted. He lies there all night. Towards morning he is found by some Indians, a feeble, simple race, who in uncouth kindness offer him food and drink. But before he accepts either, he rises to his knees, and there says matins and baptizes them in the Catholic faith. And then it occurs to him to ask them where he is, and he finds that he has penetrated into the unknown land. This was Padre Junipero Serra, and the sun arose that morning on Christian California. Weighed by the usual estimates of success, his mission was a failure. The heathen stole his provisions and massacred his acolytes. It is said that the good fathers themselves sometimes confounded baptism and bondage, and laid the foundation of peonage; but in the bloodstained and tear-blotted chronicle of early California, there is no more heroic figure than the thin, travel-worn, self-centred, self-denying Franciscan friar.

If I have thus far refrained from eulogizing the virtues of another characteristic figure, it is because he came later. The Heathen Chinee was *not* an Argonaut. But he brought into the

Argonaut's new life an odd conservatism. Quiet, calm, almost philosophic, but never obtrusive or aggressive, he never flaunted his three thousand years in the face of the men of to-day; he never obtruded his extensive mythology before men who were skeptical of even one God. He accepted at once a menial position with dignity and self-respect. He washed for the whole community, and made cleanliness an accessible virtue. He brought patience and novelty into the kitchen; he brought silence, obedience, and a certain degree of intelligence into the whole sphere of domestic service. He stood behind your chair, quiet, attentive, but uncommunicative. He waited upon you at table with the air of the man who, knowing himself superior, could not jeopardize his position. He worshipped the devil in your household with a frank sincerity and openness that shamed your own covert and feeble attempts in that direction. Although he wore your clothes, spoke your language, and imitated your vices, he was always involved in his own Celestial atmosphere. He consorted only with his fellows, consumed his own peculiar provisions, bought his goods of the Chinese companies, and when he died, his bones were sent to China! He left no track, trace, or imprint on the civilization. He claimed no civil right; he wanted no franchise. He took his regular beatings calmly; he submitted to scandalous extortion from state and individual with tranquillity; he bore robbery and even murder with stoical fortitude. Perhaps it was well that he did. Christian civilization, which declared by statute that his testimony was valueless; which intimated by its practice that the same vices in a pagan were worse than in a Christian; which regarded the frailty of his women as being especially abominable and his own gambling propensities as something originally bad, taught him at least the Christian virtues of patience and resignation.

Did he ever get even with the Christian Argonauts? I am inclined to think that he did. Indeed, in some instances I may say that I know that he did. He had a universal, simple way of defrauding the customs. He filled the hollows of bamboo chairs with opium, and, sitting calmly on them, conversed with dignity with custom-house officials. He made the amplitude of his sleeve and trouser useful as well as ornamental on similar occasions. He evaded the state poll tax by taking the name and assuming the exact facial expression of some brother Celestial who had already paid. He turned his skill as a horticulturist to sinful account by investing rose bushes with imitations of that flower made out of carrots and turnips. He acquired Latin and Greek with peculative rather than scholastic intent, and borrowed fifty dollars from a Californian clergyman while he soothed his ear with the Homeric accents. But perhaps his most successful attempt at balancing his account with a Christian civilization was his career as a physician.

One day he opened a doctor's office in San Francisco. By the aid of clever confederates, miraculous cures were trumpeted through the land, until people began to flock to his healing ministration. His doorways were beset by an army of invalids. Two interpreters, like the angels in the old legend, listened night and day to the ills told by the people that crowded this Hygeian* temple. They translated into the common tongue the words of wisdom that fell from the oracular lips of this slant-eyed Apollo.* Doctor Lipotai was eminently successful. Presently, however, there were Chinese doctors on every corner. A sign with the proper monosyllables, a pigtail and an interpreter, were the only stock in trade required. The pagan knew that no one would stop to reason. The ignorant heathen was aware that no one would stop to consider what superior opportunities the Chinese had for medical knowledge over the practitioners of his own land. This debased old idolater knew that these intelligent Christians would think that it might be *magic*, and so would come. And they did come. And he gave them green tea for tubercular consumption, ginger for aneurism, and made them smell punk for dropsy. The treatment was harmless, but wearisome. Suddenly, a well known Oriental scholar published a list of the remedies ordinarily used in the Chinese medical practice. I regret to say that for obvious reasons I cannot repeat the unsavory list here. It was enough, however, to produce the ordinary symptoms of sea-sickness among the doctor's patients. The celestial star at once began to wane. The oracle ceased to be questioned. The sibyls got off their tripods. And Doctor Lipotai, with a half million in his pocket, returned to his native rice and the naïve simplicity of Chinese Camp.

And with this receding figure bringing up the rear of the procession, I close my review of the Argonauts of '49. In their rank and file there may be many who are personally known to some of my hearers. There may be gaps which the memory of others can supply. There are homes all over the world whose vacant places never can be filled; there are graves all over California on whose nameless mounds no one shall weep. I have said that it is not a pretty story. I should like to end it with a flourish of trumpets, but the band has gone on before, and the dust of the highway is beginning to hide them from my view. They are marching on to their city by the sea—to that great lodestone hill that Sindbad saw,* which they call 'Lone Mountain.' There, waiting at its base, one may fancy the Argo is still lying, and that when the last Argonaut shall have passed in, she too will spread her white wings and slip unnoticed through the Golden Gate* that opens in the distance.

HOW I WENT TO THE MINES

I HAD been two years in California before I ever thought of going to the mines, and my initiation into the vocation of gold digging was partly compulsory. The little pioneer settlement school, of which I was the somewhat youthful and, I fear, the not over-competent master, was state-aided only to a limited extent; and as the bulk of its expense was borne by a few families in its vicinity, when two of them—representing perhaps a dozen children or pupils—one morning announced their intention of moving to a more prosperous and newer district, the school was incontinently closed.

In twenty-four hours I found myself destitute alike of my flock and my vocation. I am afraid I regretted the former the most. Some of the children I had made my companions and friends; and as I stood that bright May morning before the empty little bark-thatched schoolhouse in the wilderness, it was with an odd sensation that our little summer 'play' at being schoolmaster and pupil was over. Indeed, I remember distinctly that a large hunk of gingerbread—a parting gift from a prize scholar a year older than myself—stood me in good stead in my future wanderings, for I was alone in the world at that moment and constitutionally improvident.

I had been frightfully extravagant even on my small income, spending much money on 'boiled shirts,' and giving as an excuse, which I since believe was untenable, that I ought to set an example in dress to my pupils. The result was that at this crucial moment I had only seven dollars in my pocket, five of which went to the purchase of a second-hand revolver, that I felt was necessary to signalize my abandonment of a peaceful vocation for one of greed and adventure.

For I had finally resolved to go to the mines and become a gold-digger. Other occupations and my few friends in San Francisco were expensively distant. The nearest mining district was forty miles away; the nearest prospect of aid was the hope of finding a miner whom I had casually met in San Francisco, and whom I shall call 'Jim.' With only this name upon my lips

I expected, like the deserted Eastern damsel in the ballad, to find my friend among the haunts of mining men. But my capital of two dollars would not allow the expense of stage-coach fare; I must walk to the mines, and I did.

I cannot clearly recall *how* I did it. The end of my first day's journey found me with blistered feet and the conviction that varnished leather shoes, however proper for the Master of Madrono Valley School in the exercise of his functions, were not suited to him when he was itinerant. Nevertheless, I clung to them as the last badge of my former life, carrying them in my hands when pain and pride made me at last forsake the frequented highway to travel barefooted in the trails.

I am afraid that my whole equipment was rather incongruous, and I remember that the few travelers I met on the road glanced at me with curiosity and some amusement. The odds and ends of my 'pack'—a faded morocco dressing-case, an early gift from my mother, and a silver-handled riding-whip, also a gift—in juxtaposition with my badly rolled, coarse blue blanket and tin coffee-pot, were sufficiently provocative. My revolver, too, which would not swing properly in its holster from my hip, but worked around until it hung down in front like a Highlander's dirk,* gave me considerable mortification.

A sense of pride, which kept me from arriving at my friend's cabin utterly penniless, forbade my seeking shelter and food at a wayside station. I ate the remainder of my gingerbread, and camped out in the woods. To preclude any unnecessary sympathy, I may add that I was not at all hungry and had no sense of privation.

The loneliness that had once or twice come over me in meeting strangers on the traveled road, with whom I was too shy and proud to converse, vanished utterly in the sweet and silent companionship of the woods. I believe I should have felt my solitary vagabond condition greater in a strange hostelry or a crowded cabin. I heard the soft breathings of the lower life in the grass and ferns around me, saw the grave, sleepy stars above my head, and slept soundly, quite forgetting the pain of my blistered feet, or the handkerchiefs I had sacrificed for bandages.

In the morning, finding that I had emptied my water flask, I also found that I had utterly overlooked the first provision of camping,—nearness to a water supply,—and was fain to chew some unboiled coffee grains to flavor my scant breakfast, when I again took the trail.

I kept out of the main road as much as possible that day, although my détours cost me some extra walking, and by this time my bandaged feet had accumulated so much of the red dust that I suppose it would have been difficult to say what I wore on them. But in these excursions the balsamic air of the pines always revived me; the reassuring changes of scenery and distance viewed from those mountain ridges, the most wonderful I had ever seen, kept me in a state of excitement, and there was an occasional novelty of 'outcrop' in the rocky trail that thrilled me with mysterious anticipation.

For this outcrop—a strange, white, porcelain-like rock, glinting like a tooth thrust through the red soil—was *quartz*, which I had been told indicated the vicinity of the gold-bearing district. Following these immaculate fingerposts, I came at about sunset upon a mile-long slope of pines still baking in the western glare, and beyond it, across an unfathomable abyss, a shelf in the opposite mountain side, covered with white tents, looking not unlike the quartz outcrop I have spoken of. It was 'the diggings'!

I do not know what I had expected, but I was conscious of some bitter disappointment. As I gazed, the sun sank below the serried summit of the slope on which I stood; a great shadow seemed to steal *up* rather than down the mountain, the tented shelf faded away, and a score of tiny diamond points of light, like stars, took its place. A cold wind rushed down the mountain side, and I shivered in my thin clothes, drenched with the sweat of my day-long tramp.

It was nine o'clock when I reached the mining camp, itself only a fringe of the larger settlement beyond, and I had been on my feet since sunrise. Nevertheless, I halted at the outskirts, deposited my pack in the bushes, bathed my feet in a sluice of running water, so stained with the soil that it seemed to run blood, and, putting on my dreadful varnished shoes again, limped once more into respectability and the first cabin. Here I found that my friend 'Jim' was one of four partners on the 'Gum Tree' claim, two miles on the other side of the settlement. There was nothing left for me but to push on to the 'Magnolia Hotel,' procure the cheapest refreshment and an hour's rest, and then limp as best I could to the 'Gum Tree' claim.

I found the 'Magnolia' a large wooden building, given over, in greater part, to an enormous drinking 'saloon,' filled with flashing mirrors and a mahogany bar. In the unimportant and stuffy little dining-room or restaurant, I selected some 'fish-balls and coffee,' I think more with a view to cheapness and expedition than for their absolute sustaining power. The waiter informed me that it was possible that my friend 'Jim' might be in the settlement, but that the barkeeper, who knew everything and everybody, could tell me or give me 'the shortest cut to the claim.'

From sheer fatigue I lingered at my meal, I fear, long past any decent limit, and then reëntered the bar-room. It was crowded with miners and traders and a few smartly dressed professional-looking men. Here again my vanity led me into extravagance. I could not bear to address the important, white-shirt-sleeved and diamond-pinned barkeeper as a mere boyish suppliant for information. I was silly enough to demand a drink, and laid down, alas! another quarter.

I had asked my question, the barkeeper had handed me the decanter, and I had poured out the stuff with as much ease and grown-up confidence as I could assume, when a singular incident occurred. As it had some bearing upon my fortune, I may relate it here.

The ceiling of the saloon was supported by a half-dozen wooden columns, about eighteen inches square, standing in a line, parallel with the counter of the bar and about two feet from it. The front of the bar was crowded with customers, when suddenly, to my astonishment, they one and all put down their glasses and hurriedly backed into the spaces between the columns. At the same moment a shot was fired from the street through the large open doors that stood at right angles with the front of the counter and the columns.

The bullet raked and splintered the mouldings of the counter front, but with no other damage. The shot was returned from the upper end of the bar, and then for the first time I became aware that two men with leveled revolvers were shooting at each other through the saloon.

The bystanders in range were fully protected by the wooden columns; the barkeeper had 'ducked' below the counter at the first shot. Six shots were exchanged by the duelists, but, as far as I could see, nobody was hurt. A mirror was smashed, and my glass had part of its rim carried cleanly away by the third shot and its contents spilt.

I had remained standing near the counter, and I presume I may have been protected by the columns. But the whole thing passed so quickly, and I was so utterly absorbed in its dramatic novelty, that I cannot recall having the slightest sensation of physical fear; indeed, I had been much more frightened in positions of less peril.

My only concern, and this was paramount, was that I might betray by any word or movement my youthfulness, astonishment, or unfamiliarity with such an experience. I think that any shy, vain schoolboy will understand this, and would probably feel as I did. So strong was this feeling, that while the sting of gunpowder was still in my nostrils I moved towards the bar, and, taking up my broken glass, said to the barkeeper, perhaps somewhat slowly and diffidently,—

'Will you please fill me another glass? It's not my fault if this was broken.'

The barkeeper, rising flushed and excited from behind the bar, looked at me with a queer smile, and then passed the decanter and a fresh glass. I heard a laugh and an oath behind me, and my cheeks flushed as I took a single gulp of the fiery spirit and hurried away.

But my blistered feet gave me a twinge of pain, and I limped on the threshold. I felt a hand on my shoulder, and a voice said quickly: 'You ain't hurt, old man?' I recognized the voice of the man who had laughed, and responded quickly, growing more hot and scarlet, that my feet were blistered by a long walk, and that I was in a hurry to go to 'Gum Tree Claim.'

'Hold on,' said the stranger. Preceding me to the street, he called to a man sitting in a buggy, 'Drop him,' pointing to me, 'at Gum Tree Claim, and then come back here,' helped me into the vehicle, clapped his hand on my shoulder, said to me enigmatically, 'You'll do!' and quickly reëntered the saloon.

It was from the driver only that I learned, during the drive, that the two combatants had quarreled a week before, had sworn to shoot each other 'on sight,' *i.e.*, on their first accidental meeting, and that each 'went armed.' He added, disgustedly, that it was 'mighty bad shooting,' to which I, in my very innocence of these lethal weapons, and truthfulness to my youthful impressions, agreed!

I said nothing else of my own feelings, and, indeed, soon forgot them; for I was nearing the end of my journey, and *now*, for the first time, although I believe it a common experience of youth, I began to feel a doubt of the wisdom of my intentions. During my long tramp, and in the midst of my privations, I had never doubted it; but now, as I neared 'Jim's' cabin, my youthfulness and inefficiency and the extravagance of my quest of a mere acquaintance for aid and counsel came to me like a shock. But it was followed by a greater one. When at last I took leave of my driver and entered the humble little log cabin of the 'Gum Tree Company,' I was informed that 'Jim' only a few days before had given up his partnership and gone to San Francisco.

Perhaps there was something in my appearance that showed my weariness and disappointment, for one of the partners dragged out the only chair in the cabin,—he and the other partners had been sitting on boxes tilted on end,—and offered it to me, with the inevitable drink. With this encouragement, I stammered out my story. I think I told the exact truth. I was too weary to even magnify my acquaintance with the absent 'Jim.'

They listened without comment. I dare say they had heard the story before. I am quite convinced they had each gone through a harder experience than mine. Then occurred what I believe could have occurred only in California in that age of simplicity and confidence. Without a word of discussion among themselves, without a word of inquiry as to myself, my character or prospects, they offered me the vacant partnership 'to try.'

In any event I was to stay there until I could make up my mind. As I was scarcely able to stand, one of them volunteered to fetch my pack from its 'cache' in the bushes four miles away; and then, to my astonishment, conversation instantly turned upon other topics,—literature, science, philosophy, everything but business and practical concerns. Two of the partners were graduates of a Southern college and the other a bright young farmer.

I went to bed that night in the absent Jim's bunk, one fourth owner of a cabin and a claim I knew nothing of. As I looked about me at the bearded faces of my new partners, although they were all apparently only a few years older than myself, I wondered if we were not 'playing' at being partners in 'Gum Tree Claim,' as I had played at being schoolmaster in Madrono Valley.

When I awoke late the next morning and stared around the empty cabin, I could scarcely believe that the events of the preceding night were not a dream. My pack, which I had left four miles away, lay at my feet. By the truthful light of day I could see that I was lying apparently in a parallelogram of untrimmed logs, between whose interstices, here and there, the glittering sunlight streamed.

A roof of bark thatch, on which a woodpecker was foolishly experimenting, was above my head; four wooden 'bunks,' like a ship's berth, were around the two sides of the room; a table, a chair, and three stools, fashioned from old packing-boxes, were the only furniture. The cabin was lighted by a window of two panes let into one gable, by the open door, and by a chimney of adobe, that entirely filled the other gable, and projected scarcely a foot above the apex of the roof.

I was wondering whether I had not strayed into a deserted cabin, a dreadful suspicion of the potency of the single drink I had taken in the saloon coming over me, when my three partners entered. Their explanation was brief. I had needed rest, they had delicately forborne to awaken me before. It was twelve o'clock! My breakfast was ready. They had something 'funny' to tell me! I was a hero!

My conduct during the shooting affray at the 'Magnolia' had been discussed, elaborately exaggerated, and interpreted, by eye-witnesses; the latest version being that I had calmly stood at the bar, coolly demanding to be served by the crouching barkeeper, while the shots were being fired! I am afraid even my new friends put down my indignant disclaimer to youthful bashfulness, but seeing that I was distressed, they changed the subject.

Yes! I might, if I wanted, do some 'prospecting' that day. Where? Oh, anywhere on ground not already claimed; there were hundreds of square miles to choose from. What was I to do? What! was it possible I had never prospected before? No! Nor dug gold at all? Never!

I saw them glance hurriedly at each other; my heart sank, until I noticed that their eyes were eager and sparkling! Then I learned that my ignorance was blessed! Gold miners were very superstitious; it was one of their firm beliefs that 'luck' would inevitably follow the *first* essay of the neophyte or 'greenhorn.' This was called 'nigger luck;' *i.e.*, the inexplicable good fortune of the inferior and incompetent. It was not very complimentary to myself, but in my eagerness to show my gratitude to my new partners I accepted it.

I dressed hastily, and swallowed my breakfast of coffee, salt pork, and 'flapjacks.' A pair of old deerskin moccasins, borrowed from a squaw who did the camp washing, was a luxury to my blistered feet; and equipped with a pick, a long-handled shovel, and a prospecting pan, I demanded to be led at once to my field of exploit. But I was told that this was impossible; I must find it myself, alone, or the charm would be broken!

I fixed upon a grassy slope, about two hundred yards from the cabin, and limped thither. The slope faced the magnificent cañon and the prospect I had seen the day before from the further summit. In my vivid recollection of that eventful morning I quite distinctly remember that I was, nevertheless, so entranced with the exterior 'prospect' that for some moments I forgot the one in the ground at my feet. Then I began to dig.

My instructions were to fill my pan with the dirt taken from as large an area as possible near the surface. In doing this I was sorely tempted to dig lower in search of more hidden treasure, and in one or two deeper strokes of my pick I unearthed a bit of quartz with little seams or veins that glittered promisingly. I put them hopefully in my pocket, but duly filled my pan. This I took, not without some difficulty, owing to its absurd weight, to the nearest sluice-box, and, as instructed, tilted my pan in the running water.

As I rocked it from side to side, in a surprisingly short time the lighter soil of deep red color was completely washed away, leaving a glutinous clayey pudding mixed with small stones, like plums. Indeed, there was a fascinating reminiscence of 'dirt pies' in this boyish performance. The mud, however, soon yielded to the flowing water, and left only the stones and 'black sand.' I removed the former with my fingers, retaining only a small, flat, pretty, disk-like stone, heavier than the others,—it looked like a blackened coin,—and this I put in my pocket with the quartz. Then I proceeded to wash away the black sand.

I must leave my youthful readers to imagine my sensations when at last I saw a dozen tiny star-points of gold adhering to the bottom of the pan! They were so small that I was fearful of washing further, lest they should wash away. It was not until later that I found that their specific gravity made that almost impossible. I ran joyfully to where my partners were at work, holding out my pan.

'Yes, he's got the color,' said one blandly. 'I knew it.'

I was disappointed. 'Then I haven't struck it?' I said hesitatingly.

'Not in *this* pan. You've got about a quarter of a dollar here.'

My face fell. 'But,' he continued smilingly, 'you've only to get that amount in four pans, and you've made your daily "grub." '

'And that's all,' added the other, 'that we, or indeed *any one* on this hill, have made for the last six months!'

This was another shock to me. But I do not know whether I was as much impressed by it as by the perfect good humor and youthful unconcern with which it was uttered. Still, I was disappointed in my first effort. I hesitatingly drew the two bits of quartz from my pocket.

'I found them,' I said. 'They look as if they had some metal in them. See how it sparkles.'

My partner smiled. 'Iron pyrites,' he said; 'but what's that?' he added quickly, taking the little disk-like stone from my hand. 'Where did you get this?'

'In the same hole. Is it good for anything?'

He did not reply to me, but turned to his two other partners, who had eagerly pressed around him. 'Look!'

He laid the fragment on another stone, and gave it a smart blow with the point of his pick. To my astonishment it did not crumble or break, but showed a little dent from the pick point that was bright yellow!

I had no time, nor indeed need, to ask another question. 'Run for your barrow!' he said to one. 'Write out a "Notice," and bring the stakes,' to the other; and the next moment, forgetful of my blistered feet, we were flying over to the slope. A claim was staked out, the 'Notice' put up, and we all fell to work to load up our wheelbarrow. We carried four loads to the sluice-boxes before we began to wash.

The nugget I had picked up was worth about twelve dollars. We carried many loads; we worked that day and the next, hopefully, cheerfully, and without weariness. Then we worked at the claim daily, dutifully, and regularly for three weeks. We sometimes got 'the color,' we sometimes didn't, but we nearly always got enough for our daily 'grub.' We laughed, joked, told stories, 'spouted poetry,' and enjoyed ourselves as in a perpetual picnic. But that twelve-dollar nugget was the first and last 'strike' we made on the new 'Tenderfoot' Claim!

EXPLANATORY NOTES

3   *Hogarth's familiar cartoons*: William Hogarth (1697–1764), English painter and engraver distinguished for his satirical portraits of the high and low life of his day.

7   *two bowers*: in euchre, the jack of trumps and the jack of the other suit of the same colour are known as the right and the left bower and are the two highest-ranking cards in the game.

8   *Raphael*: Italian Renaissance painter (1483–1529) famous for the delicate beauty of his portraiture.

9   *Romulus and Remus*: in Roman legend, twin sons of the god Mars who were suckled by a she-wolf after floating ashore in a basket set adrift in the Tiber. They founded Rome.

    ex officio: by virtue of one's office or position.

11   *Sacramento*: a port on the Sacramento River, the state capital, and a major jumping-off point for the mines of the Central Sierra.

14   *Las Mariposas*: the Mariposa lily, or *Calochortus*, grows throughout California and is related to the tulip.

19   *Parthian volley*: the Parthian empire (250 BC–AD 226) extended from the Euphrates across Afghanistan to the Indus River. Parthian horsemen were famous for the effective and deceptive use of their arrows.

23   *sotto voce*: in a low voice.

24   *cachéd*: stored in a hiding-place, usually underground.

    Convenanter's: in Scottish history, Covenanters were groups of Presbyterians bound by oath to support each other in defence of their religion.

26   *son of Peleus*: Achilles, greatest of the Greek warriors in Homer's *Iliad*. Dipped by his mother in the River Styx, whose waters armoured the body against harm, he was held by the heel and so left vulnerable in that spot—his 'Achilles heel'. Hence the pun on 'Ash-heels'.

29   *Virginia City*: site of the discovery of the Comstock Lode (1859) in Nevada Territory.

    Washoe: the region—eventually the county—in which the Comstock Lode was located.

30 *Hibernian*: Irish.

32 '*the sere and yellow leaf*': the quotation is from Shakespeare's *Macbeth* (V. iii), where, as his opponents close in, Macbeth says: 'my way of life | Is fallen into the sere, the yellow leaf'.

34 *Caliban . . . Miranda*: in Shakespeare's *The Tempest*, Caliban, a native of the island ruled by the shipwrecked magician Prospero, performs menial tasks for him and for his daughter, Miranda.

35 *Una and her lion*: in Spenser's *The Faerie Queene* (Book One), Una, who stands for faith and the true Church, is attended by a faithful lion.

36 *Memnon*: a statue at Thebes in Egypt, believed by the Greeks to represent the warrior Memnon, which gave forth a sound once a day when touched by the rising sun.

42 *chaparral*: dense thickets of shrubs and dwarf trees covering the California foothills and mountains, deriving their name from the Spanish word for a place where the evergreen oak (*chaparro*) grows.

45 *Euchred*: beaten, as in the card game euchre, played by two sets of partners.

47 *cortège*: ceremonial procession.

51 *staccato*: composed of abrupt parts or sounds.

53 *quondam*: former.
   Delilah's shears: in the Old Testament Book of Judges, Delilah deprives strong-man Samson of his strength by having his long hair cut while he sleeps.

54 *Vestal's temple*: in Roman religion, the cult of Vesta, goddess of the hearth, was maintained by Vestal virgins, girls chosen from prominent families and sworn to a vow of chastity.

55 *Adolphus*: literally, noble wolf; noble hero.

60 *Marius*: Roman general (157 BC–86 BC) known as a friend of the people; he paved the way for Julius Caesar.

61 *Hebrew in the legend*: the Wandering Jew. In Christian folklore, the Jew who mocked Jesus on his way to the cross and who was condemned to wander the earth until Judgement Day.

66 *Asiatic peak*: Mount Ararat, in modern-day Turkey, the peak where, after a misreading of Genesis 8: 4, Noah's ark is believed to have come to rest after the flood.

68 *Laura*: first seen by the poet Petrarch in 1327 at Avignon, Laura became the inspiration for his love poetry and a figure for the woman worshipped from afar.

71 *peste!*: a French exclamation of disgust; literally, 'a plague on it!'

   '*Parbleu!*': by God!

72 *Norma . . . Casta Diva*: Bellini's opera *Norma* premiered in December 1831 in Milan. Set in Gaul during the Roman occupation, the first act begins with Druid soldiers and priests waiting for the rising of the moon. It rises during a moderately slow (*andante*) chorus, after which Norma sings the famous aria to the chaste goddess (*Casta Diva*) of the moon.

   Joshua: in the Old Testament Book of Joshua, Joshua commands the sun to stand still during the battle of Gibeon. See 'Mliss', p. 98.

   Diana . . . Endymion: in Greek mythology, Endymion was a young shepherd beloved by Diana, goddess of the moon. In her nightly visits she put off her light before entering his bower or cave.

73 *horses of the night*: in Marlowe's *Doctor Faustus* (v. ii), Faustus cries out: '*O lente, lente currite noctis equi.*' Facing perpetual damnation, he asks 'O run slowly, horses of the night.' The cry was originally uttered by Ovid, who wanted to prolong a night of love.

74 '*Medora*': the captivating and doomed heroine of Byron's 'The Corsair' (1814).

84 *moiety*: portion.

89 *monk's-hood*: or aconite, a poisonous plant with hooded flowers.

99 *Ceanothus*: wild lilac of the buckthorn family prevalent from the Sierra to the coast.

108 *Toledo*: the Toledo sword, originating from the Spanish city of the same name, was famous for its strength, elasticity, and craftsmanship.

110 *aguardiente*: liquor.

   sembi cuacua: or semi-cuaca, an intricate Spanish dance.

114 *Te Deum*: the chief hymn of rejoicing in the Roman Catholic Church.

115 *Hippocratic face*: the face of a doctor, after Hippocrates, the father of medicine.

116 *ex parte*: a statement made in favour of one side of an argument.

117 *deseño*: map of Spanish land grant.

121 '*riata*': lasso, rope noosed around itself.

122 *machillas*: a loose skin or cloth cover for a saddle; saddle-bags.

    vaquero's: cowboy's.

123 *Cassius-like bovines*: in Shakespeare's *Julius Caesar* (I. ii), Cassius is described by Caesar as having a 'lean and hungry look'.

    casa: house.

125 *Que bueno?*: How nice!

    corregidores: magistrates.

    llano!: flat surface, land.

127 *Lido*: island with fashionable beach resort separating Venice from the Adriatic.

    Bianca: Katharine's sister in Shakespeare's *The Taming of the Shrew*; any charming and strong-willed heroine.

128 *Howard Society?*: a charitable organization active in Sacramento in the 1860s.

133 *valda*: skirt of the hill; see p. 117.

    chimisal: chamisos; a thicket of thornless shrubs.

134 *Poco a poco*: gradually.

135 *'chupa'*: cup or bowl of stew or chili.

    Sancho-like: Sancho Panza, the loyal, down-to-earth companion of the knight-errant, Don Quixote.

139 *Moorish King*: the Moorish king Boabdil looked back at Granada and its hills in his moment of exile and issued the 'last sigh of the moor'.

140 *Junipero*: Junipero Serra (1713–84), Franciscan missionary and padre who founded the first missions in California.

    Vulgate: the most ancient extant version of the whole Bible and the official, Latin version of the Roman Catholic Church.

    R-isons: pun on 'orisons', prayers.

    immortelles: or everlastings, numerous plants with papery flowers that retain their form and colour when dried.

143 *paletot*: a loose outer garment for men or women.

145 *Circassian*: a Muslim people originating in the Caucasus whose women were famous for their beauty.

    Lake: a pigment of reddish hue.

146 *dos à dos*: two by two; together.

146 *Saccharissa*: a poetical name given by the poet Waller (1606–87) to Lady Dorothy Sidney; an object of poetic desire.

158 *infelix*: unfortunate.

159 *Sister Anne's 'flock of sheep'*: a reference to the fairy tale 'Blue Beard'. In Perrault's version of the tale, the wife, under sentence of death from her husband, calls out to her sister: 'Anne, Sister Anne, do you see nothing coming?' Her brothers have promised to visit her that day. Sister Anne, who had been overlooked by Blue Beard as a marriage choice, answers that she sees 'a great cloud of dust which comes this way'. It turns out to be the brothers, but on again being asked what she sees, Sister Anne replies, 'it is but a flock of sheep.' The allusion implies, then, that what is seen is not what is waited for.

168 *Bacchus*: Roman god of revelry and wine.

170 *chef d'œuvre*: masterpiece.

175 *John Jacob Astor*: American merchant (1763–1848), founder of the American Fur company, and the wealthiest man in the United States at the time of his death.

187 *pasear*: leisurely journey.

196 *Astrakhan fur*: pelt of the new-born Persian lamb; mohair.

199 *'No sabe!'*: 'Don't know.'

200 *Confucius*: Chinese sage of the 6th century BC.

   Mencius: major disciple of Confucius; 4th century BC.

203 *Webster*: Daniel Webster (1782–1852), US Senator from Massachusetts famous for his oratory.

205 *Malvolio*: in Shakespeare's *Twelfth Night* (III. iv), Olivia refers to her fun-killing steward Malvolio as 'sad and civil'—grave and sedate.

211 *douceur*: sweet.

219 *coulisses*: wings of the stage; backstage; place behind the scenes.

232 *eagre*: tidal wave of unusual height caused by the rushing of the wave up a narrowing estuary.

   tules: water reeds of the Central Valley.

235 *sabe*: understand.

240 *Strephon*: a shepherd lover in Sidney's *Arcadia* (1590); a poetic name for a swain.

248 *Arcadian*: simple, natural, pastoral.

249 *Sally Lunn*: a light, egg-based yeast bread.

261 *Argonauts of '49*: this essay was written by Harte as a lecture for American and English audiences and first given in 1872. The participants in the California Gold Rush were commonly called Argonauts, after the crew that accompanied Jason on the Argo in his quest for the golden fleece.

Rio de Los Reyes: river believed to flow from the Great Basin through central California to the Pacific Ocean.

De Fonte . . . Maldonado: early Spanish explorers credited with voyages in search of the Strait of Anian, a water route across North America. The voyages did not occur, and the strait did not exist.

iron-bound coast: the coast of California was called 'iron-bound' by sailors because of the lack of sheltering harbours and the prevailing winds that made northward navigation difficult.

largest bay . . . Francis Drake: Drake's Bay at Point Reyes, where Sir Francis Drake may have dropped anchor in 1579 on his circumnavigation of the world.

262 *Lothario*: character in the *Fair Penitent* by Nicholas Rowe; an amoral seducer of women.

263 *day laborer at Sutter's Mill*: on 24 January 1848 John Marshall discovered gold in the South Fork of the American River while building a sawmill for his partner John Augustus Sutter.

Brigham Young: after succeeding Joseph Smith as President of the Church of Jesus Christ of Latter-Day Saints, Young, in 1846, led his followers from Missouri and the already-abandoned city of Nauvoo in Illinois to the valley of the Great Salt Lake.

British frigate: Commodore John Sloat (1781–1867) raised the American flag over Monterey on 7 July 1846 to forestall a British takeover during the opening days of the Mexican War.

264 *Pizarro*: Spanish conquistador (1471–1541) and the conqueror of Peru. Prescott's *The Conquest of Peru* contains no reference to the burning of ships; the allusion is perhaps to the desperate stand that Pizarro took on the island of Gallo, where, abandoned by the supporting ships from Panama, he drew a line in the sand and said, 'I go to the South.'

Colchian wharf: Jason's Argo docked at the Colchian wharf while he went in search of the golden fleece.

265 *two gentlemen*: in Shakespeare's *Macbeth* (III. i), Macbeth commissions the two murderers to kill Banquo and his son Fleance. In

III. iii they are joined by a third murderer and kill Banquo while Fleance flees. Later, the murderers kill Lady Macbeth's son.

267 *Telegraph Hill*: the hill rises 274 feet above the north-east San Francisco shoreline and is named for the semaphore erected there (1850) to signal the arrival of ships from the Bay.

270 *Circean*: in Homer's *Odyssey*, the enchantress Circe seduces Odysseus after turning his men into swine.

Theocritus: 3rd-century Greek poet and originator of the pastoral, a poetic form involving a dialogue among shepherds.

Rembrandtish: Dutch painter (1609–69) famous for his command of light and shadow—his *chiaroscuro*.

271 *Stanislaus and Merced*: rivers flowing from the Central Sierra to the San Joaquin.

272 *Charles II*: the Cavaliers who supported the Restoration (1660) of the Stuart king wore their hair long and it became the fashion at his court.

Delaroche's Saviour: Hippolyte (Paul) Delaroche (1797–1856), French history and portrait painter. No painting by the title of 'Savior' has come down to us; the reference is perhaps to a work in Delaroche's cycle of paintings of the Passion and the Crucifixion.

Meissonier: Jean Meissonier (1815–91), French genre and military painter famous for his battle scenes of the Napoleonic Wars.

Danaë-like shower of gold: in Greek myth, Danaë gives birth to Perseus after being raped by Zeus, who comes to her in the form of a shower of gold.

273 *Damon and Pythias*: two Greek youths whose loyalty to each other symbolizes true friendship.

276 *Thomas Starr King*: Unitarian minister (1824–64) whose popular preaching helped persuade California to join the Union side in the Civil War.

277 *theodolite*: a surveying instrument for measuring horizontal and vertical angles.

278 *Charles V*: 1500–1558, Holy Roman Emperor and King of Spain. The Spanish empire in the Americas expanded greatly under his rule.

279 *fandango*: ancient Spanish dance done in triple time by a single couple to the accompaniment of castanets.

scrip: paper money.

281 *Hygeian*: healthy.

    Apollo: in Greek religion, Apollo is the god of medicine.

282 *lodestone hill that Sindbad saw*: in the *Arabian Nights*, Sindbad the Sailor makes seven voyages. The reference is to the Magnet Mountain, a lodestone that had a 'love of iron' and could pull nails out of the hulls of ships.

    Golden Gate: the entrance to the San Francisco Bay.

284 *dirk*: dagger.

THE WORLD'S CLASSICS

A Select List

HANS ANDERSEN: Fairy Tales
Translated by L. W. Kingsland
Introduction by Naomi Lewis
Illustrated by Vilhelm Pedersen and Lorenz Frølich

JANE AUSTEN: Emma
Edited by James Kinsley and David Lodge

Mansfield Park
Edited by James Kinsley and John Lucas

J. M. BARRIE: Peter Pan in Kensington Gardens & Peter and Wendy
Edited by Peter Hollindale

WILLIAM BECKFORD: Vathek
Edited by Roger Lonsdale

CHARLOTTE BRONTË: Jane Eyre
Edited by Margaret Smith

THOMAS CARLYLE: The French Revolution
Edited by K. J. Fielding and David Sorensen

LEWIS CARROLL: Alice's Adventures in Wonderland
and Through the Looking Glass
Edited by Roger Lancelyn Green
Illustrated by John Tenniel

MIGUEL DE CERVANTES: Don Quixote
Translated by Charles Jarvis
Edited by E. C. Riley

GEOFFREY CHAUCER: The Canterbury Tales
Translated by David Wright

ANTON CHEKHOV: The Russian Master and Other Stories
Translated by Ronald Hingley

JOSEPH CONRAD: Victory
Edited by John Batchelor
Introduction by Tony Tanner

DANTE ALIGHIERI: The Divine Comedy
Translated by C. H. Sisson
Edited by David Higgins

VIRGIL: The Aeneid
Translated by C. Day Lewis
Edited by Jasper Griffin

HORACE WALPOLE: The Castle of Otranto
Edited by W. S. Lewis

IZAAK WALTON and CHARLES COTTON:
The Compleat Angler
Edited by John Buxton
Introduction by John Buchan

OSCAR WILDE: Complete Shorter Fiction
Edited by Isobel Murray

The Picture of Dorian Gray
Edited by Isobel Murray

VIRGINIA WOOLF: Orlando
Edited by Rachel Bowlby

ÉMILE ZOLA:
The Attack on the Mill and other stories
Translated by Douglas Parmée

A complete list of Oxford Paperbacks, including The World's Classics, OPUS, Past Masters, Oxford Authors, Oxford Shakespeare, and Oxford Paperback Reference, is available in the UK from the Arts and Reference Publicity Department (BH), Oxford University Press, Walton Street, Oxford OX2 6DP.

In the USA, complete lists are available from the Paperbacks Marketing Manager, Oxford University Press, 200 Madison Avenue, New York, NY 10016.

Oxford Paperbacks are available from all good bookshops. In case of difficulty, customers in the UK can order direct from Oxford University Press Bookshop, Freepost, 116 High Street, Oxford, OX1 4BR, enclosing full payment. Please add 10 per cent of published price for postage and packing.